THE
QUEEN
OF
KENTUCKY

alecia whitaker

poppy

LITTLE, BROWN AND COMPANY

New York   Boston

Poppy

Hachette Book Group
237 Park Avenue, New York, NY 10017
For more of your favorite series and novels,
visit our website at www.pickapoppy.com

Poppy is an imprint of Little, Brown and Company.
The Poppy name and logo are trademarks of Hachette Book Group, Inc.

First Edition: January 2012

Library of Congress Cataloging-in-Publication Data

Whitaker, Alecia.
The queen of Kentucky / by Alecia Whitaker. — 1st ed.
p. cm.
Summary: Fourteen-year-old Ricki Jo, a Kentucky farm girl, learns that popularity is not all she hoped it would be when the huge changes she makes in her personality and style seem to do more to drive away old friends than to win new ones.
ISBN 978-0-316-12506-2
[1. Popularity—Fiction. 2. High schools—Fiction. 3. Schools—Fiction. 4. Farm life—Kentucky—Fiction. 5. Dating (Social customs)—Fiction. 6. Friendship—Fiction. 7. Kentucky—Fiction.] I. Title.
PZ7.W57684Que 2011
[Fic]—dc22
2010045840

10 9 8 7 6 5 4 3 2 1

RRD-C

Printed in the United States of America

This one's for Mom and Dad.

CHAPTER ONE

"When we get to high school, I want you to call me Ericka," I say, taking off my tan leather work glove to wipe the sweat from my brow. I've been blabbing to my best friend, Luke, all day because A) talking makes the time go by faster, and B) I'm a jabber-jaw; but I might as well be talking to one of our cows. Luke just sort of moseys along down the row of tobacco next to me, nodding every now and then and chomping on his bubble gum. He has been totally unsympathetic to almost every gripe I've had today, from the sad state of my grubby fingernails to how humiliating it is to have to pop a squat in the weeds every time I have to pee. But *this* is serious. "Did you hear me, Luke? I'm for real. It's Ericka."

He nods and swings his tobacco knife at the base of the huge stalk in front of him. I hate talking to his back, his white T-shirt soaked through so that I can actually see the freckles spotting his shoulder blades, but unlike the rest of the day's conversations, this is one thing I really need him to hear me on.

"Luke Foster!" I shout, stamping my boot in the dirt.

"What, Ricki Jo?" he says, exasperated. When he jerks up to look at me, sweat drips down around his clear blue eyes and his sandy blond hair falls across his forehead and sticks there. I fight the urge to step into his row and push it back, mostly because I'm in making-my-point mode, but also because once he stretches up to his full height of six foot two, there's no reaching it while maintaining my dignity.

So, calmer, I repeat myself: "When we get to high school, I want you to call me Ericka."

"Yeah, great, whatever, Ricki Jo," he says, pulling a bottle of water out from the back pocket of his jeans.

"E-rick-a," I correct, pointing my dirty tobacco knife at him and arching the prissier of my two eyebrows.

He smirks in response and swallows. "We aren't in high school yet."

"It's to-morrow!" I say.

"Then to-mor-row," he mocks, "I'll call you Princess E-rick-a. 'Til then, it's plain ol' Ricki Jo."

I roll my eyes and grab my own water bottle, totally not expecting a guy with a simple name like *Luke* to understand where I'm coming from. I'm starting HIGH SCHOOL. First impressions are important and double names are, I don't know, babyish. It's not that I hate my name, but *Ricki Jo* doesn't have that…*swagger*. It doesn't have the sophistication that *Ericka* does.

I pull my glove back on and stretch, pushing my arms up and my chest out, willing my tiny frame closer to the blue sky. Squinting against the sun, I can't help but feel defeated. So. Much. Tobacco.

Cutting is the pits. I mean, nobody likes spending her free time working with her dad, her little brother, and dirt-covered men of varying ages. But cutting tobacco? A nightmare. First of all, Kentucky in late August boasts temps in the mid-nineties with a hundred percent humidity, so, yeah, it's hot. Second, the tobacco is at full size, meaning each stalk is weighed down with sticky green leaves every bit as long as my arm and as wide as my hips. Bent over just about the entire day, a girl like me can expect sore shoulders from swiping at the thick base of the tobacco with a short knife, a sore back from hefting the chopped-off seven-pound plant upside down, and entire-body aches from then heaving said plant onto an inch-square splintery stick…a stick she is squeezing between her legs the entire time in some sort of sick balancing act.

"You gotta be kidding me," I grumble, noticing a splinter in the meaty part of my palm. I wipe my knife on my T-shirt and dig into the flesh with the tip, the splinter both a major annoyance and a welcome distraction. "I hate — *hate*—cutting tobacco," I gripe to no one in particular. (If I've said it once today, I've said it a million times, so I've kind of lost my audience.)

"Me, too," I hear from behind me. Surprised, I turn around to see my little brother, Ben, struggling, his brow knit in a combination of fury and despair as he teeters down my row, dropping sticks for me to eventually load up with tobacco. "I wish I were playing video games."

I can't help but smile. Misery truly does love company, even if it comes in the form of elementary-school-aged monsters. Most summers, I'm the one dropping sticks (a way easier job), but this morning my dad decided that Ben is "of age," so he's been dragged to the fields for tobacco initiation and I got lumped in with the guys to cut.

"Back to work, kids," my dad says sternly, appearing out of nowhere. Ben's shoulders droop as he wobbles away like a miniature tightrope walker, the long gray sticks bouncing over his little eight-year-old forearms. Before bending down to start my next stick, I give my dad my most exaggerated eye-roll/heavy-sigh combination, to which he responds with his age-old don't-push-it expression before stepping over to his own row.

Fuming, I reach for the stick at my feet; however, this is the precise moment that a small black garter snake slithers out in front of me. I do what any normal fourteen-year-old girl would do: scream my head off, dance in spastic horror, and throw my tobacco knife into the dirt—completely missing the snake. I look to Luke for help, but he's laughing hysterically, which really gets my already hot blood boiling. Wrists on sweaty forehead, breathing totally out of control, I walk around in a circle until the disgusting little reptile slithers away.

I am — officially — over it.

"Ugh! I hate this job! I hate this job!" I shout.

"Then go drop sticks with your lil' brother," Luke calls over from his row, a not-so-cute smirk playing all over his lips. "Cuttin' is man's work, anyway."

I glower at him, pick up my knife, and carry on.

At Luke's farm I'm the lone female, since his older sister, Claire, got pregnant last fall. She and I used to gossip nonstop to pass the time, but her brothers aren't so chatty. I really could've used her this summer, too. If she were here, she'd tell me which teachers are cool and which are jerks, she'd give me advice about how high school is different, and she'd totally get why I'm basically freaking out. I swipe at the stalks in front of me and try to put myself in her shoes. Would I rather be changing a diaper right now or cutting tobacco? *Hmmm...*

At the moment it's a tough choice, but in reality, the tobacco eventually all gets cut, and quitting time always comes. But not for Claire. She's 24/7 now — all baby, all the time. She was actually pretty popular in high school, but most of her friends jumped ship when she started showing. A couple of jocks started mock-interviewing her for *Teen Mom*, this MTV show about underage girls getting knocked up. Luke says she took it all really well, that she was strong and just laughed 'em off, but if it taught me anything, it's that high school is scary and that I should get in good from the beginning.

Which is why I'm so nervous. Which is why I want to make new friends, and be popular...or at least not *un*popular. Which is why I need to make a really strong first impression tomorrow. And why I'm totally beyond ticked off about this god-awful farmer's tan!

As I bend, cut, lift, and spear, I'm fit to be tied. It's five o'clock in the afternoon and the sun has not quit. I'm red from its rays, I'm red from slapping at bugs all over me, and I'm red from my temper. As I lift yet another huge stalk of tobacco up and spear it onto the stick between my legs, I can't help but be mad. *Even this doggone tobacco is taller than me! Even tobacco has hit puberty!*

"I don't see why we're helping y'all out, anyway!" I holler to Luke while rolling my white T-shirt sleeves up onto my shoulders for the millionth time today. "We don't farm anymore. My dad took a factory job. This sucks!"

A low voice growls too near. "We didn't ask for your charity."

I turn and see Luke's dad standing over me, a mean scowl on his face. I can smell the alcohol on his breath and see Luke in my peripheral vision, stepping quickly into my row, alert. The father and son couldn't be more different. Although they're both tall, Mr. Foster has that man weight on him that, at fourteen, Luke hasn't grown into yet. Luke is dirty, wearing muddy boots and jeans and a once white T-shirt—I probably look exactly the same—but his dad wears coveralls stained from chew and dip, no shirt underneath, an old flask sticking out of one pocket and a faded handkerchief out of the other. Basically, Luke's clothes were clean when we met at the barn this morning, and his dad's weren't.

"We're happy to help," my dad says, coming to the rescue, my row suddenly the life of the party. Mr. Foster grunts, spits, and ambles off. Luke cuts a couple of stalks near me, all former teasing and eye sparkle gone. He mumbles an embarrassed "Sorry" and finishes off my stick. I roll my eyes and shake my head, totally annoyed.

"Yeah, real happy," I mumble.

My dad's hand lands firmly on my shoulder and I look up. "Watch that smart mouth, young lady. I can always lower it to five dollars an hour instead of six," he threatens, staring me down until I finally break eye contact.

I march over to grab my next stick with all the silent rebellion I can muster, my dark blond ponytail sweat-soaked and smacking me on the shoulders.

Why are we even out here?

My dad farmed his whole life, but this winter he got a job at the new Toyota plant in Georgetown, about a half hour away. With the government buyout and outrageous lawsuits against Big Tobacco, farming isn't a stable way to make a living in Kentucky anymore. My dad's always talking about all the vacant land around our county nowadays that used to thrive, but "a man's gotta provide for his family," so he gave it up. A lot of guys think he sold out, but when he first told us, I was happy as a lark! We'd still have cattle, a garden, and a small orchard, but no more tobacco. It meant he'd have to work nights, but he'd get a steady paycheck, no matter what the market did with the price of our state's cash crop...and, more important, it meant that I was permanently off the hook from planting, pulling, setting, suckering, topping, cutting, housing, and stripping tobacco. Deliverance!

Or so I was led to believe.

Yet here it is, August, and although I'm getting paid now I've been a little tobacco fairy all summer long, flitting around the county on grudging wings. We've helped the Taylors, the Fischers, the Motts, and the O'Caseys. My dad is "too old to start sleeping during the day," so he catnaps here and there and zombies himself from farm to farm, dragging Ben and me along in his shadow. I don't know if he misses the farming itself or the idea of being a farmer, but I really wish he'd get over his identity crisis. *Get a Porsche! A toupee! A tattoo! If you're gonna do a midlife crisis, do it right!*

I swing at the base of stalk after stalk, pushing each of them over like Godzilla storming through Tokyo.

I hate—
Swipe!
hate—
Hack!
hate—
Cut!
hate my life!

CHAPTER TWO

"You have the most adorable freckles," my momma tells me that night as I sit on the floor between her legs and she rolls my hair. With a day out in the Kentucky sunshine comes a splatter of freckles all over my nose and cheeks. Not something I love, but not something I hate, either. My big ears, I hate. Freckles, I can live with.

"Yeah, too bad they came from a day of work instead of a day at the swimming pool," I complain.

"You don't even like swimming! You can't jump in without holding your nose," she points out.

True. But if I were at the country club with the other kids my age, I would glide in from the shallow end or just plain jump in and drown. At least I'd die cool. But the country club is only for the "well-off," and besides, our farm is way out in the boondocks, out by the county line, so it takes about twenty minutes just to get to town. And with gas prices killing my dad's bank account (and therefore my social life), there has to be a pretty good reason to go—church, school, birthday party, etc.

"Can you still smell the lemon juice?" I ask Momma as she combs my wet hair over my face. It's naturally wavy, but I want true curls for the first day.

"Uh-uh," she murmurs, sectioning off another piece. "You excited for school tomorrow, baby?"

Humph. Talk about your understatements. I've been counting down the days 'til high school all summer long. I try to nod, but she's holding strong to the next strand of hair to be wrapped and snapped in pink sponge.

I guess I'll be a new kid, but I've actually lived in this town all my life. And it's a small town. We've got one movie theater that plays one movie all week long; a Fashion Bug and a Walmart (though not Super); and McDonald's, Dairy Queen, and KFC. Yeah, we've got a few stoplights, but I personally think they're just for show. Stop signs usually do the trick. Breckinridge, Kentucky. The epicenter of Nowheresville, USA.

The reason I'm "new" is because I've gone to private Catholic school since first grade. Our town is a big Southern Baptist kind of place to grow up, but there is our one little cathedral and our one little K–8 school. There are a few other kids from my school who'll be going to the high school, too, but other than that, everybody will already know one another. When you've got just one public school for the whole county, most of the student body has been acquainted since finger painting in elementary school and staring at one another at junior high dances. Everybody knows everybody. And starting tomorrow, I'll be an everybody.

"Your hair used to be straw yellow." Momma sighs.

I pass her another roller and think about what I'll wear tomorrow and who I might already know. There are a few kids from 4-H, one of the few social clubs I'm allowed to participate in as a non–public schooler. Over the years, I've tried basket weaving and shown cows, but mainly I crochet and sew; and although I'm not talented, I love modeling my scarf/sweater/oven mitt creations at the county fair every July. I've also signed up every year for rec-league softball and basketball, since our little school didn't have much in the way of extracurriculars (or school spirit in general), so a few of those kids know me okay. I'll probably recognize a lot of faces, just from growing up here my whole life, but I'm still nervous about hardly *knowing* anybody.

"Now it's just that dishwater blond," my mom continues as she snaps the last roller into place.

I get up and kiss her on the cheek. "Thanks, Momma," I say, looking in the mirror over the mantel to check my pink plastic Afro head. *Dishwater? Seriously? Way to build the self-esteem before the most important day of my life,* I think; but what I say is, "I'm gonna go get ready for bed."

"Okay, sweetie," she says, gathering up her comb and

spray water bottle. "And don't forget to read your Bible!" she calls as I head down the hall to my room.

Right.

It feels like I just went to sleep. The sun is up and the air is electric. It's the first day of school. I feel like I'm going to throw up.

Having strewn my entire wardrobe all over my room last night, I now wade through the mess and stand in front of my full-length mirror. My skin looks quite tan against the modest white summer dress I chose, my toenails are a pretty pink in simple brown sandals, and, best of all, my face is zit free. I lean in close to the mirror and check my eyes (big and hazel), my nose (long and freckled), and my teeth (straight, finally!) to make sure they are clean and clear. I dip one skinny finger into a jar of Vaseline and smooth it over my full, chapped lips—gloss for the creative girl. I shake my head and then grin as my dark blond curls bounce from side to side, although I'm worried it may look like I'm trying too hard. Hmmm…I cross my arms over my shoulders, then pose like I'm telling Luke a dramatic story, then put my backpack on and take it off again, all while keeping my eyes on myself in the mirror. Lots of bounce. Yep, looks like I'm trying too hard. I quickly snatch a flimsy headband from around the doorknob and slide it on. Better. I take a step back and give myself one last up and down before deciding that I am as close to perfect-first-impression as I'm going to get.

The dress isn't new, but the training bra is. I smile every time I think about it.

Preston County High School, here I come. I'm in high school. Agh!

My younger brother and I stand on the front porch for our obligatory first-day-of-school pictures. Momma makes us do this every year, but whereas Ben is going to our old school, I am starting fresh. She arranges us like always: on the swing, in front of our flagpole, and at the bottom of our driveway where we wait for the bus. I oblige her scrapbook-in-the-making enthusiasm, but we made a deal that once the bus rounds the bend, the camera disappears.

"Ricki Jo!" my dad yells from his four-by-four Dodge. Ben and I scoot back into the grass as he pulls into the gravel driveway, making it home from third shift at the factory just before the bus comes. He parks but leaves the truck idling, diesel engine gurgling, and I know he must be in a hurry because that's such an out-of-character wasteful gesture (the gas money, not the fumes). With a huge smile on his face and a gleam in his eye, he heads over to where I stand, navy blue denim jacket in hand. "Look what I found."

I look.

"It's my old FFA jacket! Look at the embroidery. Clark Winstead — FFA President, 1986."

I stare.

His face goes from excited to expectant to confused.

"I thought you might wanna wear it today. Talk to Mr. Holland about joining FFA. You'll fit right in."

I gape.

FFA—Future Farmers of America. I'm fourteen, I'm four eleven, I weigh eighty-nine pounds, I have no boobs and no period, my ears don't fit my face, and, to tell the truth, I've got a plantar wart on the bottom of my left foot. This is the first day of HIGH SCHOOL. And my father thinks I might want to wear his FFA jacket.

"It's awful hot out, Clark," Momma says, fanning herself like she's suddenly stepped into a sauna.

My mother and I fight—a lot—but at this very moment I love her more than chocolate, new shoes, and MTV (which I have only seen twice).

"There's the bus!" my little brother squeals.

"Oh my god," I whisper. I get butterflies in my stomach and I feel the throw-up sensation again.

My dad tosses his old jacket back in his truck and shrugs his shoulders, his pride stung. "Same bus you've taken since first grade, Ricki Jo. Exact same bus," he says.

I climb on the first step and wave at my folks. Then, up two more steps and to a seat in the back. "Different destination, Daddy," I say to myself, looking at him through the window. "Different destination."

CHAPTER THREE

"Meet you after school," Luke says as we split at the front door. We've ridden the bus together our whole lives, but I always got dropped off before they made the high school rounds. I wonder if I'll have classes with any of the other kids on our bus, and I really wish I had homeroom with Luke. At least then he could introduce me to some people; but it's all divided alphabetically, so I'll be with the W–Z's and he'll be with the E–G's.

The hallways are a jumble of high fives and *how was your summer*s and giggles and hugs and community. I weave in and out of the throng, offering up weak smiles and weaker *excuse me*s. In Mrs. Wilkes's room, however, there is quiet. I take a seat at a table for six and wait for the bell.

Hi! I'm Ericka, I practice. *Ericka Winstead, yeah, hi! Nice to meet you.*

The bell rings and the doorjamb seems to stretch wide as bodies squeeze through and my classmates take seats all around me. Two girls sit at my table and continue a conversation about somebody's possible hickey from somebody else's possible boyfriend. They don't speak to me, but I listen, looking for a space to introduce myself.

One of the girls, Kimi, is grown-up. Seriously. She has an enormous chest and broad hips, yet her waist pinches in just right, so that she's not exactly pinup material but doesn't look heavy, either. In contrast to her body, her facial features are sharp. She has a tall forehead and a straight nose and high cheekbones that perch beneath almost black eyes. Her jet-black hair is cut in a short bob, the kind that's longer in the front by her chin and angles up in the back. She is the most interesting person I have ever seen, not drop-dead gorgeous but intriguing, like you don't want to look away.

She's talking to Sarah, who actually lives way down the road from me. I really only know *of* her. Her folks have a horse farm and go to Keeneland meets every fall and spring and are fixtures at the annual Kentucky Derby. *If I had to be a farmer's daughter, that's the way I'd rather go.* Their Thoroughbreds are gorgeous and they live in a mansion down a long, gated blacktop driveway. She's not necessarily prettier than I am, but she's tall and toned, and... well... rich. She's obviously a gymnast; her build is almost masculine. Her brown hair hangs limp to her shoulders, but she keeps blowing her thin straight bangs out of her eyes and then straightening them across her forehead again, which would drive my momma crazy. I think that as far as friend material goes, she's in my league...except for the whole millionaire thing.

"Hi. My name is Mackenzie. I'm new."

I jump. I've been staring at Kimi and Sarah so fiercely that I didn't notice the girl with movie-star looks who sat down next to me.

"Oh! Hi! I'm Ericka," I say. "I'm new, too...sorta."

Mackenzie looks exactly the way I want to when I grow up...which I'm hoping will be any day now. She is the perfect all-American girl. Her eyes sparkle blue and her smile is perfectly symmetrical, spread across straight white teeth. Her hair is not too thick or thin, but kind of looks like she may have come straight from a salon. I don't know if the blond is real, but it's definitely not dishwater.

"What do you mean, 'sorta'?" she asks.

"You're Ricki Jo Winstead, right?" a girl asks on my other side. It's Laura Wagner, another face I recognize and someone I've actually hung out with a few times before, though not since she started wearing so much makeup. She has long auburn hair and a friendly round face; she's the kind of person who nods her head a lot when you talk. We both have chipmunk cheeks and she's considered short, too, although she still has a few inches on me. Our parents play Rook together every now and then, but she obviously didn't get the memo that I'm trying to reinvent my image here.

"Um, yeah. Ericka, actually," I reply. Laura smiles and makes what I thought would be an awkward moment really easy.

"That's cool. I'm glad y'all are finally integrating. Your class size just went from — what? — five to two hundred?" We both laugh, although Mackenzie seems confused, and I'm feeling good about my first day. Laura may be popular and a master at smoky eyes, but she also seems really down-to-earth.

"This is Mackenzie," I say.

"Yeah, her folks are members of the country club. Wasn't that end-of-season pool party last night totally lame?" Laura asks.

Mackenzie nods and giggles. " 'Pool Olympics.' Ha! Your dad was great in water aerobics, though."

Laura fake gags and puts her head down. I feel like genuinely gagging and crawling under the table. I'm second string to a true, actual, just-moved-here new girl. Mackenzie's from Minnesota, says her O's in a really weird way, and already has more friends than I do.

"So you're new but you already live here?" she asks.

I tell her about our little Catholic school and how the rest of the kids have kind of been together their whole lives. Laura tells her that even the four boys from my school joining PCHS is a mega way to enlarge their dating pool. We laugh and Mackenzie tells us a little about her old school. She cheered, and so does Laura, and of course this bit of information is enough to pull Kimi and Sarah from their intense who-gave-whom-which-hickey conversation. They all babble on about "state" and "formations" and "tumbling" while I smile and nod. When in doubt, smile and nod.

"Good morning, lovely ladies."

I turn my head and feel my smile falter, my heart skip a beat, and my breath catch in the back of my throat. I have never seen him before, but I am convinced that the boy grinning at us from an arm's length away must have materialized directly from my head as the ultimate man of my dreams.

"Girls' table only, Wolf," Kimi says, flirting; she clearly wants him to stay.

"That's why I'm taking the last seat. I am your sheik and you all are my harem." The other girls giggle and roll their eyes, but I focus on bringing my lower jaw up so that my mouth can actually close.

This guy, "Wolf," is already my boyfriend...in my head. He's about a foot taller than I am and moves like liquid, smooth and sure. He's lean, too—probably has a six-pack. His skin is like that of a bronzed god, and you can tell it's that way all year long. His short dark hair spikes up here and there as if he doesn't style it at all, but he probably worked on it for at least fifteen minutes. He makes lookin' good seem effortless. Like, he lives in that lookin'-good zone. I think I'll wear a long white gown and a short veil, and he and his groomsmen will wear sharp charcoal tuxedos. We'll get married on my farm and—

"No, it's Ericka. She doesn't want to be called Ricki Jo anymore," I hear Mackenzie remind Laura.

Oh, god. Wolf is looking right at me, wearing a lopsided, perfect, melt-me-into-a-pool-on-my-seat grin.

"Hello? Erick-y Jo?" he teases, waving a hand in front of my face, breaking me from my trance. The girls laugh and I flush a deep red, feeling it all the way to the tips of my massive ears. I giggle a little and open my notebook absentmindedly.

Then I take a deep breath, will my head up, force my eyes in his direction, and choke out, "Hi. Sorry, my name's Ericka Winstead. Nice to meet you."

"I'm David Wolfenbaker. And it's really my pleasure," he says—and he winks. He winks at me!

I somehow control the impulse to squeal in delight. Instead, I look at Kimi and Sarah and introduce myself the same way. It's so weird because we recognize one another, but we don't *know* one another.

"So, girls," Wolf says, leaning back in his seat. "Which one of you will end up being my date to homecoming?" We all giggle, and as I look around, I realize that I'm not the only one under his spell...but I am surely the least likely to win him over.

As Kimi finds some excuse to show him her new belly-button ring, I doodle on my notebook and pray for the bell to sound. I want to die or be trapped on a deserted island with David Wolfenbaker. One or the other, but I've got to get out of homeroom.

*　　*　　*

"It was awful," I tell Luke at his locker. It's on the other side of the hall and I really feel like the air is cleaner over here or something. I almost suffocated trying to stuff my book bag into my own locker, squeezed right between Kimi and her voluptuousness and Wolf and his sexual-awakening-me-ness.

"Is everything at this school gonna be alphabetized?" I complain.

Luke smirks at me and shuts his locker. "What's wrong with a little order?"

"The girls in my homeroom are gorgeous. Way outta my league. They're all cheerleaders, and every one of them wears makeup and name brands. I gotta talk my mom into taking me to the mall in Lexington."

"Why? You wanna be like those girls?" Luke asks, looking over to where Mackenzie, Laura, Kimi, and Sarah stand huddled around Wolf's locker.

"Well, yeah! I mean, they're popular, they're beautiful—"

"They're stuck-up," Luke finishes.

"Not all of them," I say defensively. "I mean, Mackenzie's new—from Minnesota new—and she's really nice. And that girl Laura is cool, too."

"Yeah, well, I'm just saying that the Fabulous Four looks to be assembled already."

"You don't think there's room for a fifth?" I ask.

We head down the hall toward first period and I suddenly feel all their eyes on us. *Oh, god. Did they hear me?*

The four girls stare at us as we pass and then start to giggle. I feel my face flush, hoping they aren't making fun of me.

"Hi, Luke!" Laura calls. The whole gaggle of girls cracks up and the blush Laura's wearing seems to intensify. I slow down so Luke can talk to her, thinking he will, too.

"What's up?" Luke asks, but he doesn't stop. Instead, he continues down the hall. I sort of stand near the girls, watching them watch him as his lean frame ambles through the throng of students. Whereas everyone else is dressed up, wearing their best for the first day, Luke is totally comfortable in a pair of deeply worn-in dark jeans, a white V-neck, and cowboy boots. The only thing mildly fashionable on his whole body is the thin leather bracelet that he never takes off. He turns back, realizing I'm no longer at his side, and gives me a head jerk, a kind of let's-go signal that makes his sandy blond hair flip over his forehead. I give the girls an awkward wave and hurry to catch up.

Once I'm at his side again, he drapes his long tanned arm on my shoulder, easy and comfortable. I start to feel better.

"Why do you care about girls like that, anyway?" he asks.

"They're cool," I say. "I dunno. I'm the new girl and I'm nervous and I wanna fit in."

"You wanna fit in with some kids in our class or you wanna fit in with those specific girls?" he asks.

I think about it. *What do I want?*

I want a boyfriend. I want a date to the homecoming dance. I want a first kiss—one with tongue, one that is not decided by the spin of an old Coca-Cola bottle. I want to be cool.

"Those specific girls," I say. I affirm. I make my goal. Ericka Jo Winstead is on a mission to become popular. So it is written.

"You're on your own, then. See ya at lunch!" And just like that, Luke heads into a classroom and fist pounds a couple of guys. I watch him fold his tall body into a desk, see how his long face lights up around his old friends, and envy the sparkle in his blue eyes, how easy his first day of school is. Squaring my shoulders, I look for room 124 and hold tight to my smile-and-nod method.

"It's so cool that you're going to our school now, Ricki Jo!" My friend Candace, from the 4-H Club, is in my Spanish class, and I'm so happy to see a familiar face that I don't even mention the *Ericka* thing. After a long day of standing up, period after period, stating my name per new-girl fashion, I'm just glad to be talking to someone I really know. Candace and I shared bunk beds at 4-H camp and bonded over that week of basket weaving, hiking, and campfires. She's a little rough around the edges, lives in the trailer park over behind the nursing home, and has the thickest country accent I've ever heard, but she's smart and has a really good heart.

"Yeah, my dating pool just went from four to four hundred!" I exclaim, stealing a bit of Laura's humor. But it's true. Today, I've gaped and gawked at every turn. From freshmen to seniors, my head has been on constant swivel mode, though no one has compared to Wolf.

"From the looks of your folder, I'd say you've got your eye on a particular freshman who just happens to be in this class," Candace says, pulling her frizzy red hair into a giant puffy ponytail. I look up to see Wolf enter our classroom and strut toward the back, cocky and fascinating. "I'd rethink the heart-shaped *D.W.*, Ricki Jo. Not a tough code to crack if he sees your notebook."

I touch his initials and grin. "He's pretty cute, right?"

"Cute." She shrugs and leans back in her desk. "And knows it."

"Confident," I say.

"Arrogant," she replies.

Señorita Jones brings our class to attention and goes over our syllabus. She tells us that we need to pick our Spanish names and turn them in by the end of class. I want my name to be something really exotic sounding. Candace and I flip through our Spanish books and look at English to Spanish translations. Henrietta—Enriqueta. Mary—María. Alice—Alícia. I see a picture of two gorgeous Argentine sisters, dressed in sexy black lace gowns, demonstrating a passionate tango. I can't decide between the two and choose both names for myself: Rosa Juana.

"What's up with you and double names?" Wolf asks from behind me. He turns in his name at the same time—Davíd, real original—and follows me as we head back to our seats. I am very self-conscious as I step over the backpacks strewn in the aisle. *Do not fall. Do not fall.*

"And from now on, class," Señorita calls, "we'll be sitting in alphabetical order by last names."

I stop, stunned, and look back at her. *Seriously?*

Wolf smiles down at me. "Guess you're stuck with me, Rosa Jo." I barely feel him squeeze past me. *David Wolfenbaker will be sitting directly behind me the rest of the school year.* I struggle to understand the nausea in my gut, but find my wits quickly enough to sit down and scribble out his initials. We'll probably talk every day now, maybe sneak notes during class. I look up to God and whisper a little *gracías.* I'm going to need perfume, lip gloss, and a new notebook ASAP.

CHAPTER FOUR

School is out! I survived the first day. I run from the bus and up my driveway, excited to drop my books and head over to Luke's. We're off the hook for the next few days as far as work is concerned, so I'm taking my bike over and drilling him about anything and everything he knows about David Wolfenbaker. I trade out my dress for shorts and a T-shirt, get my bike out of the garage, and take off.

Luke lives right over the hill, but it always feels like miles. Why? Because between my driveway and his driveway is the Gumbels' driveway...which is often guarded by their pack of wild dogs. There are at least five of them, and the leader of the pack looks like a big black bear. My dad says to avoid eye contact and continue on in a steady manner, so as not to show fear. He says animals smell fear. I sniff and get a little whiff of sweat and deodorant, but no fear. Not yet.

Up, up, up the road, past the small creepy cemetery, and I hear them barking. *Please be chained up today. Please be chained up today.* At the crest of the hill, I see them running at me, full speed. *No fear, Ricki Jo. No fear.* I try to pedal steadily, but they circle around me and I'm afraid I'm going to run over one the way they keep darting everywhere. I wish a car would come. I glance down and see the leader, mouth foaming, teeth bared, and lose my balance, swerving my handlebars and crashing into the shoulder of the road.

As I lie there shielded underneath my bike, they circle around me, barking low and loud. I shout, "Get back! Get back!" but they only get more excited. Two of them dart toward me at the same time and then start to fight each other. I try to get up, but the leader jumps on my bike, effectively pinning me beneath him.

I scream. I cry and scream and scream. All I hear is barking and my own screaming, and I can taste my tears. I feel like I'm going to die.

Then I hear another voice, not screaming, but yelling. The voice is angry. The dogs forget me for a second and I hear yelps. I crane my head up and see Luke running down the road toward me, throwing rocks at the dogs and cussing them out. I know they can't understand, but I appreciate his filthy admonitions. I release the huge breath I didn't realize I was holding, let my head drop back into the ditch, and weep.

*   *   *

"I hate those dogs," I mumble, wiping my nose with the sleeve of my shirt.

Luke nods, rolling my bicycle into his yard. "I hate their owners. No leash? Irresponsible morons."

We go inside Luke's house and his momma props me up on her kitchen counter with a wet rag for the back of my neck and a cold Coke for my nerves. I've been coming over here since I was a little girl, my momma and Luke's being good friends from when they went to school together. She's the nicest lady, always treating me like one of her own.

"Took a pretty hard spill," she notes now, as she picks the gravel from my knees and hands and pours peroxide on my scrapes.

"I showed fear," I say. "Ow!"

"Now you listen to me, Ricki Jo Winstead: It ain't your fault. Those crazy beasts came running up on my Ava just the other day. My grandbaby! Not even old enough to run away! Playing in her pen in the front yard one minute, screaming from the middle of their pack the next. Scared the living daylights out of her and me both! In my own front yard!" She stops and looks out the kitchen window, her mouth set in a hard line. "There's something mighty wrong when you don't feel safe on your own property."

"You gonna call the sheriff again, Momma?" Luke asks.

"I don't know what I'm gonna do, son." She sighs, turning her attention back to me and unwrapping a huge Band-Aid.

"What about Animal Control? They gotta do something," he insists.

Just then the screen door from the back porch slams shut and his mom tenses up. "Mattie!" we hear his dad growl.

"All done, sugar. Y'all hustle on outside and play. I'll figure something out about those dogs later."

"My supper ready, Mattie?" I look up to see Luke's dad leaning unsteadily against the door frame. His eyes are bloodshot and angry.

"Dad, it's only four o'clock," Luke reasons.

"I told y'all to get outside. Shoo!" Mrs. Foster ushers us out in a hurry and gives us a *don't come back* look that makes me really uneasy. Luke hesitates, unsure. "Get!"

And we go. We walk slowly; we can hear shouting, but we don't look at each other and we don't look back at the house. We hear glass break. We shudder. We walk through his backyard and climb the plank fence, headed for the pond behind his house. We walk on a grass trail, yellow and matted down from our long summer of traipsing this same route. We walk slowly, hear shouting, don't look at each other and don't look back at the house.

At the pond, we skip rocks. Watch them sail across the smooth glass top of the water. Long, quiet minutes stretch between us.

Finally the shouting stops and Luke speaks, bitter and angry: "There's something mighty wrong when you don't feel safe on your own property."

I look over at him, but don't see my friend at all.

CHAPTER FIVE

"So cheerleading tryouts are Monday after school in the gym," Kimi tells us matter-of-factly. Mackenzie eagerly writes the time down in her notebook and the girls start talking about what to expect. I, of course, smile and nod, and then—

"Ow!" I cry.

It feels like someone just walked up behind me and flicked me on the side of my face. Looking down at the table in front of me, I see a thick triangular paper. I pick it up and look at Wolf, who is grinning devilishly, as usual.

"What was that for?" I demand, lightly touching my temple. Kimi and Sarah giggle.

"I don't know." He shrugs. "These girls are boring me to death with all their pom-pom chitchat. Wanna play paper football?" Their giggling abruptly stops and I abruptly soften.

"Sure," I say. He makes a goalpost by putting his thumbs together and lifting both forefingers in the air. I balance the paper triangle on one tip, then flick it hard.

"Ahh!" he yells out, clapping his hand over his right eye, obviously hurt.

"Oh my gosh!" I yell, my hand immediately flying to my mouth. It was a direct hit.

He tilts his head back and pushes off of Laura's chair, leaning his own chair way back on two legs. Laura looks at me wide-eyed and I freeze, stone still, next to Mackenzie. Kimi leans toward him over the table, her cleavage coming out to save the day, and Sarah just blows air through her bangs, looking totally bored. When Wolf puts his front chair legs back on the floor and lowers his hand from his face, we are all shocked, and relieved, to see that he's laughing. He's laughing really hard.

"I am so sorry!" I exclaim. *And so embarrassed.*

He blinks a few times and rubs his eye, really amused. "That's the nature of the game, babe."

I sigh, feel the heat in my cheeks, and look at the clock. Wolf asks me to play a game with him—me! out of all the girls at our table!—and I injure him. Flick him right in the eye. I mean, he's obviously not mad, but the football made its way to his front pocket pretty quickly, and then he put his head down on his books. I try to focus on the exhilarating fact that David Wolfenbaker just called me "babe" and not on the fact that he probably won't talk to me ever again. The bell rings and he's out the door before any of us. As I sling my backpack up over my shoulder, I watch him walk away. Game. Over.

"See you at lunch, Ericka?" Mackenzie asks.

"Yep," I say, snapping back to attention. "I'm already hungry." She laughs and bounds off toward first period with Laura.

I make my way through the masses to my locker, where Kimi is spritzing her bangs in her locker mirror and Sarah is flirting with an older-looking guy. I slide in and drop my book bag to the ground.

"Okay, thirty-four, twenty-five, thirty-six," I mumble to myself, trying to work my new combination from memory. My locker pops open and then—WHAM!—slams shut.

"Whoops." Wolf appears next to me, leaning against his own locker.

I give him a *not funny* look and try again, a little more nervous this time as I spin the dial. So he *is* still talking to me. *Thirty-four, twenty-five, thirty-six.* Pop and slam.

"Man! These new lockers are touchy, huh?" he says.

"Wolf! I'm gonna be late!" I protest, a little annoyed and a lot liking the attention.

I give it a twirl again, and just then I see a cloud of big red hair rushing toward me out of the corner of my eye. It's Candace, and although she's definitely wearing a fashion "don't" (even *I* know not to wear pleated jean shorts), her big smile makes up for it. Lost in her own world, she hip checks Wolf out of the way and grabs my arm.

"Hey! Are you still taking piano lessons, Ricki Jo?" she says excitedly.

"Piano?" Wolf asks, eyebrows arched, clearly entertained.

"Um, yeah," I falter. "I mean, like, every now and then."

"Well," she begins, as if she has the best idea of her life, "band tryouts for new kids are Monday after school and I totally think you should go! I mean, we get to go to all the home games, and we've won state the last five years in a row. And it won't matter that you don't know the marches, 'cause the keyboardists stay put up front. It's really fun and I can introduce you to lots of people!"

I look from Wolf to Candace, thinking about how I like them both, and how they couldn't be more different if they tried.

"Um, yeah, sounds like fun!" I say.

Behind her, Wolf's eyes bug out and he shakes his head no.

"I mean, maybe," I recover, my smile fading and my confusion growing. "I mean, yeah, I don't know." Candace looks stunned, but Wolf gives me a thumbs-up behind her. That makes me feel a little better, but then I wonder why Wolf's opinion matters so much. Because it does.

Candace is hurt, I can tell, but she covers quickly. She takes a piece of gum out of her purse, unwraps it, and pops it in her mouth before looking back up at me with a blank expression. "Yeah, sure. I don't care. It was just an idea."

I nod. "Thanks. Really."

"Whatever. See ya in Spanish," she says and walks away, blowing a big defiant bubble even though the hallways are crowded with teachers. I watch her go, feeling helpless. Feeling awful. And I'm not even sure why. I shake my head and turn back to my locker. Fitting in—trying to fit in, I mean—is really hard.

I reach for my locker dial once again, but a tanned hand with thick veins and strong fingers covers my own. Wolf is directly behind me and begins to work my lock, his arm definitely touching my side as he twists. His chin is maybe one inch from the top of my head and I am keenly aware of his body heat. I want to run away. I want time to stand still.

"Thirty-four, twenty-five, thirty-six," he mumbles, and my locker pops open. I don't move, blink, or breathe. "Listen, Ericka, I know you're new here and you seem nice, so I'm gonna give you some advice." His breath is warm in my ear. "Cool girls aren't in band, okay?" I look up and over my shoulder at him, my body frozen in place. "Cool girls cheer."

I could kiss him. I'm that close. *I could kiss David Wolfenbaker right now.*

"See ya in Spanish!" he says, flicking that paper triangle into my face and strutting off to class.

I shake my head, awake from the trance, and realize—

"Hey! How'd you know my combination?"

He half turns, midstride, and grins. Ah, that grin. I feel red and hot and tingly and in love all over my body. I close my locker and hurry off in the other direction.

It's not until the late bell rings that I realize I never got the book I need.

CHAPTER SIX

"Ricki Jo, get over here," my dad shouts. I squint up at him through watery red eyes, cranky all over again. We're helping Luke's family house the tobacco we cut a few days ago and I am less than thrilled.

Housing is about as much fun as cutting. After the tobacco sits out in the field for "three dews," we load it onto the trailer and haul it to the barn. The men shimmy up, climbing higher and higher into the old wooden rafters, and plant themselves for a long day's work. At the bottom, the smallest of us grab sticks, laden with six heavy tobacco stalks each, and pass them up. Then the men above pass them up and up and up, dirt and small leaves falling with each pass. The guy at the top levels each stick horizontally so that it fits right across the rafters and the leaves hang down straight to cure.

I would like to hit puberty sometime this century,

but right now I am thankful that I'm too small to be up high in the barn. The only problem with the bottom position is that it gets really dusty in here when we house and I end up sneezing my head off...which is why my dad brings along a white surgical mask for me to wear.

"Dad, no, I'm okay," I protest...then sneeze.

"Wear it," he demands, and then pulls himself up into the barn. I grudgingly pull the stretchy part over my head and pinch the small metal strip to fit over my nose, effectively trading my dignity for sinus relief.

I meet Luke's gaze and can tell he's trying not to laugh. "That mask drives me crazy, Ricki Jo," he teases quietly. "Really sexy."

I take a swing at him, but he's up in the rafters in the blink of an eye, laughing down at me.

"What're we waiting for?" Mr. Foster hollers down gruffly from above.

I grab a stick and pass it up, and even though it's super heavy, I try my best to stab Luke, who reaches for it like a hot potato.

"No goofing around, kids," my dad's voice warns.

And we settle. Grab a stick and pass it up. And pass it up. And pass it up.

I miss the days when Luke's older sister, Claire, worked with us — back when I wasn't the only girl and had somebody to talk to, and to look up to. I miss the days before she was pregnant and stuck — stuck in this town, in this life. I grab a stick and pass it up. Pass. Pass the time in a steady rhythm.

When the trailer in the barn is half empty, my dad yells down to me, "Ricki Jo! You and a couple boys go get another load."

Gladly. I'm out of the barn, mask off and hair down, before he changes his mind and sends someone else. I climb up into the seat of my dad's John Deere tractor and wait 'til Luke and his older brother Paul hop onto the empty trailer hitched behind me.

I complain a lot about working, but I actually love driving the tractor. It's a powerful feeling, and even though I have to completely stand, pulling up hard on the steering wheel while putting my entire body weight down on the brake to stop the dang thing, I feel in control. Nothing but waving bluegrass hayfields on one side and cattle-specked rolling green hills on the other. Put-put-putting over the fields, in absolutely no hurry, I soak up the sun and have a lot of quiet time to daydream while the boys lie stretched out on the empty trailer, exhausted.

I follow the gigantic wheel treads leading back to the front field, pull up to the row where we left off, kill the engine, and lock the brake.

"We're already here?" Luke groans.

I turn around in my seat and look down at the two boys, covered in dirt, sweat, and pieces of tobacco. Luke has one arm behind his head and one thrown over his face, blocking out the sun. Paul hops off the trailer and heads for the tobacco, while I climb down from my perch and up onto the trailer next to Luke.

"Wake up," I say, singsong.

"Just five more minutes," he groans.

I touch his forehead and giggle when I pull it away to see a finger-shaped white spot fill in red again. "You got burnt."

"Sunscreen's for sissies," he replies. Then he moves his arm a little and squints up at me, a mischievous look on his face. "You hungry?"

"Starved."

"Let's go," he says and springs to life. I follow him in the dirt, his footprints nearly twice the size of mine. Luke tells his brother that we'll be right back and I hear Paul mumble something about "kids." Whatever. He can kill himself in the tobacco field if he wants, but I'm going with Luke.

Where the dirt ends and the grass begins, we head toward a small wooded area. I'm hesitant, worried it's going to be some kind of gross boy-type surprise like a dead squirrel or something, but Luke motions me on. I step between a couple of walnut trees and see it in the shade—an orange cooler with a white top.

"You've got food in there?" I exclaim.

Luke nods smugly. "Peanut butter and jelly sandwiches. Mom made some for all the guys up at the barn, but I swiped a few just for us. And a couple of Cokes. We gotta hurry, though."

Hurry we do. I don't know if it's the fact that we're

sneaking around or that we're truly famished, but I start laughing as I watch Luke inhale his PB&J.

"You look like some kind of monster!" I giggle.

He starts shoving the food into his mouth, getting jelly all over his face, and growls and claws the air like a wild animal. I can't help myself; I fall down laughing, and Coke comes out my nose.

"It burns!" I cry. "Stop! It burns!"

I roll over on the ground, howling. I have a sharp pain in my side and my cheeks hurt. Luke plops down next to me and we sit back to back, propping each other up. As we catch our breath and finish our snacks, I figure this is as good a time as any to get the 411 on David Wolfen-baker, aka my future husband.

"How well do you know that guy Wolf?" I ask as non-chalantly as possible, taking another bite of my sandwich.

"Why do you wanna know?" he asks, suspicious.

I shrug my shoulders against his and swallow. "I don't know. I mean, he's kind of friendly."

Luke spins around to face me and I fall back, the solid weight of him gone from behind.

"You like him," he states.

I steady myself, take another bite, and nod, although I can't really look at him. It feels weird talking about boys with Luke.

He looks away, too, and I flick my eyes over his face, trying to read his thoughts in the deep creases across his forehead. He takes a minute, then looks back at me. "Let's just say I'd play ball with the guy any time, but I'd never let him date my sister."

"Would you let him date your best friend?" I ask teasingly.

He looks down at his Coke, then drains it, stands, and crunches the can under his foot. When he looks down at me, it's like he's explaining why two plus two equals four. "They call him 'the Wolf,' Ricki Jo," he says, "and it's not just because of his last name."

I pop the last bite of my sandwich into my mouth and drain my own Coke. He crunches my can for me, then tosses them both back into the cooler. The last thing I want to do is get back out in the field under the blazing sun, but things seem to be getting just as uncomfortable in our wooded hideaway. I follow him back to the field and jump up on the trailer as he joins Paul, throwing a full stick over his shoulder, the two of them looking like those old caricatures of hobos who carry everything they own tied to the end of a stick.

We work wordlessly for the next half hour, the guys passing the full sticks up to me, me arranging them against the back of the trailer, in an easy rhythm. I think a little bit about what Luke said . . . and a lot about Wolf's heart-stopping grin.

Obsessing over a boy makes the time fly. I grab the last of the load and hop down, my head in the clouds and my smile unfamiliar out in the tobacco fields. I heave myself up onto the tractor and get her going again. As the tractor roars back to life, I still can't wipe the grin from my face. Ricki Jo as she is now may not be able to snag a guy like Wolf, but the new and improved Ericka will be. I just need to upgrade: Me 2.0.

As the steering wheel slides back and forth through my fingers, loose like it's got a mind of its own, I guide us through the fields and up toward the barn, giddy at the thought of no more tobacco 'til it gets colder. No more gum-stained fingernails or farmer's tan. Not another whiff of this stuff 'til strippin' season. That's two full months to metamorphosize.

CHAPTER SEVEN

"Okay, so *if* I make the squad, we'll have practices after school, and maybe a couple of Saturdays," I tell my folks.

The breakfast nook is my courtroom, and my parents are the judge and jury. I pace back and forth, having planned my case thoroughly during Mass this morning. Tryouts are tomorrow and the homily was on why God gave us free will, so I'm making my move while the iron is hot.

"As it gets cold, I won't be able to run around outside or ride my bike, so it's an excellent way to get exercise. You can't be on the squad without good grades, so of course I'll stay on top of that, too. I've saved enough money this summer that I won't have to ask for spending money on away games. And apparently cheerleading is really important to the girls at school, meaning I'll be making the kind of friends who value work ethic and doing their best."

As my dad takes a bite of blackberry cobbler I think I see him trying to hide a grin under his mustache, and my heart skips. *This is working!* So I continue, really hamming it up.

"Now, you might be thinking, 'Why the sudden interest in cheerleading, Ricki Jo?' Well, we all know that what I lack in height and size, I make up for in spunk. I really want to fit in at my new school, and I figure that cheerleading is the best way to boldly display my intense school pride to my peers. Four-H just isn't gonna cut it anymore."

I pound my fist into my palm, furrowing my brow. My dad chokes on his dessert. I am emboldened.

"I want to wear the maroon and gold—the same maroon and gold you two wore when you fell in love all those years ago. Without that maroon and gold, you never would have fallen in love at prom, and I never would have been born. I *am* maroon and gold."

The drama builds.

"I have spirit! Yes I do! I've got spirit, how 'bout you?" At this, I wildly wave fierce spirit fingers and heartily attempt the splits.

Key word: *attempt.*

"Ow!" I cry, my crotch a foot from the floor, pain burning my groin.

At this, neither of my parents can hold it in anymore

and, along with their eye rolling and head shaking, there is gut-wrenching laughter. I fall over to one side—sweet relief.

My dad pushes his cap back and wheezes, "What are we gonna do with this girl, Toots?"

My momma wipes at the tears in her eyes. "Don't ask me. She's your daughter."

My dad slaps at his knees and my momma starts snorting. Snorting! *I've got 'em. I've so got 'em.* I get up off the floor, sit down at the table, and cut myself a piece of cobbler. My work here is done.

Trying out is one thing; making the squad is another thing altogether. I walk into the gymnasium and freeze. All around me, ponytails and gym shoes are back-flipping, round-off-back-handspringing, and toe-touch jumping. I don't see a whole lot of "cheering," per se, but I'm seriously rethinking the marching band idea.

"Ericka! Over here!" Mackenzie waves me over to where she and Laura are stretching. I force one tennis shoe in front of the other and walk toward them, terrified.

"Are you okay?" Laura asks, wrangling her long auburn hair into a tighter ponytail. "Your face is white as a ghost!"

Mackenzie offers me her water bottle, but I shake my head. "I'm just a little nervous," I croak.

I sit down beside Laura and begin to stretch out, mimicking her every move. Mackenzie is going on about how worried she is as a new girl, whether or not she'll fit in with the Kentucky style of cheering, but all I hear is *blah, blah, blah* and the strange buzzing sound in my ears that I usually get right before I vomit. A whistle blows from somewhere in the atmosphere, bringing me back to my senses.

"Ladies!" Coach Thomas yells, her voice authoritative. She reminds me of a beauty pageant queen past her prime. "We'll see one tumbling pass, a short group number to the fight song, and then your individual chants. Let's go!"

As Coach passes out sheets of paper printed with our chants, I grab Mackenzie's elbow and pull her aside. "I think I'm gonna get out of here."

"What? Why?" she asks, her hands suddenly tight on my biceps.

"I just think maybe it was a bad idea. I can't do all those crazy flips, and I've never learned a dance routine. I don't even know the fight song!" I assert.

"Neither do I," she reminds me. *Hmmm...I should've pulled Laura aside.*

"Listen, can you do a cartwheel?" Mackenzie continues. I nod. She perks up. "Awesome! So for your tumbling pass, you'll do as many cartwheels in a row as you can. And if you want, end it with a round-off—it's basically just a cartwheel where you bring both feet down at the same time. Okay?" Her vigorous head bobbing is intoxicating.

I nod along, involuntarily.

"Then, for the group routine, stick by me and Laura.

When we go through the practice with the senior girls, just keep the count in your head. Count out loud if you need to; just keep the count. One through eight, over and over again. It won't be super dance-y; it'll probably be more like motions and angles." She demonstrates a few arm movements that look pretty easy. I'm feeling...less nauseous.

"Finally, the individual chant. Sounds scary, but I bet it'll be your best part. You've got tons of energy, you've got a huge smile, and you really want this. That'll go a long way," she assures me.

"But we have to do a jump in the individual chant!" I remind her.

"You can't touch your toes?" she asks. I shake my head, embarrassed. "Can you bring your knees up like this?" She demonstrates a tuck. It looks possible. I take a deep breath and try it.

"Perfect! Just do a tuck jump!" she squeals. "Listen, the secret to great cheerleading is confident head nodding and nonstop smiling."

The whistle blows and we take our places among the masses in a three-row formation to learn the dance. Mackenzie squeezes my hand, her blue eyes sparkling, then tightens her salon-blond ponytail. That girl's one helluva cheerleader.

Following the seniors as they dance to the Lady Gaga party mix blaring from the gym speakers, I count to eight like my life depends on it. The majority of my previous dance experience consists of one preschool ballet recital and self-taught moves to Top 40 hits in front of my full-length mirror at home. After thirty minutes of learning and rehearsing this routine, I've decided to never show my aforementioned self-taught moves to the public. Today's dance style seems to involve a dash of bump and a cup of grind, with a heavy dose of attitude...ingredients I haven't incorporated before. Not having cable television can really keep a girl out of the loop.

"Watts! Whitman! Wilson! Winstead! Let's go!"

Mackenzie, Sarah, Kimi, and I take the floor. Sarah looks awake and focused, and even unconcerned about her bangs for the first time since school started. And Kimi is the picture of confidence in an old cheer T-shirt that she's cut deep at the neck and tied up into a knot in the back. All three girls are smiling fiercely and standing at perfect attention, so I pull myself up to my full height and flash my biggest smile to the coaches as the music starts again.

"Five, six," Coach counts. "Five, six, seven, eight."

The music is blaring, and I'm glad Coach counted us in. With each mark, I bump, hit, and grind as hard as my little body will let me. The angles aren't a problem—I'm all knees and elbows—but "rolling my body" just feels creepy and unnatural. Still, truth be told, the dance routine isn't as awful as I'd imagined it would be. A few jazz squares and grapevines, but mainly a lot of hand slicing in the air. It's kind of like karate mixed with aerobics. The eight count is brilliant, and Mackenzie's smile-and-nod method, although a bit perkier than the one I've been using at school, is a tool with which I am already comfortable. There are a few moments of borderline flailing, but overall I gallop off court feeling okay.

My tumbling pass is another story. My confidence wavers as I watch Mackenzie's nonstop back tucks and Sarah's sky-high back layouts. Then Kimi and Laura back-handspring their way across the floor without a hitch. On my turn, I take a deep breath and manage eight cart-wheels before ending with my first ever round-off (which I nail). Looking up excitedly at the judges, I see shock and pity in their eyes. So I do the only thing I can do: smile wider, wiggle spirit fingers ferociously, and give a few controlled fist pumps into the air, shouting, "Let's go! PCHS! Number one!"

The hour and a half that we've spent in the gym has flown by; I guess self-discovery is a fast-paced affair. I'm getting a lot of encouragement from the other girls who are trying out and feel good about myself for trying something new. As I watch my classmates go through their individual chants, I'm glad to be a W for the first time in my life: It allows me to watch everyone else and learn from their routines. I go through the words over and over in my head and mark the motions modestly on the sideline.

"Winstead!" Coach Thomas calls out.

Now or never.

I muster up all the spunk I've got and run/skip to center court, prepared to give the performance of my life.

"Ready? O-kay!" I head nod with all my might and plaster the biggest smile you've ever seen across my face. Then I freeze.

I am mid-court, by myself, all kinds of pit stains and body odor, when I see Wolf saunter into the gym with some other guys from our school. He's wearing a Stallions basketball jersey, probably his older brother's, and his lean body climbs up the bleachers quickly and effortlessly. The cheerleading chant has something to do with our team, winning, and yelling, but my mind is void of all but the killer grin laser beam he gives me when he sits down. He passed me a note today in Spanish—"*Buena suerte.* Good luck."—and signed it with X's and O's.

"Miss Winstead?" Coach Thomas's voice echoes over the loudspeakers and I snap to attention. *Does she really need a microphone?*

I smile and begin again, my focus strong and my will to impress even stronger.

"Ready? O-kay!" *(fierce head nod)*

"Cheer for the Stallions!" *(pom-poms up in a V)*

"Cheer for a win!" *(poms down in a V, spin)*

"Come on, crowd!" *(crazy uncontrolled pom-pom air chops)*

"Yell go, fight, win!" *(and the tuck jump of my life)*

There is the briefest pause before I hear Mackenzie and Laura cheering for me. The coach seems more curious than pleased, and I gallop off the floor, yelling, "Let's go Stallions! Go, fight, win!" and pumping my pom-poms in the air.

Back at the sidelines, Mackenzie gives me a huge hug. "I'm so proud of you, Ericka!"

Laura gives my thick ponytail a playful tug and says, "Yeah, you hustled us out there!"

I feel incredible. Seriously, I know I'm not the best, but I did *my* best, and I'm on top of the world. *I'll get better with practice. I'll work hard.* I grab a Gatorade and soak it up. Tryouts are officially over. My pulse can finally slow down.

From the bleachers comes a screeching male voice: "Let's go, Stallions!" We all look up and see Wolf, surrounded by a small group of guys, all of them cracking up. Coach gives him a quick, stern look, he waves and gives a big thumbs-up, and she turns back to the tabulation table with the other coaches. Once her eyes are off him, he stands and ties his jersey in a knot, puts his hands on his hips, and flashes a wicked smile. None of us knows what to expect, but Mackenzie and I share a look. After just a week of school, we know he's got "mischief" written all over him.

"He's gonna get in so much trouble," she whispers to me, and I nod in agreement.

"Ready? Okay!" he starts, slapping his hand against his outer thigh.

I can't help but giggle.

"I am a redneck! New to this school!" he yells. "I wanna be a cheerleader, so I can be cool!"

His motions are herky-jerky, fists balled up tight, shooting directly out at me. I feel them like punches in my gut.

I originally thought that the guys around him were looking in my *general* direction, but at this moment, I fully comprehend that those knee-slapping, laughing-their-butts-off idiots are looking in my *exact* direction. And now a few of the girls are, too.

I feel the blood rush to my face and know I'm bright red. I want it to stop. I need him to stop.

"I'm just a farm girl, short and flat!" he continues, hands smoothing down his own chest.

A whistle echoes through the gymnasium, high and angry, effectively cutting him off. For a beat, all eyes leave my face for Coach Thomas's. I take the opportunity to blink.

This is not a dream.

I don't think he's finished, or maybe he can't find a word to rhyme with *flat*, but Coach is furious and making her way up the bleachers two at a time. "Basketball tryouts aren't for another twenty minutes! If you can't behave like a gentleman, then you can wait outside. Wolfenbaker, out of here! Now!"

He slides out of his row, getting high fives and fist pumps along the way, and exits the gym a general hero, blowing a kiss at me as he leaves. His bleacher posse erupts.

Coach's whistle takes the brunt of her anger; she

blows it shrilly over and over as she explodes. "That's it! All of you, out of here! Let's go!"

Wolf's pack exits the gym in a fit, blowing air kisses to me or throwing up mocking spirit fingers. My face and ears are on fire, and I can't look down or the big tears that line my lower lids will definitely fall. I lean back against the wall padding behind me, keeping my chin as up as it will go, and stare at the far basketball hoop until we're dismissed. I feel small and ugly and country.

In the tunnel behind the bleachers, I finally crumble, knees up, head on arms, and let the tears fall.

CHAPTER EIGHT

"You've been crying," Momma says as I get in her blue Corolla.

"I don't wanna talk about it," I reply, slamming the door shut and staring out the window at the water tower. My dad once told me that as a teenager my granddad climbed it with his buddies and swam around in it to impress a girl. Boys are so dumb.

"Well, sweetie, we're proud of you no matter what," she says, patting my hand. I know this is one of those moments that she wants to hold it and try to make everything okay. I slide my hand out from under hers and fish around in the glove box for my shades. I can't look at her.

Waiting is the worst. There's nothing to do but keep our eyes on the front door of the high school, where the list will be posted once this year's cheerleaders have been selected. Nothing to do but wait, replay the most horrifying moment of my life over and over again in my head, and listen to soft rock.

"You sure—" Momma starts again.

"Ma!" I give her a foul look, one of my specialties, and she backs off.

Instead, she takes up the issue of cheerleading skirts, how they were much longer in her day and she only had to shave up to her knees. Meanwhile, "Girls today flash their panties to the crowd with every rah, rah, rah." I try to imagine my mother, the farmer's wife, as a cheerleader. When she starts on bikini lines, it all gets very uncomfortable; and yet, it's still better than waiting on the front lawn with the other girls. I'm not in the mood for sympathy or awkward chitchat.

Finally, Coach appears. She tapes a white sheet of paper to the door and the girls claw past one another to get at the results, like a pack of wolves fighting over a piece of meat. *Wolves*, I think bitterly.

"Go ahead, Ricki Jo," my mom fusses. I open the door slowly and make my way up the sidewalk. Mackenzie sees me coming and bounds toward me maniacally. Obviously, she made the squad.

"Ericka!" she cries and slams into me with a huge hug.

"Congratulations," I say, hugging her back and faking a smile.

"You made it! You made it!" she squeals.

I pull back from her, my mouth open wide. I watch

her blue eyes twinkle and see her mouth moving, but my brain is struggling to understand. *"I made it?"*

She bobs her bouncy blond ponytail so hard that I worry for her neck and we race to the list eagerly, so I can find my name. It's there. It's actually on there. Ericka Winstead—Junior Varsity.

I made it.

"Can you come over?" I ask Luke on the telephone. "I've got some big news."

He agrees and I run out to the back deck. My brother's little hand is full of plastic spoons and he really concentrates as he sets one beside each bowl on the patio table. I ruffle his light hair and walk over to my dad, who's manning the grill.

"Hamburgers *and* hot dogs?" I ask.

"Hey, it's a big night! Uncle Jim and Aunt Bev are bringing the kids over, too. We had ice cream and a cookout on call, just in case you made it," he says and kisses my forehead. "I knew you would."

I float on cloud nine over to the grapevine by our plank fence. Although my momma is controlling and my dad is corny and a workaholic, I feel really blessed. I look over our farm toward Luke's, eager to see his frame appear on the horizon. I pop grape after grape into my mouth. After a little while, I hear my uncle and his family show up and soda cans crack open. *Luke should be here by now.*

"I'll be right back!" I call to the group assembled in my honor.

"We're eating in a few, Ricki Jo," Momma warns.

I head over to Bandit's doghouse and unleash him. He's a Heinz 57 — a true mutt, fifty-seven varieties of dog — but I love him. He howls and jumps and runs in front of me through the field. He catches a scent and takes off through the high grass. I catch glimpses of his brown and white splotches as he hunts rabbits in the weeds, but as I walk farther and farther from the rabbit trail he gives up and comes back for a scratching. He never wanders too far. I grab a stick and throw it, then run in the opposite direction, toward Luke's. Bandit is always torn — the stick or me — but today he goes after the stick and then runs like hell to bring it back to me.

"Good boy," I purr, scratching his head. It may sound silly, but Bandit really is my best friend. I tell him everything, and even though we can't share clothes, he's a great listener and loves me unconditionally. He flops down on my feet and rolls over, all four paws up in the air, just like he used to do as an attention-starved puppy. I bend down and scratch his belly, watching his right leg, which always goes berserk and really makes me laugh. I grab the stick and toss it again, then climb onto the top rail of our wood plank fence to wait for Luke. Sitting on my perch at the highest point of our land, I'll be able to see him coming, and I'm still in earshot in case Momma calls. As the sun dips down lower and lower, I absentmindedly play fetch with Bandit, and wonder where in the world Luke is.

"To Ricki Jo Winstead. The best little cheerleader in the county!" Dad toasts.

"Not a bad little worker, either," my uncle adds.

We all take hearty sips of my momma's homemade sweet tea and I feel great. Uncle Jim and my dad exchange a proud look and I know it won't be long 'til they're reliving memories of their farm-boy glory days. My cousins drag Ben out to the backyard for a game of Wiffle Ball and my momma and Aunt Beverly trade recipes.

"Got room for one more?" I hear from behind me.

"Well, hey there, Luke!" my dad says, standing up and offering a handshake. "We've got plenty!"

Luke ambles over to the grill, following my dad. For as tall and lean as he is, he's not awkward like a lot of the boys in my class; instead, he's got a sort of easy, laid-back stride. Plus, he's just a regular down-to-earth guy, which is probably why it's so easy to be his friend. He grabs a paper plate and two hot dogs before heading over to the table.

" 'Bout time!" I say, moving over and passing him the buns.

"Sorry," he mumbles.

"What happened to your lip?" I ask. The top part's swollen, for sure.

"Busted it," he says, shrugging it off. "It's nothin'."

He grabs the hot dog buns and loads up his plate with

chips and potato salad. I get him a Coke from the cooler and think about our walks down to the pond behind his house...and about the shouts we always hear.

"Did something...?" I start, but can't find the words, exactly. "No, I mean, did you...?" He looks at me, waiting, and I finally break eye contact to retie the bag of buns.

"It's nothin', Ricki Jo," he says simply. And that's that. We sit in silence for a bit, letting the conversations around us fill the space. I don't know what to say, and he's not the kind to offer up personal information. His lip looks awful and the cut's fresh, but I know not to push. "This is quite a cookout, huh?" he finally asks, snapping me from my thoughts.

"Yeah! Oh my gosh! I forgot! That's why I called," I say excitedly.

"Uh-huh," he says, squeezing a grotesque amount of ketchup and mustard on his hot dogs.

"Huge news! Gigantic news!"

I pause for effect. He takes a bite and looks at me.

"Well?" he asks, his mouth full.

"I made the squad!" I squeal. "I'm a cheerleader! I'm a Preston County High cheerleader!"

I can't help it. I'm clapping. Clapping and squealing.

"Congratulations," Luke replies. He is unfazed, and polishes off the first hot dog.

"That's it? You're not happy for me?" I ask.

"Happy for you? Sure," he says simply. "Surprised? No way. You said you were trying out. I knew you'd make it."

I don't know how to explain the flip-flopping of my stomach, except that maybe my momma put too much sugar in the sweet tea, but Luke's compliment is really nice to hear.

"Thank you," I say, reaching for a brownie and letting my dark blond hair fall forward to mask the gigantic smile stretching across my face.

So Luke's not the clap-and-squeal type. At least he believes in me. I decide not to mention the whole Wolf-being-a-vile-human-being scene. Seems like Luke's in a brooding mood as it is. Plus, it'd kind of ruin the moment to hear, "Told ya so."

Completely stuffed, my sweet tooth satisfied, I curl up in bed and pile all of my pillows behind me. I am officially a Preston County High School Junior Varsity Cheerleader. I grab my new journal from the drawer in my headboard and turn to the first clean page. I started keeping a diary last year, but I hardly ever wrote in it, and now the things I did write seem childish. I didn't want to start off high school by writing in that same old diary, so when we went shopping for school supplies, I begged my momma for a new journal from the Barnes & Noble in Lexington. I love it. It has a black leather cover that seems more serious than the pink one with a lock and key that I used to have. Plus, the pages are a faded off-white color, with frayed edges. Totally serious. And a lot of serious things are happening this year already.

I've been writing almost every day since school started. I want to be able to look back on these pages in a few years, once I'm popular, and remember every moment so I can see how far I've come. I've written about the girls in home-room, and Wolf, obviously, and how different things are from my K–8 private school, but today has been the most action-packed day at PCHS so far and I have tons to tell.

Tryouts ended up a success, although the humiliating Wolf moment was a lesson learned: That kind of guy doesn't date girls like me…yet. Plus, he's only fourteen and really immature. Also, I hate him now.

I realize that I've already used three full pages talking about Wolf and frown.

But I have made some really great new friends.

I turn the page and chew on the end of my pen. Over-all, things are good. Reinventing Ricki Jo is not a mission to take lightly. There are going to be bumps, like growing pains (which I'd love to experience sometime soon). I think about people like Ellen DeGeneres — she used to sell vacuums — and Bill Gates — I mean, he was probably a nerd in high school. And, on *America's Next Top Model*, they all start off plain and awkward before Tyra helps them find their inner fierce selves.

I've got the desire. What I need are goals....

Project Ericka —
10 Goals by the End of This Year

1. Be best friends with the girls in homeroom
2. Learn how to do a back handspring
3. Start my period
4. Grow (height and bust, please)
5. Make straight A's
6. Get a real job (*no más tobacco!*)
7. Get asked to homecoming
8. Pray for Wolf
9. Get first kiss (by Wolf??? — if he changes)
10. Get a hickey / Give a hickey

I look things over and feel pretty good about some, and worried about others. I sigh and tuck my diary...um, I mean *journal*...under my mattress, then lean back and stare up at the ceiling. My Bible is open on my lap, just in case Momma comes in to check on me, but I'm too emotionally discombobulated to concentrate. I feel awesome for making the squad, but I feel stupid for thinking Wolf could like a girl like me—and even stupider for liking him still.

And I think I know how Luke busted his lip...or, rather, who busted it for him. I just don't know what to do about it.

♛
CHAPTER NINE

"Boys' Varsity is totally where you want to be as a freshman," I hear Kimi say as I walk down the hallway. She's standing at her locker facing Mackenzie, whose eyebrow is cocked, her foot tapping. I give a little wave and bypass the convo. Kimi on a soapbox is something I've already learned to avoid; Mackenzie obviously wasn't as successful.

School feels different to me today. It's probably the rain; the hallways seem darker, and tennis shoes squeak nonstop. Wet hair hangs down unhappy faces and a few boys engage in an umbrella duel. I used to beg for rain to get out of work, but now that I'm a cheerleader, I can get out of it rain or shine. I'll have practice after school three times a week!

I pop open my locker, throw my umbrella up top, and grab the wad of Silly Putty I keep on the upper shelf. I tear off a small chunk and paste it to a funny picture my momma printed from the cookout. It's me and my whole family doing cheerleading poses, the highlights being Clark Winstead in a stunning lunge and his wife a vision in a standing liberty. Luke and Bandit didn't participate, but they're both smiling at the camera. I laugh, pressing the photo onto the inside of my locker door.

And then someone slams the door shut. Guess who.

"I'm not talking to you," I say, picking up my back-pack and walking away, my stomach flutters multiplying exponentially.

"It was just a joke!" Wolf calls as I head over to Mac-kenzie. I see Sarah occasionally nodding along while Kimi waxes philosophical about some "cheerleading hier-archy"— *bo-ring*—but I don't feel safe at my own locker. Wolf is wearing a white button-up, looking like he stepped right out of an Abercrombie & Fitch catalog, and I forgive too easily.

"I mean, yeah, I only made Girls' Varsity, which means I'll totally have to work harder next year. But I'm super glad you guys made it," Kimi lies, bobbing her head vigor-ously, as if she is convincing herself.

"Hey, girls. Congratulations!" I say, being ultra-cute.

"Thanks!" Mackenzie says and hugs me. "You, too!"

"Well, I mean, yeah, but it's only JV," Kimi says. Mac-kenzie looks as if she can't believe what Kimi just said. I feel my own smile, and confidence, falter.

"Kimi!" she scolds. Laura walks up and puts an arm around my shoulders.

"What?" Kimi asks innocently. "I mean, it's a great starting point, 'cause you're new to cheering, right?"

I gulp and nod.

"Okay," she continues. "So your squad will cheer for boys who are new to sports. Freshmen, or just kids who aren't good enough for Varsity. And it won't matter that you kind of suck 'cause nobody goes to those games, anyway."

"Kimi!" Laura and Mackenzie say together.

"What?" she asks, exasperated. "This is exactly what I was talking about. PCHS has a cheerleading hierarchy. Junior Varsity is bush league."

"Let's get to homeroom, Ericka," Mackenzie says, trying to lead me away.

"Wait," I say weakly. "So, there are levels?"

"Totally," Kimi explains dramatically. "Now, Sarah and Mackenzie are Boys' Varsity — as freshmen. Freaking awesome. They get to cheer at the big football and basketball games. You know, the ones the whole town cares about." She looks for a way to explain it better. "Oh! It's like they're in the upper class. And, like, Laura and me, we're Girls' Varsity, so we get to cheer for soccer and girls' basketball. And soccer is totally getting big in the U.S. now with, like, David Beckham on the scene. So it's not the best, but still cool."

"Middle class," I state.

"Exactly." She beams, and then adds, "Well, more like upper middle class."

"And so JV," I say, dreading the answer I already know.

The bell rings and students start heading into classrooms, thinning the hallway traffic. Kimi gives me a thumbs-down and shrugs her shoulders. "No offense, Ericka."

"And now, for your starting lineup!" a booming announcer voice comes from behind us. "A six foot freshman, number twenty-three, at point guard...David Wolfenbaker!" The girls all laugh, which just eggs him on. He brushes his shoulders off and does the John Wall dance, holding the pose and kissing his biceps. I would usually think this is funny, but not today. I look away and remind myself how much I hate him right now. "That's right. Starting freshman. Who's the man? Who's the man?"

Kimi is in fits. "You're the man, Wolf!"

"That's right. That's right," he says, as the girls clap for him.

After the mood-shattering conversation I've just had with Kimi, the last person I want to talk to is Wolf. I slip between Mackenzie and Laura, eager just to get to homeroom, but he pushes Laura to the side and grabs my wrist.

"Whoa, whoa, whoa!" he says, turning me back around toward the group and draping his arm across my shoulders. "My best new girl hasn't even said congratulations."

I flush a deep red, anger and hurt pride and teenage hormones all fighting inside. I roll my eyes and look away, completely aware of the swoon-inducing cologne he's wearing. Then a perfect finger touches my cheek, where he draws an imaginary twenty-three. I shiver at his touch.

"Paint that on before every game, you little vixen cheerleader," he says. I finally cave, grinning and giving him my best *ha, ha* look. And then he says, "Oooh! That's right. You're JV."

Kimi and Sarah burst out laughing and I look down at my shoes. Wolf leans close to my ear and whispers, "Maybe marching band was a good idea after all." I shrug him off, move to the other side of the hallway, and hate that I tingled at the sensation of his breath in my ear.

Mackenzie follows me and says, "Forget them."

"Who am I?" Wolf shouts and does a cartwheel in the hallway, nearly kicking Mrs. Wilkes in the process.

"Homeroom, people. Now," she grumbles.

Kimi is hysterical at this point. "Oh my god! You're Ericka! Except your cartwheel is actually better!" Sarah giggles and then they follow Wolf into homeroom, Kimi winking back at me as if I'm in on the joke and not the actual joke itself. *Yeah, right.*

Tears make their way to my eyes, again. Mackenzie fishes in her purse for a tissue while the last few stragglers give me weird looks.

"Don't let them get to you," she says. "Wolf's probably just flirting, anyway. Guys always act so weird around girls they like."

I think her theory has more than a few flaws, but I sniff and nod, appreciative of her support. I wipe my cheeks and blow my nose, trying to take deep breaths. She fluffs my hair, then hands me her lip gloss.

"There, that's better," she says. "You want to look good for school pictures, right?"

I nod, dab my eyes one last time, and give her a shaky smile. Even though I almost missed the bus this morning trying to find the perfect outfit for school-picture day, I'd already forgotten that I had to take them first period.

High school is actually turning out to be a total nightmare.

With each day, I meet more people. The problem is, most of them already have best friends. A lot of my classmates are really nice, but I still feel lonely. No one to confide in, pass notes to, or talk about boys with. Mackenzie is probably my closest friend, since she's new, too, but we don't have any of the same classes. Plus, she's made friends with the upperclassmen girls on her squad. Our friendship basically revolves around homeroom and time spent together in the hall between classes.

"Ericka!" she says as Wolf approaches his locker. I'm putting my umbrella away for the third time this week and feeling like I'm over the rain already. "You're so lucky to have naturally wavy hair. Mine goes to pieces in this weather."

In truth, her hair is flawless as always, but I still love the compliment. More than that, I appreciate what she's been doing for me. Whenever I'm at my locker and she sees Wolf, she comes over to run interference. "He's a scumbag," she says, which always makes me laugh 'cause it sounds so funny in her Yankee accent.

"Yeah, your hair really is pretty, Ericka," Wolf agrees, leaning around her.

I check his eyes, his mouth. He seems sincere. *Whatever.*

"Gonna be late," I hear from behind me. I know that voice without turning around.

"Hey, Luke," I hear Laura say, her voice going up an octave. Looking over, I see her grinning from ear to ear and standing on her tiptoes, her legs crossed like she has to pee.

"Hey," he replies, then leans over my shoulder to get a look at the cookout picture. He chuckles.

"I love that picture," Laura says, with a touch of desperation in her voice. "You guys are, like, best friends, right?"

"Yeah," he murmurs.

"One big happy family, huh, Luke?" Wolf says.

Luke gives Wolf a nod and says, "Let's go, Rick—uh, Ericka."

I slam my locker and we head down the hallway.

"Real smooth, Don Juan," I say sarcastically, looking up to see if his face will give anything away. "I think Laura likes you—no, it's obvious that she likes you—and you say, 'Hey.' "

"Don't question my skills, RJ. It's called playing hard to get."

"Laura Wagner Foster," I tease. "You like the sound of that?"

"Shut up, Ricki Jo," he says and nudges me into the oncoming foot traffic so that I bump into a really big-chested senior girl.

"Watch it, jerk," she says.

Nice.

"That's one I owe ya," I tell Luke, stepping on his foot as we head into Earth Science.

The after-school routine is just another way to divide the popular from the less than. Behind the gym is the student parking lot, where freshman girls like Sarah saunter out with their older boyfriends for a ride home. Anyone lucky enough to have a sibling who's an upperclassman, like Wolf, can also be found heading in that direction. These lovely people delight in the acts of honking and hollering out their windows at us as they pass.

Then you've got the kids who live within a mile of the school and can walk home. Although this may not sound glamorous, it still beats my place on the totem pole: the bottom. Yes, we of the bus routes find ourselves in a general throng outside the auditorium, where all who pass may mock us. We look forward to an hour-long ride of picking up and dropping off loud middle schoolers and louder elementary kids and peeling our hamstrings off the pleather seats over and over again in the heat.

I see Candace waiting for her bus and walk over to join her conversation.

"Hey, what's up?" I say.

She looks at me in surprise, like I'm some kind of alien, and then narrows her eyes. "You sure you wanna be seen talking to band geeks?"

I shake my head, caught off guard by her attitude. "Huh?"

"Forget it," she says. "There's our bus." Her friends roll their eyes and smirk in my general direction as they follow Candace toward the sea of school-bus yellow. I've seen this persona of hers before. She calls it "trailer park proud." It's this attitude she gets with people who cross her, and although I've seen it, I never expected to be on the receiving end.

"Candace, wait a sec," I say and run to catch up. "Are you mad at me for something? 'Cause I didn't try out for band?"

We walk toward her bus and she shrugs. "Let's see, you've played piano since you were little and never cheered a day in your life. I tell you about band tryouts and you look at me like I've got cooties, and then run for the nearest set of pom-poms."

"It's not you, Candace!" I say. "Or the band," I add for the benefit of her scowling entourage. "I didn't mean to hurt your feelings. I just wanted to try something new."

She softens a little and lets the other kids board ahead of her. "Listen, I'm sorry to be nasty. It's like this automatic defense or, I don't know, wall or something I put up when I'm hurt." She sighs loudly.

"Candace!" one of her friends calls. "Let's go!"

"Look, I know you're new and it's probably hard," she says, her words rushing out all at once, "but you're already running with the wrong crowd, Ricki Jo. I hate those kids. They're all stuck-up and fake. I actually bunked with you for a full week at camp, and we've talked on the phone all summer, yet all I get is a head nod in Spanish while you throw yourself at Wolf. It's like you want to fit in with those snotty kids in your homeroom so bad that you're *changing.*"

A couple of kids around us snicker, and I feel my face flush again. Usually I can take her blunt, borderline-rude comments with a grain of salt, but today, I snap.

"What's your problem, Candace?" I'm mad. I can't help it. I'm not changing, I'm upgrading. Trying to be a better me.

She stiffens and I see her jaw tighten. "My problem?" she asks incredulously. "I'm not the one with a problem. But if you think cheering at the JV games is gonna win you Miss Popularity, you better think again."

And with that, she turns on her heel and boards her bus, smacking me with her fiery fluff of a ponytail. And then I get angry. Really angry.

Screw everybody! I'm a freshman! What's so wrong with cheering for freshmen?

As if this moment can't get any worse, my head is

suddenly engulfed by a tanned forearm and I squirm ferociously under what I can only describe as a noogie.

"Leave me alone!" I scream up at the face attached to the offending hand.

Luke puts both hands up in defense, his leather bracelet sliding down his arm a little to reveal an untanned white strip near his wrist. "Whoa! Take it easy, champ."

"Bye, Ricki Jo!" I hear Candace shout obnoxiously from the back window as her bus pulls away.

"It's Ericka!" I holler at the top of my lungs, long and loud.

Smoothing my hair into place, I look back at Luke, ready for a fight.

"Hey, I know. It's Ericka. Got it," he says, eyebrows to his hairline, backing away from my wrath. I sigh heavily and walk toward our bus with him, completely broken down.

"Ericky Jo!" I hear someone sing. "I love you, Ericky Jo!" I look up and see Wolf hanging out the passenger window of his older brother's Audi SUV, blowing me kiss after kiss, the boys in the backseat laughing like maniacs.

I don't know what comes over me, but my middle finger is up before I can blink an eye.

CHAPTER TEN

"I guess it sounds like a pity party, but being the new girl sucks," I tell Bandit. I'm sprawled out on an old blanket by the creek that divides our property from Luke's and from my uncle's. It's always been a good spot to go and think. The water trickles over the rocks in a soothing melody and the maple trees here provide the perfect shady nook.

"I mean, really, Bandit, anybody at school could be my new best friend. I just got thrown in with the W's, and those girls seemed like a good place to start." I pluck petals off of a dandelion and plead my case to my dog. "It's not like I don't wanna be friends with Candace, you know? I just don't want to be in the band! Big deal."

Bandit has been very attentive, but suddenly he howls like crazy and darts off. I lean up on my elbows and see the cause. Luke and his beagle mix, Bessie, are walking along the creek in our direction. I like watching Bandit and Bessie together. They always run to each other as if it's been years, and Bessie likes to show her dominance with an awkward, yet fascinating, humping technique. We always joke that Bandit and Bessie are married, the way they carry on when they're together.

"Mind a little company?" Luke asks.

I lean back and cross my arms behind my head. "Make yourself at home."

He settles down on the blanket, his body diagonal to mine, and we're head to head, looking up through the branches above.

"Rough day?" he asks.

"Rough week," I reply.

"Wanna talk about it?"

"Nah," I say. "It's nothin'."

He knows. In these moments, we both know. The dogs walk over us, licking our faces, and we swat them away. I consider fetch, but just don't have it in me.

"You guys finish housing yet?" I ask.

"All but the one small field by the red barn. Irrigate all summer, and then it finally rains when it's time to house," he gripes.

"It's clearing up."

"Yeah. But work's boring without you there to complain about it," he teases.

"Ha! Well, I'm sure my dad will have me out in it tomorrow," I say bitterly.

We're both quiet for a while. A slight breeze shuffles

the leaves above us. Sometimes I feel a security on our land that I don't feel anywhere else. No one can hurt me here.

"I've never seen you flip the bird, RJ," Luke says.

I can't stop the little smile that creeps onto my lips. I really don't know what came over me. I've never been the vixen. I'm always one hundred percent good girl.

"Yeah, it felt weird. And wrong. And awesome."

"Well, you're lucky Mr. Bates didn't see you. Principals usually frown on that kind of sign language." He laughs.

"Mr. Bates can suck it," I say defiantly.

"Whoa!" Luke replies and we both laugh. "Have you been watching wrestling with Ben again? Admit it, Ricki Jo. You love oiled-up fat guys in unitards."

"Ew!" I scream and flick him in the head. He leans up and frogs my forearm, which can only be followed by my famous elbow drop, which turns our joking into an all-out wrestling match. As skinny as Luke is, his rough hands are strong; however, let it be known that I can give any opponent a run for his money. The dogs circle us and bark like crazy while we writhe around on the checkered quilt.

"One! Two! Three!" I count, proud of myself for pinning someone twice my size. I know he is holding back, but it feels good to get out my frustrations.

Looking up at me, he smiles an easy, genuine smile and says, "You got me, Ricki Jo."

And suddenly, things feel weird. Not bad, just different for the first time. Luke's like a brother to me, but something feels strange. He's staring, boring a hole through me, and just barely smiling so that I can see how his front bottom teeth are a little bit crooked. And I'm on top of him, holding his wrists out to the sides, with my face just a foot above his. My heart skips. *Whoa.* I feel Luke's pulse quicken in my hands and I let go of his wrists, look away, take a minute. I am suddenly hyperaware of my entire body and fight a weird pull to turn my face back to his. To kiss him.

No. I shake my head and flop over onto the blanket, running the stupid thoughts out of my head and feeling thankful he can't read my mind. How embarrassing. Luke doesn't like me like that. Too weird. He'd laugh me out of the county if I told him the stuff that just crashed through my mind, and really, I've had enough humiliation for one lifetime. Plus, I like Wolf anyway. *I like Wolf.*

I lean back on my haunches and lighten the mood, clasping my hands together and swinging them from side to side in sweet victory. "Ladies and gentlemen! Your new lightweight champion of the world!"

And then, in the midst of my due self-congratulations, I double over and clench at my abdomen. "Ow, oh!" It feels like someone is wringing out a dish towel right below my belly button.

"Are you okay, RJ?" Luke asks, bewildered.

And then it hits me. It's so obvious! And I get up and

run, leaving him, the dogs, my journal, and my blanket without a second thought. I've got to get home.

"This is it," I whisper to myself, wriggling out of my jeans in the bathroom. "This has got to be it."

I sit squarely on the cushiony soft toilet seat and look at the crotch of my panties, stretched between my shins, but do not see the red splotch I hoped for. Nothing. Still.

When I was in the fourth grade Momma explained all about periods and sex using Christian literature, so I figured that the cramps I felt out by the creek would mean that I'd gotten my period. A period means puberty, which brings with it bigger breasts and a possible growth spurt. But nothing. Still!

"Ricki Jo?" Momma calls from outside the bathroom door. "You okay in there?"

Gosh, I've only been in here for, like, four minutes max!

"Momma, I'm fine!" I call back, irritated.

"Oh, well, you ran through the house so fast, I thought something might be wrong."

I roll my eyes and flush the toilet, just for the sake of my audience. Pulling up my pants, I unlock the door for Momma and head to the sink. I don't know how she does it, but she can tell that I'm disappointed.

"Ricki Jo," she begins in her Dr. Phil voice, "your body is going through a lot of changes."

"Ugh, Momma, please don't," I groan, shaking the water off my hands and wiping them on my shirt, hoping that my not using the hand towel will distract her from where she's going with this...which is obviously a puberty talk...which I *obviously* do not need.

I walk past her and cross the hall to my bedroom. In this sanctuary, I sit at the desk by my window and open up my pre-algebra book, though it's kind of impossible to concentrate on basic equations after the day I've had. Why does becoming a woman have to be such an ordeal? And why do I have to ask my mom about this stuff? I truly need a best friend for things like this, but I'm too embarrassed to call Mackenzie or Laura, and Candace isn't exactly speaking to me. This is the problem with being a tomboy. I can't really call up Luke and ask him about cramps. Ugh. This is exactly why I need Internet in my room.

"Ricki Jo?" My momma knocks at my bedroom door a few minutes later.

Oh, great. Round two of Knowing Your Body, *by Debbie Winstead.* I lay my forehead on the cool pages of algebra homework in front of me and yell, "Come in!" bracing myself for the worst. This has not been one of my best days.

She sets a glass of sweet tea on my desk and sits down on my bed. "Ricki Jo, is everything okay?"

Her tone is super serious, and I roll over on my cheek and look at her sideways.

"Uh, yeah, Momma. Why?"

"Well, just how upset you were after tryouts the other

day, and then the kind of maniacal look in your eye this afternoon when you opened the bathroom door."

I sit up, feel the page of my textbook peel slowly off my cheek, and take a drink of sweet tea. "I'm fine, Momma."

She reaches over and tenderly tucks my hair behind my ear. "Has it been hard being the new girl, sweetie?"

Most of the time, when I get hurt or sick, I suck it up. I'm tough. I'll get through it. And then my momma comes in the room or gets on the phone and I just lose it. I don't know what triggers it or what kind of hold this woman has over me, but once my momma's in the picture, the tough girl caves. I start to cry.

"I don't know. I mean, there's this one girl, Mackenzie, who's really new. I mean, legitimately new. All the way from Minnesota! And she's already one of the most popular girls in our whole school. She's pretty and nice and her parents are in the country club and—"

Momma passes me a tissue and I take a break to blow my nose and wipe my eyes. She is on her knees next to me now, not shushing me but letting me cry it out and scratching my back, which she knows I love.

"I mean, I just want to fit in, you know?" She nods. "I want to have friends and be accepted and...I don't know."

"Ricki Jo, you're a beautiful girl," Momma purrs. I roll my wet eyes. She *has* to say that.

"And you've got a big heart," she continues, "and you make people laugh, and you're a hard worker and someone who always makes us proud."

Okay, even though she has to say all this stuff, it feels good.

"I think I'm an okay person," I admit, sniffling. "I'm not that pretty yet, but I think I've got potential. If I could just get my period!"

"You know, hon, with a period comes pimples."

Eye rolling has become an art for me, basically due to parental statements such as these. Leave it to Debbie to point out the negatives. Pimples, huh? For boobs and curves? Bring it on!

"Whatever, Momma. I'm fine. It's just been a tough couple of weeks," I say. I love my mom, but we've had our moment and now I'd just rather drown my sorrows in $(a + b) + c = a + (b + c)$.

"I've got an idea," she forges on. Sweet. I love my mom's ideas. "Let's go to Lexington this weekend. Just you and me. Whatever money you made this summer working for your daddy, I'll match toward back-to-school clothes. I imagine we missed the rush, so there should be some good sales."

My eyes bug out and, for a second, I'm not sure I heard her right. A trip to Lexington! To the mall! There is nothing to do but bolt from my chair and fling myself at my mother. I hug her tightly and can't stop saying *Thank you, Thank you, Thank you.* And yeah, I'm crying again.

CHAPTER ELEVEN

"Since when did you become a morning person?" my dad asks me at breakfast.

It's Saturday morning and four hours 'til Momma and I head up to Lexington. The day is clear, the sun is shining, and I've got a skip in my step. Sure, I've got to work a little bit first, but whatever I make, my momma's going to match.

"Since I get to go shopping," I say, scarfing down my biscuits and gravy.

He smiles and downs the rest of his orange juice.

"Let's go!" I say to Ben. "We're burning daylight."

Ben sticks his tongue out at me before finishing his milk. He's annoyed. I would be annoyed with myself, too, if I weren't so fired up. I'm thinking new jeans, new shoes, new tops, new everything! He's thinking: *Work sucks.*

I hop on the back of my dad's huge four-wheeler and Ben revs up his mini-ATV. We drive over the fields and the wind catches in my hair. I throw my arms back and face the sun. I feel like Leo in *Titanic*. 'Course, it only takes one pothole to snap me out of that little fantasy, and I hold on tight.

Up at the barn, we stomp through the dewy grass and meet the others: Luke, his dad, his sister, his four brothers, and us. This being a small field, we'll be done before you know it. And even if we're not, I'll be done at eleven. Mrs. Foster unloads a couple of coolers and kisses Claire and each of her sons before climbing back into their old pickup. I love that. All tall and rail thin, each of them has to bend down to let her peck him on the forehead.

Everybody knows his or her place. The guys climb up into the rafters, Ben and another kid clean up around the barn, and Claire and I unload the trailer, passing the tobacco up.

"I'm so glad you're out here today," I tell her. It's nice to have another girl around.

"Yeah, being a mom is no joke," she huffs. "I left Ava with my mom today. I mean, I never thought I'd say this, but I miss working out here sometimes."

I cock an eyebrow and give her one of the special looks I usually reserve for Momma. "You have officially lost your mind."

We work steadily. Our breathing is labored, but we don't stop talking. I tell her stories about school and she tells me about changing dirty diapers, and our tales are equally glum. I've always looked up to Claire. She looks a lot like her brothers—same sandy blond hair and bright blue eyes—except she's got a few womanly curves here and there. She could be a model—*could've* been a model—but when she got pregnant her senior year life changed for her. Everything changed.

"You like working at the day care?" I ask.

"It's cool," she says. "I mean, I get paid and—"

She is cut off by the longest-sounding four-letter word I've ever heard in my life. The F word, the baddest bad-boy cuss word of all time, long and low and getting closer, as if time is standing still, followed by an empty-sounding thump and a scary crack. Then silence.

"Dad!" I hear Luke yell.

Claire and I hop off the trailer and run over to Mr. Foster, who is sprawled out on the floor of the barn, wincing in pain. Thud after thud registers on the trailer behind us as the men thunder down from the rafters.

"My leg!" Mr. Foster shouts. "I think I broke my damned leg!"

I back away from the crowd assembling around him. Mr. Foster's right leg is bent out in a way that makes me a little nauseous. My dad is already on his cell phone, calling 911, and he motions for me to pull Ben away. I look at Luke, bent over with his brothers.

"I just passed it up!" I hear someone defend himself.

"The weight threw me off," Luke's dad says.

"You been drinking, Daddy?" one of the boys asks.

The silence says it all. Every blond head hunched around Mr. Foster hangs. Of course he's been drinking. And it's only eight thirty in the morning.

Luke stands up, puts his hands behind his head, and turns away.

CHAPTER TWELVE

At the mall, Momma and I started off with cinnamon-covered pretzels, and that's the last thing we've agreed on all day. Everything I try on is too short, or too low-cut, or shows midriff when I lift my arms. Momma goes right for the sale rack, while I go for whatever the mannequin is wearing. She picks out flowery prints and muted colors, while I tend to go for the opposite of anything she likes. So far, we've agreed on two pairs of jeans and a headband.

"Too revealing," my mom says, shooting down the hundredth cool top I've tried on this afternoon.

"Revealing what, Momma?" I exclaim. Frustrated, I place my palms down flat on the two minuscule bumps on my chest. "I've got nothing to reveal!"

"Your father won't like it, Ricki Jo," she says in her *and that's that* voice.

"He doesn't have to wear it," I smart off.

Her eyebrows cock up angrily, and I storm back into the dressing room.

To tell the truth, this whole day has been a nightmare. First, Luke's dad fell in the barn and broke his leg, putting us down two workers: Mr. Foster and Claire, who went with him in the ambulance. Nobody said a word the rest of the morning, but it was all anybody was thinking about. Work dragged on, punctuated by the swish of the leaves as each stalk was passed up and the clack of the sticks as they were leveled across the rafters. Over and over again, feet shuffled against the rough wood above, but no words were spoken. Nothing. Not a peep.

Until eleven o'clock.

My momma's Corolla isn't ideal for off-roading, so she pulled over on the shoulder by the red barn and laid on the horn.

"Ricki Jo! Ricki Jo!" she hollered.

I froze mid-grab when I heard her, breaking the rhythm of our work. Luke was hunched over above me, waiting for the next stick.

"That's my momma," I said up to him, apology in my eyes.

"I'm moving down!" Luke yelled up to the other guys, and then he swung down to the trailer by me. The guys above grumbled and rearranged themselves in the barn.

"I don't have to go, Luke," I told him. "I'll just run and see if we can go next weekend or something."

But Luke just reached past me and started passing tobacco from the trailer up into the barn, filling my shoes and not missing a beat.

"Y-yeah," I stammered on. "I'll just stay, seeing as how you're already down two workers...."

"It's a small field," he stated, not looking at me. He was passing up the heavy sticks draped in tobacco much faster than I had been, like a man on a mission, intense, like he needed the rhythm. I stood there a few minutes watching him, until my mom started honking again.

"Just go, Ricki Jo," he said. I hesitated, reached toward his arm, but he brushed me off. "Just go. Okay? I'm fine."

His set jaw, tense back, and hunched shoulders said he was anything but fine, but the anger in his eyes told me to back off.

The car ride was quiet. As soon as I got in I told Momma exactly how it all had happened in the barn, and she said, "Poor Mattie," feeling sorry for Luke's mom. It didn't feel right going shopping while Luke's family was in a bind, but we kept going. She fell silent and I followed suit, staring out the window and letting my eyes unfocus a little. We whipped down Beer Can Alley and over to Russell Cave Road in a flash, and I kept my eyes out the window, watching the Kentucky landscape blur past. Each rolling hill boasted green fields, horses, cows, hay, and ponds. Most of the houses we passed were regular ones like ours, modest farm-type places; but I looked forward to the big ones, older out our way and more modern as we got closer to Lexington. I liked to imagine myself getting married on the big balconies or throwing a fancy party in the huge rooms.

The drive to Lexington was a short one, partly because I was daydreaming about Wolf, but mostly because of my momma's lead foot, meaning she took each back road curve like Danica Patrick, the Indy Car princess.

And now, as if the day can't get any worse, my momma and I are locked in a staring contest. I'm in an adorable lacy-strapped tank top and she's sitting in a plush purple chair shaking her head ferociously. I break eye contact and launch the loudest, most obnoxious, heaviest sigh of my life before marching back into the dressing room.

"This is gonna take all day!" I call out as I throw off the tank and wiggle into a floral dress my momma is forcing me to try on.

"Which one are you trying?" she calls.

I step out of the dressing room and stand in front of her, shoulders hunched, a look of disgust on my face. I save the model poses and cheery smiles for the outfits I want her to buy. She checks me out approvingly.

"That is just adorable, Ricki Jo," she says, which is all I need to hear.

"I hate it," I say, turning around.

"You hate that?" a young salesgirl asks incredulously. "Vanessa Hudgens is totally wearing something just like that in *Us Weekly*. You just need to accessorize. Look."

She reaches over my momma to the rack above and

pulls down a cropped tux jacket. "Hmmm...size zero, I'd say. Now, hold on one sec."

She hands me the jacket and I put it on while she bounces over to the register for a belt and bracelet, bopping her head to the pop song blaring over the store speakers. Momma and I watch her work, skeptical. The girl looks over at me, two belts in her hand. She holds up one at a time, closing one eye, then puts one back and heads over enthusiastically. As she wraps a subtly studded belt around my waist, I start to feel like an empty canvas under the hands of Michelangelo. No! Like a swimmer who's gone out too far in the ocean being pulled back to shore by a fashion lifeguard.

"What size shoe do you wear?" she asks, handing me a swirly gold cuff bracelet and powering her compact figure over to the back wall.

"Six and a half," I shout.

"Okay, some sexy strappy shoes, and this outfit's the bomb dot-com," she says, making her way back over. I giggle.

"Nothing sexy," interjects Momma, the ever-present buzz kill. The salesgirl turns back around without missing a beat.

"Well, then, black ballet flats would kill! And it's getting cold soon, anyway, so actually, these are more practical. You're totally right," she says to my mother, who looks confused but flattered.

"I am?" Momma asks.

"Totally," the girl affirms, handing me a cute pair of black slippers.

I put them on, turn toward the three-way mirror, and almost don't recognize myself. I never would have put any of these things together, or worn any of them separately, but the outfit actually works. And the salesgirl is beaming behind me, which doesn't hurt. I look over at my momma, throw my shoulders back, stand up straight, and smile wide.

"What do you think?" I ask.

She pauses, takes it all in, and replies simply, "I love it."

We are both stunned. The tension is gone and the day is saved as I turn back to the mirror and twirl from side to side, checking myself out from every angle. My momma gets up and stands behind me, her reading glasses on, examining the price tags on each of the newly added items. Once she's finished taking inventory, she leans in toward the salesgirl to read her name tag, then closes her glasses and picks up her purse.

"You know what, sweetie? I think Rachel here probably knows a little more about teen fashion than your dear old mom. And the mall closes in about an hour and I still haven't figured out my Sleep Number for our new bed. So how 'bout the two of you pick out about five more outfits while I head down to that mattress store across the way. Sound good?"

I squeal, a sound that just comes out when I'm at my happiest.

"Now, Rachel," Momma continues, "you work on commission, right?"

Rachel nods.

"Okay, then. You're about to get a big paycheck, honey, but only if you follow a few rules. No midriff when she raises her hand, as if to ask a question at school or something. Nothing shorter than this mole here on her right leg. And absolutely nothing low-cut, got it?"

I sigh again, while Rachel nods and smiles. "Yes, ma'am!"

"Ricki Jo, I should be back in no time, but use the phone here to call my cell if you need me. And I'm going to want a fashion show before I swipe the plastic, got it?"

"Yes ma'am," I say, with much less enthusiasm than Rachel.

Following Rachel from rack to rack is an education in and of itself. As she pulls different jackets, skirts, and tops, she tells me why each one would work for my frame and why certain items would not. She talks to me about accentuating my good qualities and downplaying the body parts that aren't really working for me yet. From behind the counter, she grabs the aforementioned *Us Weekly* and lets me leaf through it as we shop.

"From a fashion standpoint, just look at the young stars, like Miley Cyrus or Taylor Swift," Rachel says, holding up a cute pink dress.

"Way too short," I say, my momma's voice in my head.

"Not with these underneath," she replies, grabbing a pair of black tights from a basket on top of the rack. "Leggings are totally in right now," she says, talking more to herself than to me, "so we'll get black, gray, and one lacy pair...ankle- and calf-length. Ooh! Bangles!"

And she's off again. I follow along, flipping through the glossy pages of the magazine, fascinated by the "Stars, They're Just Like Us" section. I also definitely like the way Rachel gets around my momma's rules. I should take notes.

Back in the dressing room, Rachel calls Momma while I start trying things on. We're going to build my wardrobe around a few strong pieces that can be interchanged with different accessories to look like totally different outfits. My dad would appreciate Rachel's thrifty take on fashion, but I think she's just trying to get me as much bang for my buck as possible. Looking down at the crumpled clothes I wore to the mall today, I realize she probably feels like she's doing a good deed.

"All in all, I'd say it was a pretty successful trip," Momma says as we unload the car. "But baby, I'm beat."

I stretch and yawn, exhausted myself and longing for my bed. It's been a full day, but worth it for sure. On the way out of the mall we walked past Abercrombie & Fitch and I stopped cold, sure that Wolf was right beside me. Guess that's where the boy buys his knock-me-dead cologne. I took deep breaths of it 'til I felt my lungs would explode and then floated outside. And on the way home my daydreams of us together at homecoming were interrupted only by a stop at the Wendy's drive-thru for a chocolate Frosty—the perfect way to cap off the perfect day.

"Definitely," I agree, gathering up the clothing that has spilled all over the trunk. (My momma + curvy roads = wear your seat belt.) She helps me stuff the previously folded clothes back into the gigantic shopping bags and we loop the handles over our forearms. Then, she finds Rachel's copy of *Us Weekly*.

"What's this?" she asks, holding it to the light in the trunk.

"Just a magazine," I say, grabbing it and stuffing it in a bag.

"Looks like you've got a few of them," she says, finding the copy of *Seventeen* I bought while she was in the bathroom.

"Just a little reading material, Momma," I say, quickly grabbing the last bag and closing the trunk. She holds it up and reads by the light of the full moon.

"'Hookup Report—What Guys Really Expect.'" She cocks an eyebrow at me, then sighs and shakes her head. I wait, breathless, hoping she won't take it away. I've been thinking about that article all the way home. Finally, she rolls it up and tucks it into one of my bags. "Just don't let your father see," she says, and heads inside.

"Luke!" I whisper, tapping on his bedroom window. It's cracked at the bottom, and if he doesn't open it soon I'm going in. I've been out here tapping for what seems like forever and know he can't be asleep. He never sleeps when he's stressed.

"Luke, I know you're awake," I whisper again. Tap. Wait. "Luke!"

"For God's sake, Luke, answer the damned girl," I hear his older brother groan.

Finally, Luke comes to the window and opens it. "What do you want, Ricki Jo?"

"Come down to the pond," I say.

He gives me a look I can't quite interpret, lowers the window again, and disappears.

"Luke!" I whisper again.

"Damn it, Ricki Jo! Let me put some pants on!" Luke yells, and then I see a pillow fly at him from across the room.

I take this opportunity to back away from the window and sit on the grass with Bandit. I'm not much on sneaking out—things seem scarier in the dark—but I got home too late to call Luke and ask him about his dad. I couldn't sleep, worrying about it and wondering if he's mad that I left, so I unchained Bandit and started hopping fences. Bandit's an awesome sidekick, and besides, a full moon makes the farm look more like a black-and-white photo than a forbidden forest.

"That dog better not start barking," I hear a grumpy voice say from behind me. Luke is standing over us, barefoot and bare-chested and obviously in a bad mood. "Let's go."

I hop up and follow him down his backyard to the plank fence. We climb it and head down our grass trail 'til we get to the edge of the pond, the stars sparkling on its smooth surface. I take a deep breath of his farm, filling my lungs with this countryside. I just love it here. Luke plops down on the soft grass and I join him, feeling secure, leaning back under the biggest sky I've ever seen.

"Lot of stars out tonight," I say.

"Yep," he replies, leaning on one elbow and splitting thick blades of grass with his fingers.

"You wanna talk about it?" I ask softly.

"The stars?" he asks.

"No, Luke."

"Oh. Your fabulous day at the mall?" he asks, sarcasm heavy.

"Hey! I said I wouldn't go!"

He sighs, sits up, and rests his skinny elbows on the knees of his old jeans, his head down. He takes a deep breath and fidgets with the worn leather band around his wrist. Looking out over me and the pond, he says, "It's broken. In three places. He can't hardly walk, Ricki Jo. How's he gonna work? Feed cattle? Cut hay? Think it'll be all healed up by the time we gotta strip tobacco? Think it'll be better by Thanksgiving?"

His voice gets stronger and louder and angrier, and his left leg is twitching up and down. I lie still, looking up at the face I know as well as my own, but seeing that hardened edge again.

"You think that lazy fat-assed SOB is gonna get better anytime soon?" he asks, finally looking down at me. "Or you think he's gonna sit around the house all day, boozing and back-handing my momma?"

This time, I look away, over at the cattail reeds that line the pond. He's scared—scared in his own house—and angry. I was going to tell him how mad I was at Momma when she wouldn't let me get a makeover at Macy's today, but his momma…

"And you know it'll be in the paper," he spits.

"How? I'm not gonna tell anybody, and my dad won't, either," I say.

"Come on, Ricki Jo," he says. "In the *Times* they put school lunch menus and a full page of records. You don't think the town drunk falling out of a barn is big news?"

"You mean, 'cause of the hospital records?"

"It'll be in next week's paper. I guarantee it."

We sit quietly, both knowing he's right. Our town paper, *The Breckinridge Times*, comes out once a week and prints about seven pages of everything from new births to the honor roll. My dad was just in the "25 Years Ago Today" column for winning the County Fair Tractor Pull when he was in school, and I was on the front page in fourth grade for winning the Soil Conservation Essay Contest. Unless the cops find marijuana in somebody's tobacco crop, the word *news* has a loose definition.

"I just wish she'd leave him," Luke says quietly. Bitterly.

I jerk up on my elbows. "Divorce?"

"What?" he asks me. "You call that a marriage?"

"I don't know," I say, shocked. I can't imagine my parents getting a divorce. I mean, I guess you'd get two Christmases, two birthday parties, two bedrooms, and all that; but you couldn't watch TV together, or play euchre, and you'd have to tell everything twice instead of just one time over dinner. I shudder. "I think divorce sounds scary."

"Yeah, well, I think a drunk for a dad is scary," he says. "And I can't just sit by watching my momma get knocked around."

This is the closest Luke's ever come to the topic of the shouts we hear in his house sometimes and the busted lip he brought to my cookout. I try not to breathe or look him in the eye 'cause I want him to feel like he can talk to me. I need my big mouth to stay quiet and my big ears to just listen.

"I'm just about a man now, you know?" he says quietly. I nod.

"And you think a real man sits back and watches while his mom shoves her kids behind her to take blow after blow? Or you think a real man shoves his mom back and takes the blows for her?"

I do not know the answer to either question, so I don't respond.

"Or just maybe," he says, standing up and brushing the grass off his butt, "a real man fights back."

I hop up fast and touch his arm.

"Don't fight back," I say before I can stop myself, feeling the worry etched all over my face.

He drapes his arm over my shoulders and leads me toward my house. We walk quietly, in sync, a happy Bandit leading the way, his brown and white tail wagging while an unhappy couple follows him, quiet and sad. I feel guilty and stupid. Guilty for having good parents, and stupid for complaining about them. Guilty for wanting lots of new popular friends, and stupid for not noticing the nightmare my true best friend is living. I wrap my arms around his waist as we walk, and squeeze.

"I'll never touch a drop of that stuff," he vows. He pulls away and looks down, staring me right in the eyes. "On my life, Ricki Jo. I'll never drink a drop."

CHAPTER THIRTEEN

"Let's take a quiz," I say to Luke as he sits beside me on the bus. I am determined to cheer him up, so my new *Seventeen* magazine is open, and my pen is ready to record his results.

"Save the quizzes for school, Ricki Jo," he grumbles. "I'm too tired for your girly games."

"No! This is really fun! I promise!" I plow on. "Okay. 'Two of your girls are fighting. You A) Ask them for details'—"

"Or B," Luke interrupts, "get new friends."

"Okay, so this one isn't good for guys," I concede, flipping back to the index. "Oh, but your horoscope! Okay, okay, okay. Here it is! 'Taurus: Jupiter will send you a boost of confidence on the seventeenth, and you'll finally find the courage to tell your crush how you feel!'"

Luke rolls his eyes.

"Okay, listen to mine. 'Gemini: Drama will run rampant in your life this month! You'll meet a new guy and instantly like him.' Oh my gosh! It's so true!"

Luke the Skeptic eyes me. "How is it 'so true'?"

"You need to tell your crush—aka probably Laura—how you feel, and I have drama with Wolf. Agh!" I exclaim, holding the magazine to my chest.

Luke looks over at me, amused. "You really believe that stuff, Ricki Jo?"

"Uh, yeah! It just totally nailed us both. Wait 'til you hear the 'Traumarama' section," I say, flipping to the right page. "Kissing goofs!"

"Kissing goofs!" Mackenzie exclaims. "Read another one! Oh my gosh, I would die."

Seventeen sprawled on the table in front of me, I delight the girls at my table by reading the "Traumarama" section aloud. They are much more receptive than Luke was, and Laura actually has tears in her eyes. Even Kimi is paying attention to me. *Does this count as bonding?*

"Morning, girls," Wolf says, taking his place at our table across from me.

I look up, but no one else does.

"Come on, Ericka!" Mackenzie begs. "Read another one!"

Pleased, I begin a horrid tale of a girl being shoved into a dark closet to play "70 Seconds in Heaven," only to find out she'd been making out with her first cousin. Wolf interrupts the story once, but Sarah shushes him.

"Seriously? Ugh, Kissing Cousins!" Laura cries giddily and fake spits, as if trying to get the incest out of her mouth.

"Who cares about some dumb magazine?" Wolf asks.

"Let's do a quiz," Sarah says. I am amazed at how little attention she is paying to her bangs and how engrossed she is in what I have to say.

"No! Let's finish these stories first!" Kimi demands. "They're hilarious!"

I wait, poised over my magazine, willing to acquiesce to either of their requests, when suddenly Wolf jerks it out of my hands.

"Hello?" he says, standing over the table, obviously worried about his charm wearing off.

"Grow up, Wolf," Kimi bosses, grabbing the magazine back and handing it to me.

Just then, Mr. Bates comes over the intercom with his boring-as-usual morning announcements.

"Keep reading," Kimi whispers, leaning forward on her forearms. The other girls huddle closer as well. I steal a look at Mrs. Wilkes, but she's nose deep in grading papers, so I lean forward and keep reading. We have to cover our mouths to keep from cackling out loud, and I notice that even Wolf seems to be leaning closer, actually enjoying the subject matter.

"'...so, I made an excuse and sprinted out the door

with my hands covering my butt!' " I read, and we all crack up, totally losing it.

"Hey, was that story sent in by your mom?" Wolf asks Kimi. "I remember her leaving in a hurry last night."

"Ha, ha," Kimi answers sarcastically. "My mom likes her guys with a little more muscle and a lot more facial hair."

And to my immense surprise, Wolf is put in his place.

These stories are hysterical, and at the same time, a little horrifying. Unlike the other girls at the table, I have zero boyfriend/make-out experience, and feel sick at the thought that any of these true tales of horror could happen to me.

As I begin the next woeful story, about a girl who bit a boy's tongue during a make-out gum exchange, I am interrupted.

"Miss Winstead," comes the stern voice of our homeroom teacher. "If that magazine does not disappear in five seconds, I will make it disappear. Understood?"

"Yes, ma'am," I say and hurriedly stuff it in my backpack, my pulse racing. There's no replacing this thing, so I can't get it taken away.

All the girls lean back disappointedly and give in to lame morning announcement time.

"That sucks," Wolf whispers to me loudly. "I was hoping you'd get to the sex tips."

I flush deep red.

"And let's have a good day here on the hilltop," Mr. Bates finishes, machinelike.

"Oh my gosh!" Kimi says dramatically and leans forward. There is mischief in her eyes, and we all huddle over the table again, even Wolf. "I've got a story that could totally be in *Seventeen*."

I fit in. In this moment, I fit in. I look around the huddle at the anxiously waiting, openly happy faces of my new friends and feel my heart beating in my throat. I can't stop smiling.

Kimi proceeds to tell us about the time she was babysitting for her parents' friends and had her boyfriend meet her out back in their pool. They took off all their clothes and started skinny dipping while the baby napped, but then the parents came home early and caught them in the act.

"I would die!" I cry. "Oh my gosh, I would totally die!"

"Yeah, and that's not the worst part," she says, really getting into it and taking off her sweater. She goes on with her story, but I don't hear another word. I'm wearing one of my new outfits—my favorite new outfit, to be exact: a yellow dress with a lacy neckline, an empire waist, and cropped sleeves. To my horror, Kimi—curvaceous and delicious and all things I hope my body will one day be—is wearing the same exact dress.

"Ericka?" I hear. "Ericka, Earth to Ericka."

Kimi is waving her hand in front of my face and I snap back to reality.

"Huh?" I say.

"I was just saying, I like your dress!" she jokes. "Twinsies!"

The girls laugh good-naturedly. I choke out a crazy guttural sound that one could easily mistake for a laugh, but I really want to crawl under the table.

"I love the way it blouses on you," she says, in what sounds like a sincere tone.

"Ha!" says Wolf. He looks at me. "That's just another way to say you don't have boobs."

"Wolf!" Kimi says, wide-eyed. "No, I really like it on her. I'm going to have to put my sweater back on so I don't feel bad."

She smiles nicely at me.

"Give the sweater to her!" Wolf protests. "Why should the guys at this school be punished because y'all have the same dress?"

I pick up my backpack and clutch it to my chest, looking up at the big round clock above the door. The bell rings, and not a moment too soon. I consider not going to my locker, but Mackenzie's arm is linked through mine before I can detour.

"You know you look adorable today, right?"

I nod halfheartedly.

"Your accessories are way cuter," she continues at my locker. "I didn't even notice at first, so it's obviously not like she looks better in it or anything. Just different."

"No," Wolf chimes in matter-of-factly, hanging on my locker door. "It looks better. It definitely looks better on her." Then he leans in to make sure Kimi can't hear and whispers, "But your face is prettier, Ericka. She kind of looks like a dude. I mean, just in her face. Obviously." He winks, does a weird shooting kind of gesture, and struts away.

"I love her face," Mackenzie says, looking over at Kimi and totally missing the fact that Wolf just said I was prettier. "Isn't she, like, half Native American or something?"

"Who cares?" I say meanly and slam my locker door. I leave her gaping and weave my way through the student body to Luke's locker, my safety zone.

"Hey, I meant to tell you this morning," he says, looking down at me with a lopsided grin. "You look really nice today."

I roll my eyes and lean against the locker next to his, letting the back of my head slam against it. "Kimi Wilson looks nice today, Luke. I look like an idiot."

"Me gusta tu pelo," comes a breath behind me. I half turn during Señorita's lecture and see Wolf leaned all the way up on his desk so that he is inches from the side of my face. "You mad at me again, Ericka?" he asks.

I shrug. I always want to be mad at this boy, and I always want to kiss him. Like I know I should be treated better, but I allow myself to be treated like a dog just because he's the most beautiful creature I've ever seen.

Of course, being totally incapable of saying any of this out loud, I say, "Yeah, I think so."

He grins. "Are you mad, mad? Or playing hard to get, mad?" he whispers.

I'm sure the look of complete shock registers on my face as I whip all the way around. "What are you talking about?"

"I'm just saying"—he shrugs and leans back—"I like your hair." Then he raises his hand and gives Señorita the present tenses for the verb *gustar* (to like), without missing a beat.

Gracías, I write on his notebook.

I face front again and think about page forty-two of *Seventeen*—"50 Secrets to Flirty Hair."

And I smile.

CHAPTER FOURTEEN

"I can't believe they were voted off!" my dad exclaims.

We just finished watching our favorite network reality show, and my parents are bummed. The couple they liked best were high school sweethearts (go figure), and didn't complete their challenge in time, totally letting down their entire team. I would've kicked them off, too. It took the woman, like, a million years to weave a potholder, and she kept complaining about her manicure. Pathetic.

"I'm glad," I say. "I want the two male models to win, anyway."

"Teenagers," my momma says, shaking her head.

"Hey, she can root for male models," my dad says, winking at me. "She just can't bring any home."

"I want the brother and sister to win!" Ben hollers, scoring major points with me. I reach over and give him double high fives, marveling at the fact that his eight-year-old hands are almost the same size as mine.

"Okay, off to bed, kids," my dad says, scooping Ben up and hanging him upside down, sending him into a shrieking fit. "It's late."

I get up from the couch and grab the popcorn bowl and Coke cans while Ben flees the tickling hands of my father. I'd actually like to get back to my room and write in my journal. I want to try to turn Kimi's embarrassing babysitting story into something like we read in *Seventeen*, just to see if I can.

"And don't forget to read your Bible," my momma calls.

"We know," Ben and I say in unison.

Teeth brushed, face washed, and pajamas on, I crawl into bed and grab my Bible, my journal, and my magazine. I look at *Seventeen* and try to copy their style as I jot down Kimi's story as if it were my own. I actually start giggling all over again (it's pretty funny), and think that it'd be cool to do this all the time. Maybe I could be a magazine writer one day. It's fun and takes no time, as long as I have a source for the real-life trauma. It couldn't exactly be anything from my personal experience, seeing as I have none, but hopefully that will all change in high school.

I sigh as I close the journal and slip it under my mattress. I toss the magazine over toward my backpack and open the Bible right smack down the middle.

Ever since I could read, my parents have encouraged me to end each day in the Word. I've read it through twice, but I prefer to randomly pick sections, letting it fall open where it may. There are actually some good stories in the Bible, but it's not exactly something I'd bring up at school. People would think I'm some kind of religious zealot or Jesus Freak or something, crazy and preachy and all the stereotypes I see on the news. And I seriously doubt Wolf would find it sexy.

Sometimes, the daily Bible reading can feel like a real chore. But most of the time, especially this year, it's kind of nice that the last thing I read before falling to sleep are promises that I'm never alone.

Tonight, the Good Book falls open to Song of Songs, and I'm instantly hooked. I sort of feel guilty, like I'm doing something wrong. It's a short book, and it's never made an impression on me before, but I'm reading it through for the second time already tonight and can't understand what it's doing in the Bible.

For example, the man says to the woman:

How pretty you are, how beautiful; how complete the delights of your love. You are as graceful as a palm tree, and your breasts are clusters of dates. I will climb the palm tree and pick its fruit. To me your breasts are like bunches of grapes, your breath like the fragrance of apples, and your mouth like the finest wine.

Right? I mean, he says he's going to climb her tree and pick its fruit!

Okay, and then *she* says:

Then let the wine flow straight to my lover, flowing over his lips and teeth. I belong to my lover, and he desires me.

Seriously! The "wine" is her mouth, and she wants it to flow all over him! *All* over.

I actually find it curious that this reading material is encouraged by my parents while teen magazines are frowned upon, although I would die of embarrassment to mention it. I close my Bible and think about what in the world made this woman's breasts so holy that they were written about in sacred text. Are they like Kimi's? I bet they are. I wait for the lightning to strike and feel kind of tingly all over, especially in my own "bunches of grapes," which could actually use a jump start. I pull at the neck of my T-shirt and look down, hoping to see some improvement.

"Ricki Jo?" my dad knocks at my open door and clears his throat. I jump a mile, eyes open wide, and clutch the fabric of my pj's to my neck. He looks confused but has that expression where he'd rather not know. "Telephone," he says. "Make it quick."

I wait for my dad to walk away before pulling back the covers and getting out of bed. *Not exactly a Hallmark father-daughter moment.*

"Hello?" I say into the phone in the living room.

"Ericka!" comes Mackenzie's voice through the receiver. "Oh my gosh, I'm so glad you're still up! I just talked to my parents and they agreed to rent out the roller rink for my birthday party. That's awesome, right?"

It is totally awesome.

"Totally!" I squeal into the receiver.

"Good, 'cause the other girls said the roller rink was *the* place to have a birthday party, but I wasn't sure. I mean, I don't even think there is one in Minneapolis, and if there is, no one would be caught dead there."

I frown. I mean, I don't know much about big cities, but the roller rink in our town is on the way to my house, and it's always jammin'.

"Well, I've been to a couple of parties there and they were pretty fun," I say, less enthusiastically than before. "And sometimes I go with my family, but never on the weekends, 'cause it's always so packed."

"Awesome!" she trills. "It's so cute and small-town! This is going to be the *best* birthday."

"Ricki Jo," my dad says in his low parental voice. He's tapping his watch and hovering. I roll my eyes and turn around. Dads.

"Okay, I *had* to call you 'cause you *have* to come," she gushes. "You're, like, my new BFF. We're, like, the New Girls Club! Ha!"

"Ha!" I reply, letting the words register. "Yeah! Totally! We are!"

"So it's this Saturday afternoon, but my mom said I

can have you over afterward for a sleepover, too! Isn't that great? Can you come? I hope you can come."

I can't see her, but in my mind, she is jumping in place, her blond hair full and bobbing.

"Uh, maybe," I say. I hope. I really, really hope. "I'll have to ask my folks."

"Okay," she says. "I'll wait."

I hadn't meant that I would ask them right at this moment; I'm still feeling a little awkward after the whole dad-walks-in-while-I'm-checking-out-my-chest fiasco. But Mackenzie is waiting, and I don't want her to get impatient and ask somebody else to stay over after the party.

"Ricki Jo," Momma says, "who's on the phone? Tell them it's past your bedtime."

I cover the receiver and look over my shoulder at my folks. *Right. 'Cause having a ten o'clock bedtime is something I want to shout from the mountaintops.*

"My new friend Mackenzie is having a birthday party this Saturday afternoon and a sleepover after," I say. "Can I go? Please?"

My parents look at each other, each trying to read the other's eyes.

"It's at the roller rink," I singsong, knowing that's where they had their first kiss. My mom's lips curve up and my dad's shoulders relax a little.

"I think that sounds like fun," Momma says, and then hip checks my dad. I turn around before any more parental flirting causes me to go blind.

"They said yes!" I tell Mackenzie excitedly.

"Cool. So, the rink, this Saturday, four o'clock," she says. "I can't wait! We're going to have so much fun!"

I hang up the phone and saunter back to my bedroom, sassy and saucy. "New Girls Club," I sing to myself, jazz voice rasping, hips swinging, attitude on high.

"You going to Mackenzie's birthday bash, Rosita Jo?" Wolf asks me in Spanish class.

The days this week have dragged by. Every night, I go through my wardrobe and plan optional skating party outfits. In *Seventeen*, there's this whole article: "Look Great on Any Date." They've got outfits for dancing, gaming, bowling, and concerts, but nothing about skating. I'm leaning toward a statement tee and skinny jeans (bowling gear), but think a team tee and faded boot-cut jeans might be more comfortable (gaming). I mean, it's not like her party is even technically a date, but the article is still a good resource. And a girl should always look good when roller-skating with potential boyfriends.

"Most definitely," I say to Wolf.

We've been paired up to do Actividad Numero 15, something about food and drink.

"Yeah, me, too," he says. "I heard a lot of upperclassman will be there. You know, her older brother Mark's friends, and then the girls from her cheerleading squad."

"Oh, yeah?" I say nonchalantly. "Anybody you got your eye on in particular?"

"Huh," he snorts. "You think the Wolf would tie himself down to one woman so early in the game? I'm still checking out all the inventory."

"You're disgusting," I tell him, and he laughs.

"Nah, I'm just kidding," he says. "Hey, I'm a freshman. The girls at her party want a guy with wheels, and I don't mean roller skates. Stunning good looks only get you so far."

We both laugh.

I don't know what it is about Spanish class—maybe it's that there's nobody around to impress—but Wolf's usually a pretty normal teenage guy between two and two fifty PM. He's actually smart, which I like, breaking the dumb-jock stereotype. With the whole alphabetical system the school is married to, we're always doing group work together. He totally participates and does his share when we're paired up, but acts like an absolute slacker when we're in a bigger group. I almost think he's just like me as far as his image goes, that maybe he's trying to mold himself into the cute, talented basketball star who doesn't need school.

"Ooh, I'd like to get her alone in the locker room," he says, licking his lips and looking out the window at a senior girl in the parking lot.

And then he says things like that.

"Ricki Jo!" my mamaw yells.

That woman has the loudest voice from here to Timbuktu,

and she trills my name at the top of her lungs. She is waiting for me when I step outside of school at the end of the day, her sturdy frame standing by the passenger door of my papaw's small truck, waving. Yes, waving — wildly, with both arms in the air, and catching herself on the door when she loses her balance.

Mortified, I attempt a nonchalant wave to the other girls on my squad. Practice actually went well today. I like the girls and I'm on top of all the pyramids, which is cool.

What is not cool is my grandmother shouting my name and motioning at me like an escaped mental patient who has taken a day job landing planes. I sprint over to their truck, which is parked diagonally across two handicapped spots, as quickly as I can.

"I'm here, gosh! Stop yelling," I say.

"Come here, baby," she says, and before I know it, she's pressing me against her massive bosom in a bear hug, slapping my back and cooing into my ear. "You're Mamaw's baby, ain't ya? Yes, Mamaw's sure happy to see you."

There is no escape. Because I am too short and scrawny and no match for her brute grandchild-love strength, I wait it out. As soon as I feel her loosen up the tiniest bit, I pull away and throw my backpack in the bed of the truck. Since it's not an extended cab, it's a tight fit. I slide onto the bench seat next to my papaw, a thick, quiet man who has both hands on the wheel, even when the truck is in park. Once Mamaw's eased her body onto the seat, pinning me in so tightly that a seat belt would just be redundant, we head out of the parking lot and onto the open road. Mamaw and Papaw have agreed to take me shopping for Mackenzie's birthday present, and we're heading out to The Square at the breakneck speed of thirty-four miles per hour.

"Slow down, Frank," my mamaw commands, patting my knee. "We've got precious cargo."

He eases up on the gas and I throw my head back and close my eyes, anxious and frustrated. I have to find the perfect gift and I have to find it today. The party is in twenty-four hours and it'll probably take that long just to cross town!

I begged my momma to take me back to Lexington, but there was no way. By the time she got off work, picked me up, and drove me up to the mall, it'd be closing. Short notice doesn't work in this town, but I guess Mackenzie will catch on soon enough. 'Til then, my grandparents are my best bet.

As Mamaw starts singing a little a capella Hank Williams Sr., I focus on the task at hand. Against the backs of my eyelids, I use imaginary chalk to calculate just how much money I have and how much I can afford to spend on a gift for Mackenzie. I blew most of my savings on the shopping spree of the century last Saturday, so my cash situation is a little tight. I've got forty-five dollars to show for an entire summer of breaking my back in the hot sun. JV girls don't cheer at away games, so cheering won't cost me anything, but as a member of the student body, I totally plan on supporting our school at all the Varsity games, which means I'll need moolah for tickets and concessions. Plus, if I keep making friends (or even snag a boyfriend!), I'll need an emergency fund in the event of *their* birthdays.

Friends are expensive, but important. I decide I can spend fifteen dollars.

As Papaw deftly pulls into The Square's parking lot, I look around at our meager selection. Walmart is the shopping center's anchor, while a long strip mall juts out from either side filled with a Fashion Bug, a stromboli shop, a bank, a Sally Beauty Supply, and a few locally owned shops. There are also some clothing stores, but I don't know Mackenzie's size and, let's face it, I'm no fashionista. I could probably find something at Sophie's Candle, but a candle seems so...anybody. And at Linda's Card Shoppe, I could get a pretty picture frame, which promises the hope of future photo ops together, but that may be presumptuous.

"You wanna just go right to Wally World?" Papaw asks, steering the pickup in that direction. Walmart is his favorite store of all time. He power walks the large aisles every morning and then makes excuses throughout the day to go back, always running into people he knows and keeping his finger on the pulse of small-town life.

"Um, I don't know," I answer, looking around The Square.

I am starting to sweat. I don't know if it's because I

can't move or because I have no idea what I should buy for my new BFF. Seems like Best Friends Forever should have an idea of each other's interests, but I was only just informed of this development in our friendship a few days ago. I'm sure we'll learn all about each other at the sleepover, but in the meantime, I'll have to get creative with what I know so far: She likes cheerleading, she has pierced ears, and she is from Minnesota.

It's not a lot to go on.

Finally, I give in to my papaw's longing gaze and we head over to Walmart. Right away, Mamaw chats up the greeter and Papaw makes a beeline for the fish and tackle department. I head straight to electronics, my stomach in knots. I see Mrs. Wilkes waiting for her photos and duck behind a video-game machine so she doesn't see me. Whenever I see my teachers out in the real world I clam up, get a sort of weird feeling, and look for the nearest exit.

"I love this movie! Oh my god, it's a classic!" I hear a girl squeal from behind me. She's in electronics, holding up a copy of *Mean Girls* and waiting for her friends' reactions. I see college girls, a whole gaggle of them in matching sorority sweatshirts, giggling over by the DVDs. College girls! Experts in all things cool! They're like a light at the end of the tunnel. I wander closer, feigning interest in the new releases but staying close and taking notes.

"No, what about this?" another girl answers, grabbing *Dirty Dancing*.

"Ladies, we need something dramatic, maybe something we all saw together, but with lots of eye candy," says a beautiful girl who is obviously their ring leader. She stares at the movies, concentrating fiercely, and then picks up a movie with Channing Tatum on the cover. They all squeal and jump around. I smile. That's the exact reaction I want from the birthday girl.

Once they're gone, I fly over to the stand and grab the last copy of the very same movie, *Dear John*. I heard this movie was actually kind of sad, but I also read that Channing Tatum is shirtless most of the time, so I guess that's the appeal. Maybe we'll even watch it after the party when I sleep over, although I'll totally act like I saw it in the theater.

Skipping through the store to the birthday-card section, I grab a gift bag and find a great card: a sexy lifeguard with oiled-up abs. *Perfect!* I search the store for my grandparents and then wrangle them back to the front, confident in my mature, yet fun, gift—a college-approved movie.

"Twenty-one-oh-nine," the checkout girl slurs, going to town on a huge wad of blue gum.

The total is a tad out of my budget, what with the DVD, card, and gift bag. I hesitate a second before grabbing a few more bills from my billfold. "Never thought I'd say this," I say to my mamaw, who is hovering over me, "but I can't wait for strippin' season."

The girl gives me my change and I grab my purchases,

keeping both hands full in case Mamaw tries to hold one as we head for the parking lot.

"Mamaw thought you hated workin' in tobacco, honey," she says, third person being her favorite point of view.

"Yeah, well, Mamaw's right," I say. "But Ericka doesn't like being broke."

CHAPTER FIFTEEN

The outside of the rink is plain; it's an old building with white paint peeling off. The sign out front is faded from the sun and doesn't look to have been repainted since this place opened in the seventies. But the inside...

I walk through the front door and feel butterflies swarm through my stomach. Pop music blares from the speakers, and kids are everywhere. I get in line with Luke to wait for our skates and stare out at the roller rink, checking out the competition. I don't know if Mackenzie invited Luke because he's my friend and therefore hers, too, or if it's because Laura has a crush on him. Either way, I'm glad he's here.

"You know, you clean up nice," I tease him. He's wearing a pair of distressed jeans that look like they were bought that way, but I know they were actually worn in by long days working on the farm. And he's wearing a button-up, albeit a really casual one, but the pastel blue looks really nice with his eyes and light hair. I hardly ever see him in anything other than a T-shirt of some kind, so I can't help but rib him just a little.

"Yeah, I just hope the ladies can keep their hands to themselves," he says, popping his collar.

I roll my eyes and fake gag, and he blushes a little and shakes his head. We both crack up.

"Ericka!"

I turn at the sound of my name as Mackenzie hobbles over to me on her skates.

"I'm so glad you're here!" she says.

She hugs me and almost falls. I steady her, while trying to keep my own tennis-shoed feet out from under her wheels.

"Happy birthday!" I say. "It looks amazing in here!"

The space has been completely transformed. Pink streamers stretch from corner to corner and wind around the rails of the rink. Giant columns of pink and white balloons are tied up outside the skating area, and the entire ceiling is covered with more balloons. Blown-up pictures of Mackenzie are taped up on the walls, and the cake is definitely not a grocery-store job. This party is the real deal.

Mackenzie grabs my shoulder and rolls forward with me as the line we're waiting in for our skates dwindles. Her head is on swivel mode as she takes in the party and her guests, flashing a perfect smile at anyone who makes eye contact.

"There're a lot of people here," I comment, absorbing the scene with a little more awe.

"Get your skates!" the overjoyed birthday girl squeals.

I giggle and turn to the counter.

"Six and a half," I say to the owner, who I've known since I was little.

"Try not to be a show-off, kid," he says with a wink, and passes me a cute white pair of roller skates with pom-pom shoelaces.

"Wait, are you good?" Mackenzie asks, looking almost worried.

Before I can answer, though, an older girl from her cheerleading squad rolls up a few people away and yells her name. Mackenzie screams and hobbles toward her, grabbing every shoulder waiting in line to pull herself forward until she finally dives into the girl's embrace.

The truth? I'm magic on eight wheels. My momma and daddy met at this roller rink and bring us skating about once a month for "family time." I can skate backward and spin around like a ballerina in a jewelry box, and I always win the limbo. (It helps that I'm already the closest to the floor at my full height.)

I settle down on a wooden bench that skirts the rink and feel my adrenaline pumping. I can't get my skates on fast enough, but Luke looks a little worried.

"I hope I don't break my neck," he says, eyeing his skates dubiously.

I smile encouragingly. "You'll be great."

From the looks of our fellow classmates, he's not the only rookie in the room. Some kids are getting around okay, but I can see the fear in their eyes. A couple of girls look like they're on tiptoe, walking around on their front wheels and brakes. Lots of kids skate with their arms out wide, poised to catch themselves in case of a fall. I make a mental note to avoid those particular skaters, 'cause those are the ones who will take the closest kid down with them.

"What's up, Ricki Juana?" my favorite Spanish partner asks as I finish lacing my skates. Wolf leans against the rail and looks down at me with his full-on sexy grin. He's wearing a classic plaid shirt under a vintage A&F hoodie, looking ultra-fine and somehow managing to pull off cargo shorts with roller skates. I get a whiff of his cologne and my hands shake a little. "You gonna save a skate for me later?"

Luke grunts as he pushes himself up off the bench, gives Wolf a curt head nod, and wobbles out into the throng looking a little bit like a baby giraffe taking its first steps. Usually, I'm self-conscious around Wolf, all nerves, but today the nerves feel more like adrenaline. I'm in my new dark boot-cut jeans and a flirty pink tank with sheer petal details around the neckline. I feel pretty and know I can skate, so I stand and put a hand on my hip, looking up at Wolf with more confidence than I've ever had around him.

"Think you can keep up?" I tease and circle around him in a flash, my skates pointed outward.

"Whoa!" he exclaims, looking over his shoulder and losing his balance a little.

"Let's really get this party started!" the owner yells over the speakers. "We've got a room full of teenagers, so let's do some Hokey Pokey!"

I scream. "The Hokey Pokey! Wolf, let's go!"

I tug at his sleeve and take to the floor, forgetting to be nervous and awkward around him for the first time since we met.

"Wait, you're excited about the Hokey Pokey?" he calls, his hand still hesitantly holding on to the rail. "Isn't that kind of lame? Like a kid's game or something?"

"Yeah, you're probably right," I say, rolling back toward him with a smirk on my face. "Me totally showing you up out there today is going to be bad enough, but if I schooled you at something as lame as the Hokey Pokey, your reputation would never recover."

"You're going to school me?" he asks haughtily. "On what planet?"

"Okay, guys and girls. Time to par-tay!" the owner yells again over the microphone, starting the Hokey Pokey song . . . which, yeah, is actually kind of silly.

"Ericka!" Mackenzie yells from the center of the floor, motioning to me with her megawatt smile and bobbing blond head to join her. I beam at her. If the Hokey Pokey's lame, the super-pretty birthday girl didn't get the memo. She's holding on to a wobbly Laura with one hand and a cute boy with the other. "Come on!"

The music starts and I look back at Wolf. "So, how 'bout it, Wolf? You gonna Hokey Pokey, or are you too scared?"

"Yeah, right," he says and starts to move out onto the floor. "Let's do this."

I clap my hands and jump, then twirl around and race to the middle, leaving him to stare after me.

"Did you just *jump* in those?" an incredulous Wolf calls after me, slicing his arms back and forth in an effort to propel himself forward. He looks like the sexiest idiot I've ever seen.

I backward scissor skate around a few kids and stop right in front of him as the chorus starts. I mimic his signature "Wolf Wink" and he cracks up. I can't help but show off. Finally, he and everybody else can see that Ricki Jo Winstead—um, make that *Ericka* Winstead—is really good at something.

With Wolf right next to me, I shake it all about like my life depends on it.

"Happy birthday, dear Mackenzie. Happy birthday to you!"

I sing at the top of my lungs along with a huge crowd of fellow well-wishers. This is, by far, the best birthday party I've ever attended. Mackenzie blows out the candles and we all cheer. Her dad cuts the cake and her mother passes slices around. I've already had two Cokes, but I grab another. It's a celebration!

"Dude, this cake is crazy good," Luke says.

"Yeah," I agree, my mouth full. "I'm definitely gonna get another slice if there's extra."

Flashbulbs have been going off like crazy all afternoon. As I stuff my face with a too-big bite of cake, smearing chocolate icing all over my mouth, Mrs. Watts captures the moment.

"Cute!" she trills.

Meanwhile, Mackenzie's dad has been making a dent in the gift pile by passing beautifully wrapped presents her way. She reaches into bags and peels open envelopes and appears to be thrilled with each present. Plus, Mrs. Watts snaps a photo of her with each gift-giver, which is going to make for one thick scrapbook.

"What'd you bring?" I asked Luke.

He shrugs. "I gave her a card at school yesterday. Good thing, too, 'cause now I can avoid the paparazzi."

"Oh my god! I love it!" Mackenzie squeals, turning my attention back in her direction. She's holding a movie up for the camera and hugging Sarah. "Thank you so much!"

I gasp.

"What?" Luke asks.

"Well," Sarah is saying to Mackenzie, "I know you got a Blu-ray player, so you have to have this for your collection. Did you see it? It's so good and, seriously, Channing Tatum is so hot."

All the kids laugh, and a few girls giggle in agreement.

"Oh my god," I whisper in horror. "I got her the same thing."

And, as if on cue, Dr. Watts passes a gift bag covered in smiley faces Mackenzie's way.

"It's from Ericka!" Mackenzie yells. "Come over here, girl!"

"What'd you get her, Ericka?" Wolf calls playfully. "Skating lessons?"

Everyone laughs and the sea of partygoers in front of me parts. I roll forward weakly, feel sweat form on my upper lip, and fidget next to her as she digs into the tissue paper.

"Oh my god!" she squeals, holding up the movie and hugging me. "How funny! It's the same one I just got from Sarah. Great minds think alike, huh, girls?"

"Yeah, but that's a DVD," Sarah points out, and the crowd gets quiet. "Not Blu-ray."

I cringe.

Which is, of course, the moment Mrs. Watts takes the picture.

"Score!" Luke hollers, holding his hands up high as a lime-green air hockey puck clangs into my goal. When the lights were dimmed for the couples' skate, we left the hot and horny party guests out on the floor and made our way over to the arcade.

"Hey, guys," Laura says, skating up to the edge of the table. Her long auburn hair is curling down in front of her left eye and it's all I can do not to tell her to get it out of her face. I hate that I'm becoming my mother. "Nice shot, Luke," she purrs. Her flirting needs work.

"Uh, thanks," Luke says, fishing around in his jeans pocket for more quarters.

"You wanna play?" I ask, offering her my chunky white paddle and giving her big matchmaking eyes. Luke jerks his head up and gives me a murderous look.

"Um, no thanks," she says and smiles at me kindly. She really is cute as a button. Then she turns to Luke and takes a big breath, then flips her hair over her shoulder. "I was actually wondering if you might want to skate the next song with me?"

She is looking up at him with mild desperation in her charcoal-lined eyes, and even on roller skates, she's leaning in on tiptoe. He looks over at me, six feet two inches of total fear, and I sell him out—sell him right down the river.

"Yeah! You all go skate," I say. "I gotta go to the bathroom, anyway."

Laura's chipmunk cheeks go even rounder as she beams at me. Without hesitation, she grabs Luke's hand and pulls him toward the rink, and although she's at least a foot shorter than he is, she's able to move him along based on the strength of her determination. He turns and shoots me a hateful look, while I hold my arms up and mouth, *Score!*

But helping Laura means losing my wingman, and the only thing left to do is wait out the ridiculously long couples' skate. Leaning against the rail and watching the other kids roll past is absolute torture. The lights are low and the DJ plays sappy R&B slow jams over the speakers.

When Justin Bieber's "That Should Be Me" comes on, I totally relate. I have proven that I can out-skate any girl at this party, yet I'm on the sidelines right now. The couples' skate is obviously not about skill. The magic is in the hand-holding and the disco ball.

"Whew!" Wolf says, slamming up against the rail beside me, totally catching me off guard.

I jump back and scream, which sends him into fits of laughter. I get myself together and put my hand on my hip, flirty pose engaged.

"Lookin' good out there," I say, wishing I were on his side of the rail.

"Why aren't you skating?" he asks.

I don't think it'll help my cause to say *'Cause nobody's asked me*, so I shrug and play it off. "Too good, I guess. Would put all the boys to shame."

He laughs. "You're pretty competitive, aren't you, Ericka? Like, you hate when I get a better grade than you in Spanish."

"Once," I remind him. "You scored one point higher on one quiz."

"And I'll never let you forget it," he says, his cocoa eyes sparkling. "But seriously. You haven't skated with anybody, and you're really good. It's kind of hot, to tell you the truth."

I blush, which is a minor reaction considering that my blood is flowing like raging hot lava through my veins.

He puts both hands on my shoulders and looks directly

into my eyes. "Why don't you ask some good-looking guy to take you for a twirl?"

I can't believe what I'm hearing, but it's pretty clear that Wolf is hinting that should I ask him to skate. *What the what?* I tuck my hair behind my ear, then remember that *Seventeen* says that only accentuates big ears and pull it loose again. I lick my lips and take a deep breath. Asking Wolf to couples' skate is like bungee jumping without a cord—it may be the bravest thing I've ever done in my life.

Or it could be the stupidest.

There's only one way to find out.

I look him dead in the eyes, summoning up both my courage and my sense of reckless abandon, but before I can even squeak out one syllable—

"Oh!" he says, looking over one shoulder and dropping his hands. "Kaitlyn's free now. I gotta get over there!"

He rushes off, blowing me an air kiss.

My mouth should get used to falling open when he's around, either from his good looks or from his total lack of comprehension of all things polite. *Did that just happen?*

My face in my palms, I lean on my elbows against the rail, invisible, and fall into an intoxicating state of self-pity.

I can't watch anymore...and yet I can't stop watching. Like a rubbernecker slowing down traffic by staring at a gruesome accident scene, I can't peel my eyes away. Mackenzie has not skated with the same boy twice and yet has not stopped skating. Sarah is glued to her boyfriend's side (well, his tongue), and Kimi is unsuccessfully trying to skate, hold hands, and text message at the same time. Laura and Luke have gone around a few times, both threatening to fall at any moment and take the other down with them, but both seeming to enjoy themselves as well. I find myself wishing Candace were here. I'm not very good at making fun of people, but she's a pro—she feels no remorse—and although I think it's wrong, she really makes me laugh.

"Are you Ericka?"

And then, there is a boy. A cute boy. A cute boy with green eyes and curly brown hair. And he's talking to me.

"Yeah, I am," I say, straightening up and blushing for sure.

"I'm Mark," he says, holding out his hand for me to shake. "I'm Mackenzie's brother, um...a sophomore at your school, um...our school."

He's really nervous.

I'm really flattered.

"Anyway," he continues, "um, Mackenzie said you're really cool and nice and...um...you want to skate with me?"

I don't know why I ever closed my mouth after Wolf skated off, because it's officially hanging open again. I nod, attempting to breathe, and he takes my hand. After one lap, I feel comfortable and pretty. I look over at Mark's profile and smile. He doesn't have Wolf-esque model looks, but he's cute and nice and nervous. *I make him nervous!*

In front of us, there is a small traffic jam of idiots on wheels. Mark tenses up, clutching my hand a little tighter. I see Wolf holding the pole near the end of the oval floor, trying to swing Kaitlyn around for lap two. I feel cocky and proud, and I want to show Wolf what he's missing.

"Excuse us," I say, and then I spin around, grab Mark's other hand to face him as I skate backward, and lead him through the bottleneck. We weave easily through the throng of skaters and I feel Wolf's eyes on me before I turn and see him fall. I can't help but giggle as I look over at Mark again.

"You're pretty good," he says, allowing himself to be pulled around the rink.

"You're not so bad yourself, Yankee Doodle," I tease, wondering how many first kisses have occurred under the magic spell of the disco ball.

CHAPTER SIXTEEN

"Wow," I whisper as Dr. Watts drives up the tree-lined driveway to Mackenzie's house. It's right by the hospital and sits back off the road, a towering home that looks like it could be right out of *Gone with the Wind* or something. A home so fancy that it has a name: Chesswood Manor.

I'm squished in the backseat of the minivan between the window and Kimi. As the skating party died down, I realized that the BFF sleepover included more than just the New Girls when I saw Sarah, Laura, and Kimi waiting at the front door with their sleeping bags and totes. And now I'm in the very back, Kimi turned away from me to face Sarah, constantly elbowing me as she complains non-stop about how Sarah's boyfriend was looking at other girls at the party. Mackenzie, Mark, and Laura are squished in the seat in front of us, loaded down with gifts and balloons, while Dr. Watts drives and Mrs. Watts goes through the pics on her digital camera.

"Home sweet home," Mackenzie's dad announces, putting the minivan in park. We climb out one by one, and I stretch outside on their cobblestone driveway. My momma would love this place.

"Just take your things straight down to the basement, girls," Mrs. Watts directs us as we enter their chandeliered and wood-floored foyer. To my left is a formal living room, complete with a baby grand piano and velvet settee, which I have previously seen only in the movies. To my right is the formal dining room, with a china buffet and a long oak table, the polish gleaming under yet another chandelier.

I lug my sleeping bag and backpack down the stairs in front of us alongside the rest of the girls, but I'm dying to know what's upstairs and to see the rest of the house. Their kitchen is probably like one out of a restaurant or something. I bet they have a pool.

Yet all thoughts of the upstairs are banished when I see the basement. It's completely finished, decked out from floor to ceiling with pictures of Mackenzie and Mark. I look around and see a small gym, a pool table, a Ping-Pong table, a foosball table, a gigantic flat-screen TV, and a huge wraparound couch. The basement is teenager heaven. It's also pretty much the size of my whole house.

"This is awesome," I say to Mackenzie, setting my things down in a corner.

"Yeah, it's pretty cool." She shrugs. "I liked our house in Minnesota better, but this is good 'cause Dad's so close to the hospital. We get to see him a lot more."

I wonder what kind of doctor he is. Probably a surgeon, like on TV. In fact, he's kind of handsome, in an older-guy, McDreamy sort of way.

"He's a heart specialist," Mackenzie says, as if reading my mind. I nod casually, making a mental note to block all telepathic vibes I may be sending into the universe. It would be pretty creepy if she knew I think her dad's sort of hot.

"Ericka, help me move this," Mackenzie orders, snapping me out of my thoughts. I walk over to the Ping-Pong table and help her fold it up and push it against the wall. Then we push a recliner and reading table out of the way as well.

"What are y'all doing?" Sarah asks from the sectional, the noise we're making apparently pulling her away from the constant texting she's involved in on her iPhone.

"Making room to tumble!" Mackenzie exclaims, and then she does an impromptu aerial, right there, without warning.

Everybody screams and runs over to Mackenzie. Sarah and Laura are already pulling their hair back into ponytails and Kimi searches her bag for an elastic headband. Before I know it, they are taking turns doing tumbling passes down the lush carpet of the basement alley Mackenzie has created. I am in awe of them, and feel super self-conscious.

"Not too high," Mackenzie warns Sarah, who must have springs attached to her heels. "I basically just want to help Ericka."

All four of them look at me, and then collectively light up. It dawns on me that I am their project. And then it dawns on me that I'm okay with that.

"Okay, so you need to get the back handspring down," Laura says, planting herself across from Mackenzie. "Stand in front of us."

I do as I'm told. At first, I feel pretty scared. Call me crazy, but something about throwing myself blindly backward seems not so smart. I can't see where I'm going, and it's hard to fearlessly toss my entire weight back. Then Kimi, in all of her bossiness, takes control of the situation and basically threatens my life if I don't do it. I don't want to look bad in front of these girls; plus, I tell myself, I'll be one step closer to accomplishing the ten goals of Project Ericka.

Deep breath drawn, prayers said, I lean back over their arms... and voilà! I do a back flip! (A very slow back flip—kind of like a back bend over Mackenzie's and Laura's arms where I get stuck, leaving Kimi and Sarah to grab my calves and heave me over—but a back flip nonetheless!)

We spend an hour working on tumbling, and then we cheer. Mackenzie and Sarah teach the rest of us some of their Boys' Varsity cheers, since that's what we all aspire to. I find the motions and chants easy, but the jumps and splits impossible. I see a trampoline out back and think how cool it'd be to have one of those. I could practice my jumps on that thing all the time.

Worn out, we all grab bottles of Gatorade from the fully stocked downstairs fridge. I crash on the oversized ottoman, which is the perfect size for me, and the other girls sprawl out on the couch. I feel like part of the group, one of the girls, a friend. I push my sweaty bangs back off my forehead and sigh, content. Mackenzie cracks the back patio door to let the September breeze cool us down.

"Are we gonna eat soon?" Kimi asks.

I lean up and look over at her, stunned to see that she's standing there in her bra, rubbing lotion on her arms. Her boobs are enormous—they really are. And now I've seen them...well, the top halves, anyway. I don't know if I'm imagining it, but I think I feel my own nipples sink back into my chest—which sucks, because lately they've really been making some headway.

"Yeah, let's order pizza. Is that okay?" Mackenzie asks. We all nod in agreement and I hope to God that Mark doesn't come downstairs. If he sees Kimi the Exhibitionist, he'll forget I exist. Not that I have a crush on him or anything, but it was nice to be noticed. When Mackenzie picks up the phone to call in our order, I grab my pajamas and go change in the downstairs bathroom, wary of getting involved in any group nakedness.

Now, maybe it's just me, but I feel that when going to bed alone, as most freshman girls do, one need not worry about what one wears. Yet, as I come out of the bathroom and carry my party clothes back over to my bag, I notice everyone else changing into actual pajamas and/or night-gowns, ranging from flirty to sexy. Kimi's wearing a lace-trimmed zebra tee with matching boy shorts, Sarah's wearing polka-dot satin pajamas, Mackenzie's pulling a cute cotton sleep shirt over her head, and Laura is in flannel pants and a tank top with a built-in bra. Meanwhile, I have on an oversized University of Kentucky basketball T-shirt and sweatpants. Compared to the other girls, I look like a small boy.

As I berate myself for not scanning *Seventeen* for sleepover wear, I walk over to the couch area and plop myself down next to Laura, who's uncoiling the head-phones to her iPod. Mackenzie is flipping through this month's *OK!*, and I make a note to get my hands on that magazine before the night is over. Sarah is back to texting on her iPhone, and Kimi has moved from lotion applica-tion to painting her toenails. The way she has her leg hiked up, her knee pushes against her chest so that one of her C-cups is thrust out into the spotlight. It is seriously hard not to gawk, so I ask Laura to show me her favorite playlist.

"Oh, definitely this one," she says enthusiastically, passing me one of her earbuds. "I call it Make-Out Jams, and it's awesome."

Make-out jams?

"Ooh, what's on yours?" Kimi asks, her black bob flicking up out of her face and her dark eyes sparkling at the mention of male groping.

"You know, kind of a variety, 'cause you never really know the guy's taste. So, like, Mariah Carey's 'Touch My Body'—"

"*Love* that song," Sarah pipes up without missing a beat as her thumbs fly across her phone's screen.

"'Sex on Fire,' by Kings of Leon."

"Now *that's* a jam for when it's really getting hot and heavy," Kimi interrupts knowingly. She secures the cap of her nail polish and stretches out her short but toned legs, admiring her handiwork.

"And Dave Matthews's 'Crash Into Me,' even though it's a total oldie." Laura looks at me and sort of winces, as if she's embarrassed.

I nod and feel like I have to say something. "But it's a classic," I manage, all sorts of false confidence. Make-out jams? Seriously? I wouldn't care what I was listening to. I'd just be stoked about making out.

"My guilty pleasure is John Mayer's 'Your Body Is a Wonderland,'" Mackenzie confesses. "I mean, whenever I'm thinking about a boy I like or something, I put that song on."

"It's on here," Laura says, thumbing through her play-list, and almost immediately I hear it in my right ear.

"What boys *do* you like?" Sarah asks pointedly, looking up from her iPhone for the first time in half an hour. She pulled her bangs back with a bobby pin when she washed her face earlier and I can't help but think how much prettier she looks without all that stringy hair in her eyes.

"I don't know," Mackenzie says, curling her legs up under her on the couch and majorly blushing. She's obviously embarrassed, and obviously lying. We all *oooooh* and suddenly the room is abuzz with boy talk. I love it.

"Come on, Mackenzie," I goad her, feeling mischievous. "Who do you like?"

"Nobody!" she squeals, putting her hands up over her face. Laura and I laugh and clap, and Kimi reaches over to swat Mackenzie's legs with her magazine.

"Seriously," Sarah says, all business. "You're new, so I'm sure you've been checking out the guys. And you, too, Ericka. I mean, there are a lot more boys at Preston County than there were at Saint Pat's."

"Yeah, did you ever make out with any of the Saint Pat boys?" Laura asks me, her round face flushed with excitement. " 'Cause I think Trevor Barker is sort of cute."

My eyes go big and my smile gets a little goofy. I liked this game better when it was all about Mackenzie. I mean, yeah, I have a major crush on Wolf, but I don't know if I want to announce it to the world, especially since these girls have all seen what a jerk he's been to me. I would look so stupid. And as far as my experience with the boys at my old school, holding hands with Mike O'Conner at the sixth-grade ice cream social probably doesn't count for much.

"Oh!" Kimi interjects. "You all tell us who you like,

and we'll tell you if we've hooked up with them already. Or who else has. Or if they're, like, a good kisser or whatever."

The three of them look back and forth between my face and Mackenzie's, waiting for some good gossip. I take a sudden interest in the loops of Mackenzie's plush shag carpet and she seems suddenly preoccupied with an imaginary hangnail. This is obviously not going the way Sarah had hoped, and she sighs dramatically.

"Okay, fine. You don't have to say your main crush. Let's just do a top five. Like, for me, I'm obviously in love with Jimmy, and I don't like anybody else."

Kimi snorts and Sarah shoots her a nasty look before she continues. "However, if you put a gun to my head and made me name five boys, I'd say Jimmy first—'cause we're totally exclusive no matter what *some people* might think—and then I'd go with four other seniors: Ben Roth, Joey Beach, Greg Grammer, and...um...oh, Brad Jones."

She says all this flippantly, as if it's no big deal. As if telling four other girls, two of whom she just met this month, that she likes four other guys besides her boyfriend is no big deal. I'm in awe.

"Okay, now you, Ericka," she says, turning her gaze my way.

I gulp, not really feeling the gushy girl bonding I was expecting tonight. I'm fourteen, the same age as these girls, but I've never been kissed, so I definitely don't have a playlist of make-out jams, and I've never really had a boyfriend. Of course, that's the last thing I want to admit. I'm sure the Fabulous Four, as Luke calls them, will find my lack of experience more pitiful than fabulous.

I shrug. "I don't really like anybody," I lie, feeling my cheeks flame red.

"Oh, come on!" Sarah says, exasperated. "It's not a big deal, Ericka. Like, okay, if you ask Kimi, she could name at least fifteen off the top of her head! And she's probably been felt up by half of them already."

"Soooo jealous," Kimi spits under her breath.

"So just name a few guys, Ericka. It's easy." Sarah looks at me and waits. All of them look at me and wait. Finally she blows air through her lips and rolls her eyes. "Ericka, it's top secret. Like, we'll pinky swear and all that. Nobody tells who's on your boys list. Girl code."

"Pizza's here!" Mark calls down the stairway. I jump at the sound of his voice, hoping he hasn't heard any of this. He couldn't have come at a better time, though, and judging by how fast Mackenzie springs off the couch, she couldn't agree more.

"Coming!" she yells, bounding over to the stairs.

"Like Mark," Sarah states simply.

Mackenzie stops cold and jerks her head over toward us. I avert my gaze. *Awkward. All so very awkward.*

"Whatever," Sarah says, almost challenging Mackenzie. "It's obvious he's totally into her, and she's your friend, right? So who cares?" Her phone beeps and, showing how serious she really is about all this, she shoves it in between the couch cushions without checking her message and keeps her eyes on Mackenzie.

"Yeah. Who cares?" Mackenzie finally says, looking over at me and shrugging before disappearing up the stairs.

I watch her go and kind of feel like she cares; but Mark is really nice, really cute, and, apparently, "totally into" me. And as quiet as Sarah usually is, she's obviously unrelenting about boy talk, so I cave just to get her off my back.

"Okay," I say timidly. "Well, then, Mark Watts."

"You two were soooo cute couples' skating earlier," Laura chimes in, bobbing her head ferociously.

"Good, who else?" demands our resident boy-talk interrogator, Sarah. Kimi and Laura are both grinning from ear to ear, eager to learn more of my juicy secret desires.

I take a deep breath. Just four more to go. The name *David Wolfenbaker* is going off like fireworks in my head, making my heart beat extra fast and causing me to sweat a little. He's the only guy I really, really like, but if he knew, if anybody were to tell him, I would absolutely die.

"I don't know that many guys yet," I stall.

"Well, I think you like Wolf," Kimi says, her eyes sparkling.

And there it is. Out there. Because although I didn't confirm it with my mouth, they all *oooooh* at the same time, which means that burning sensation I feel in my cheeks, ears, and neck has indeed given me away. So I nod, and then I do the only thing I can think to do, which is rush through this torture and save myself. "Okay, so Mark, and Wolf, and his older brother, too, and I guess that guy you said, Joey Beach, or whatever."

"And?" Kimi asks.

I don't want to blow it with this top five game, but I'm drawing a real blank and feel like I could break out into hives at any second. The only other boy I can really think of is Luke, and I mean, he's cute, but he's like my brother. Right?

"Ericka, just say somebody," Laura says, getting antsy.

Right. That's the other thing about Luke: Laura likes him.

"That guy who's always hanging around with your boyfriend at the lockers," I say quickly, looking at Sarah. "I mean, he's not exactly my number one, but he'll do."

The girls all giggle at that, and Kimi pipes up, "Well, he may not be Orlando Bloom, but he's really quite talented with his tongue . . . and creative, too."

Everyone cracks up, and Sarah hits her with a throw pillow. I feel like I can finally breathe. Mackenzie comes back downstairs and I start to relax a little again. I don't know why that was so stressful for me, but I guess it's like this: I already feel out of place around these girls. I mean, Sarah and Mackenzie are super rich. Laura is cute, and Kimi is both cute and experienced. I totally want to fit in, but it's like I'm three steps behind.

Mackenzie puts the pizzas on the coffee table, and

they smell delicious. I'm famished. I grab a Coke from her fridge while the other girls huddle around the pies. Then I make my way over and snatch a paper plate, which is when I see the selection: mushroom-pepperoni and supreme. And I'm allergic to mushrooms.

"I'm glad you guys weren't picky," Mackenzie says, biting into a slice. "That was the easiest pizza ordering I've ever done. All my friends back home were always like, 'half this, half that, no this, light on that, sauce on the side, etc.' So high maintenance!"

The last thing I want is any more attention on me, so I grab a lesser-of-two-evils slice with pepperoni, take a seat at the far end of the couch, and start picking off the mushrooms as stealthily as possible.

"I'll go next," Laura says. "It's probably kind of obvious, but I really like Luke Foster."

She pauses and I realize that she's looking right at me. I've just taken a huge bite and don't really get what she's looking at, so I shrug and give her a greasy thumbs-up. She smiles super big, looking totally relieved. "Okay, so my top five goes Luke Foster, Trevor Barker, Wolf, Tommy Parks, and Keith Miles."

I can't believe she paused, all worried like, because of Luke—Luke!—when the real reason I'm about to choke on my pizza is because *she* likes Wolf, too!

"So I'm picking five guys I haven't made out with before based entirely on looks and not because I actually want to go out with them, okay?" Kimi says, glancing over at Sarah as if she's about to do something wrong. "Jimmy is really cute." Sarah narrows her eyes, and Kimi rushes on, "But I don't like him like that; I'm just saying. Then Wolf, Trevor, Mark, and Matt Wright."

Wolf?

"I thought you weren't dating freshmen," Sarah says, calling her out. "And you said Wolf's a pig."

"Wolf *is* a pig," Kimi says, eyeing Sarah evilly, "but we can't all date the sleazeball quarterback, and I like to keep my options open."

"That 'sleazeball quarterback' was your first pick."

"Based only on looks."

"Whatever." Sarah seethes and looks at Mackenzie. "Go."

The tension is obviously back, and not just between Sarah and Kimi. So far almost everybody has Wolf in their top five. I'm dying.

Mackenzie takes a deep breath, looks around at all of us nervously, and then screams, "Wolf, Wolf, Wolf, Wolf, Wolf!" hiding her face with a couch pillow and kicking her legs in the air.

I feel my jaw fall open and my eyes bug out, and I make absolutely no effort to hide the surprise and terror splashed all over my face. My Best Friend Forever likes my True Love Always!

"Oh, brother, I'm glad these things are secret, or he'd never get his jersey over his big head," Sarah grumbles.

Everyone laughs and then Kimi goes into a long tirade

about how much better a thong is versus all other styles of underwear, but I tune her out completely. I don't know if it was all the birthday cake, the tumbling session right after, or a rogue mushroom from the pizza, but I cover my mouth and run to the bathroom, vomiting a little in my hand before I make it.

Getting picked up early from Mackenzie's is the worst. I feel like such a little kid, waiting upstairs at the kitchen counter with Mrs. Watts. The other girls were concerned, but pretty grossed out as well. When I came out of the bathroom, my lips were a little swollen and I smelled like puke. They all said their good-byes downstairs after I called my mom, and I can still hear them laughing and squealing from up here.

"You sure you don't want some more Sprite?" Mrs. Watts asks.

"No, ma'am," I respond, holding washcloth-wrapped ice to my swollen lips.

"Careful with all those manners," Mark says, coming in for a glass of milk. "You're going to get me in trouble around here."

Mrs. Watts chuckles and wrings my shirt dry in the kitchen sink. She was really great with the whole "vomit-gate" episode, giving me an old cheer shirt of Mackenzie's and rinsing out my own.

"I'm going to throw this in the dryer until your mother comes," she says and disappears around the corner. How can she be so jolly about cleaning up my puke?

Mark stays put by the fridge, nervously tapping on his glass and looking out the window over the kitchen sink. I stay perched on a tall kitchen stool, searching for something to say, looking at the breakfast nook windows over his shoulder. It's pitch dark outside and the lights are bright in here, so we're both basically just looking at our own reflections.

"You going home?" he finally asks.

"Yeah," I say, my heavy sigh and drooped shoulders speaking volumes.

"That sucks," he says.

I nod in agreement. It does suck. Finally getting invited to a cool slumber party, where the most popular girls in our class want to help me with my cheers and talk to me about boys, is awesome. Getting sick in my hand in front of those very same girls and calling my momma in the middle of the night is anti-awesome.

"You want a tour before you go?" he asks, finally looking at me.

I sit up straight and meet his gaze. "I'd love one," I say, standing up and moving around to his side of the counter, keeping my Angelina-times-ten lips as covered as possible.

"Just try not to throw up on anything, okay?" he teases.

I punch him in the arm and giggle.

He leads me from the kitchen to the breakfast nook and toward their spacious den/movie room, where Dr. Watts is watching the Discovery Channel in surround sound. We wind through the ground floor and I feel like I'm a princess inside a gorgeous castle. If I lived here, I wouldn't take any of it for granted. Mark indicates that I should go up the stairs first, which makes me keenly aware of my butt placement in relation to his eye line. We walk down a long hallway, lined with guest room and bathroom doors. He shows me Mackenzie's room, which is massive, with a huge canopy bed and cheerleading trophies on wraparound shelves. Her dresser is covered with pictures of her old friends from Minnesota, and she actually has a walk-in closet...with enough clothes to fill it. His parents' room is off-limits but has beautiful French doors.

At the door of his own bedroom, he touches the knob and leans in close to me. Like me, he has tiny freckles on his nose. I hold my breath and hope to God that I don't smell like barf.

"I'm not supposed to have girls up here," he says, blushing and looking confused as to whether or not he's breaking a rule. I blush, too.

But the doorbell rings and saves him from any possible punishment.

And I want to kill my mother.

CHAPTER SEVENTEEN

Okay, Red Alert: Operation Restore BFFness.

It's after lunch and I can't wait any longer to call Mackenzie. This morning would've been too early, and maybe would've made me seem a little desperate. And it's all I could think about during Mass, then over lunch at KFC, and then throughout a lovely family trip to the grocery store. I would have called on the way home from church, but I'm the last teenager on the planet without a cell phone.

I don't know what spontaneous acts of sleepover vomit do to new friendships, but it can't be good. I press the living room phone tightly to my ear and nervously wind the cord around and around my finger while it rings.

"Hello?"

It's Mackenzie.

"I'm so embarrassed!" I cry.

"Ericka, don't be!" she says. "I hate that you got sick, but don't be embarrassed."

Relief washes over me and I realize that the circulation in my first finger is being cut off. I unwind the cord and flop down on the couch.

"I don't know," I respond, still depressed over the whole thing. "I was so excited to spend your birthday with you, and we were having so much fun...."

"Yeah, it was a good birthday." She sighs contentedly.

Too contentedly? In the pause of looking for something to say, curiosity gets the best of me.

"So, what'd you guys do after I left, anyway?" I ask in a casual tone, but dying to know what I missed.

"Oh my gosh, it was so crazy," she gushes. "Kimi brought a Ouija board and we turned down all the lights and lit candles and spoke to Sarah's dead grandfather, which was really sad, but totally incredible. She started crying and we all felt awful. I've never talked to a dead person or spirit or whatever. It was so wild. Like, really wild. We kind of got spooked, so we changed gears and asked it all sorts of questions, like who's going to be the first to have sex and who's going to ask us to homecoming. But then we realized it was just yes or no questions, so we had to get really specific." She giggles. "Let's just say, it's looking good for me!"

I gasp.

"Not about the sex!" she assures me. "About homecoming." Which actually makes me feel worse, knowing exactly who is on her top five—in all five spots.

"What else did you do?" I ask, sitting up straight and abandoning my casual facade.

"Um, we stayed up all night and gave each other mani/pedis and watched movies. It was really fun." And then, as an afterthought, she says, "But we all really missed you!"

"Yeah, I missed you guys, too," I say, meaning it more than I've ever meant anything. One mushroom allergy and the next thing I know, the guy I like is spiritually conjured into going to homecoming with my new bestie.

"See you in twenty," I say into the phone and hang up. I grab a tote bag and stuff it with my journal, a pen, a bottle of water, and my iPod. "I'll be at the creek!" I holler down the hall to whoever cares and head outside.

Feeling sorry for myself after talking to Mackenzie, I called Luke and asked him to meet me at our spot by the creek. It's not like he'll know what to think about it all, but he's a guy and he'll make me stop overanalyzing everything. He'll say either, "Yeah, it's pretty bad. You suck," or "Ricki Jo, it's no big deal. Just a little puke." I'm hoping for the latter.

I whistle for Bandit and he comes flying around the side of the house as if it were on fire. He's the kind of dog whose ears flop when he runs and whose mouth is in a sort of constant smile. I don't really feel like feeling better just yet, but I grin involuntarily at the sight of him and bend down to rub his belly. We get to the creek in about five minutes and I figure I've got a little while to pour my aching heart out onto the blank page. If I were the editor of *Seventeen*, I'd write an article called "How Bad Is Too Bad?" and put real-life stories like mine in it and have friendship experts weigh in. For example, I didn't steal anything or kiss anyone else's boyfriend, so it can't be that bad, right? I start a loose outline for the article in my journal, just for kicks, drawing a sort of chart with pizza vomit being really low and killing a cheerleader being really high.

"Beat it, Bandit," I say for the millionth time. He's fixated on my journal and keeps trying to bite it. He's already drooled all over the pages and I can tell he's not going to let me get very far. I sigh and finally just put it back in my bag. "Someone's needy today," I say, rubbing his head so that his ears flop wildly.

I grab a stick and lie down, pacifying Bandit with a halfhearted game of fetch. I throw and he runs, retrieves, and races back, dropping the stick on my chest.

And then, halfway to the stick, he stops, perks up, and howls like crazy. I lean up on my elbows and see Luke and Bessie, who trump both the stick and me as Bandit races toward them, Bessie already running in the opposite direction. She's got a good game of hard to get going on, and Mr. Needy Dog is suddenly all "Ricki Jo who?" (He can call me that—we have history.)

"So you had fun at Mackenzie's?" Luke asks, staring down at me.

"Yeah, but I got sick and had to go home early," I tell him.

"You okay?" he asks, concerned.

I look up at him and nod. "Yeah, nothing to worry about. Just a little mushroom incident."

"Ah," he says, knowing all too well what that entails.

Luke holds out his hand and hefts me up. We walk, me swatting at the tall grass with a long, skinny stick and pouting. It's late afternoon and the air is crisp. I smell fall on the breeze, sweeping away the last days of summer. Depressing.

"So did the Fabulous Four initiate you?" he teases. "Are you the Fab Five now?"

I stare up at him with narrowed eyes, hand on cocked hip.

"As a matter of fact," I say, "I think we are. Mackenzie called me her best friend, so, yeah. Things are good in that department."

"So you're fitting in," Luke states simply.

"I think so," I reply.

"I mean, I can tell a difference," he says, looking away.

"What do you mean?" I ask.

"Well, I don't know," he starts, looking down and then up again, anywhere but at me. "Like, for example, your new clothes. It's like a whole new you. You dress more like those girls now."

"I just want to look nice!" I defend myself.

"No, not that that's a bad thing, Ricki Jo!" he says, glancing down at me and then back over his shoulder.

"You look great. Really pretty, actually. Just, you didn't care before and you were still"—he stammers on—"y-you know...pretty."

I smile. Honestly, hearing that makes me feel like every part of my body has lungs and just got a deep breath of fresh air. My folks call me pretty sometimes, but it sounds totally different coming from a boy—even if that boy is just Luke. Looking up at him, I see the back of his neck redden a little and think it's really cute the way his hair curls back there when it's time for a haircut. He's still looking in the opposite direction, but he's fidgety.

"Are you okay?" I ask, tapping his leg with the stick in my hands.

"Yeah," he says looking back at me for a quick second. "Yeah, fine, just, you know. I don't want you to get mad or anything."

"Why would I get mad?" I ask.

"You know," he says quietly. "'Cause you're turning into those girls on the outside, and I'm afraid you're gonna start changing on the inside, too. That's all."

I think about what he says. Of course I want to look like those girls—they're beautiful and popular guy magnets. I mean, I don't want to be as bossy as Kimi or let a guy rule me like Sarah does, but it wouldn't be bad to be more like Mackenzie or Laura. They're really nice and they have that something. *Seventeen* calls it the "It Factor": the inner quality stars have that makes them shine. I could use some shine, and I feel like the more I rub elbows with those girls, the better chance I have of some of that It Factor rubbing off on me.

Speaking of Laura, she *did* ask me a little favor before I disgracefully bowed out of the sleepover....

"Did you have fun with Laura at the party?" I ask, fishing.

Luke looks me directly in the eye. "I had fun at the party, and Laura is nice, but we're just friends."

"Well, I think she's pretty and I think she likes you and—"

"I think it's none of your business, Ricki Jo," he interrupts.

"Ericka," I correct.

"Ericka at school," he says, "but you're still Ricki Jo out here. My normal, fun, best friend Ricki Jo."

He goes in for a noogie, but I maneuver my way out of it and jump on his back. He spins around a few times and I swing out from his body, my arms gripped tightly around his neck, shrieking. As we go round and round, I start to laugh. I laugh so hard that I let go and collapse in the grass. He picks up my stick and pokes me.

"Stop!" I shriek, crab-walking back to the edge of the creek. He follows, poking my sides. "Stop it!"

I wrench the stick away and throw it in the water, ruining his little game. I stick out my tongue and roll over on my stomach, resting my chin on my hands and searching the water for minnows and crawdads. Luke grunts and falls down next to me, poking a long finger in the water.

"Why do you think they always walk backward?" I ask, peering at a huge crawdad that's moving toward a big rock.

"I don't know." He shrugs. "Crawdaddies are probably all teenagers. Teenage *girls*."

I chuckle and flick cool creek water at him. He gives me a warning look and I put my arms up in surrender. The last thing I need is a water fight.

He's right, though. A lot of the time, I feel totally backward. Like everything I do is inside out. I dress wrong and have to go back to square one to catch up with the style. I've never been kissed, so I read articles about other girls' stories. Everybody I know is growing, while I seem to be stuck in the body of a ten-year-old boy. And my new friends all have crushes on the boy I'm in love with.

Luke and I fall into one of our comfortable silences. My mind races as I watch life move below the water's surface. Luke's forehead is all crinkled up as he swirls his finger around in circles. The grass swishes in the wind, a constant, soothing, brushing sound.

Twenty minutes sneak by, and then I yawn and stretch and roll over onto my back. Big, fluffy clouds blow across the sky in a hurried fashion. It's going to storm.

"Yeah," I finally say, looking over at Luke. "Being fourteen kind of sucks."

He nods, hypnotized by the water. "Old enough to know better, but too young to do anything about it."

There's definitely a storm on the way.

"It's golden blond, Ricki Jo," my momma laments. "You can't even see it."

I have used my momma's Nair on my legs a few times before, and the hair just floated away in the shower; but my first JV game is after school tomorrow and I want to shave my legs. For real.

"It's just gonna grow back thicker, and black," she warns.

"Momma, you don't have to stay in here," I complain. "I can do it on my own."

She snorts and crosses her arms. "You'll cut yourself to pieces."

After supper, I sneaked into my parents' bathroom and stole her Venus razor and shaving cream. Back in the privacy of the bathroom I share with Ben, I foamed up my left leg and propped it on the sink. But after the first stroke I felt a terrible stinging and saw blood pouring out of a gash by my ankle. That's when I freaked out and hollered like hell for my momma.

"Okay, first of all, you have to use a new blade," she says now, showing me how to click off the old one and replace it with a new one. She hands me the razor and I prop my leg back up on the sink. Then she tries to guide my hand up my leg. She actually tries to shave my legs for me!

"Momma," I whine. "I can do it myself!"

She lets go and backs away, her hands in the air in

surrender, and sits down on the edge of the tub. As I start again at the bottom of my shin, she leans forward. "Now, you don't need to bear down so hard. And make sure you stay in a straight line."

I sigh heavily. She cleaned up the blood, I've calmed down, and now I wish she'd just leave me alone. She's probably afraid I'll bleed all over the white bath mat or something. I try to ignore her as I swipe, rinse the razor, and swipe again. She's right about my leg hair—it's totally blond—but it's there. And it's long. And every other girl I know shaves her legs already.

"Ricki Jo!" my dad yells from outside the bathroom door. "Telephone call."

"Who is it?" I yell back, almost finished with my left leg.

"It's your friend Mackenzie," he replies.

"Oh! Okay, hold on!" I call, sliding the razor around in my excitement and nicking my knee. "Ow!" These Venus razors are nice, but three blades is a little excessive.

"Take a message, Clark," Momma yells, leaping forward to blot the new cut with an old washrag.

"No! Pass the phone in, Daddy!" I shout, swatting at my momma to give me the rag and go get the phone.

She shakes her head, a total basket case over nothing, and unlocks the door. My dad passes her the phone and she hands it to me, clearly annoyed.

"Hello?" I say nonchalantly, as if I don't have one leg cocked up and bleeding or an overbearing mother sucking all the air out of the room.

"Hey, Ericka!" Mackenzie starts, excited. "I'm calling up the girls to go down to the movie theater for the seven o'clock."

"It's always the seven o'clock," I tell her. "And only the seven o'clock."

"Oh." She pauses, clearly thinking she's back in Minnesota, where there are movie theaters that show more than one movie, more than once a day. "Well, whatever, that's the one. You want to go?"

I look at my momma and know there's nothing doing. For one thing, I have school tomorrow. Two, my right leg is still in Sasquatch mode. Three, she would have to drop me off and then wait around town 'til it's over to pick me up. And anyway, I already saw this week's feature. Dad took us Friday, for the family Friday five-dollar special.

"Um, I don't think I can make it," I say sadly, "but thanks for inviting me!"

"Totally," Mackenzie says. "We'll miss you."

Worried that I might be replaced in my absence, I say, "New Girls BFFs, right?"

She giggles. "Totally. New Girls BFFs for-eva!"

CHAPTER EIGHTEEN

Another rookie mistake on my part. Awesome. Turns out going to the movies isn't at all about the movie itself. Who cares if I'd already seen it? I should've begged and pleaded to go again. If I had, I'd be taking part in the wild laughter going on between the girls—yeah, okay, the Fab Four—around Kimi's locker. Instead, I stand outside their circle, looking for an in and trying to catch up with the incredible amount of drama that must've gone down last night.

"I can't believe he tried to hold my hand," Laura whispers.

The other three squeal and whisper over one another. *Who? Who tried to hold her hand?*

I try to follow along, standing up on tiptoes as far as I can go, my entire torso pressed up against their Red Rover–esque embrace, but it's no use. The four of them are huddled tightly around Kimi, oblivious to the rest of the world. Jimmy James approaches Sarah and she actually waves him off. Apparently, nothing interrupts a good social recap.

"Where were you last night?" Wolf asks, loudly banging his fist against the locker behind me and making me jump.

I turn from the girls and face him, feeling encouraged that he missed my presence, but still not my usual swooning self. I may have smooth legs, but I just lost the foothold I had in my quest for fabulosity. It sucks feeling left out—and all because a PG repeat wasn't worth seven dollars.

"I'd already seen it," I tell him weakly.

"Ah," he says, opening his locker.

I lean my head back against my own locker and close my eyes. Conversations roll past, steady, volume increasing and decreasing, the student body an ocean lolling through the hallways. Wolf leans over to me and lowers his voice. "Want to know a secret?"

I open my eyes and nod. He leans in even closer and puts his hand up to the side of my face, moving a piece of hair away from my mouth. There's that cologne again. There's that spearmint breath.

"I saw you at the movies on family night," he says.

I turn and look at him, stunned, and try to remember what I wore on Friday. Then horror washes over me as I remember my momma and daddy wearing their matching I'M WITH JESUS T-shirts.

"Why didn't you say something?" I whisper.

"Eh, I don't know." He shrugs, his attention back on his locker. "You were holding your dad's hand, and I didn't know what to say."

Oh. My. God. He's right. In a moment of blind ignorance, I so desperately wanted a snow cone that I held my dad's hand to butter him up for the three bucks. I had just spent more on Mackenzie's gift than I meant to and I'm a sucker for frozen ice and blue syrup.

Before I can explain, Mackenzie interrupts, the other three girls flanking her.

"Hey, Ericka," she says, and I smile. "Do you feel better?"

"Yeah, totally," I say, not wanting to explain my mushroom allergy in front of Wolf.

Kimi breasts herself forward, aiming right for Wolf, but nearly taking my eye out.

"Did you like the movie last night, Wolf?" she asks, and her gaggle giggles.

He hangs on his locker, grinning at them, cocky as ever. I want to work my fingers down each button of his polo. I'm not sure what I would do after that, but I'm sure he looks good with his shirt off.

"What movie?" he asks mischievously.

All the girls giggle again and I look up at him, confused.

The bell rings, lockers slam, and we head for homeroom. Wolf grabs my arm and pulls me back while everybody else leaves.

"I go on Friday to see the show," he explains, grinning like the Cheshire cat, " 'cause *if* I go again on Sunday, the movie is the last thing on my mind."

"Who made out with Wolf?" I want to know.

That's all that's on my mind. The cafeteria is buzzing and I'm sure that one of the girls here has tasted his lips and I want to find and kill her. And knowing the top fives of this particular crowd, I am emboldened and want answers.

"I didn't recognize the girl," Sarah says.

"How could you?" Kimi asks. "You were too busy kissing Jim-Jim."

They all laugh.

"Or James-James," Mackenzie adds.

They all laugh again.

I feel like missing the sleepover part of the sleepover was a major blow to my place in the clique, but skipping movie night *really* knocked me off my game. The girls are all friendly enough, but these inside jokes are starting to wear on my nerves. Mostly because I'm on the outside. Plus, as the fifth wheel, I have no one to whisper secrets to when the others pair off doing the same.

"All of us but Sarah had him on our top five boys list, and none of you sat by him or saw who he was with?" I ask incredulously.

"All I know for sure is that she is either an upperclassman or from another county," Laura says confidently. "I stared for a long time, but I just could not place that ponytail."

Inexcusable. Frankly, I question Laura's right to have him on her list at all. Popping Tater Tot after Tater Tot into my mouth, I seethe.

The final bell has come and gone and I wait for Luke at his locker. Today sucked. Really sucked. I never thought I would say this, but I can't wait to get on the school bus. I just want to get out of this building and go home. Maybe I'll skip rocks with Luke or go four-wheeling or play basketball outside the Fosters' black barn. I don't care, as long as I'm doing something to get my mind off of how hard making new friends is...and how bad I wish Wolf had been kissing *me* last night.

When Luke's lanky frame turns the corner in front of me, I smile. When I see the redheaded girl at his side, my smile falters.

"What's up?" he asks, messing up my hair.

"Ugh! What's up with you?" I ask, frogging him hard on the forearm.

"Ow!"

"Hey, Candace," I say, not really sure what else is appropriate.

"Hey, Ricki Jo," she says. I stiffen, but I sense more indifference than malice on her part, so I let it slide.

Luke bends down to trade books out of his bag while Candace and I stand on either side of him, opposite each other, silent and awkward. Minutes pass. I look down and see Luke fiddling with his backpack zipper, obviously stalling. I sigh loudly, realizing that he's waiting for us to make up, so I look for something to say to Candace.

"What's new?" I ask. Lame.

"Nothin'," she answers.

"Didn't you say something about the school paper, Candace?" Luke asks, looking up at us and obviously leading her.

"I already asked her to join band and she thought it was dumb," she replies, looking down at him defiantly. "What makes you think our new cheerleader is going to think the school paper is any better?"

"School paper?" I ask, knowing she's a good writer. She's had two letters to the editor published in *The Breckinridge Times*. "Are you on it?"

"I think I'm going to go to the meeting Thursday, you know, just to see what it's all about," she says, guarded.

"That's cool," I say, forgetting our feud and feeling kind of psyched about the paper. "I didn't know freshmen were allowed."

"Yeah." She shrugs. "You just gotta submit a letter of interest and a work sample."

"Cool," I say again, thinking about the story I just wrote in my journal about Kimi and the great babysitting fiasco. "So, you turn it in at the meeting?"

"Basically."

"You should go, too, Ricki Jo," Luke says, flicking his blond hair off his forehead and looking up at me.

"Nah," Candace says. "She's too big-time. And probably *really* busy with cheerleading and her fake friends."

I blow a frustrated sigh through my bangs and face Candace. "Look, Candace, this is dumb. We were friends before and I'm sorry I'm not in band and I'm sorry you don't like cheerleaders and I'm sorry I haven't called as much lately and I'm sorry that you hate me for trying to make new friends, but we were friends before and I'm the same person, okay?"

That was the longest run-on sentence of my life, and I need a breath. I want to say so much more, like how frustrating it is to base my friendships on extracurriculars or how hard it is to please everybody. And I feel guilty that she thinks I've blown her off, but also angry that she's being so judgmental. But mainly, I just don't have enough friends to have enemies. And I actually like Candace. And I want a truce.

"Yeah, whatever." Candace sighs, scraping the black nail polish off her thumbnail. "It's a stupid fight."

"Thank you," I say, leaning back against the locker next to Luke's. I watch a few kids walk by and realize that I'm starting to recognize some of the faces in the crowd.

"And, I don't know," I continue, looking over at Candace. "The school paper might be a good way for me to meet some more people."

"That's true," she says, softening the teeniest bit.

"I kind of have a column idea in mind," I go on, "but I don't know how much they let freshmen write."

She glances at me, the closest we've come to eye contact. "From what I hear, they actually base it on skill, and not class. So you probably have a good shot."

"Yeah?" I say, loosening up. "Well, you're a good writer, too, and I think it'd be a fun thing to do together."

Candace lightens up a little more. When she relaxes her shoulders and lets her facial muscles go slack, it's like talking to a whole other person. I don't know what makes someone that guarded, but it reminds me a little of Luke. I hope he's never hurt as bad as someone must've hurt her. I shudder.

"Anyway," she says, "it's in Miss Davis's room on Thursday during lunch, so you should probably bring some food from home that day."

"Aw, man!" I groan. "And miss out on Salisbury steak?"

We both laugh and Luke stands up looking self-satisfied. He closes his locker and we walk toward the back of the building.

"I think they do the yearbook, too," Candace says thoughtfully.

"Oh! That'd be fun," I say, imagining a shot of myself on top of the pyramid at tonight's JV game. Then I think about Photoshopping a pic of Wolf and me together in the yearbook: Best Couple. *In your face, mysterious ponytailed wench.* "That'd be *really* fun."

"Did you know that Sunday night is, like, make-out at the movies night?" I ask Luke once we're settled in a seat at the back of the bus. We slide down low and put our knees up against the seat in front of us, blocking out all the other kids and making our own world.

"Uh, how do you think Claire got pregnant?" he asks.

"At the movie theater?" I exclaim, stupefied.

"Good Lord, Ricki Jo, you're so gullible." He laughs. "No, not *at* the movies. But seriously, the movies, The Square, wherever. Horny teenagers will go anywhere to get it on."

As we bump through the west side of our county, he asks me about my classes and cheerleading and I ask him about his classes and how things are going at home. Not surprisingly, I do most of the talking. When we finally get close to his stop, he asks me to get off with him.

"Um, I can't go down to the pond in my school clothes," I say. It's always been a lame rule, but now that I buy clothes with my own money, I take it a little more to heart. Plus, kitten heels aren't really made for farm life. "Let me go change and we'll meet after."

"Come on," he says. "Thumper had babies and I want to show you."

Luke's little brother has a black rabbit, and the thought of seeing its bunnies convinces me to go with him. I take off my shoes and follow him down the ribbed rubber aisle of the school bus, trying to avoid any candy or gum that the screaming munchkins sitting up front may have dropped.

We climb down the bus stairs and cross in front of it

to Luke's yard. I see that pack of mean dogs in the road up ahead and, not long after, hear the bus driver yelling at them to get out of the way. Claire is on the front porch swing feeding her baby girl, and their little brother squats nearby playing with his Tonka trucks.

"I heard Thumper's a momma," I say, grinning down at him. "Let's go out back. I want you to show me the bunnies and tell me all their names."

He looks up at me but doesn't smile.

"What's wrong, buddy?" Luke asks, bending down and ruffling his sandy hair. Looking up at Luke, the little guy's eyes fill with tears. When we look over at Claire, we know something's wrong.

"Where's Momma?" Luke asks.

"Taking a bath," she answers.

"And Daddy?"

She looks him in the eye. "Out back."

Luke looks away, his face hard, fists clenched. "He hit her?"

She sighs and looks over at their little brother, who is focusing intently on his trucks. "As soon as the boys went out to feed, he came hobbling in the living room, looking for a fight," Claire says softly. "He always waits 'til the boys are gone."

"I should've been here," Luke says.

Claire stands up, baby on her hip, and walks over to Luke. She's about his height, and she looks him straight in the eye. "Lukie, you've got a big heart, but he's a big man. And ain't nothing you can do about it. Understand? Nothing you can do."

I stand in the yard, the grass cool between my toes, and look away. *I am not supposed to see this.*

I turn from the porch and look over toward the back of my house, way over the hills, way over what's happening in front of me, way over Luke starting to shake in Claire's arms. I think about the times the Fosters had "tiffs" and his momma sent us down to the pond. I think about Luke's busted lip at my cookout.

I know Mr. Foster gets mean when he drinks, cusses and throws things (that's why I'm not allowed to work his farm without my dad being there, and why I can't be over at Luke's if his momma isn't home), but it didn't seem real before. Even when Luke talks about it, which is hardly ever and not in detail, it still seems far away, like one of those things that only happens in the movies.

Tears spring to my eyes before I realize it, startling me from my trance. I wipe my eyes and face the road, my back to this nightmare. Knowing Luke and his pride, he won't want my pity.

And he won't want to talk about it later.

Dad's diesel truck hiccups its rough rhythm all the way to town. We sit quietly, just the two of us, eyes trained hard on the same green scenery we drive by every day as if this were the first time. From the passenger window, I watch the sun slide down in the sky slowly, slipping behind houses and barns and the new subdivision near the city line. My mind works overtime.

I try to concentrate on my cheerleading chants, marking the motions in my seat and blocking out the memory of the look on Luke's face when I left this afternoon. Momma curled my hair before I left the house, so that my ponytail has a perky, spirally bounce. I feel pretty in my uniform—a sleeveless maroon tank with PCHS across the chest in gold, and a pleated maroon skirt with gold trim. Momma's right, the skirts are short, but we get to wear these cute maroon panty-type things over our real panties so we don't flash anyone.

I am the image of pep.

So why do I feel so lousy?

My dad finds a spot near the back door of the gym and Momma and Ben pull up next to us. Dad, decked out in his Toyota uniform, can stay only a little while before he has to go to work.

"It means a lot that you can make the first quarter at least," I say to him, grabbing my pom-poms from the backseat.

"I wouldn't miss it," he says and winks.

I shut the door and we all walk together toward the gym. I look up at my dad and think about Luke's dad. Then I put my arm around his waist, which totally shocks him, and he wraps his arm around my shoulders—but only 'til we reach the door.

When I enter the gym, my stomach flips. The boys are

warming up on one end of the court and I see our rivals shooting around on the other end. Mamaw and Papaw are in the bleachers already, and she starts cheering the second she sees me.

"Go, Ricki Jo!" Mamaw chants, high pitched, over and over. Papaw helps her up and she starts to clap and whistle between two fingers. "Ricki Jo Winstead! That's my grandbaby!"

Cringing, I give her a quick wave and then race across the court to meet the rest of my squad in the tunnel behind the bleachers.

"Winstead," Coach says, her eyes twinkling, "I'm not sure if you noticed, but your grandmother's here."

I turn beet red and the other girls laugh good-naturedly. Everybody knows my mamaw.

"She loves the Stallions," I offer up and we all laugh.

The six other girls on my squad are pretty down-to-earth, and I have a few classes with some of them. Cheering hasn't given me a ton of new friends like I thought it would, but everybody's nice and I'm getting to know them better with each practice. Now we stretch out, our adrenaline pumping, and a few girls tumble. I'm not confident enough to do my new back handspring without a spotter, so I just keep going over my chants and motions.

When the first whistle blows and the game gets under way, my nerves start to settle. I smile, nod, and jump.

"R...E...R-E-B-O-U-N-D. Rebound, Stallions! Rebound!"

I shake my pom-poms and lunge up on my toes and back. I feel like a Preston County cheerleader. Like I belong.

The first half goes pretty well…for our cheerleading squad and the visiting team. At halftime we do our big routine, and the small crowd goes nuts when I fly into the air, turn over and over tucked tightly into a ball, and lay out straight in the basket toss. Then, when they toss me back up, I falter a tad, but I stick my standing liberty. I look over at my family and see my momma wiping away a tear.

"Stallions, number one!" we shout, pumping our fingers in the air, then gallop giddily off the court. I can't stop smiling, I'm on such a high.

As we regroup on the sideline, I grab my water bottle and sit down by the other girls. "That was awesome," I say, a little out of breath.

"Totally," one girl says. And then she screams, pointing to a skinny guy climbing the bleachers. "I can't believe he came! Look! My boyfriend's here! Look!"

We all look, feeling jealous at the sight of the shy boy with long hair sipping on a Slurpee, all of us wishing we were as red-faced and nervous as she is in this moment. As the players take the court again, we take our places on the sideline and give it our all.

"Shoot for two!" *(clap, clap)* "Shoot for two!" *(clap, clap)*

I smile, nod, bob my ponytail with fierce pep, and wiggle spirit fingers all night long.

I wish Luke were here.

I wish *Wolf* were here.

We lose the game, but I float back to my family on cloud nine. My momma shows me some of the video she took and I can't wait to upload it to YouTube. Somehow, this horrible day has been saved.

CHAPTER NINETEEN

I walk into school with a little more confidence each day. Slowly but surely, I'm making friends. Slowly but surely, I'm figuring out the school and how it works. And slowly but very surely, I'm working up more and more nerve around David Wolfenbaker.

Bright and early Friday morning, I pass Kimi, Sarah, and her boyfriend to take my place at Wolf's locker in my new tan romper, studded skinny belt, and tall flat boots with knee socks ("showing a little leg without looking overexposed"—a tip from guess what mag). Wolf swaggers toward me, wary of my grin, and starts turning his dial, then suddenly stops, sensing my stare.

"You think I'm stupid?" he asks.

"Whatever do you mean?" I respond, wide-eyed.

"You're just waiting to close my locker as soon as I open it."

"Moi?" I ask, feigning great indignation and vigorously batting my eyelashes.

"Come here," he says, smiling, and quickly wraps his arm around me, pinning my arms at my sides. My face is squished up against his blue striped polo and I'm getting high on his cologne.

"There," he says, popping open his locker and planting a high-top sneaker in the bottom as a stopper. He loosens his grip and I look up at him.

"You're free to go," he says, tweaking my freckled nose softly.

I shake off the vertigo and turn to my left, coming face-to-face with a smirking Kimi, who's been watching the whole time. It's been a week since the sleepover and theater scandals, and I've made very little progress in reestablishing myself as the fifth member of the fabulous freshmen circle.

"What was that all about?" Kimi asks conspiratorially. The last thing I need is her mentioning our top fives in front of the one guy who made almost all our lists, so I try a diversionary tactic.

"I have no idea, but I'm pretty sure he ruined my hair," I say with a grin, knowing how she feels about perfect hair.

She gives me a once-over and grins back, a nicer version of her usual self, and opens her locker door wider. "Check it out," she says, indicating a large pink sparkly mirror. "I've got hair spray if you need it."

I stand on tiptoes and check my 'do. Not bad.

"I like your dress," I hear from behind me. Mackenzie's brother, Mark, is standing there, awkward, his hands tucked in his jeans pockets, his face flushed. "Or, um, your shorts. Or outfit, or whatever."

"Uh, thanks," I say, trying not to giggle. He's a cute guy, but so obviously nervous.

He tilts his head and looks around, shifting his weight to his other foot. "See ya," he says, heading off.

I watch him walk away and catch Wolf giving me a *What was that?* look. I shrug and lightly elbow Kimi, who's giggling hysterically. *Poor Mark.*

"Ericka!" Mackenzie yells from somewhere to my right.

I look over quickly, surprised by the tension in her voice as she rushes toward me, weaving through the thickening hallway traffic. I squeeze past Kimi, Sarah, and the "sleazebag quarterback" Jimmy James to get to her.

"What's up?" I say, smiling big.

"Let's go to homeroom," she answers, hushed and urgent.

I let her drag me down the hallway and we duck inside Mrs. Wilkes's room a full four minutes before the bell is set to ring. This must be super important for her to give up that much social time.

"I have to ask you something," she starts, tears in her eyes, "and I'm so embarrassed."

"Oh my gosh!" I say. "What is it? Are you okay?"

She nods and sniffs a little, looking around, but we're

completely alone. "It's algebra," she says. "You have Mr. Sox, right?"

I nod, hoping she's not flunking out. They'll kick her off Boys' Varsity for bad grades.

"Well," she says, "I totally forgot about the take-home test until I looked in my locker this morning, and I have him first period! I'll never get it done in time, and it counts for a third of our grade!"

At this, she breaks down crying. I feel awful for her. She looks at me desperately, her blue eyes swimming in tears, and I give her a hug. I don't know what else to do.

"So?" she asks, wiping her face.

I'm blank. "So . . . ?"

"Can you help me?"

And then it hits me. She wants to copy off of my test.

Not to sound like a prude, but I'm not a cheater. I mean, I'm not a holy roller, but I'm a hard worker. I spent hours working on my test, and we've had them since *last* Friday. It just seems unfair to hand my work over to somebody else who spent time at the movies flirting with cute boys instead of doing her own homework.

"I mean, I had my birthday party and everything. I had to clean up for you guys to come over, and then clean up all over again after you left. . . . I had a lot going on," she laments.

This is so awkward. I mean, I did vomit at her house last weekend, but Mark told me they have a housekeeper. Plus, she had all week to finish the test.

"I don't know," I say, feeling sick to my stomach. Oh, Lord, I *cannot* barf again.

Mackenzie clutches my arm. "I would never ask for something like this, Ericka," she says, "if it weren't so major. And even though I'm totally embarrassed, you're my best friend and I would, in a heartbeat, help you out in a pinch. You know that. You *know* I would."

I sigh heavily and swing my backpack up onto our table. Who am I kidding? I could never let a friend down, even if that friend is asking me to do something that brings with it mild nausea. I pull out my math folder and hesitate. She sits down, fishes a pencil out of her purse, and looks up at me, life-or-death desperation written all over her face.

I pass my test to her, take my seat, and feel dirty as I watch her duplicate my formulas. She starts to fill out the top section and looks up at me again, smiling broadly.

"You're such a good friend, Ericka."

I smile weakly and continue to watch her, feeling miserable. The bell rings and the tables all around us fill. When Kimi sits down, she sees the test and lights up.

"Oh my gosh! Is that Mr. Sox's take-home? I didn't get the last one."

Before I know it, Mackenzie is giving Kimi the last page while she continues scribbling down my other answers. Laura and Sarah take out their tests and begin comparing their answers. When Wolf sits down, he sees the expression on my face and looks puzzled.

"What's wrong?"

"Nothing," I say, grabbing a piece of my hair and searching for split ends.

"Is that Mr. Sox's take-home test?" he asks.

I roll my eyes. *Him, too?*

"Yeah!" Kimi exclaims. "You want to look at it?"

She holds it up to him and Mackenzie snatches it back, not missing a beat as she scribbles furiously.

Wolf looks at me, disappointed. "That yours, Ericka?"

I gulp — *He actually said my name right* — and then nod my head, guilty as charged.

He shakes his head and lays it down on his books. "Unbelievable," he mutters.

I feel sick. Sick*er*, I mean.

"Thank you *so* much, Ericka," Mackenzie says, finally handing me back my test with a flourish. "You totally saved me."

Wolf twists sideways in his chair, turning his back to us, facing the door and the clock above it.

"What's with him?" Kimi whispers.

I shrug. "I guess he's got something against copying."

Mackenzie makes a face. "Weirdo." To me, she smiles and holds up her pinky finger. "New Girls BFFs?" she asks.

This is what I want, right? I wrap my pinky around hers and smile. "Foreva!"

And to my surprise, she squeals and gives me a gigantic hug.

                              *   *   *

I missed the bus on purpose today. My life sort of flip-flopped in the course of six periods, and I'm not up for an hour-long ride home. I'd rather walk the mile to Mamaw and Papaw's house and fake sick so they'll fawn over me. They have a freezer full of popsicles, and cable television — just what the doctor ordered.

Not that I'm sick. I just feel sort of, I don't know, lousy. I mean, I am now totally sure of my standing in the Fab Five — and yes, we are definitely five. Kimi and Sarah gave me a mini-makeover at the lockers today before lunch (together, they have enough makeup to open a small cosmetics store), but I keep wondering about what Luke said the other day, about me changing on the inside. I don't want to change on the inside. I want to be myself, but I'd like myself to be popular, too, if that's an option.

Ugh. I don't know. I shake my head and make my way down the hall, dodging Luke. We still haven't talked about what happened at his house Monday afternoon, which has made every conversation we *have* had this week totally awkward. And besides, I'll feel pretty lame complaining about my problems when he's obviously got a lot more going on. I just need to think.

As I walk to the back door of the high school I pass the gym. I hear sneakers squeaking and kids milling around, so I pop in. Looks like most people are going to an extracurricular activity or just hanging out after school for a while. I drop my book bag on the bleachers and walk over to a rack of basketballs near the sidelines. I guess somebody's got practice soon.

I pick up a ball and slam it with one palm. It's firm and has that new-ball smell. I press it down in a dribble a few times and head toward the free throw line.

Swish!

Feels good. I grab my own rebound and line up a jump shot.

Swish!

Nothing but net. The ball comes back to me and I take an eight-footer.

Swish!

I go after my rebound and feel a little better, a little less tense. A little more like Ricki Jo... uh, Ericka... *Ericka?*

"Not bad, Winstead."

I turn and see Wolf standing near the three-point line in a wifebeater and Nike shorts. Now I know who's got practice. I bounce pass the ball to him.

"Oh, you talking to me now?" I ask.

"What?" he asks innocently, his cocoa eyes wide. "You noticed my *silencio* treatment in Spanish class?" He takes his shot, sinking it.

"Yeah, I noticed when I had to do Actividad twenty-two by myself, as both waiter and customer," I say, catching the ball and passing it back to him.

He dribbles a little around the arc, looks at me, and

shrugs from the top of the key. "I was just disappointed, I guess."

"Kinda like I am when you play dumb in our Spanish big-group work?" I say as he lines up his shot.

Swish!

"I don't know," he says, wiping his brow with the bottom of his shirt and showing the beautiful six-pack I had assumed was there all along. "At first, I thought you were just gonna be some redneck. Then, I don't know, we have homeroom and Spanish and whatever, and I kind of got to know you and I thought you were smart, and funny."

I grin, glad to be having a normal conversation and sure that *smart* and *funny* probably equals *marriage material*... although he also said that *redneck* was his first impression.

"And now," he continues, "I don't know what to think. I just didn't peg you as the kind of girl to sell out."

I lose the grin, grab the ball, and chest pass it to him, hard and direct. "Sell out? How? I was just helping out a friend."

"Looked to me like you were peddling your smarts to *get* friends."

"Ha!" I scoff. "And you hide your smarts to keep friends."

He shrugs and shoots, totally showing off. I grab the ball and pass it to him again, as hard as I can.

"And maybe you wanna get in good with Mackenzie's brother," he says, lining up a ten-footer. "I saw him at your locker today. What? Homework for a homecoming date?"

He closes his eyes and sinks the jump shot, making my blood boil. I guess this is why he's a freshman starter for Varsity, but he has officially ticked me off.

I rebound for him again, but this time I dribble the ball out to where he's standing, crossing it between my legs, which is pretty awesome considering the previously mentioned tall boots with tall socks.

"Horse?" I ask, challenging him to a shot-for-shot game in which one person shoots from anywhere on the court, in any style. The other person has to match the shot or take a letter. The first one to spell H-O-R-S-E loses.

He shrugs. "Should I go ahead and take a couple letters?"

"I don't need a handicap," I say, offended.

"Oh, yeah. You take the two letters, then, since you're so willing to help out your *friends*."

He sinks a jumper from the hash mark near the free throw line. I pull my thick hair back with the ponytail holder on my wrist.

Game. On.

CHAPTER TWENTY

"He Wants You to Make the Move!"

This is what the headline of October's *Seventeen* says, anyway. I've combed through September's issue so many times the pages are starting to fall out. When Mamaw saw how down I was yesterday after school, she asked me what would make me feel better.

"A trip to Walmart," I answered, to the extreme delight of my papaw, who shot up in his recliner like he'd won the lottery.

And now here I sit, spending a lazy Saturday afternoon in my favorite spot by the creek with the newest issue of my all-time favorite reading material ever, anxious to find out "The #1 Guy Mistake [I'm] Making."

The signs seem pretty obvious. Apparently, guys don't always have the confidence to ask us out, so they clue us in to their attraction in four easy ways:

1.) He does the "look back."
2.) He says something stupid.
3.) He tilts his head.
4.) He uncrosses his arms.

I don't know, though. At Mackenzie's birthday party, Wolf put his hands on my shoulders, asked me why I wasn't out there for the couples' skate, and stared deeply into my eyes while the disco ball and slow jams entranced us. But then he forgot all about me the instant he saw another girl, so I don't know what to make of that. According to the magazine, if his pupils were dilated, he was definitely into me. The problem is, I didn't have the magazine at the time, so I didn't to know to check said gorgeous pupils.

"Ugh." I sigh, closing the magazine, rolling it up, and stashing it in the pocket of my University of Kentucky hoodie. Fall is looming, cooling the otherwise warm day with a chilly breeze and working its way through the tall grass and around the trees, eager to settle in around the farm.

Curling my knees up to my chest and wrapping my arms around them, I stare out over the rolling hills of our farm, feeling a little lost—like I'm back at square one. I mean, Luke is obviously going through scary stuff at home, and I can't do anything to help him. My new friends are cool and popular and starting to accept me—especially when it comes to borrowing my homework, which makes me feel bad about myself. Candace is talking to me again, but we don't have that much in common anymore. Wolf apparently holds me to some kind of moral standard that he himself doesn't even observe but thinks I should. And as frustrating as that is, I still like him—maybe even more than before—because he's right. Cheating is wrong. And it's beneath me...as is leading guys on, which I think I may be doing with Mackenzie's brother, Mark. He does the look back, he always says something stupid around me, his head is on constant tilt, and he uncrosses his arms when we talk.

I sigh. *He would be such a nicer boy to like.*

I stand up and make my way back to the house, brushing the grass and dirt off the butt of my jeans. I'm getting hungry and hear a PB&J calling my name. Then I'm going to snap out of my funk. Maybe I'll go over some of my cheers in the front yard, or maybe I'll call Luke and dominate yet another innocent victim at a game of Horse. Poor Wolf. His coach walked in right when he missed that last hook shot I set up. The look on his face was priceless, although my beating him may mean a few more *día*s of *silencio.*

Back at the house, I smear creamy peanut butter over one slice of white bread and spread grape jelly over the other. Mash them together, and voilà! Lunch à la Ericka. I pour a glass of milk, shake a few SunChips onto my plate, and grab a paper towel before carrying my lunch out to the front porch swing.

The thing about being home alone with no cable is that there's not a lot to distract me on days like today when my mind is going nonstop. I finished *Gone with the Wind* last night and wish I had the sequel 'cause I tore through it so fast and am dying for more. I need to know what happens to Scarlett and Rhett—that *can't* be the end. I mean, sure, Scarlett's conniving and somewhat selfish, but she's also strong and fights hard for everything she wants. She loves to be the center of attention, doesn't take no for an answer, and is both in love with and depressed by her family's land. I love her, and I just can't let myself believe that Rhett doesn't give a damn. I really can't.

Downing the last of my milk, I wipe my mouth and hop off the swing. Standing under Old Glory, my dad's pride and joy ever since the summer we dug a hole and planted the flagpole, I stretch and soak up the last of the sunny days. I don't want to think about Luke or Wolf or Mark or any of my friends, fabulous or otherwise. I jump up and down to get my blood moving and begin pumping my fists, doing Up V's and Down V's, twisting my hips, and lunging as I practice our chants.

"Go, go, G-O! G-O! Go, go, let's go!" I shout, repeating the chant and motions over and over, the hills throwing my words back at me. I practice my tuck jump and keep working on my toe touch. I can almost do a back walkover; once I'm bent backward I have to kick off from the flagpole for the momentum I need, but I know that I'll eventually get over by myself. When I see a vehicle passing by, I shout "Go, fight, win!" extra loud down the long driveway.

I've gotten one honk, which isn't bad.

"Ricki Jo! Ricki Jo!"

I hear Luke, desperately calling my name repeatedly. I hear him shouting for me and I race around the side of the house toward his voice. What I see when I get to the backyard stops me dead in my tracks. Luke is running toward me at full speed, with blood all over his white T-shirt and carrying something small in his arms. Something about the size of a dog. Of my dog. Bandit.

"Ricki Jo! Is your dad here? Your momma? We gotta get Bandit to the vet!" he shouts, out of breath, almost over to where I stand, stunned.

I can't move.

"Ricki Jo!"

He's standing right in front of me now, panting, holding Bandit carefully against his chest. I am at eye level with my dog, the dog I picked four years ago when my uncle's dog had puppies, the one I confide in, the one whose right foot goes crazy when I scratch his belly, the one I named and feed and love. My dog. Luke is holding my dog in front of me and I barely recognize him.

"Oh, Bandit," I whisper.

His face is like some horrible cartoon, distorted and droopy. His left ear is hanging off his head, limp and sad. There is a huge gash on his jaw so that I can see every jagged tooth even though his mouth is closed. And his neck. Oh, god, his neck won't stop bleeding.

"Ricki Jo," Luke says.

I can't move.

"Ricki Jo. It was that pack of dogs. I was heading over to see if you wanted to go to the creek or skip rocks or something and I saw 'em. They were all around Bandit's doghouse. He was chained up, nipping at them from inside, but they were too much. They were all over him. I—" Luke falters. "I killed one."

I look up at his face and see that it's tortured.

"I killed one, Ricki Jo," he says again, his face white. "Oh, god."

Bandit whimpers and I look down. One eye is unfocused and dead-looking, but the other pierces me through the heart with a look of equal parts fear and defeat.

I break out of my trance, and touch Bandit gingerly. I'm relieved when I feel the slightest movement. He's still alive, but barely.

"What are we going to do?" I ask Luke. "My folks went to town. Is anybody home at your house?"

He shakes his head, clearly distraught. "They're gone. Everybody's in town. Oh my god."

Everybody's gone.

"We gotta get him to the vet, Ricki Jo. We gotta get him some help."

I look at Bandit and am filled with rage. Every breath he manages is labored. The wheezing sounds he makes torture me. I feel so angry and helpless. I look around the farm and wish my dad were here. He would know what to do. He would—

"The tractor," I say. "We can put Bandit in the bucket and raise him up and…I don't know, drive it to town."

"It'll take forever to get to town in the tractor," Luke says.

"The four-wheeler, then," I say, knowing this is the best idea. "Yeah. I'll drive, and you keep holding Bandit 'cause I don't want to move him. We can go way faster on the four-wheeler. And maybe…maybe Sarah's family is home, and we can stop by there. They have racehorses! They probably have a vet on staff! Or maybe her family could take us into town."

He nods and we're off, running up to the barn. I hear Bandit cry a little bit and know that Luke is doing his best not to jar him too much. I hop on the four-wheeler and turn the key while Luke steps carefully over the seat and kind of leans back, holding on to the back rails with one arm so that Bandit can lie flatter against his stomach. I guide us down the hills and take the shortcut across the farm to the road past Luke's house. No way am I passing the Gumbels' place right now. No way.

At Luke's backyard I power around to the front driveway, hoping like crazy that somebody's come back home, but it's empty. I do see his dad out back; he hollers something about tread marks in his yard.

"Keep going, Ricki Jo!" Luke shouts, and that's just what I do.

On the road I can really open it up, and we're flying. It's so much smoother and I'm not as afraid for Bandit as we take the curves. I am afraid of meeting a car or top-pling over, but I don't—can't—slow down. After a couple of miles I see the gates in front of Sarah's house and feel a wave of relief wash over me. Her dad is actually out front, checking the mail.

"Mr. Whitman!" I yell, gunning it. "Mr. Whitman, please help us!"

I whip the four-wheeler into the driveway and he sees Luke and Bandit and all the blood right away. "Oh my god," he says, his voice a whisper.

"My dog's been attacked," I start, words racing out of my mouth at ninety miles an hour. "He's hurt bad and he's still alive, but he needs a doctor and I'm really scared and our parents aren't home and—"

He holds up his hand. "Wait here."

We watch him run past the open gate and down the long tree-lined driveway. It looks like a lot of people are outside on their wraparound porch, and I'm so relieved that they're home.

"It's gonna be okay, Bandit," I say, turning around and looking down at my dog. "Mr. Whitman's gonna help us, okay? Okay, puppy?"

I look up at Luke and he looks at me, and I can't take the darkness in his eyes, the fear. My emotions finally spill over. I don't want to cry, but I do. Bandit whimpers and I cry harder. Luke reaches out to touch my hand, but his own is covered in blood and he stops himself. I grab it anyway, and hold on tight.

"Please don't let my dog die," I pray out loud. "Please, God, please don't let my dog die."

"He's coming," Luke says, and I turn back around to see Mr. Whitman flying down his driveway in a silver Mercedes-Benz. I let go of Luke's hand, wipe my face on my sleeve, and shake my head, trying to get it together.

Mr. Whitman stops the car and hurries out of the driver's side toward us. "We're gonna put him on the back floorboard, okay, kids?" he says. "I put some newspaper down, and I want you to lay him down on top of that, okay?"

I slide off the four-wheeler to give Luke room and he carefully stands, swinging his leg over, being super gentle with Bandit.

"I'm going to need you to take off your shirt, son," Mr. Whitman says before opening the back door. Luke's hands are full and he pauses for a second, trying to work out the logistics.

"I'll help you," I say. "Squat down some."

He does and I peel the bloodied T-shirt off his back and over his head, wrapping it around Bandit. Mr. Whitman opens the back door and Luke sets Bandit down as carefully as if he were handling dynamite. Mr. Whitman closes the back door and opens the front one, throwing a beach towel to each of us.

"For the seats," he says, and heads back around to the driver's side. I take my towel and walk around the car to the back. I want to ride with Bandit.

Luke and I spread our towels over the seats and get in. I've never been in a car this nice and it still has that new-car smell. We buckle our seat belts and Mr. Whitman takes off, handling the curves like he's on the NASCAR circuit. I breathe, and pray, and try not to cry. I lie down on the seat, forgetting about my towel, just getting my whispers as close to Bandit as I can. I tell him I love him and he's going to be okay. I keep telling him over and over because I have to keep telling myself. Mr. Whitman lets Luke borrow his cell phone to call his momma and then my folks. I close my eyes and keep whispering to Bandit, rolling with the rocking of the car, hoping that we'll make it in time.

The girl at the front desk only needed one look at the shirtless, frightened teenage boy holding a bloodied dog to page the doctor and get Bandit right in. The waiting room was actually a little more crowded than I would have expected, but no one minded us barging in when they saw our terror and, frankly, all the blood. Luke laid Bandit on a steel table in a small back room and Dr. Switzer asked us to leave, saying that Bandit needed "immediate attention," which we later found out meant surgery.

When my parents finally showed up, I broke down; I started crying like crazy. My momma pulled me in and rocked me and stroked my hair, murmuring in my ear. My dad stuck out his hand for the usual man-to-man handshake he and Luke always share, but then shocked us all by pulling him in for a long hug. Luke blinked full eyes, pulled away, and walked over to the windows. Then Mr. Whitman approached my folks with a calmer version of what actually happened. I watched the grown-ups huddle together to discuss the situation and decided after a minute that it was all too much.

"Let's go out back," I said to Luke.

And now we're perched on a black rail, waiting for word.

"Bandit was fine this morning," I say, sniffling. "I fed him and took him water, and he was happy as a lark." I wipe my nose on my shirt sleeve, a habit my momma hates. "Seriously. He's such a good dog. I don't know why I didn't take him with me to the creek. I always take him with me. I should have taken him."

"It's not your fault," Luke says, looking over at me. "You know that, right?"

I shrug, but I can't shake the guilt. "It feels like my fault."

"Yeah," Luke says, swinging his legs and looking out at the horizon. "Sometimes things feel that way. You know, you just think there must've been — must *be* — something you can do. But in the end, you just gotta do the best you can, when you can."

I look over at him and see his sharp jaw settling into a deep frown. His pep talk is forced, as if he's trying to convince both of us...as if he's not talking about Bandit at all.

"Is that how you feel about the stuff with your mom and dad?" I ask quietly.

He jerks his head toward me and looks at me hard, his blue eyes flashing betrayal. I inhale sharply, shocked by his intensity.

"I'm talking about Bandit, okay?" he says.

I nod quickly.

"God, Ricki Jo!" he says, standing up and turning away. "It's like I've said a million times: I don't wanna talk about it. But hey! Here we are again, you trying to talk about it. So, okay, you wanna talk about how I feel? Let's do it. My dad's a drunk and a jackass. I get it. And you get it. End of story. Jesus Christ!"

He rams his foot into the gravel drive and a few rocks fly out into the yard. I feel stupid. Awful. I *have* asked a million times about his dad, his momma, his feelings. He never wants to talk about it, never opens up. And I don't know; it just doesn't make sense to me, living like that— living *with* that. I would want to talk about it.

"I'm sorry," I say.

He turns around to face me, his arms cocked back behind his head. He lets them fall and exhales loudly— it's as if he's deflating right here in front of me. His head hangs, his shoulders droop. He nudges the gravel around a little with the toe of his boot, sniffs, and spits.

"Me, too," he says, almost a whisper.

I watch him for the next few minutes, digging a hole in the back lot. Steadily, he digs.

I finally stand up and walk over to him. I lean in so that our arms and sides are pressed together, and he leans into the contact. We stay like that for a few seconds, until he pushes a little harder and I push back—until we're smiling half smiles and breathing steady breaths. With the side of my tennis shoe I knock his rock pile over, refilling the emptiness he's created in the back lot, moving the stones back a few at a time.

When I stomp the last of the gravel back in place, Luke speaks, softly.

"I killed one," he reminds me.

I look up at his face, at his deep anguish, and see his eyes searching mine, asking me things he won't let himself say out loud: if he's a good person, if any of this is his fault. I think about what would've happened to Bandit if Luke hadn't come over. My heart hurts again, and I put my arms around him and hug tightly. I scratch his back lightly, press the side of my face against his still bare chest, and cry for us both.

CHAPTER TWENTY-ONE

"This is one of those days when I wish my mom would let me wear makeup," I say. Luke and I are waiting to get off the school bus, and I realize now that checking myself out in the gigantic mirror the driver uses to keep us all in check was not a good idea. My eyes are bloodshot and really puffy underneath. Even though the vet told us that Bandit's outlook is more positive than negative, I've cried myself to sleep the last two nights in a row, which I'm pretty sure would be a *Seventeen* magazine Beauty Don't.

"I think you look all right," Luke says, climbing down the stairs.

I don't usually care for liars, but I have a sudden appreciation for the value of the little white lie and give Luke a small, grateful smile.

We cross the back parking lot quickly and, as the first bell rings, we join the foot traffic, heading off to our respective homerooms. I wanted to play hooky today, but my parents said that "moping won't help Bandit" and "school will be a good distraction." Actually, I have a Spanish test today and I'm not feeling very *preparado*; plus, I sleepwalked my way through my science lab last night, which is not encouraging. So school is less of a distraction and more like a whole new form of stress, since the balloons under my eyes will probably prompt people to ask me what's wrong all day long.

"It's gonna be a hard day." I sigh, and Luke nods.

We weave through the hallways and I use him as a shield so I can duck into Mrs. Wilkes's room unseen. I'm anxious to be alone, and unable to pretend to care about anything other than Bandit. I put my head down and soak up the next five quiet minutes. Then, when the bell rings again, I sit up and brace myself for what will probably be a very long day.

"Oh my gosh, Ericka!" Mackenzie says, rushing toward me. She sets her books on the table and sits down next to me as our homeroom fills up. "I heard about your dog. I am so sorry. Are you okay?"

I shake my head, surprised. "You *heard*?"

I almost don't believe her. I mean, she didn't call me this weekend or anything. How could she have heard?

"Yeah," she replies. "Mr. Whitman told us when he got back from the vet. It must've been awful."

Mackenzie is rubbing my arm and looks genuinely concerned.

"You knew?" I ask again, incredulous. "Why didn't you call?"

Mackenzie opens her mouth, but has no response. I wait. Her mouth twitches.

"Oh my god, Ericka!" Sarah says, rushing into homeroom and sitting down at our table with Kimi and Laura. "My dad said your dog might die! Are you okay?"

"Yeah, I went down and looked at your four-wheeler, and it was covered in blood," Kimi adds. "Disgusting."

I look around at their faces and feel what can only be described as betrayal. "Wait a minute," I begin. "So, you all knew. And none of you called?"

The other girls freeze up, much like Mackenzie did a few moments ago, and have nothing to say. Not "I'm sorry, Ericka," or "I suck," or "I lost all the feeling in my fingers and couldn't dial a telephone." Nothing!

I can't believe what I'm hearing. In fact, I can't believe what I'm *not* hearing. They knew. Mr. Whitman told them. All of them.

Wait, Mr. Whitman told *all* of them?

"So you had a party?" I ask Sarah. "And you were all there? Just down the road from my house?"

And I wasn't invited.

"Well, it was a last-minute thing," Sarah says uneasily.

And just like that, a lightbulb goes on over my head. They're back to being the Fab Four, with no room for a fifth, for a country girl whose folks aren't members of the country club, who doesn't have a cell phone, who hasn't hit anything close to a growth spurt, who can't even do a back handspring.

"Are you—" Mackenzie breaks off, worried, then continues. "Are you okay?"

I look at this girl and feel the most hurt by her, the one I thought I knew best. My "BFF."

"No, Mackenzie," I say, letting her see all the pain in my eyes. "I am not okay. My dog has not recovered from his surgery. He may not live, and if he does, he will never be the same. My heart is breaking. I cried myself to sleep the last two nights. And you knew, all along, and you never called."

Mackenzie looks as though she might say something, but then shakes her head and gulps hard. She just stares at me, almost pleadingly, looking like she feels awful.

I hope she feels awful.

"I'm sorry," she finally says quietly.

I put my head down on my arms and shut them all out.

"Hello, ladies," Wolf says, making his daily loud entrance, slamming his books on the table. The noise jars me but I keep my head down. He's just one more person I don't want anything to do with today.

"Did anybody get the science lab?" he asks.

I hear the other girls murmur and shuffle some papers, but no one offers the homework up to Wolf. Despite myself, I'm proud of them for keeping their work to themselves. Maybe it really was a onetime thing.

"Ericka," Wolf says. "Hello?"

He ruffles my hair and I sit up quickly to get out of his reach. I smooth my hair back down and shoot him a killer look, my eyes daggers. "Stop."

"Whoa! What's up with your face?" he asks.

"Please. Not today," I say, defeated.

"Did you get beat up or something? Fight somebody?"

I roll my eyes and put my head down.

"No, no, okay, I'm sorry," he says. "Late night, whatever. But Ericka, seriously. Did you get the science lab?"

"Yes," I say into my arms, the sound muffled. "Why? Did you suddenly have a change of morals?"

He chuckles. "Me? No. But I thought you might want to help out your *friends.*"

I look up at the other girls and realize that they all have their science labs out but not one of them has anything filled in. I shake my head, completely stunned. I got through my homework between sobs and thoughts of my dying dog, but I guess parties at Sarah's house take a lot out of a gal. I look at each of them in turn, and only Mackenzie can't meet my gaze, although the others are squirmy.

"Unbelievable," I say, shaking my head in disgust, surprising Wolf and obviously putting a major kink in the girls' plans to borrow my homework again. I put my head back down.

"Okay, gang," Mrs. Wilkes says. "When I call your name, come up to my desk to pick up your school pictures. Morning announcements were short, so if you can keep the noise to a mild roar, I'll give you the rest of homeroom to cut out the wallets I'm sure you're dying to swap. I've got a lot of scissors up here, but remember your kindergarten days: Share, and don't run with them."

Great. School photos. Usually this is a really fun day. I mean, you never know how your picture is going to turn out, but I like passing them out and collecting them from my friends. Unfortunately, I'm a bit limited in the friends department...especially today.

When I return to my desk and look at my picture, I find I'm actually pleased at the way it came out. My eyes are open, my smile is braces-free, my curls are full and frizzless (thanks to the tips I got from the "Wild, Yet Tame" article in *Seventeen*), and I love my outfit. Mackenzie and Laura are furiously working on their science labs while Kimi and Sarah are going gaga over their own pictures. Wolf is smugly cutting wallet-sized photos of himself from his photo sheet. I hesitate, then grab the other pair of scissors to start on mine. At least Luke will want one.

"Ericka," Kimi says, "here's mine. Can I have one of you?"

I look over at her with a smirk, not willing to trade a two-by-three photo for my homework.

"Oh, me, too!" Sarah joins in. "I want one of all the girls. Our little exclusive club."

She and Kimi giggle. "The W's!"

I look at them, bewildered. Didn't they forget to invite me to a slumber party a couple miles away? Didn't they know about my dying dog and not call me? Weren't they just ready to use me for my science lab? It's like none of that affects their view of the Fab Five—like it's up to me how long I want to be mad.

I choose to be mad for a while. I deserve to be mad for a while.

But not forever.

"Wait! First put your name on it, and the year," Kimi demands. "We're gonna think these are so funny when we're seniors."

I cut out a couple more photos and turn them over, scrawling my name and the date on the backs. I stay quiet; I don't want anyone to get the wrong idea. I'm still mad.

Sarah and Kimi slide pictures over to me, and then to Wolf and the other girls. I pass around my photos, too. I'm starting to feel a smidge better—well, more like a sliver of a smidge, really. Mackenzie and Laura get into the photo-day excitement and give up on science. It's actually cool looking at everybody's pics. Mackenzie looks like a knockout, as usual. Laura and Sarah love theirs, too, and Kimi is being a sport, even though she's a little upset about a long flyaway in her normally perfect bob.

"Wolf, let's see 'em," Kimi says.

He grins and picks up his stack of photos. Then he clears his throat dramatically and starts talking like an old game show host.

"Hmmm," he says. "First, to Miss Minnesota. We're all so glad you came to Preston County High."

Ugh! I hate it, but my heart deflates. I'm new, too!

He passes a pic to Mackenzie. As it slides past me, I notice he's wearing that killer white polo that brings out the natural tan of his skin. Just looking at his pic, at that patented smile, makes me want to pick it up and kiss it a million times.

"Then, to Kimi, for your lovely curves," he says, and I nearly gag. *Gross.*

"Laura and Sarah, here you go, my beauties. Enjoy."

All the girls laugh at his creepy little game, but then he tucks his pictures into his shirt pocket and looks up at the clock.

What? Wait, what about me?

"Hey, Wolf," Mackenzie says, "what about Ericka?"

I look down, trying to act uninterested.

"She doesn't get one," he says.

Wow. I almost can't believe what I'm hearing. His words bounce around my head, a constant echo: *She doesn't get one. She doesn't get one. She doesn't get one.*

"Wolf!" they all protest in unison.

I honestly can't believe it. I feel ridiculous. I hadn't expected this day to get worse in only the first fifteen minutes. I tuck my picture folder in my backpack and wait for the bell.

"Are you serious?" Sarah asks him.

The bell rings, and not a moment too soon.

"Yeah, I'm serious," he says, his grin set to super evil. "I gotta ration these babies out."

He pats his shirt pocket and I breeze past him, chin

up, as if he doesn't exist. But I want to pull the tiny pictures out of his pocket and slide them all over his beautiful face, paper cutting his ego in half.

"Thought you might want backup," Luke says quietly. I toss him a grateful smile and bend down to get the books I need.

"Hey, Luke," I hear Wolf say. "I just want to say I'm sorry to hear about your dad, man."

I look up in shock.

"Ah, yeah, it's all good," Luke says, trying to brush it off. His father's story was in last week's paper, like we knew it would be, but at least it didn't make the front page. Luckily, the city council is thinking about working with the government on a bypass highway, which is way bigger news.

"I read it last week, but I haven't really seen you," Wolf continues, putting out his hand. "At least he's okay, though, right? Could've been a lot worse than a broken leg, huh?"

Luke nods and shakes Wolf's hand. I look at them, feeling angry at myself because every time I want to hate Wolf, he does something human and I warm to him again. He's such a jerk, most of the time, but deep down, he's a good guy. I know he is. Every now and then, in moments like right now, he can't hide it.

"Here, man," Wolf says, pulling out a wallet pic for Luke.

I don't believe it.

"Uh, thanks," Luke says, obviously feeling awkward. He slides the photo into one of his books without even giving it a glance.

"Ericka," I hear and look in the direction of the sound, grateful for the distraction. Luke scoots toward Wolf a little as Mark works his way over to me.

"Later, man," I hear Wolf say as he saunters off, snapping right back into jock mode.

Mark leans down and puts his hand on my back. "Listen, Mackenzie just told me about your dog." He squats next to me and moves his hand up to my shoulder. "I am so sorry to hear that. If you need anything, if I can do anything, let me know, okay?"

I gulp. And nod. Mark Watts is a good guy a hundred percent of the time.

"Thank you," I say.

"Picture," he responds.

My confusion must be evident on my face because he starts to turn red.

"Uh, no, sorry," he says. "Here, I don't know if you want one, but I don't know that many people yet, and — here's a school picture."

"Oh," I say, giggling. *He says something stupid*, the *Seventeen* voice in my head reminds me. "Here's one of me, too. We'll probably laugh at these when we're seniors."

He chuckles, stands up, and starts to walk away. Then . . . he looks back! He always does the "look back." I grin and put the last book in my bag, stand up, close my locker, and look at Luke. He crosses his arms over his chest and cocks his right eyebrow up high.

"I don't like him like that," I say.

"Sure," Luke teases as we walk off.

"Hi, Luke!" Laura shouts, holding a picture out to him before we get very far.

He gives her a nod and takes the picture. Just like with Wolf's, he puts it in his book without looking at it. Then— and this looks painful—he pulls one of his own from his back jeans pocket and hands it over to his very cute, very bubbly, and very obvious admirer.

"Oh, it's really good," Laura gushes, looking down at the wallet-sized version of her blond-haired, blue-eyed crush...totally absorbed and basically ignoring the real thing towering over her as she turns to stick it in her locker.

"See ya," Luke says quickly, seizing the opportunity to grab my arm and jerk me along with him, working our way back into hallway traffic. I cock my own eyebrow and smirk up at him.

"I don't like her like that," he says, mocking me.

"Sure," I tease, giving him a taste of his own medicine.

It's funny how Luke is with girls. I mean, Laura is cute and really nice (even though we're kind of in a fight right now), but he acts like a girl liking him is more of a hassle than anything else. I don't know; maybe it's all timing or something. Like I would like Mark if I weren't hung up on Wolf...which is totally annoying.

"Why can't I like good guys, like Mark?" I wonder aloud.

" 'Cause good guys finish last," Luke states.

"Then what's the incentive to be a good guy?" I ask.

Luke drapes his long arm around me and looks down. "Good guys get awesome best friends," he says, and we laugh. I put my arm around his waist and we walk to first period. Thank God for Luke.

"Is he okay?" Candace asks before Spanish class starts, as we wait for the final bell.

"No," I say, shaking my head. I can't stop thinking about Bandit, and I can't stop thinking about the Gumbels. I want to toilet paper their house or shoot it up with paint balls or have them arrested. I expected all this sadness, but I am surprised by the anger. I am *really* angry.

"They don't know for sure if he's gonna make it," I say, trying not to cry.

"Aw, I remember that picture you had of him at Four-H camp," she says. "He's a real mutt, but cute enough, I guess. Are you gonna get a new dog?"

My mouth falls open. The thing about Candace is that she means well. She has a good heart. Tact, however, is nonexistent in her world. Plus, she has diarrhea of the mouth, which is why I can't tell her a secret. For instance, at 4-H camp a horrifying case of poison ivy found its way to my backside—and this news was broadcast at every cabin.

"We're just gonna take it one day at a time," I say. I look around at all the other kids in my class, grouped together, gossiping and laughing. And then I catch Wolf's eye as he walks into class and quickly direct my gaze back to Candace.

"Oh!" she says suddenly, as an idea comes to her. "This Thursday, when we find out if they liked us and if we get on the school paper, maybe you could start, like, a pet obituaries column or something. You know, if he doesn't make it."

I gasp involuntarily.

She recognizes her thoughtlessness, and I can tell she feels horrible. One hand flies to her mouth and the other grabs my hand. "Oh my gosh! I'm so sorry. I just mean, you know, that dogs and cats and stuff are like best friends, like family sometimes, and you could help a lot of kids at school by doing a pet obits thing."

"You always say exactly what's on your mind, don't you, Red?" Wolf says, stepping between us to take his seat.

"Yeah, I do," she snaps. She crosses her arms over her maroon PCHS PRIDE T-shirt and cocks out a hip defiantly. "Like, for example, her dog was way cuter than you think you are."

"I'm still cuter than I think you are," he retorts.

The last bell rings and Candace squeezes my hand and moves toward her seat.

"Oh, and too much hair gel, brother," she adds. "You look like you drowned in a salon."

I glance back at him to see his eyes twinkling. He loves getting a rise out of people and actually takes most digs as well as he hands them out. I quickly face forward again, not in the mood for sparring with Wolf.

"Hey, Rosa Jo," he whispers, leaning up close to my ear. "I didn't know about your dog. Sorry. I was a jerk today."

I spin around in my seat to look at his face, to search for sincerity. It's there.

"Here," he says, holding out a picture to me.

I look down at it and sigh. It's adorable. That signature melt-me grin. Those sparkly brown eyes and small, perfect ears. And too much gel or not, I love his perfectly spiked hair. I feel an involuntary urge to reach out for the picture. I want to put it in my locker, blow it up and paste it on my bedroom wall, practice kissing on it.

"*No gracías*," I manage to say, and I turn back around, sitting firmly on my trembling hands.

"I really am sorry," he whispers in my hair.

I give a swift nod but don't turn back around, because I don't trust myself, and I will not cry.

CHAPTER TWENTY-TWO

"Our Father, who art in Heaven, hallowed be thy name," I pray along with my family. My eyes are sealed shut so tightly that the black is turning purple and neon fireworks are going off on the insides of my eyelids. That's how fervently I'm praying. That's how bad I need God to hear my prayer.

My parents picked Ben and me up from our schools today and we stopped by church before heading to the vet's office for an update. Momma led us up front and we each lit a candle for Bandit, our footsteps echoing eerily in the empty cathedral. I open my eyes and find that I can't stop looking at my candle now, as Dad leads us through the Lord's Prayer. It's beneath the Virgin, the fourth one over in the second row, its flame flickering for Bandit.

"Hear our prayer," I whisper, gripping tightly to the rosary in my hand. "Hear our prayer, please."

"His outlook is good," Dr. Switzer tells us in the waiting room, and we breathe a collective sigh of relief. "He's got a long road ahead of him," the doctor warns, not wanting our hopes to soar too high, "but he'll pull through."

I hug him. I can't help myself. I hug him with all my might. "Thank you, thank you, thank you, thank you, thank you," I mumble into his white coat.

Dr. Switzer pats my back and then pulls away some. He squats down and looks me dead in the eyes. "Now, Ricki Jo, he may never be the same Bandit he was before. He won't be able to run and play for a long time, and then, when he is able, he may have some psychological issues that you can't feed into. Don't pity him. He may be fearful, he may be jumpy, but it'll be up to you to snap him out of it. Don't feel sorry for him and he won't feel sorry for himself."

I guess he sees the mortified look on my face — *Can I get a little bedside manner here?* — because he awkwardly pats the sides of my arms and tries to smile.

"But, you know," he continues, "we can talk about all that once he's feeling better. He should recover well, and although you'll have to watch him, clean his wounds, and give him medicine, he should be back on the farm in about a week or so."

I bite my lip and nod. *Poor Bandit.*

Momma and Ben stay out in the waiting room (my folks worried about how my little brother might take seeing our dog so battered), but Dad and I follow Dr. Switzer down a small hallway to a caged area out back. I hear barking in the kennel as Dr. Switzer opens the back door. All the barking makes me jittery and I hold my dad's hand, gripping it tightly, hoping Bandit is awake and that if he is, he isn't scared, too.

"He's still very weak," Dr. Switzer warns us as he leads the way to a big cage off to the side, away from the ruckus.

On a long work table, Bandit rests in a big, clean cage. My eyes fill with tears when I see my dog lying there, his chest and face shaved close so that, even under all the bandages, I can see scratches, stitches, and bite marks. Thick black stitches crisscross his ear and a shaved ring circles one eye.

"We hope we can save it," Dr. Switzer says, reading my mind. "He'll need another surgery."

I gulp and nod, scooting closer and wrapping my fingers around the wire of Bandit's cage.

"And the tube?" I ask. A thick ivory tube sticks out from his upper chest, and then again near his neck.

"Infection," my dad answers, putting his hands on my shoulders. "The tube helps drain the infection, sweetheart."

I look over at Dr. Switzer and he confirms this with a swift nod.

I let it all sink in. This is not quite what I imagined when we were told that Bandit's outlook is good. I watch his belly move up and down slightly and take encouragement from the steady breaths, trying to block out the persistent wheezing. I wish I could touch him, wish he would open his good eye and see me, wish I could take him home.

"We'd better get going," my dad says gently.

I sniff and nod, wiping my eyes. "Bye, Bandit," I whisper. "I love you."

My dad shakes the vet's hand at the front door, while Ben and I follow my momma out to the car. On the way home Dad explains that Bandit had major surgery on his neck and chest and needs to stay a few nights for observation. He starts to go into details that make my stomach turn along with the curves on our road, and I stop him. I saw the ear, the eye, the jaw, and all the blood. I *saw* how bad it was. The only thing I need to *hear* is that Bandit's outlook is good. That, I can cling to. That, I can accept.

"Where's Dad?" I ask Momma as I sit cross-legged on the floor next to her.

I already halfheartedly finished my homework, so I dive into the warm heap of towels that just came out of the dryer. I love the smell and warmth of just-washed bath towels. I can't help but put my face into each one before I fold it and add it to the pile. It's one of those things, like comfort food, that makes me feel better instantly.

"Did he already leave for work?" I ask again, worried. Dad usually kisses us before heading over to Toyota, and it's late. I really hope he didn't leave without saying good-bye.

"He had something to take care of," Momma says matter-of-factly. She folds faster, more militantly, and her face is set and determined.

"Oh," I say, understanding. A cold chill runs up my spine and I grab another warm towel. "He went to see the Gumbels, huh?"

She looks up at me, surprised, and then shakes her head and resumes folding. "He went to see the Gumbels. And Animal Control is with him."

"He called them?" I ask, frozen in place.

"He called them," she answers, not missing a beat. "Animal Control came over here for the dog that…didn't make it…and they took it over to the Gumbels' house together. Your father is very angry, Ricki Jo. It could easily have been you or Ben."

My mother's words bounce around in my head. *It could easily have been me or Ben.* It's almost been me before, actually, but I doubt telling her that will make her feel any better. The fact is that it was Bandit, and now he'll never be the same.

I am happy to hear that justice is knocking on the Gumbels' door, but I worry about my dad at the same time. The Gumbels are mean, and they will still be our neighbors after the folks from the pound are long gone. And they won't like it much that Luke killed their biggest dog.

Luke killed their biggest dog. I don't know what came over him, but my dad said he found a bloodied piece of firewood near Bandit's doghouse with black hairs all over one end. Luke must've grabbed the first thing he could get his hands on, and with the woodpile being right there, nature's baseball bat was the weapon of the moment. Which means he got really close to the dog tearing at Bandit's neck. Which means he practically killed a dog with his bare hands.

I shiver again and wrap a beach towel around my shoulders. My momma raises an eyebrow, but I just grab a washcloth and keep folding in silence. I can't believe Luke won't talk about it.

CHAPTER TWENTY-THREE

"So the meeting's today, then?" Luke asks me on our way into the gym.

"Yeah. I'm pretty pumped," I say. "I mean, I don't know how much they'll actually let me write, but it should be fun, and I can meet new people."

"Oh, trading in the Fab Four?" he teases.

"No, sir," I say, pulling a dollar bill out of my purse for a Coke. "We're still fabulous—and we're five, by the way—but I'm broadening my horizons. And you know I love to write."

"I know," he says, leaning up against the vending machine. "And if you publish anything like what you write in your diary, it should be a pretty juicy read."

I stop cold. "You read my journal?"

He tries to keep a straight face, but he's a horrible liar. When I see his telling smile, I relax. I can't believe I bought it for even a second, 'cause obviously Luke would never do that. Still, I just can't let it slide, so I lift up his shirt and stick my cold cola can right up under it, freezing his abdomen.

"Hey! Ow!" He squirms. I laugh hard and hold tight to keep his shirt down over the can. He's jerking around like a spaz, all flailing right angles, and it's hilarious.

"I didn't read it, okay?" he screams. "Hey! Stop!"

I stick out my tongue and retrieve my Coke. "Serves you right."

"I'm gonna get you back for that, Ricki Jo," he warns, grabbing his book bag from the floor and backing down the hallway, bumping into a few kids as the tunnel behind the gym starts to fill up. "I'll get you."

"Bring it on, Foster!" I sass and head back out to the hallway.

On my way to Miss Davis's classroom, I cut through the cafeteria to see my crew. From the way she's waving at me from our table across the room, Mackenzie looks like she's landing planes. I smile and wave back, really appreciative of the effort the girls have made this week. My parents are starting to complain about all the phone calls I've been getting at home (which I'm hoping will open their eyes to the brilliance of buying me a cell phone), and it seems Kimi found another girl for them to get homework from, which is a huge relief.

"Can't today, girls," I say, holding up my brown bag. "I'm going to a meeting for the school paper."

Kimi wrinkles her nose. "Ew. The paper? You're such a nerd, Ericka."

Sarah elbows her, hard.

"Just kidding," Kimi says quickly, rubbing her arm and glaring at her best friend.

I shake my head and roll my eyes. "Whatever. I think it'll be cool. I'll meet new friends, and hopefully get to write a cool column."

"What do you mean?" Mackenzie asks. "We're your friends."

"Yeah, I know," I say. "I just like writing, and I think it'd be cool to do the kind of articles we read in *Seventeen* and stuff."

"Oh my god!" Kimi says, almost spewing her Diet Coke. "Yes! You didn't say you were going to write something *chic* in the paper, you know, to actually make it worth reading. I'll give you tons of hair and makeup tips if you need them. Just ask."

"Thanks," I say, spotting the editor, Mitch Mills, leaving the cafeteria. He's an upperclassman, effeminate and well-dressed. Some kids say he's gay, but I don't know how you can tell that just by looking at a guy. "Catch y'all later."

I turn to go, not wanting to be late, and almost run into a tray full of mystery meat.

"Where you going?" Wolf asks, his confident grin slipping. "I was about to join y'all."

"Take my place, then," I say coldly. "Poor substitute, but whatever."

I leave him standing openmouthed at our table and weave my way through the hungry throng, my heart pounding like crazy. Part of me is proud that I've managed the cold-as-ice treatment toward the crush of my life all week, but the other part is completely ticked off that the one time Wolf decides to eat with us instead of with the ball players, I've got a meeting.

I hustle down the hall and blow into Miss Davis's classroom out of breath and am relieved to see that they haven't started yet. Candace perks up and pats the seat next to her. I collapse into it and smile at the kids around the table, surprised to see a really diverse group, from jocks to wallflowers.

Mitch looks at the clock and then down at a sheet of paper in front of him.

"Well," he says, clearing his throat a little, "let's get started."

I pop open my Coke and take out my lunch, nibbling as I wipe all thoughts of Wolf from my brain. I want to focus completely on Mitch as he explains his vision for this year.

"First things first. We read the freshman samples and would like to welcome the two of you to our staff," he says, and heads nod all around him.

I smile. I mean, I kind of figured they wouldn't have invited us back just to reject us in front of everyone, but you can never be sure. I let out the huge breath I didn't realize I'd been holding and slouch back into my chair. It feels good to be accepted so easily.

Mitch goes on about the deadline for this month's issue, but since I'm new, I have no responsibilities this go-round. Still, it's interesting hearing everybody give input and offer up suggestions, and I really like putting faces with some of the bylines. Like, I didn't realize that the sportswriter is actually Mayor Green's son. That makes him the biggest celebrity I've ever met, which I do recognize as totally pathetic.

The meeting is going well and I'm so focused on what Mitch is saying that I completely forget about the Bandit situation until he asks if anyone wants to pitch a new column idea. Candace grabs my hand and raises her other one.

"Mitch?" she asks. "I, um, kind of have an idea. My good friend is dealing with a very sick dog, and I know we can all get so attached to our pets, like family, and I thought it might be really nice for their owners to be able to see an obituary for that family member in the event that they pass away."

The room is still for a moment.

"Not that Bandit will," she adds quickly, looking over at me.

I smile. I actually think it's a really sensitive idea, and even though she didn't pitch it as well in Spanish class, I know she got the idea because she has a big heart.

"So, I'd like to do a pet obits column," she finishes, "if you don't think it's stupid."

Mitch's too-thin face cycles through a bunch of

expressions in rapid succession as he thinks it over. Then he asks for comments and the group weighs in with pros and cons, although it looks like most people are behind the idea. One girl does say that we'd want to limit the space, keep the obits short.

"True," Mitch says, rolling his eyes and smoothing his swept-over hair. "High school is depressing enough."

I tend to agree.

"Anyone else?" Mitch asks.

"Actually," I say, "I'd really like to do a column, too."

I take a deep breath and put on my best smile. *You could sell ice cubes to Eskimos,* my dad always says, and looking at this crowd, I think I'm going to have to be quite the salesman.

"Okay," I say, standing up, which only puts me at the same height as the beast on my other side. (I think he throws shot put.) Another deep breath. And go.

"A lot of people delight in the misery of others," I begin.

This statement triggers a mini-uproar of facial expressions, although no one makes a noise. *That was kind of awesome,* I think to myself before moving on.

"So, what I want to do is a 'Traumarama' column, like the one in *Seventeen* magazine. Except I would open it up to be accessible for guys, too. I was thinking that I could create an e-mail account for submissions, and kids could send in their tragic stories. I would edit them, exaggerating here and there, you know, adding my own flair. They could send in all kinds of mortifying experiences, like with kissing, parents, sports, whatever! We'd keep it light, and I would edit them to be even juicier and funnier. The original e-mailer's identity would remain anonymous, of course."

"Example?" Mitch asks.

"Uh…" I wrack my brain. "Okay, like I could write about being new to this school and feeling really self-conscious already, you know, 'cause I'm new and haven't really gotten my growth spurt yet…in any capacity."

This gets a few chuckles and I plow forward.

"Then, at this meeting, maybe some cool, hot jock is sitting next to me and asks me to stand up, only to have the entire classroom staring at me as I say, 'But I *am* standing up!' Except, you know, funnier."

A few kids giggle and the big guy next to me grunts, "Pretty funny."

I smile over at my new comrade and smack his massive shoulder like we're old friends. I'm going to have to get his name.

"I mean, obviously it'd be better than that. But I just think it'd be good comic relief," I add, doing what my dad calls laying it on thick. "And we could put it near the pet obits to balance out all the high-school-is-depressing-enough vibes!"

Now the laughs are easy and everyone's smiling, and I feel myself loosen up a bit. Just like Mom and Dad with cheerleading, these folks are cracking under my spell, and I start really amping up the drama.

"And I know I couldn't use 'Traumarama' as a title since *Seventeen* already does, but I'm thinking 'Trauma and Drama—Terrible Tales of Teenagedom,' or something like that, with some real-life gossip mixed in."

I can tell the idea is taking off because another girl I don't know adds that we could have monthly themes (which I'd already thought of, but I'm delighted to let her think it was her idea if it means she's in my corner).

"I like it," Mitch says. "I'll work on it with you at first, actually, as you get a feel for the staff and how we run things around here. Girl, you will get so much gossip and dishing that you may want to consider being anonymous as well. People will be breaking down your door wanting to know who really said what."

"I'll think about it," I say. But people breaking down my door to talk to me? Sounds to me like I *have* to have that byline.

Mamaw and Papaw have picked me up from school every day this week, now that I demand to see Bandit as soon as the last bell rings or practice is over. Squished between my grandparents and moving at thirty miles an hour is a small price to pay to get to the vet's office, but today Luke begged to come along, so Papaw is driving even slower than usual. With Luke hunched down behind us in the bed of the truck, obviously without a seat belt, Mamaw keeps her eye on the odometer and yells about "precious cargo" every time the needle nears twenty.

At Dr. Switzer's office, Luke and I get our books out and start studying. Mamaw watches over us like a hawk, determined to make us focus on our "lessons" until they let us in to see Bandit, while Papaw occupies himself with a copy of *Field & Stream* magazine that the staff left out in the waiting room.

On my first few visits, I just did my homework until my momma came by, getting to see Bandit briefly before going home. They let me pet him while he rested and talk to him and mash up his medicine in his food. But yesterday was different: Bandit was totally awake and hobbled around out back a little, yelping weakly and excited to see me. When I told Luke, he was determined to come visit.

"We can probably take him home this weekend, depending on whether he'll need the eye surgery," I whisper to Luke when Mamaw gets up to use the bathroom. "The staff is watching him around the clock."

"He's lucky," Luke says.

"Yeah," I agree. "And I'm lucky to have parents and a doctor who are willing to save him instead of saving money by putting him to sleep."

"Absolutely," he says, nodding firmly.

"And, you know"—I shrug my shoulders and start tapping my pencil against my science book involuntarily—"I—well, *we*—are all just...I don't know. We owe you one. A big one. If you hadn't found him when you did, hadn't saved him..."

I'm working toward "thank you," but my throat closes

up. I know I can get it out, but the only way to open up my throat is to open up my tear ducts, and I really don't want to cry again.

A warm hand covers mine and my pencil clacking stops. "I know," Luke says.

I glance over at him and nod, then turn back to the clock.

"Miss Winstead?" the girl at the front desk asks. "Would you like to see Bandit now? He's up and walking."

A smile explodes across my face and, of course, a couple of tears spill out, but I play them off as tears of happiness.

"I'd love to," I answer, quickly wiping the back of my hand across each cheek.

We put our books in our bags and leave them with Papaw. Then we walk down the hallway to the outside kennel, me leading the way. At the back door, Luke stops cold when he sees Bandit through the thick glass. He still has the tube through his chest and neck and he's wearing a bandage on his left eye. Plus, there are lots of stitches.

"I know," I say, grabbing Luke's arm and pulling him a little. "But really, he's a lot better."

I open the door and Bandit howls when he sees us, whipping his tail back and forth like crazy. I force myself not to run, but walk calmly over to him and put my face close so that he can give me kisses. I'd like to hug him and wrestle with him and kiss him right back, but Dr. Switzer has warned me many times to remain calm and be gentle. Bandit doesn't realize the extent of his injuries, so we can't overexcite him. I can tell Luke is worried about touching him at all, but as soon as he sits down, Bandit hobbles in between his long legs and licks his chin.

"I can't believe it, Ricki Jo," Luke says to me, his face a sea of astonishment. "I . . . I didn't know if . . ."

"I know," I say. "You saved his life."

Luke looks out over my shoulder at the back lot, which separates the vet's parking area from the nursing home's. He is intensely focused on something, but when I turn around to follow his gaze, I don't see anything. And then, when his eyes darken, I get a cold chill.

"Hey," I say softly, reaching out to touch his knee. "Are you okay?"

"I saved his life," he says, "but I took a life, too."

I sigh and look over at Bandit. He waddles out from between Luke's legs and over to a caterpillar making its way across the ground.

"I know," I say quietly.

"I killed one," he says, still not looking at me. "I picked up a piece of wood from your dad's woodpile and beat that big black dog. His teeth were just—"

He pauses to look at Bandit, involuntarily raising his hand up to his own neck.

"Just latched on," he continues. "Bandit didn't have a chance. His head was like a rag doll's, just hanging there in that killer dog's mouth while the others were barking him on and taking swipes and bites at Bandit's side and—"

Luke shakes his head hard, closes his eyes, and shakes it again. I can almost see the whole scene being tossed out of his mind, being driven out by that need to get out from under the hold something like that would have on a person. He shakes his head yet again and opens his eyes, finally looking at me. I shiver.

"I gripped that piece of wood," he continues shakily, "hollering like a madman, and just whacked him as hard as I could. His skull cracked, Ricki Jo. He just fell— dropped limp. Bandit, too. They just fell right there on the spot."

I flip my ponytail over my shoulder and run my fingers through it absentmindedly, listening and afraid to interrupt since Luke is usually a closed book. I don't know what to say, because all the things I want to say— *You did the right thing, Thank you, You saved his life*—might make him stop talking.

Luke sighs as Bandit follows the caterpillar around him, smacking him in the back with his tail.

"I can hear that crack when I go to sleep at night," Luke says really softly. "It kind of haunts me. Like, I know I had to do something to help Bandit, but then, after I whacked that other dog, I didn't even check on him, didn't even give him a second look. I just pried Bandit out from his grip and ran. I just left him there."

At this point, I feel a little of that old anger bubble up in my gut. I mean, I'm glad Luke's talking to me, 'cause he always keeps everything so bottled up, but seriously?

Am I supposed to feel sorry for that stupid attack dog, who shouldn't have even been on our property in the first place? Supposed to feel sorry for a five-on-one fight where my dog was tied up the whole time? No! I'm glad Luke didn't check on that other dog. To be honest, I'm glad he killed it, and I wish he'd killed them all.

"You can't think like that," I finally say, trying to keep my voice steady, trying to keep the bitterness at bay. "If you hadn't stopped him, he would've killed Bandit. He almost did. And anyway, blame is a weird thing. I mean, if I'd untied Bandit that morning, or taken him with me to the creek, he wouldn't have been there to be attacked in the first place. And if he weren't chained up, he would've at least had a fighting chance. And then you wouldn't have had to kill that monster. So, whose fault is it really?"

"Well," Luke says, "it's not your fault."

"Sure feels like it."

"Well, it's not."

"Yeah, but I could've prevented it. Right?" I ask. "I mean, I could've stopped it from ever happening."

Luke looks at me hard. Then he looks off behind me again, past sun-kissed old cars parked in the nursing home lot across the way. I see his jaw tighten, see the storm clouds roll over his blue eyes. He stares out and I stare at him, and we sit, silent.

"It's my fault then," he finally says. But I can't tell if it's a statement or a question or a challenge.

"I'm sorry?" I say.

"I don't prevent my momma from getting knocked around, so it's my fault."

"Luke," I start, "that's totally dif—"

"No," he says angrily. "You've seen it now. You heard it before, maybe assumed it, but the other day, you actually saw it. Saw what I come home to, or what happens sometimes right there in front of me. And I always just let it happen."

"Luke."

"That's what you're saying, right, Ricki Jo?" His voice is getting louder. "You said you didn't prevent it, so it's all your fault. So if I don't stand up to my pathetic excuse for a father, then the bruises on my momma's face and arms are my fault."

"Luke," I say, leaning up on my knees, trying to make eye contact. "Luke, look at me."

"He beats her," Luke says, turning his head to look directly into my eyes. "He drinks and becomes a different person. A monster. An animal that waits until my older brothers are gone to pick fights with my momma. To knock her around." He takes a second, looks away, and then looks me straight in the eye again. "Ricki Jo, I'm afraid he's gonna kill her."

"Luke."

"No. It's like with Bandit. He didn't have a chance in that fight. Just like Momma."

"Luke."

"I've got to stand up to him. Fight him. Grab a piece of wood, or whatever it takes. Fight force with force."

"Luke," I whisper, because I don't know what else to say and he's scaring me. I put my hands on his face and stroke his cheeks with my thumbs. He looks at me, looks right through me, and I feel like he can see all the way into me, to the blood racing in my veins. I am kneeling in front of him, eye to eye, locked. I want to tell him with my eyes that it's not his fault. That he's the best person I've ever known. That—

"Luke" is all I can choke out, all I can say.

He softens, though. He hears everything I want to tell him in the quiet between us. Then he takes my hands from his face and rocks me back 'til I'm on my heels again. I see that his eyes are full before he drops his head into his hands, hunching over his long legs. Bandit stops still between us and looks at Luke, curious. And I guess he can sense our emotion, 'cause his tail drops and drapes itself between his back legs. He whimpers and limps over Luke's legs again, up between his skinny arms, snuggling into his lap as best he can. I hear Luke let out a soft sob and I spin so that I'm facing the other way, knowing that's what he wants. We sit there another ten minutes, Luke crying and me pretending not to hear.

CHAPTER TWENTY-FOUR

"You want to help me feed, Ricki Jo?" my dad asks Saturday morning.

I'm sprawled out in front of the television, watching cartoons with Ben, totally zoned out. I look over at my dad and consider my options.

"Are you asking if I *want* to help you feed, or are you telling me to help you feed?" I ask.

"Up to you, kiddo," he says. "The cows have missed you, and your dear old dad likes having you around, but it's completely up to you."

Guilt trip. Great.

I lug myself off the couch, tired of SpongeBob anyway. "Give me a second, Dad."

"I'll meet you in the shop," he says, smiling, and heads down the hallway to his man-cave.

It's a bright morning, brisk but clear. As I put on a

flannel shirt and old jeans, I think about how little I love the smell of manure, but also how great my dad's been about Bandit. That last surgery yesterday wasn't necessary for Bandit to live, but Dad gave the go-ahead anyway and Dr. Switzer was able to restore partial vision in his left eye. So feeding the cows isn't glamorous or mentioned anywhere in *Seventeen* when they're talking about how to snag boyfriends or become popular, but it's a good way to show my dad that I appreciate everything. Plus, he usually tells pretty great stories when we're out on the farm alone.

In the garage, I pull on my work boots and grab a pair of my dad's old leather work gloves. As I am making my way across the backyard to my dad's shop, he meets me with a Coke and a Little Debbie, and I can't help but smile. Every now and then, he mixes business and pleasure in the perfect way. We make it to the electric fence before I hear Momma yelling for me.

"Ricki Jo!"

I turn back and see her on the deck with the cordless phone in her hand.

"Yeah?" I holler.

"Telephone!"

I look at my dad. "Want me to tell her to take a message?"

It's the right thing to say with my voice, but he can see in my eyes that it's the exact opposite of what I really want to do.

"That's okay," he says. "Go take the call, and then meet me up at the barn."

I hug him and kiss him on the cheek. "Thanks, Dad."

"Teenagers," he mumbles.

"Just a second, Momma!" I call, running to her at breakneck speed.

"Who is it?" I ask, completely out of breath.

She covers the mouthpiece and holds the phone away. The smile on her face and the twinkle in her eye make me nervous...like she's up to something.

"A boy," she says.

I freeze. *A boy?*

"And it's not Luke," she continues.

I wrack my brain, wondering who the mystery boy could be.

"Want me to ask who it is?" she whispers.

"No!" I yell. I'm still trying to control my breathing when she finally hands me the phone.

I take the phone and walk toward the other end of the back deck, eager to get far away from my mother, and even more eager to find out who's on the phone. I'm guessing it's Mark. I mean, that's the only logical person besides Luke, because I think he sort of likes me, and he could've asked Mackenzie for my number. No other guys know my phone number. I mean, they could look it up— there aren't that many Winsteads in the phone book— but why would they? Who would?

"Hello?" I pant into the phone, keeping an eye on my momma, who doesn't seem to be in any hurry to give me privacy.

"Yo puedo hablar con Ericka?"

Oh.

My.

God.

All the blood rushes from my face and then floods back a second later. Momma steps closer when she sees my reaction and I wave her away.

"This is she," I answer, knowing that voice and that god-awful hick Spanish accent.

"Hey. It's David," the voice says. "Um, Wolf."

I pause to scoop my lower jaw off the deck and sit on the bench to stop the yard from spinning.

"Hello?" he asks.

"Uh, I'm here," I say.

"What's up?" he asks.

"Um, not much," I say, my head reeling. "Just finished up some homework."

"That's cool," he says.

"Yeah," I say.

Then we both just sit silently on the phone. I use this pause to go back inside and shut myself safely in my room, away from the nosy interference of my momma. I cradle the phone between my shoulder and my ear and wipe my sweaty hands on my flannel shirt, all the while watching the big clock on my headboard as thirty slow seconds tick by. I've dreamed of this phone call for months, and now that it's here, I have nothing to say.

I am crazy about this boy, and although he knows I'm

alive, he seems to use that knowledge for evil. I'm still pretty mad about the school picture thing, but it's hard to be angry with him right here, right now, when *he's called me* and *he's on the other end of the phone line!*

"I'm sorry," he finally chokes out.

"What?" I say, thinking I misheard him.

"I'm sorry," he says again. "I don't always act like a nice guy, but I do feel bad about your dog. Is he okay?"

"He's getting better," I say, smiling in spite of myself— tingling in spite of myself. "Still at the vet's, but we hope he can come home this weekend."

"That's cool," he says.

"Yeah," I say, and we go into another marathon pause.

"So..." he finally says. "Think you can start talking to me again?"

"Oh, so you noticed the *silencio* treatment?" I tease. My horoscope in *Seventeen* this month encourages me to "take a romantic risk," so I'm going for it.

"Yeah, I noticed when I had to do Actividad thirty-three as both fruit vendor and customer," he says, and I can hear him grinning through the phone.

"Well, payback's a you-know-what," I say, giggling.

"I know, I know," he says with a lighthearted laugh. "But I didn't talk to you for one class period. You've ignored me all week!"

He noticed. Hmmm...

"So, anyway, that's all," he says. "Just don't be mad anymore, okay?"

I only wish I *could* stay mad at him.

"Okay," I agree. "Took you long enough, though."

"What?"

"You were a jerk, and it took you five days to admit it," I tease again. "Just sayin'."

He chuckles. "Well, first of all, I'm not used to apologizing. Second, girls usually forgive me faster. All week I've gone out of my way to talk to you and you've been, like, stone cold. I thought you'd crack."

I laugh. I can't help it. It's so funny to me that I've thrown off his game. "Were you starting to feel you'd lost your touch with women?"

"Ha!" he answers. "Not possible. Come on, Ericka, you know the ladies love me."

"Gag!" I gurgle, dramatically faking a gagging sound. "Ugh! I'm gagging!"

We both laugh and suddenly I remember that I'm talking to the love of my life on the telephone. My poor carpet; I'm pacing it threadbare.

As we come down from laughing, there's another little pause. I guess this is where we should get off the phone, but I don't want to initiate it. I could sit silent on the phone with him forever.

"You going to homecoming next weekend?" he asks out of the blue.

Oh!

My gut explodes and I fall back on the bed as if someone has punched me in the face. David Wolfenbaker just

used the word *homecoming* in a personal phone call to me.
He's gonna ask me to homecoming. He's about to ask me to home-
coming. Oh my gosh!

I play it cool.

"Uh, yeah, I think so," I say, furiously kicking my feet
in the air. "You?"

"Yeah, it should be pretty fun," he says.

"Yeah, should be," I say.

Pause, pause, pause, heartbeat racing. I can't catch my
breath.

"You know who you're going with?" he asks.

I'm sorry, but OH. MY. GOD.

"Nah," I say, pulling off nonchalance like a pro. "You
know me; it's hard to choose when half the school is beating down my door."

He chuckles. "I don't doubt it."

Beat down my door, Wolf. Beat it down right now. I'll say yes!

"What about you, Mister Player?" I say instead, rolling
over on my side and fluffing my hair. "You got your eye on
some pretty young thang?"

"Eh, sorta," he says, clearing his throat. "I'm thinking
about asking Mackenzie Watts to go with me. Her brother's trying to take my spot on the basketball team, and it'd
probably piss him off pretty bad."

What?

Who?

I stop smiling, stop breathing, stop listening. He's still
blabbing about how much he hates Mark Watts and how

sucky he is at basketball *(Who cares?)*, which I interpret as *Blah, blah, kill me now, blah, blah, my life is over, blah, blah, blah.*

The ceiling spins and I hear a loud buzzing in my ears. I feel nauseous.

"Ericka?" he asks. "Are you there?"

"Uh, yeah," I manage.

"So, what do you think?"

What do I think? I think you're in love with me and you're too stupid to see it! I think I want to marry you and I know I'd make you happy and I really, really, really want to make out with you after homecoming and I am in love with you! I think Mackenzie could have any boy in our whole town and I'll kill her if she takes mine! I think I want to die.

"Whatever," I say flippantly, suddenly eager to get off the phone. "I think Mark's a nice guy."

"Well, yeah," he says, "he's nice to you. You're best friends with his sister."

"Oh, he can't be nice to me just 'cause I'm a good person?" I ask heatedly.

"I mean, sure, I guess," he says. "You're pretty funny and stuff, but he's the kind of guy who's gonna ask a cheerleader to homecoming. I mean, uh, a Varsity cheerleader. No offense."

"I gotta go, Wolf," I say abruptly.

"Oh, okay. Well, see you at school on Monday. And you better start talking to me again or I'm gonna fill your entire locker with Silly String or something," he teases. "Remember, I know your combination."

"Actually," I say, feeling sour, "I'm surprised you haven't already."

He laughs. I don't. And we get off the phone.

I roll over on my stomach, completely defeated, and smother my face in a pillow.

"Nooooo," I groan into the pillow. "No! No! No! No! No!"

David Wolfenbaker is going to ask Mackenzie Watts to homecoming. Not new-girl me, but new-girl Minnesota. Damn that stupid Ouija board.

No, you know what? Damn those stupid mushrooms!

I call Mackenzie immediately—I need to know if he's already asked her—but she's not home. I call Laura next and find out she's not home, either. Before calling Sarah, I can't help but wonder bitterly if everyone's just down the road again, having another awesome sans-Ericka get-together, but Mrs. Whitman tells me she's staying with a friend tonight. Which leaves only Kimi, the last person I want to call, but I can't stop myself as I punch in the numbers of her cell phone.

"Hello?" she answers.

"Hey, Kimi, it's Ericka."

"Oh my gosh!" she squeals. And then she whispers to someone in the background, "It's Ericka."

I was going to ask her if she knows where Mackenzie is, but then, when I hear her tell someone that it's me on the phone, I stop cold. I don't want to believe it, but I have to know.

"Are you having a party or something?" I ask, hoping not to sound desperate.

"No," she says really quickly. "No, not at all. Why? What's up?"

"Um, nothing," I answer, and then realize that I really don't know what to say. I don't want to tell Kimi that Wolf's going to ask Mackenzie to homecoming, but—

"I gotta go, Ericka," she says, cutting me off before I can even think through my game plan.

"Oh! Okay."

"Bye," she says abruptly and hangs up the phone, though not before I hear some giggling.

Great. This is just freaking awesome. Obviously, the Fab Four—who, let's face it, may not be so fab after all—are hanging out without me again. It's like, they act like they love me at school. I mean, they're always laughing at my jokes, and they've all called all week asking about Bandit. But weekends must be sacred or something, and five's a crowd. Whatever.

I lie back on my bed and stare up at the ceiling fan, trying to focus on just one blade as it goes around and around. I was just reading in *Seventeen* about how cliquey girls can stir up a lot of drama.

I grab my journal and thumb through the pages, taking a deep breath as the smell of the leather cover fills my nostrils. Lately, I've been writing a lot about Bandit. A bunch of those pages are smudged, but my last entry is especially hard to read:

Luke scared me today, the way he talked about standing up to his dad. I can't imagine living in a house like that…in fear like that…constantly worried, not so much about yourself, but for someone you love.

Depressed, I flip through to earlier in the journal and rediscover Project Ericka and my ten goals for this year. As I look over the list, I sink deeper into a funk. I'm making straight A's—but that's it. No period, no boyfriend, and the most pathetic back handspring you've ever seen.

The last thing I want to do right now is relive my phone call with Wolf and the subsequent conversation with Kimi, so I toss my journal back under my mattress and head outside. Might as well help my dad; at least it'll get my mind off my sucky "BFFs." In reality, my real best friend is at his house and has to build fence all day with his brothers. My other loyal friend is at the veterinarian's office hobbling around with a tube stuck in his chest. And actually, those are the only real friends I've got. Pathetic.

At the back door, I look over across the living room and see my momma staring out the front window like she's looking for someone, probably my dad. When she sees me, she can't help herself.

"Who was on the phone?" she asks, all high pitched and girly. *Ugh.*

"Just this boy from school," I say.

She makes a face, like she wants more juicy details.

"Spanish," I say and shrug my shoulders.

She smiles, as if part relieved, part disappointed to hear that it was just about schoolwork, and goes back to looking out the window. I can't help but grin to myself as I walk out back. My knack for bending the truth is a gift.

Outside, I see my dad coming back down from the barn and realize that I must've been inside a lot longer than I'd realized. He sees me and smiles.

"Sorry, Dad," I say, joining him in the yard.

"Not a problem, girl," he says. "They were all up at the barn waiting for me, so it didn't take that long today."

His cell phone rings and I roll my eyes. Cowboys in the old days wore guns on their belts; my dad whips his cell phone out of a leather case clipped to his belt, like his very own six-shooter. So not cool.

He's only on the phone a couple of seconds, though, before he puts his arm around me and leads me around front with a big, goofy smile. "Come here, Ricki Jo. I want to show you something."

I don't know what he's up to, but I walk with him around the side of the house. An old tree house perches by the plank fence and I remember how long I begged for it as a kid, and how infrequently I actually used it once my dad built it. It's funny how that seemed so important at the time. Makes me wonder what I'll think when I look back at my freshman year of high school. *Please feel just like this.* But I'm afraid high school is way more serious than a dumb tree house. *I should be building a reputation and making friends and getting French kissed!*

I shake my head. I shouldn't be thinking about kissing around my dad. That's gross.

At the front of the house, I'm surprised to see Momma and Ben out on the porch swing. Dad leads me over to Old Glory and I look up, thinking maybe he wants help taking her down from the flagpole. Instead, he just stands there and crosses his arms, his eyes fixed on the road, his lips twitching. I look around at everybody (obviously they're all lunatics) and start to feel like something's up. My momma won't stop smiling and my dad is now starting to chuckle. Ben is so fidgety, he finally climbs off the swing and cranes his head to look down the sidewalk to the driveway. Which is when I finally notice the minivan sitting there.

Wait. I know that minivan.

"SURPRISE!"

The door slides open and I see them. My friends. Mackenzie, Laura, Kimi, and Sarah all climb out of the van with balloons and flowers and backpacks and sleeping bags. I look from my momma to my dad, my mouth wide open in shock.

"What...?"

Momma joins Dad and me by the sidewalk and they both put their arms around my shoulders, leading me toward the driveway.

"We know things have been hard this week," she says, "with Bandit and everything. So I got your friend Mackenzie's phone number off the caller ID, and she helped us put together this surprise slumber party for you."

At this point we're by the van and Mackenzie throws herself at me and encloses me in a huge hug.

"Are you surprised, Ericka?" she asks, bouncing up and down on her toes.

"Yeah, are you shocked?" Kimi asks. "We were totally freaking out when you called me."

"Oh my gosh!" Sarah screams. "We were driving out of my driveway! We were so close!"

"She's totally shocked," Laura states. "You're totally in shock, aren't you?"

The girls hug me one by one, and I can't help but smile like mad. All of their voices are running together and pretty soon we're all holding hands and jumping up and down. I'm not sure why; it just seems like the perfect thing to do. A minute ago I felt like I had no friends, and now I feel like I'm on top of the world.

The bubbly as ever Mrs. Watts is nearby with her camera, snapping away.

"Get together, girls," Mrs. Watts shouts. "Smile!"

We scrunch together in front of the minivan and I become starkly aware of the red-and-black checkered flannel shirt I'm wearing. But at this point, who cares? The photos are snapped and my friends are here and this is the farm, doggone it. They're the ones who are out of style right now!

"Ricki Jo, why don't you show your friends inside?" my dad suggests.

As we gather up their things, I hear Momma mutter under her breath, "It's Ericka to her friends, Clark," which I think is really nice of her.

We're like a herd of donkeys, loaded down with all their gear. I don't know how long this surprise slumber party is going to last, but based on all the stuff they brought, they might as well be moving in.

Inside, the girls compliment our house, although I know it's nothing like what Mackenzie and Sarah are used to. Still, it's "cute," "cozy," and "really homey." I smile when I hear it, happy to have them here.

"Oh, wait," Mackenzie says suddenly. "I need to go say bye to my mom."

She says this, but then she just stands there.

"O-kay," I say.

"No, like, I *need* to *go* say bye *to my mom*."

"Oh!" Laura says. "Oh, okay. Me, too. Let's all go say thanks, you know? For driving us all the way out here."

I frown at the *all the way out here* part, but I follow them back outside. *Was the drive that bad last weekend, when they went to Sarah's?* I shake the thought from my head. They're here, at my house, surprising me and making me feel special. Forgive, forgive, forgive.

"Clark, could you help me with something in the back?" Mrs. Watts asks my dad when we're all back outside. "The girls brought something special for Ericka."

I look at Mackenzie, perplexed, but she just clasps her hands to her chest and smiles at me deviously. The other girls are wearing similar looks of anticipation, and even my family is inching closer.

Then my dad opens the back door of the minivan and I gasp.

"Bandit!"

I run over to the van and stand next to my dad, more surprised than I've ever been in my entire life. Bandit looks up at me and I start to cry.

"Oh, Bandit," I cry, leaning in and kissing him on the head. "You're home. You're home."

I turn to Mrs. Watts and hug her fiercely. And then it's a regular hug-fest, cry-fest, love-fest, with our very own paparazzo getting lots of candid shots, blinding us all with the constant flashing. My parents and Ben and I pose for a pic beside Bandit, and then we carefully lift him out of the van on his brand-new dog bed.

"That's a really nice doggie bed," I say to my dad as we carry him across the driveway.

"He's an outside dog, Ricki Jo," he reminds me sternly.

"Well, maybe he can be a garage dog for a few weeks, *Ericka*," my momma cuts in, really punching my name for my dad's benefit. He starts to protest, but she puts her foot down. "Just for a few weeks, Clark. Garage."

This is maybe the best Saturday of my life.

CHAPTER TWENTY-FIVE

"Okay, so what's the plan tonight?" Kimi asks.

We're all situated in the family room. Ben was not happy getting the boot, but my parents bribed him with glow-in-the-dark stars and they're spending the evening sticking them all over his bedroom ceiling.

"Don't ask me," I say. "I didn't even know y'all were coming over!"

I look at the girls, all sitting around drinking soda and eating popcorn, chips, and chocolate. I'm having the best time, and it's only seven o'clock!

"Wait, doesn't Luke Foster live by you?" Laura asks.

All the girls die laughing and she turns bright red.

"Ooh!" Kimi squeals. "Why do you want to know? Thinking of some late-night sneak-out making out?"

Laura screams and puts her head in her pillow, completely covering her face as her curly auburn hair falls forward. Wow. I didn't know she liked Luke *that* much. And I don't want to say anything, but I don't think he likes her like that.

"Ericka?" Kimi says, waving her hand in my face. "Earth to Ericka."

I blush a little and we all giggle.

"So, seriously, E," Kimi continues, absentmindedly smoothing her jet-black bob. "What's the deal with sneaking out? Can you call Luke and his brothers? Will they be home? What time do your parents go to bed?"

"Sneaking out?" I ask.

I'm not a total dork, okay? But I don't want to get in trouble—get grounded, miss homecoming, lose any chance of getting at least one slow dance with Wolf. And, I don't know. It'd be one thing to explain sneaking out after Luke's dad broke his leg. I mean, my folks would've been mad, but they probably would've understood. But risking it so that Laura can make out with Luke? Ugh… I'm feeling that same nausea I had when Mackenzie asked for my homework—like I want to say no but have no idea how.

A knock at the door saves me, and Momma peeks in. "Ericka? I've got some frozen pizzas in the kitchen if y'all get hungry, and there's lots of Cokes, okay?"

"Thanks, Momma," I say, giving her an extra big smile for remembering to call me Ericka. Unfortunately, this special smile gives her a false sense of lovey-dovey-ness and she blows me a kiss before shutting the door again.

When I turn back to the group, expecting them to tease me, I see Mackenzie bent over to get something out of her bag.

"Mackenzie!" I scream, diverting my embarrassment. "Crack kills!"

The other girls look and we all start laughing. Mackenzie looks up and sees Sarah pointing at her butt. She flushes bright red and hikes up her jeans. Lucky for me, the conversation turns from sneaking out to skinny jeans and long tank tops and the amount of butt cracks teachers see at school, even with the dress code.

"I'm surprised we don't wear uniforms," Kimi says.

"I'm glad we don't," Laura says.

"Whatever," Kimi says, throwing a Hershey's Kiss at Laura. "Uniforms can be very naughty. Drives the boys wild."

This declaration is followed by lots of squealing and laughing. Kimi pops a Starburst in her mouth, wrapper and all, and then sucks her cheeks in and rolls her eyes in deep concentration before proudly producing the wet wrapper on the tip of her tongue. I'm pretty sure Kimi is the kind of girl my momma calls "fast." I make a mental note to get her talking about sex later. That girl's a wealth of information.

"So," Laura says, refusing to let me relax and enjoy myself. "This'll be so much fun. We'll watch the movies Mrs. Winstead got us and then, once everybody's asleep, we'll sneak over to the Fosters'. Oh my gosh, it's gonna be so scary!"

"Ooh!" they all scream.

They don't know the half of it. It's not like I haven't sneaked out before, but I've always had Bandit. And it's going to be the thumbnail kind of moon today, not God's spotlight. And without Bandit... I think about the coyotes I hear sometimes at night. And about the rest of the Gumbels' dogs, although they're supposed to be chained up now.

"Hey," Kimi says, snapping her fingers in front of my face. "God, Ericka, seriously. You zone out more than anyone I've ever met. So, it's a plan? Can you hook Laura up with Luke?"

"I can try," I say, working like crazy to think of a way to keep from sneaking out tonight without them thinking I'm a wuss. "But, um... why wait 'til tonight?"

"Huh?" Laura asks.

"I mean, they usually play basketball on Saturday nights before they go out. If we go on over there now, we'll probably catch 'em before they go."

"Oh! Yes!" Kimi claps, bouncing up on her heels. "His older brother Paul is so cute. Let's go before he meets some floozy at The Square! Let's go!"

With the proper amount of giggling, we get ready. Getting ready for barnyard basketball shouldn't require much effort, but in our case, it takes us twenty minutes to squeeze into jeans and cute tops. I go back to my bedroom and zip up a fitted sweatshirt with a cool design on the back over a PCHS T-shirt, then pull my thick, dark blond hair up into a ponytail. Done. When I get back to the family room, I see that the other girls are wearing tank tops, putting on mascara and lip gloss, and fluffing their loose hairstyles. The thought enters my mind to change, but I don't want to get cold, and I don't see any point in dressing up for the Fosters.

We pop into the garage because I, of course, want to bring Bandit along. But when he lifts his head up from his posh new doggie bed, I can tell that he doesn't quite have it in him yet. It really is a long walk for somebody who's got a tube running through his chest. And anyway, Luke's dog, Bessie, would probably overexcite him. So my friends and I pet Bandit and offer him a little puppy love before sashaying across the backyard.

Once we're outside and away from my parents' watchful eyes, I ask Mackenzie if I can borrow her lip gloss. I smack the strawberry goodness over my lips and walk through the grass with my pack of fabulous friends as if I'm walking on clouds. At the first field, I unhook the electric fence to let the girls pass, and we make our way over to the Fosters'.

"Oh my gosh, there's so much cow poop!" Kimi screams.

We all laugh and dodge cow pies and thistles, some of the girls wishing they'd taken my advice about wearing tennis shoes instead of flip-flops.

"*Seventeen* won't help you out here," I tease.

"Yeah, that should be your first article for the school paper." Mackenzie giggles. " 'What to Wear for a Day on the Farm.' "

"Actually," Kimi corrects her, "what to wear for a *date* on the farm. 'Cause that's the only reason I'm out here. To straight hook up!"

We all die laughing again, especially since we know that Kimi is absolutely serious.

I usually make it over to Luke's place a lot quicker, but the girls are really slowing things down. By the time we get to the barn, I figure the guys will stop playing soon for lack of light. The sun is setting and it's chilly up here on the hill.

"Wow, this is really gorgeous," I hear Mackenzie whisper.

I turn, surprised, and watch her survey the land. She's right. The sun flicks the last of its rays across the rolling hills like highlights, marking my farm with golden kisses. I love the way it makes the pond's surface shimmer and how the shadows are even more accentuated. I love that she thinks something of mine is beautiful.

"Hey, boys!" Kimi yells obnoxiously. Why she thought a denim miniskirt was appropriate is beyond me, but she turns her hips on supershake and heads straight for the testosterone. Sarah follows, somehow slipping her iPhone into the tight front pocket of her skinny jeans, and Laura is right on their heels, eager to get to Luke.

"You comin'?" I ask Mackenzie.

"How much of this is yours?" she asks, rubbing her arms with her hands to keep warm.

I smile and step beside her, pointing out our fields. I show her the property lines, the ponds, which fields are for hay and which are for tobacco. I motion wide, waving my arms over our land like a proud mother, the memories sweeping through my mind.

Swept up in the moment, I start blabbing. "I fell off that shed when my dad had us help him reroof it when I was nine. One time, up by that patch of woods, I found a baby fawn, must've just been born. And over there by the creek, that's the place I go to think. And all the water, well, some ponds are for fun and some are for work. Like, for instance, those over that hill are for irrigation, but that one's where we go fishing. And even though Luke and his brothers love frog gigging, I can't really bring myself to actually stab one, so I usually just hold the flashlight. My uncle's farm is right by ours so we ride four-wheelers over there all the time and my aunt still makes my grandma's famous peanut butter cookies when we visit. And you should see Bandit! He's always chasing rabbits out of their holes and pestering the cattle. It's hilarious 'cause they're, like, eight times his size, but he really gets 'em jumpy."

The sun hits Mackenzie's face, then slips down just a smidge so that I gasp. The light bounces off her eyes, blue like Caribbean water, and her freckles are like little stars. Her small mouth is turned down in a pout and I suddenly realize I've been talking nonstop.

"Oh my gosh, I'm probably boring you to death," I say.

"No!" she says, turning to me and grabbing my arm. "Not at all. Sometimes I still get a little homesick, I guess."

I nod and shove my hands into my pockets. It's getting a bit chilly.

"And, I don't know," she continues. "I guess I'm a little jealous."

This is where I almost knock myself unconscious, tapping at my head, trying to regain my hearing. I thought she said she was jealous of me, but recognizing the absurdity of such an idea, I realize that I must suddenly be stone deaf.

"Ericka," she says, laughing openly and grabbing my hand before I can give myself another knock. "I'm serious! I'd love to have all this. I mean, I'd probably trade at least one cow in for a pony, but it'd be nice to have a place to go to be alone. I mean, when we finally got up here, I stood in this spot and did a complete circle...and I didn't see one other house but yours. That's incredible! It's like your kingdom or something!"

I hear her, but don't. I mean, I love the farm, but I'd give anything to be as close to town as she is—to be able to walk down to the movies or over to other friends' houses. And she has a pool! Who'd trade a pool for a pond?

"The grass is always greener," I say.

She shrugs and we shimmy down the steep slope to where Kimi and the girls have totally disrupted a Saturday-night ball game. Luke raises his arms in an exasperated gesture, and the other guys look pretty peeved as well.

Kimi screams, "Granny shot!" and swings the ball down between her legs, bending over and giving Luke a full view of her cash and prizes. He looks like he just saw his grandma naked and covers his eyes, then stalks toward me like an angry bull.

"Listen, we've got about twenty minutes left of poor light, and our cousins are up by two," he starts yelling at me before I'm even all the way down the slope. "You know you're always welcome, but look! We start at seven, it's almost eight now, and we've still got ten minutes on the clock. Everybody wants to go out later, so they're gonna call the game pretty soon. Your girl's killin' me!"

Kimi has now cajoled Luke's older brother Paul into showing her how to shoot a free throw, complete with him wrapping his arms around hers to take aim. Her eyes are on his neck when she tosses it in the air, nowhere near the hoop.

"That's it!" Luke yells, rebounding the ball in a huff. "Paul, you're out. Ricki Jo, play for Paul. You two go get a room or something, damnit."

Kimi sticks her tongue out at Luke, but obviously loves his idea. She threads her arm around Paul's skinny waist and they stumble all over each other making their way off the court.

"Good luck, Ericka!" she hollers back to me before disappearing behind the barn. I would wish her the same, but it doesn't look like she needs it.

"Our ball," Luke demands, and the other boys are

back on the dirt court, ready to play. I look at Mackenzie and she gives me a thumbs-up as she goes over to sit on the grass by Laura and Sarah. I step up to Luke's shortest cousin, who is still five inches taller than I am, and get into the game. Luke will kill me if I screw up, and I don't want to make him even angrier...although secretly, I'm glad he's in a bad mood. I know Laura likes him and I know she's my friend, but to tell the truth, I just don't think they're right for each other.

Reading Luke's cue, I set a pick for him and then move to the top of the key, knowing he'll feed it back out to me once he drives. As I line up a three pointer from my sugar spot, I grin. *Poor Laura. Luke's just not in the mood for lovey-dovey.*

"Seriously, Ericka, you're really good," Mackenzie gushes. Her breath feels weird on my eyeball, which she has pried open. I would say thanks, but I'm too scared to move a muscle as long as that eyeliner is stabbing at my inner lower lid.

"I was actually surprised," Sarah says from the couch, her gymnast frame folded up cross-legged in front of Kimi. "You held your own with those guys and they're all, like, twice your size."

"I seriously don't know why you even cheer," Kimi says around the bobby pins stuck in her mouth. She's squatting, her fingers working through Sarah's limp brown hair, and frowning. "I mean, I cheer for Girls' Varsity, so

I'm at all their games, and they could actually use a guard like you. Seriously."

I really don't want to move my face since Mackenzie is jabbing at me like crazy with that eye pencil, but I'm pretty sure Kimi just gave me a real compliment and, against my better judgment, I blink.

"Careful!" Mackenzie exclaims.

"But I guess in reality, basketball players are all butch, and cheerleading will get you hotter boyfriends," Kimi reasons.

Ahh, that's more like it.

"Whatever, Kimi," Mackenzie says, smudging the liner on my outer lid with her thumb. "Guys dig athletes."

"Yeah," Laura says, looking up from her toes, which she's painting Cherry Berry Red. "Guys *do* love athletes. Like, for instance, you and Luke have a really weird connection, right? I mean, on the court. Like you can read each other's minds or something."

"Ooh, jealous much?" Sarah asks, wincing a little as Kimi tries to re-create a hairstyle she found on Vogue.com. Her hair is actually starting to look like the Great Wall of China. Kimi read that this style is "polished enough for work," or, in our case, school, "but sexy enough for a date"—although I'm not sure she's got the hang of it just yet. We had to open the windows when she brought out her second can of hair spray.

"I'm not jealous," Laura snaps back. "I mean, why would I be jealous? Ericka, should I be jealous?"

"Of me?" I ask as Mackenzie sharpens her eye pencil. "Of course not. He's like my brother."

"See, case closed," Laura says, although she's been in a really snotty mood ever since we got back.

Somehow, this seems to be my opportunity. The other girls know I think Wolf is cute (although they don't know just how much I like him, seeing as how I thought the rules were that I had to name four other different guys, too), but Mackenzie didn't hear my top five because she was getting the pizza. I really need to let her know how desperately in love I am with Wolf before he asks her to homecoming. Then, when he does ask, she'll want to say no out of loyalty to me.

"I mean, just like I don't need to be jealous of you and Wolf, right, Laura?" I say, trying to sound calm and confident, although my heart is in my throat as I brace myself for their reaction.

Which is, of course, collective screaming.

"I knew it!" Kimi yells, standing up and gesticulating with her hairbrush. "The way you two flirt at the lockers, and how you're always mad at each other for no reason! I mean, all week he's been following you around like a puppy dog! I knew it!"

Oh! I only admitted to liking Wolf. Is Kimi saying that he likes me, too? My stomach flips. Oh my gosh! Does Wolf like me, too?

"So, wait," Mackenzie says, a frown wrinkling her forehead, eyes, and mouth. *Wow. She's even going to be pretty when she's old.* "So, like, you and Wolf are going together in secret?"

"Oh my gosh!" I squeal. "I wish! No! Not at all!"

She sits back on her heels, pensive.

"It's just that, at your party, you were upstairs for my top five. And I didn't know you guys very well yet, and I was nervous to admit it, but"—I gulp—"I really, really, really like him. A lot."

Kimi flops back onto the couch and she and Sarah hold hands and kick their feet, screaming like banshees. It's so clear to me why they're cheerleaders. Laura, too, is grinning from ear to ear, looking relieved by my confession. But Mackenzie still seems to be in a state of shock.

"But you know I like him, too," she says. "I had him on my list."

"Technically," Sarah says, "you all had him on your list."

"Well, I named him for all five spots! So, technically, I like him more!" Mackenzie cries, near tears as she turns back to me. "And what about my brother? He really likes you, and I thought you liked him."

"I *do* like Mark," I say, surprised by her intensity. "As a friend. He's really nice and he's cute, too. I just...I don't know, I really like Wolf. I have since the first day of school."

"No, you can't like him as much as I do. I'm sorry," she says, standing up.

"But you said he's a scumbag," I say, standing up, too.

"Just because I was trying to make you feel better!"

We stand face-to-face, neither wanting to cave and neither wanting to fight and both crushing on the same boy. My brain is racing, but I can't think of anything to say.

"Ericka, you're my best friend, right?" she finally says, her voice level.

"Yeah," I say. I grab her hands. "That's why I—"

"New Girls BFFs," she goes on, "would never fight over a boy."

I exhale, relieved. "Totally. I'm so glad you said that."

"Good," she says, squeezing my hands. "Then out of loyalty to me, you'll back off since you know I'm new and don't know that many people and really only like this one boy. Right?"

Tears flood her blue eyes again and I'm totally taken off guard. I'm new, too. And she could have a million boys. And I love him…and I hate him sometimes…but only because I love him so much.

"Right, Ericka?" she asks again.

I want to rewind the last four minutes and abort this mission. My plan to leverage our friendship to garner a homecoming date with Wolf is backfiring, and I suddenly feel nauseous. Again.

I give a slight nod—a tiny, minuscule, baby nod— and she hugs me tightly around the neck, all butterflies and happy places. Over her shoulder, I see Sarah look at Kimi and roll her eyes, which kind of makes me feel like she has my back. Still squeezing me, Mackenzie bounces and says "thank you" over and over, but I really am starting to feel sick.

On autopilot, I sink back down to the floor, intensely grossed out by the fact that slumber parties, for me, seem to be so closely related to vomit. I grab a bottle of water and take a few sips, my head spinning. Wolf is going to ask Mackenzie to the dance and she's definitely going to say yes. And just look at her—he's going to fall in love with her, no question.

"Okay, look past my shoulder," Mackenzie says brightly, settling in front of me with her mascara, her tears already a thing of the past. I look at the wand and then up at her. She falters, then swallows hard.

"It's waterproof," she says quietly.

I nod and look over her shoulder, letting my eyes blur.

CHAPTER TWENTY-SIX

"So, Sarah, truth or dare?" Kimi asks.

As the night's gone by, I've resigned myself to the Mrs. Mackenzie Wolfenbaker destiny. As much as I hate it, I'm comforted by the fact that at least Wolf will be going to homecoming with my friend and not that mystery hussy he made out with at the movies.

"Truth," Sarah answers.

Smart girl. Laura chose dare and Kimi made her lick between her own toes. Disturbing.

"Okay," Kimi says, pouting. "This is getting boring. If you're all gonna keep saying truth I'm not playing anymore."

She's right. It's midnight and nobody wants to admit it, but we're all getting a little sleepy.

"I think I'm gonna get another Coke," I say, getting up from our circle on the floor. "I need my second wind."

"Bring a couple," Kimi orders. "And some cups, too."

"Yes, ma'am," I say, doing a little curtsy. She rolls her eyes and the other girls giggle.

I half skip, half drag myself from the family room to the kitchen. The house is eerily still, and it feels weird. With all the lights on inside, the windows in the breakfast nook are like mirrors and I feel creepy thinking that somebody could be looking in and I wouldn't have a clue. Of course, the alternative is turning the lights off, but walking around in the dark is even creepier. Scaredy-cat that I am, I find myself getting cold chills and run into the kitchen, sliding on my sock feet in front of the fridge. I grab a two-liter of cold Coke and five Solo cups from the counter, plus a whole carton of Double Stuf Oreos; then, I hit the lights as I hightail it back to the family room.

"Got it," I tell the girls, breathless, and drop the goods down on our blankets.

"Perfect," Kimi says. She unstacks the five cups and pours a little bit of Coke into each one. "Let's play a real game."

Yes! I love games. I dominate board games, like Monopoly and Clue. And I'm pretty stellar at charades if I do say so myself. And seriously, I'm still small enough to totally destroy everyone at hide and seek. Lame? Or kind of awesome? You decide.

"First, everybody take off all your clothes."

My jaw unhinges. *Take our clothes off? Why? What kind of sick game are we playing here?*

"Seriously, let's go," Kimi says, standing up and dropping her shorts. "We're going to streak."

I look around the group of girls and see that everyone looks just as baffled as I do, which is comforting.

"We're gonna do naked runs," Kimi repeats, exasperated. "Two people leave from this door and run through the kitchen, all the way down Ericka's hallway, and touch the wall beside her parents' bedroom. The first person back wins, and the loser has to drink."

So many bells go off in my head during Kimi's recital of the official rules of this made-up-on-the-spot game that I don't know what to address first. The fact that I don't want anyone to see me naked? Especially not a groggy dad or little brother in the event that we make too much noise. Or the fact that we have to drink? And drink what?

"Drink what?" Laura asks, reading at least one part of my mind.

"Sarah, if you please," Kimi says, giggling and pulling her shirt off over her head.

Sarah lifts up one of our couch cushions and pulls out a fifth of Maker's Mark. A fifth of bourbon from the Winstead family room sofa!

"What the—"

"Got it from Paul Foster earlier," Kimi explains mischievously. "Now let's go, ladies. Chop, chop!"

Sarah and Kimi are already in their underwear. I look over at Mackenzie, who starts unbuttoning her pajama top with an "if you can't beat 'em, join 'em" type of shrug. Laura peels her pajamas off in a rapid motion, like ripping off a Band-Aid. I sigh heavily and do the same, embarrassed by my flowery training bra but glad to be wearing it.

We stand there in a circle, looking at Kimi for further instructions.

"Everything," she says.

But this time, nobody budges.

"Ugh," Kimi groans, obviously annoyed with us. "Okay, I'll turn the lights out. Our eyes should get used to the dark, anyway, for the runs."

She goes over to the door and hits the light switch. The room goes pitch-black and all sorts of weird colors stream out in front of me as my eyes try to adjust. It's completely silent and I haven't moved an inch. Then I hear the rustling of clothes. The other girls are actually going through with it! Do or die. I sigh again, unclasp my bra, and slip out of my undies.

"Sarah and Laura, you're first," Kimi says from somewhere in front of me.

I see a human form coming toward me, arms outstretched. Assuming that form to be naked, I duck and back up so as not to get groped by one of my zombie friends, only to back my bare heinie into someone else.

"Ahh!" Mackenzie screams.

"Ahh!" I scream right back.

Ohmygosh, ohmygosh, ohmygosh. My eyes are adjusting, and I see that all five of us are jumping up and down and screaming. We would usually hug or fall into some kind of laughing pileup in this kind of situation, but in our current state, we instead sort of cover our chests with one forearm and slap at the air in front of us with the other. Then we all start shushing one another, terribly afraid of waking up anyone else in the house.

Kimi opens the door to the family room and we peek out. No sign of human life in the kitchen. I spooked myself in there only a few minutes ago, and now I'm about to run headlong into this very same nightmare naked. *What is wrong with me?*

"Go!" Kimi whispers loudly.

Sarah and Laura take off. I can't really see them but I know their challenges: One, don't wake anybody up. Two, don't run into the walls or the furniture. Three, don't touch the person running directly next to you—at all.

"Oh my gosh, this is so crazy!" I whisper to Mackenzie and Kimi.

"I know!" they both whisper back to me.

Sarah breezes into the family room, with Laura a couple of paces behind. As soon as they're safely inside, Kimi shuts the door and we all start laughing hysterically, wheezing from trying to keep quiet. I can't see much, just shadowy figures, but even if the lights were on, my eyes are too blurry. I can't catch my breath, I'm laughing so hard, and I keep wiping at the tears in my eyes. This is actually fun. I thought it would be weird, but it's really fun and wild and totally reckless.

Why, hello there, second wind!

"Okay, Laura, you drink," Kimi whispers. "Mackenzie and Ericka, let's go!"

Mackenzie and I line up at the door and I'm glad to have the home court advantage. When Kimi gives us the signal, we take off down the hall. I'd say that in a normal running match, Mackenzie would leave me in her dust; but tonight, I call upon all the inner strength I've ever possessed. I've got more at stake here. I pass the kitchen counter, hearing our bare feet slapping on the hardwood floor. We're neck and neck. But around the corner, I squeeze into the hallway first and spread my arms out so that she can't pass, barely grazing the old wallpaper as I go. At the end, I break out into a full-body sweat at the thought of being right outside the bedrooms of both my parents and my little brother, so I throw it into turbo and straight-up *fly* back toward the family room. I am on a mission. I would truly die on the spot if anyone in my family ever saw me naked.

Mackenzie is on my tail, but I barely make it back through the family room door first. Bent over and jubilant, I crash onto the blankets on the floor and try to catch my breath while the other girls giggle uncontrollably. I won! My chest is heaving and my smile is wide.

And then—

The lights are on. My first reaction is the lack of one. I'm too stunned. One second later, though, I hit the deck, pulling at the blankets below me and shielding my eyes.

"I need to find my iPhone," Sarah explains from beside the door. When the lights came on Mackenzie and Laura dove under the blankets closest to them as well, but Sarah takes her time getting back into her bra and panties and I realize how very different our bodies are. Kimi jiggles back into her own bra and shimmies into a thong (loads of coverage there), and then leans over the couch to help Sarah look for her phone. I don't stare or anything, but I see how different her body is as well. And it's not just our chests; it's the way Sarah's back muscles jut out, and the surprisingly pudgy stomach that Kimi really hides well.

"Mackenzie, you guys, stand up," Sarah demands, pulling at the covers. "Maybe it's underneath here."

Mackenzie and Laura obey, abandoning the safety of the blankets and diving for their own bras and panties. They both look totally awkward, and Laura sort of crosses her legs like celebrities do on the red carpet while she shakes her panties out of her shorts. Only a couple of inches taller than I am, she is meatier, compact, solid. Mackenzie crosses her arms as if she's cold, then turns around to snap her bra back in place.

I squirm, trying not to look at any of them, but, well, looking.

"Ericka, get up," Sarah says again.

"Can't somebody just call your phone?" I say, hunched over with the tiniest corner of a blanket covering me.

"Come! On!" Kimi yells and jerks the blanket away.

I scurry up and kind of turn away, trying to be as

collected as the others, but totally not succeeding. We all have different body types, but at least they sort of look like women. I gulp hard and figure I'm further behind than I ever imagined.

To tell the truth, I thought everyone would tease me — point at my mosquito-bite boobs or count my ribs or make fun of my bony butt. Obviously I'm not yet a woman. But no. Instead of making fun of me, everybody sat down and started talking about all the awkward body changes that come along with growing up. Like, what things felt like and how it happened.

"I started my period in the fourth grade," Sarah admits, shoveling popcorn into her mouth like it's her job. "I freaked the frick out! Mrs. Janson sent me to the nurse, and I literally thought I was dying!"

I giggle, remembering the fourth grade and the one thing I was freaking out about: retainers.

"I didn't start 'til last spring," Laura says, which actually makes me feel a little better.

We're sitting in a circle in the family room again, passing around the bourbon bottle and Coca-Cola. The Solo cups are a thing of the past. If you can run naked together, you can drink from the same bottles.

"So, obviously I have the biggest boobs," Kimi says as she takes another nip of bourbon. "It's not all it's cracked up to be, though. Like, in cheerleading, I have to wear two sports bras."

"Yeah, but you're only a C-cup," Sarah says. "They just look huge 'cause you've got a short torso. I mean, I'm almost a C-cup, too, but I'm so tall."

"Almost," Kimi points out.

I grin at the dynamic of their friendship.

"But I don't think all guys care about boobs," Laura speaks up next to me.

"You show me a boy who doesn't care about boobs and I'll show you a flying cow," Kimi says with a snort.

I giggle and pass the bourbon bottle. I can smell the sweetness of the alcohol as it whiffs past me. I've never been interested in drinking, probably because of all the stuff with Luke and because my folks hate it, but I feel tempted at this moment. I don't know; I feel safe right now, in my house, with my best friends, and everybody seems to be taking really tiny sips. I watch the bottle circle and chuckle as they make funny faces with each drink. We've been passing the booze and spilling our guts for the past twenty minutes and hardly any of it is even gone!

"Come on, Ericka," Mackenzie says. She loops her arm through mine and makes a silly face. "Take a little drinkity-drink."

We all giggle and I hold the bottle up to my nose.

What the hell.

I take a deep breath and barely tip it back, just to get a little taste and see what all the hoopla's about.

It burns! All the way down. I start huffing, like when

you blow on a fogged window, to cool my mouth. It's like drinking fire!

"The Coke," I breathe like a dragon. "Pass me the Coke!"

Mackenzie passes me the Coke and everyone cracks up. Kimi, of course, does a hilarious impression, like I'm some kind of parched survivor on a deserted island. I laugh so hard that I snort, which makes me blow Coke through my nose.

"Ahh!" I scream. "It burns!"

We fall over in one another's laps. Nobody can stop the laughing and everyone's dabbing at their tears, none of us eager to ruin our makeovers.

Then Sarah's phone beeps and she squeals like a maniac, kicking her feet in the air.

"Jimmy's here!"

I look up at her in shock.

"Here? Like, on the front porch?" I ask, totally imagining how long I'll be grounded if my dad sees him.

"No, they're parked down at the Fosters'," she whispers urgently. We all have our heads together in the middle of the room. "They wanna know where we can meet 'em."

I whisper and giggle with my friends, my heart racing.

It looks like we'll be sneaking out after all.

And at this point, I'm okay with that.

CHAPTER
TWENTY-SEVEN

"I guess we should go up to the side barn," I say, my breath clouding the air in front of me. "At least there's a security light there, and we can get to it from the road. I don't think any of us want to go trekking through the cow pastures in the middle of the night, do we?"

"Ew," Kimi replies, her nose crinkling.

We head down the driveway, trying to keep quiet as the gravel slips and crunches beneath our feet. My heart is beating wildly, both because I'm really sneaking out for the first time and because I finally feel like I fit in. Once we're on the road, our flip-flops flap against the blacktop in a way that would be totally normal in the middle of the day but sounds eerie this late at night. Once day gives way to night, everything changes. Even the crickets sound menacing.

"Wow," Mackenzie breathes, "it feels like we're in a movie or something."

The other girls nod and I watch their faces. When I try to put myself in their places, I realize how beautiful the elm and maple trees are, draping over the small country road. I admire the stone fences that line our boundaries, fences built by our Irish ancestors generations before I was even a thought in God's mind — pretty cool, even if they are crumbling in a few places.

I smile to myself and take a deep breath of the crisp country air, feeling content.

Right before the Gumbels' house we hop a small stone fence and walk up to the barn. I miss Bandit, but I'm glad those crazy dogs aren't out. It's scary enough out here at one in the morning without a pack of Cujos running around.

I spin the combination and slide the big barn door open. We walk inside and the smell of straw hits us hard. Dad keeps the hay in here nowadays, but the scent of cured tobacco still lingers. I take a big breath, then notice the other girls doing the same, filling our lungs with past and present. There is a buzz in the air.

Mackenzie throws a blanket down on the ground and we huddle together to wait for the boys. Kimi and Sarah are giggling like crazy, texting Jimmy and Paul on their phones. Mackenzie fishes through her bag while I daydream, thinking about "sneaking out" and my parents and whether or not this would count if push were to come to shove. Technically, I'm still on our property.

"Laura, jump up on that hay," Mackenzie says. "I want to take your picture."

Laura looks at me and rolls her eyes. Mackenzie is just as bad as her mother. The three of us get up and walk deeper into the barn. Laura situates herself on a square bale of hay and looks at Mackenzie, waiting for further instructions as if she's done this before.

"Now, sort of lie back," Mackenzie instructs. "Yeah! Like that! Hold it."

The flash goes off brightly in the barn and Laura quickly shields her eyes. I giggle and step behind Mackenzie to see the shot.

"Oh, wow," I say. With the makeovers from earlier and the backdrop of the barn, this picture is really cool. Like, I could totally see it in a *Seventeen* Halloween special issue or something. "You look awesome."

"Do another without smiling," Mackenzie commands.

A mini photo shoot begins. I love watching Mackenzie zoom in and out, love hearing her give Laura directions as she walks around her muse. Honestly, she has a real knack for photography. The way she positions Laura is fascinating. I mean, I would've just put her on the hay and said, "Cheese." But Mackenzie makes it more artistic, sometimes shifting the camera so that Laura is off-center, and making the blurry shots look purposeful.

"I didn't realize you were a photographer," I say to Mackenzie, kneeling down with her as she shoots Laura from below.

Mackenzie snaps the shot and looks at me. "I'm not."

"You should be, then," I say. "These are incredible."

Mackenzie shrugs and stands up, brushing the straw from her knees. "You're next."

I stare. "Me?"

"Yeah," she says, "but over by that tractor."

By the time she finishes her sentence, she's already walking over to the small red tractor. She walks around it, pensive, while I look at Laura in bewilderment. Laura rolls off the hay and stands up, brushing off her butt.

"She doesn't take no for an answer," she says, and drags me over to Mackenzie.

I look back at Kimi and Sarah, wishing one of them would take a turn instead. But they're so excited over the prospect of making out (and who could blame them?) that we are the furthest things from their minds as their busy little thumbs race across the keypads of their cell phones.

"I don't know how," I mumble.

"Don't know how to what?" Mackenzie asks, smiling. "Take a picture?" She pats the big back tire of the tractor, motioning for me to take her place.

"Model," I answer, moving over to her.

"It's easy," she says. "Here, let's just…"

Her words trail off as she goes to work. Before I know it, my T-shirt is twisted around and pulled tightly against my torso, held in a knot at my back by her ponytail holder. I pull at it self-consciously, but she keeps me from covering my now exposed midriff. She bites her lip and looks at my jeans.

"Are these old?" she asks.

I nod, embarrassed.

"Perfect!" she exclaims, bending down on one knee and putting her finger in the hole on my left thigh. I cringe, wishing I would've just spent the money at Guess, but seventy-five dollars seemed like so much for a pair of pants I would just grow out of. Oh, god, I sound like my mother—

And then, I hear the rip. Looking down, I gape at the hole, which is now the size of a half-dollar, and she keeps clawing at it, making it even more frayed.

"Sweet," Laura quips, standing nearby.

Mackenzie pops up and digs into her pocket, producing lip gloss and slapping it on my mouth. For the first time in my life, I know what a mannequin feels like.

Laura pipes up, "Now you know what a model feels like."

Hmmm . . . same thing?

Mackenzie smiles as she fluffs and teases my hair. She lifts her camera and snaps a close shot. "Fierce," she says, looking at the pic on her digital screen. "Let's get you up on the tractor."

I don't move as gracefully as Laura, but the two of them patiently direct and position me, oohing and aahing at a few of the shots. I start to loosen up as I follow Mackenzie's direction. This is fun and, I don't know, I feel . . . pretty.

"I heard there's a party up in here!"

My head snaps over to the barn door fast as lightning.

I know that voice, and a chill runs all the way up my spine and through my ears. I shudder as his shadow runs long across the barn floor and across my head, which is hanging upside down over the hood of a tractor. My mouth fights gravity and opens wide in shock. David Wolfenbaker is standing in my barn.

"Wolf!" Mackenzie squeals, standing up instantly and bounding over to him. She looks like it's Christmas morning. "What in the world are you doing here?"

"I saw Jimmy at The Square and rode out with him," Wolf says, oozing confidence as he looks down at her. She twirls a lock of perfect blond hair and cocks out one hip, oozing confidence right back.

The other girls hop up, too, as the guys trickle in, and I'm off the tractor before you can say "redneck." Paul is there, looking like he won the lottery as Kimi rubs herself all over him in a big "hug." I personally know that he hasn't had a lot of luck with the ladies over the years, so I'm glad for both of them. Jimmy James and Sarah are in a deep lip-lock as soon as their bodies collide and I'm guessing there won't be much in the way of conversation with either couple this evening.

"Ever feel like a third wheel?" Laura asks me, grinning.

"Yeah, I guess we should have been a little more diligent in the text-a-date department," I joke as I reach around my back, tugging fiercely at the knot in my shirt.

And then Luke walks in.

"Oh my gosh," Laura breathes.

His frame is impressive in the doorway, his long shadow just one of many filtering through the barn, and his boyish smile is a great substitute for the absent moon. In fact, he looks cute tonight, really cute, yet there's nothing different about him. I don't know; same V-neck, same Levi's, same leather bracelet, but somehow I don't feel like I'm looking at a guy I've known my whole life.

As he ambles toward us, though, Laura tenses up and I feel bad that he's walking straight for me, as if she doesn't even exist.

"Dang, looks like we've got a bunch of America's Next Top Models in here," Wolf says, stepping in front of Luke and leading Mackenzie over to where Laura and I stand.

I shake my head and laugh at myself. It's Luke, the same old Luke, and I figure I'm just super glad to see him, knowing this isn't really his scene. It's always nice to have another ally when Wolf is around.

"Yeah, we all did makeovers," Mackenzie says. She bats her mile-long lashes and waits for a compliment, but Wolf is staring at me. I mean, really staring. I blush under his steady gaze and avert my eyes. It's one thing to be looked at, but another to be examined. Mackenzie puts herself back in his line of vision by stepping next to me and draping her arm around my shoulders.

"Doesn't Ericka especially look gorgeous?" she says, squeezing me.

"She definitely looks... different," Wolf says.

I make a face at him. "It's really me," I joke drily, then

walk past them toward the blanket, where Luke is still standing.

"Untie this," I hiss, my back to him and my arms crossed over my stomach.

"Why you got it all hooched up like this, anyway?" he teases, fumbling with the knot behind me.

"Mackenzie did it," I whisper back.

"Oh, *Mackenzie did it.*"

"Ugh! Just shut up and untie me," I snap back at him. He chuckles and I know he's taking his sweet time, really enjoying my awkwardness.

The others walk over and take seats on the blanket, Laura looking at Luke and me through narrowed eyes and Mackenzie sitting so close to Wolf that I have to fight the urge to gag out loud. When I finally feel my shirt loosen, I jerk it down quickly and sit, grabbing Mackenzie's ponytail holder from Luke and using it to pull back my big, wild hair. I don't have a mirror, but when Mackenzie teased it she said she was going for "Zombie Glam," which cannot be a good thing.

Luke sits down next to me, flips his blond hair off of his forehead a little, and drapes one arm over his knee, a thoughtful look on his face. "I think that's the first time I've ever seen you in makeup," he says, his eyes twinkling. His smile is easy, sincere. Boy, am I glad he showed up.

"Yeah, we did this smoky-eye thing from *Seventeen.* Intense, right? My dad would kill me."

He chuckles. "He sure would."

"But you look great in makeup," Laura says loudly, almost hysterically, leaning toward us to get in the conversation. "I mean, you could totally be a model."

"Yeah, if she grew a foot, maybe," Wolf jokes.

"No, seriously," Laura continues enthusiastically, her head bobbing. "She's got a 'look.' Tyra Banks is always saying it. Like, real models aren't drop-dead gorgeous. They're 'ugly-pretty'—her words, not mine. Like, unique. Right, Mackenzie?"

I jerk my head back like Laura just slapped me in the face, hard. I shake my head. *Did she really just say that?*

"Totally," Mackenzie agrees, her perfect blond head bobbing vigorously. "She inspires the photographer 'cause she's so different from the average girl."

I gawk, caught completely off guard by their rudeness and *really* amazed that both girls are looking at me as if they just gave me the compliment of my life. It's like, we're all best friends one minute, and then a couple of guys show up and we're a bunch of chickens, pecking at one another over nothing.

"That's stupid," Luke says sharply, totally out of character, and shoots Laura a look that makes her flush red. "First of all, she's not ugly-pretty, she's just normal pretty. What a dumb thing to say. And second, she's different from the average girl 'cause she doesn't even need makeup."

Silence. Luke looks down at his arm and twirls the

leather strap around his wrist. I nudge him, and when he looks up at me I mouth *Thank you*, not trusting my voice since an unexpected lump has found its way to my throat.

"I was just saying…" Laura stumbles over the words, her voice low. "I mean… Tyra—"

"No, Luke's right, seriously," Wolf adds loudly. "Some girls wear so much makeup, you're like, 'Whoa, are you a girl or a ghoul?'" He cracks himself up and Mackenzie titters along with him. Laura is our resident makeup aficionado, a MAC fiend, and never goes anywhere without a totally made-up face. She squirms uncomfortably on the blanket, suddenly interested in her cell phone.

Two minutes ago I might have felt bad for her, but now, I swallow hard and clear my throat before asking her for the time. It's two AM.

"Ugh." I yawn, losing that famous second wind and the contented, happy, friendship feeling along with it.

"Oh, are we boring you, Miss Winstead?" Wolf asks, his eyebrows raised.

It's hard to believe that sitting next to my dream boy late at night on my own property could ever leave me feeling so blasé; but with my drop-dead gorgeous friend perched perkily on his other side, dibs officially called, my normal nervous energy gives way to exhaustion.

"Nah." I shrug. "I'm just pretty sure I turn into a pumpkin at two."

Wolf laughs at my little joke and kicks my foot with

his. I half laugh, amazed once again at how much power he has over my moods, for better or worse.

"So, Luke," Mackenzie says sweetly, "do you know who you're going to take to homecoming?"

She blinks and sort of cocks her head toward Laura, as if sending a subliminal message. I roll my eyes at the obvious setup.

"Um," Luke says, squirmy. He looks to me for help. I totally know that look, but I don't know how to help him out of this one so I just shrug my shoulders and give him my most winning smile. He shoots me a looks-could-kill stare and I have to look away to keep from busting out laughing.

"I don't know," he mumbles. "I might go stag."

Laura's face falls a little, but I don't feel bad for her. She and Mackenzie both look to me for help, but I'm still recovering from the "ugly-pretty" comments and keep my eyes on my shoes.

"Yeah, if you go stag, you can dance with anybody," I say, leaning back casually on my palms and shaking my legs out in front of me. I look over at my best friend—Luke. "I might go stag, too. Have my way with the boys."

Luke and I laugh, easily. No one else does, and that's okay.

But I notice that Mackenzie and Laura bristle.

"Yeah, like you're going alone, Ericka," Mackenzie says to me, her smile a tad forced. "Go with my brother. He's a sophomore with a car, probably going to be a starter on Boys' Varsity."

I know how much Wolf hates Mark, how defensive he is about his spot on the basketball team, and I prepare myself for a meltdown. I've seen the silent-treatment side of Wolf, but I've never really seen him get angry.

"Sophomore? Yes. Car? Yes. Starter? Hmmm, doubt it," Wolf says, a tight smile stretched across his lips but cocky as ever. Mackenzie is obviously taken aback but she composes herself quickly, batting her lashes double-time. Then Wolf looks at me, chuckles a little to himself, and turns back to her. "And anyway, what makes you think he'd want to ask Ericka?"

"Oh, like being my date would be the worst thing in the world," I snap at him.

"Because he adores her," Mackenzie gushes. "He talks about her all the time. 'Ericka this. Ericka that.'" Her eyes move around the circle and she smiles. I give her a quizzical glance, but she quickly looks away; she's a terrible liar. I know how nice her brother is and wonder if he'd appreciate her pimping him out like this. Personally, I don't get the vibe that he likes me *that* much.

"He's a great guy, and we could all go together," she plows on. "Hey! What if Ericka goes with Mark, Laura goes with Luke, and I go with Wolf? We'd have the *best* time, and my dad would get us a limo!" She says this as if she totally just thought of it off the top of her head. Laura splashes a *Wow! Great idea!* look across her face. Mega-gag.

"Wait, wait, wait, wait, wait," Wolf says, putting his hands up and looking at Mackenzie, talking to her as if

I don't exist. "Mark Watts likes Ericka Winstead? Your brother likes Ericka?"

"Geez, Louise!" I cry. "Stranger things have happened, people!"

Mackenzie leans in close to him and nods fervently. "A lot. Wouldn't they be cute together?"

I groan, sit up, and blow warm air into my palms. Sometimes I feel like I'm in the room and nobody sees me. I sigh, missing the way things were ten minutes ago, when I still felt pretty-pretty.

"Well, folks," I say, standing up and rubbing my cold hands together. "I think I'm going to excuse myself from this evening's festivities. I'll leave the back door open—"

"Wait!" Wolf says, reaching over and grabbing my calf. I freeze. "I've got a better idea."

I look down at Wolf and he flashes that evil half grin of his. My stomach flips nervously. Then I flare my nostrils angrily. For the past month and a half, that devilish grin has meant nothing but heartache for me.

"What?" I ask hesitantly, my eyes narrowed.

"What if you go with me?" he asks, cool and nonchalant.

My mouth falls open, as per the standard. My heart picks up its pace to some kind of double-time beat and I can't believe my ears.

"To homecoming?" I ask stupidly.

He laughs easily, throwing his perfect head back, and then settles his brown eyes back on mine. "No, to the moon," he says teasingly.

Even better.

I feel my jaw lock in place so that I can't speak. I really want to scream "Yes!" at the top of my lungs, but my brain is processing a million thoughts at once, and it takes me a minute to sort through them all.

First and foremost, David Wolfenbaker just asked *me* to homecoming. He's sitting right next to the most beautiful girl in our class, but asked *me*. Oh. My. God.

Which leads to my second thought, that the most beautiful girl in our class happens to be my friend—actually, my "best friend forever"—and accepting Wolf's proposal will kind of make me look like an A-hole. Plus, she might murder me in my sleeping bag later.

Not to mention that a few hours ago, Wolf specifically told me on the phone that he was only asking Mackenzie to homecoming to make her brother mad...and so he's probably only asking me out to make her brother mad... and so he probably doesn't love me and want to marry me and make out with me at the dance.

In the few seconds it takes me to stare at him and think about this impossible dream, Mackenzie cuts in, laughing in a borderline maniacal way. "Oh, no, no, no, silly," she says, pulling Wolf's arm so that he looks over at her. "Mark *really* likes Ericka."

"Well," Wolf says, his evil grin widening as he looks back over at me, "maybe I *really* like Ericka, too."

I stop breathing. It just happens. His face is perfection, his eyes twinkle in the security light shining through the barn slats, and he just said he likes me...maybe. Agh! David Wolfenbaker maybe really likes me!

I. Am. Dying.

"Well?" he asks, grinning from ear to ear. Then he gets up on one knee and grabs one of my hands. "Rosie Jo, will you go to homecoming with me this Friday?"

A sigh escapes me. A chill runs up my spine. I can't take it.

I steal a glance around the circle. Luke looks just as surprised as I am, his mouth in an O shape, like he wants to say something but can't. Laura looks hopeful, her eyes wide, like she's getting rid of her imaginary competition. And Mackenzie looks worried, leaning up on her knees, her eyes bugged out as if in warning.

I take a deep breath and know that I'll have regrets either way.

"Okay, you goofball," I say, laughing and shaking him off, powerfully fighting the urge to turn celebratory cartwheels around the barn. I squat back down on the blanket and cross my arms. "But I don't fast dance."

He laughs and surprises me by giving me a hug, wrapping me up in his soft Abercrombie hoodie and cologne... which is just about the single most perfect moment of my whole life.

Except for Mackenzie glaring at me over his shoulder.

"Where's the booze?" Paul Foster asks, breaking away from Kimi and standing over our little circle. It's obvious that he's been drinking already.

Still, as he sways unsteadily over our group, I've never been happier to see him. The last five minutes have been pretty awkward over here on the blanket. Laura has been trying to find common ground with Luke by asking about tobacco, but he's fallen into one of his quiet spells all of a sudden. I thought Mackenzie was going to cry, but then she flipped some sort of imaginary switch and went into super-cheerleader mode, babbling on and on about Wolf's team through a forced smile, all the while shooting me murderous looks when he wasn't looking.

I've tried keeping up with both conversations, but my mind is in overdrive, trying to figure out if I did the right thing. I guess I sort of feel guilty in a way, but I also feel within my rights. I mean, I know she called dibs and I said I'd back off, but I was still stinging from the "ugly-pretty" comments. Plus, she was totally manipulating the whole homecoming triple-date scenario, without asking if I even wanted to go with Mark. As her friend, I should have said no to Wolf…but as *my* friend, it wasn't fair of her to ask me to.

Ugh. It's a bad situation for sure; but if Wolf feels the tension, he seems to enjoy it, whistling the whole time and kicking my shoes with his—which sends tingles up my leg and provokes Mackenzie even more. So Paul and his need for alcohol are a welcome distraction.

"Y'all hardly drank any of it!" he exclaims, grabbing the bourbon from the blanket and holding it up. "I thought you were gonna party."

"We are," Kimi says, sauntering up behind him, "but we wanted to wait for you boys." She grabs the bottle and takes a swig, careful to avoid the herky-jerky spasms she made when drinking at my house. There is a bit of a grimace, but overall, I'd say she definitely deserves Most Improved.

"Jimmy!" Kimi yells, holding the bottle out to the entangled couple in a dark corner. "Jimmy, you want a shot of bourbon?"

The quarterback phenom comes up for air and it looks like the shadows start to rearrange themselves. Then Sarah and Jimmy come stumbling toward us and I giggle when I see that there is straw in Sarah's hair and Jimmy's shirt is on backwards.

He takes the bottle from Kimi and tosses back a drink, then passes it to Sarah. She takes a couple of pulls like a champ and passes it to Kimi, who tries to match her. Next thing I see, Paul's taking a few more gulps and Luke is looking at him with obvious disgust.

"Wolfenbaker, you drinking tonight?" Paul drawls. He holds the bottle down toward Wolf and I see that it's half empty already. I look back up at Kimi, who seems a little unsteady, and then over at Sarah, whose face is bright red, although I don't know if it's from the booze or the face-sucking.

Wolf grabs the bottle and gives me a special side grin. "Sure I'm drinking," he says, leaning against my arm. "I've got something to celebrate."

He winks at me and I shiver. He takes a drink, then shudders like a dog shaking off water. I squeeze my knees up to my chest and giggle. I love when his perfect-guy facade cracks even a tad.

"To *nosotros*," he says, and I smile at him. His face is close to mine as he offers me the bourbon, his own lips still wet. I have an urge to just take a sip, to consecrate our first date, but then I feel Luke tense up next to me. I glance over at him and see the tightness in his body, and when I look back at Wolf, it takes everything I have to decline, to pull back from the intensity in his eyes.

"Nah," I finally say, looking down at the blanket. "I'm good."

Luke on one side, Wolf on the other. Angel on one side, devil on the other.

"Ericka, you've gotta be kidding me!" Wolf persists, holding the bottle under my nose. I can smell the sweetness, and I feel electricity shooting through my veins as his shoulder leans into mine. "Aren't you Catholic? Y'all's preacher says it's okay to drink, right?"

"I don't think it's a preacher; it's a priest," Mackenzie corrects him.

"Then your priest drinks," Wolf says.

"No, they call him Father," Laura says. "I'm pretty sure it's Father."

"Ugh, then your Father drinks, whatever!" Wolf says, exasperated.

"Well, hers doesn't, but ours sure does!" Paul hoots.

He steps away from Kimi and staggers over to Luke, slapping him hard on the shoulder, cackling at his own bad joke.

Luke roughly brushes his brother off and stands up. "You know better," he mutters to Paul, giving him a hard shove into the shadows.

"Okay, seriously," Wolf says, turning back to me, his arm warm around my shoulders. "Toast us going to homecoming."

He is holding the bottle up to me again when the reality of his words seeps into Sarah's booze-soaked brain and she loses it.

"Ericka! OH! MY! GOD! I'm so happy for you!" she screams, running in place with high knees and blade arms. I can't help but laugh watching her. It feels so nice to see someone outwardly expressing exactly how I feel inside.

"So . . . ?" Wolf says, waving the bottle under my nose. I grin up at him.

"Drink! Drink!" Sarah starts chanting, doing a full lunge, complete with spirit fingers. Kimi joins in, as do their boy toys and Wolf. Pretty soon the barn is echoing, "Drink! Drink! Drink!"

I laugh hard and cave, reaching for the bourbon.

"Dude, she doesn't have to drink if she doesn't want to," Luke blurts out, bending down and ripping the bottle from Wolf's hands.

Everybody freezes, like time stops for a second. I am

shocked by the anger in Luke's voice. I look up and see him standing over me, hovering with his fists clenched like my bodyguard or something. His eyes flash, but mine do, too. I feel my cheeks burn red, embarrassed and angry and totally shocked to see this overprotective side of him. When I see Kimi and Sarah exchange glances and Wolf raise his eyebrows and lean away, I have to make a decision . . . and I still want to fit in. It's only one drink, so what's the big deal?

I stand up and sort of hip check him, trying to lighten the mood, even though the tension between us is thick. "Whoa, Buzz Kill McGee," I joke. And even though I hate the stuff, I'm trying to not piss off the few people in the barn who are actually happy for me, so I grab the bottle from Luke, though not easily, and take a big chug.

I hear the hooting and laughing, but as soon as the liquid fire hits my tongue I swallow hard and close my eyes. I try to keep my cool but it burns and I do a crazy dance in place, like an exorcism, shaking demons out of my body.

Wolf totally cracks up as I hang my tongue out in a pitiful Bandit impression and pant, longing for the Coca-Cola we left behind. As soon as I catch my breath and wipe the tears from my eyes, Kimi and Sarah each drape an arm around me.

"You've been initiated," Kimi booms. "Ericka Winstead is officially one cool girl!"

She squeezes my shoulder with one arm and pumps the other one in the air.

"Yeah!" I holler, amped by all the love. *I am officially one cool girl!*

I see Luke step back and shake his shaggy blond head, looking up at the rafters and mumbling something low to himself. He sighs, crosses his hands behind his head, and finally looks down at me with blank eyes and a half smile on his lips before joining Mackenzie and Laura on the blanket, all three of them looking defeated to some degree.

Wolf leans back on his palms and gives me one of his up-and-down looks, the kind he usually reserves for upperclassmen or girls like Kimi. "You're something else, Winstead. That's for sure."

I melt and take it as a compliment.

"The game is called Never Have I Ever," Kimi explains. Now that make-out central has come up for air, we're all circled around on the blanket. "One person says something they've never done, and if you *have* done it, you have to drink."

Sounds pretty easy, seeing as how my life is completely G-rated.

"Never have I ever seen a boy naked," Kimi starts devilishly.

But then again, my lack of life experience might be more embarrassing than owning up to some of these things. Sarah immediately reaches for the bottle and Kimi smirks. Laura and Mackenzie's eyes bug and Wolf nods his head appreciatively.

"That'a girl," Jimmy encourages as Sarah takes a sip. She blushes and gives him a quick kiss on the cheek.

When she puts the bottle down, Wolf reaches for it and holds it out to me. "Ericka?"

My cheeks flush red hot (it goes without saying that I have never seen a boy naked), but for a millisecond, I consider lying. A white lie and another tiny sip might be a small price to pay to impress Wolf; but I can't do it, and I shake my head, completely embarrassed. He grins and does the unexpected, taking a swig himself. Everyone dies, hooting and hollering.

"What? Duh. Locker rooms," he says by way of explanation.

But then the challenges get harder. "Never have I ever cheerleaded" and the girls drink. "Never have I ever worn a bra" and the girls drink. "Never have I ever streaked" and, to my extreme humiliation, the girls drink as Kimi excitedly fills the guys in on our nudist shenanigans. My mouth feels dry, and weird, like it's harder to move my lips. This makes me giggle.

"Never have I ever puked at a slumber party," Mackenzie says, her sugary sweet smile exaggerated and aimed right at me. I do a double take and stare into her icy blue eyes. I see them flash — she is clearly enjoying this moment. She holds the bottle out toward me.

"Disgusting," Jimmy says.

Mortified, I take the bottle from her. "Mushroom allergy," I defend myself weakly.

I grab the bottle and just the smell makes me shudder. Ick. I take a deep breath and down yet another drink, but realize that it's not burning as much as before. Maybe my esophagus is drunk.

"Never have I ever milked a cow!" Laura says sweetly, giggling as if it's the funniest thing she's ever said, yet looking directly at me.

"Cow teats!" Mackenzie laughs, giving her a high five.

I take another tiny drink and feel sort of numb.

"I think your friends are trying to get you drunk," Wolf says, leaning in close.

"Huh, some friends," Luke says and semi-laughs, trying to sound light, but once again filling the barn with tension. Laura looks shocked.

I shiver and snuggle closer to Wolf, which actually is really brave. Wow. I'm very brave right now. His cologne, oh my god. I close my eyes and breathe in his magic spell, feel like I could fall asleep on his shoulder. Like I could fall asleep right here in the —

"Never have I ever kissed a girl!" Kimi squeals.

A collective "Whoa!" goes out into the night air and the boys (except Luke) all drink. I watch them each take big gulps and feel relieved when I see that the bottle is almost empty.

"Thank goodness we get a break," I slur, and then

giggle. I consider trying that sentence again, but shrug it off as too exhausting.

"Aw, I was hoping one of you girls would take a drink," Wolf says fiendishly.

"Good thing Candace Baker isn't here, then," Kimi quips, and everybody laughs.

Next to me, Luke's eyes go dark. He's a laid-back guy, but now he looks like he's been pushed too far and he gives me a strong nudge.

"What?" I ask, my face scrunched up. I didn't need an elbow to the side.

He gives me a hard look and mumbles, "You know what."

As the others laugh around us, I open my eyes wide, innocent. *What's he mad at me for? I didn't say it. I didn't even laugh.* His face changes then, closes up, and he looks away. I shake my head and he splits in two for a second; then I refocus and see that his face is still tight.

"Ericka's best friends with her," Wolf says on my other side. I can feel his breath on my cheek. "Has she ever made a move, Ericka? Did you ever have a slumber party with Candace that got a little *Girls Gone Wild*?"

I feel the shock register on my face, and the circle laughs heartily.

"Never!" I scream.

"Come on, Ericka," he persists, his fingers making their way to my sides. I'm dying. "Tell the truth."

"Wolf!" I giggle, amazed at how close his face is to

mine. He starts to squeeze, and I am super ticklish. "Wolf! Stop it!"

I wiggle and try to get away, but can't.

"Tell me," he says softly, yet with lots of pressure at my waist keeping me at his side. "Tell the truth about your little lesbo friend."

Tears are streaming down my cheeks, I'm laughing so hard. No matter how much I squirm, I can't escape his tickling. I'll tell him whatever he wants to hear just to get out of this grip.

"Okay, okay!" I scream. "She tried to kiss me!"

"Oh!" The barn erupts. The boys lose it, high-fiving and fist pumping. The girls are laughing, too. I even catch Mackenzie throwing a smirk over at Laura, and then I think maybe I can sort of make the peace if I just get everybody laughing.

"Yeah!" I continue, my mouth dry. I feel like I have to yell. "And she really has a thing for cheerleaders!" I point to Mackenzie and her eyes widen. Her cheeks flush pink and she squeals.

"Lipstick lesbians—I like it!" Wolf says, leaning over to Mackenzie and putting his arm around her. She seems happy with the attention, so whatever. Let her have it for a while. I still get him for homecoming.

Jimmy and Wolf get into a conversation about the hottest moms at our school and which two they would like to see making out. The barn beams blur a little and then, to my surprise, start to spin. I feel weak from laughing so hard and collapse onto Luke's shoulder. Sarah yells something about never making out in her parents' bed and the game moves on rambunctiously. I close my eyes and sigh, happy for the brief break and suddenly feeling a little...nauseous? No, tired. It's late. I'm just tired. I think about the electric touch of Wolf's fingers on my sides and smile.

"You lied," I hear a low voice rumble above me. I lean my head back and see Luke looking down at me. His eyes are angry, but I can't help thinking that they're really pretty, too. The blue is like gray. And I like the yellow flecks by his pupils.

"Ricki Jo!" he hisses.

"What?" I say, trying to focus. I can hear the group laughing around us.

"Candace is not a lesbian," he repeats, just as low.

"Yeah, but no big deal if she is," I say, my eyes closing again as I nuzzle my head against his soft fleece jacket.

He shakes my arm. "But she's not."

"I know that," I say softly, confused.

"You should have *said* that," he says, shaking me off.

I sway and try to focus on his face. "I...what? I—"

"You shouldn't have made that up. You should have stuck up for your friend," he says again.

"She's—well, we're not that close, anyway," I mumble, hearing how lame it sounds.

"Then you should have stuck up for her because it's the right thing to do, Ricki Jo."

"Ericka," I correct weakly, not knowing what else to say.

I watch his expression settle into one of new understanding, almost like he's just woken up.

"Oh, that's right," he says. "That's exactly right. You're a different person now."

He checks his watch and stands up. From where I sit, he looks like a skyscraper. I want to talk to him some more, understand why he's in such a bad mood, but he says his good-byes and stalks out of the barn.

CHAPTER
TWENTY-EIGHT

Bang. Bang. Bang. Bang. Bang. Bang. Bang.

I peel my eyes open, and then snap them shut against the brightness of the sun coming through the family room window. It's early...feels so early. It may be a Sunday morning, but not even good God-fearing Catholics like us get up this early. I roll over on my side, my back to the window, and wiggle down deeper into my sleeping bag, pulling it completely over my head. Everything goes dark, but the pounding picks up again.

Bang. Bang. Bang. Bang.

"What?" I croak, throwing the covers off and looking over at the door. Nobody comes in and I wonder if it's one of my parents or my nosy little brother. I squint around the room and see Mackenzie and Laura sleeping on opposite ends of our couch, their feet intermingling. Kimi is curled up in my dad's recliner and Sarah lies spread-eagle beside me on the floor, her sleeping bag kicked down around one ankle and her pillow over her face.

My eyes are adjusting but the pounding won't stop.

"Who is it?" I try to shout, but my raw voice comes out in a whisper.

The door stays shut and I finally drag myself up to my knees.

Whoa.

The room spins and an earthquake cracks down my body, splitting across my forehead. "Holy crap!" I say, clutching my head and falling face-first onto of my sleeping bag. It's in that moment, with my forehead pressed against the silky material of my plush sleeping bag, that I realize the pounding is coming from within my own head. I groan.

Then, I remember last night.

And I groan again.

Still on my knees, I reach my arms out and gather the sleeping bag all around my head, balling it up so that it blocks out the light and the fabulous friends who surround me. I wish it could block out last night's events, but I feel sick from the alcohol and even sicker from the memories.

I'm pretty sure I fell asleep after Luke left. I don't know the difference between falling asleep and passing out, but I did wake up to find myself all alone in the barn, drooling. It must've just been a few minutes or so, 'cause I could hear laughter outside, and I knew my friends wouldn't really leave me. I made my way out into the night and saw the whole group running as fast as they could toward our cows. I shook my head—in disbelief, I guess, like maybe I was still passed out. Watching Sarah lower her shoulder and run headlong toward the broad side of an Angus was almost too much to comprehend. The cows were quicker—they weren't hurt, or even touched—but I lost my mind, yelling at the group to stop. (I'm sure they had no idea that cow tipping is like cow homicide.) They all looked at one another like I was an alien from another planet, but they did stop.

As I marched angrily toward my friends, the cows braying loudly in the fields, I slipped on a fresh cow patty and fell, hard, on my back. Lying there, looking up at the stars, I took a few major cuss words out for a test drive before I started to cry. The shadows became human and circled around me, looking down in a mixture of pity and disgust. I was sobbing, the ugly kind of crying that rattles my rib cage and sends mucus and saliva out in bubbles and streaks, while cow poop oozed around my shoulders. Wolf was so grossed out that he held his nose, gagged, and begged Jimmy to take him home, which made Sarah mad at me. Kimi, the most unlikely of the four, was the only friend I had left, and she helped me walk home... even if she wouldn't get within an arm's length.

Remembering this now, I groan. My mouth is cottony and tastes disgusting. I realize I'm going to vomit.

As quickly as I can (which isn't fast at all considering my condition), I crawl out of the family room and down the hall, noticing the time on the kitchen clock: six AM. *What time did we get home?* In the bathroom, I kneel in front of the toilet and heave. It burned going down, but it burns ten times worse on the way back up. With one hand, I push my hair out of the way, and with the other, I flush. I can't look at it.

When I feel good and empty, I sit down on the cool tile floor and see my shoes and clothes from last night hanging over the shower rod to dry. This could lead to questions from Momma, but at this very moment, I'm just thankful the bathroom doesn't smell like dung. My head droops, and I realize how dark the windowless bathroom is. The family room seems awfully far away. I open the bathroom cabinet, pull out a couple of beach towels, and snuggle in.

"Will you just tell him that Ericka called and to meet me by the creek after church?" I say into the phone. I've called Luke three times already this morning, but Claire seems to be covering for him.

"I'll tell him, *Ericka*," she says, sighing, and I hear her baby wailing in the background. My head is still splitting.

I snap Kimi's cell phone shut, bummed that I couldn't get past the Fosters' caller ID with a different number, and head out to the garage, where the Winstead taxi is waiting. I know Luke got a little mad last night, but right now I really don't need another frenemy.

I walk as steadily as possible to the side door of the minivan, careful to avoid eye contact with my parents, and assess the seating arrangement. Looks like I'll be climbing into the very back with Mackenzie and Laura, my biggest fans.

The van is quiet on the way to town, save for the soft rock Momma hums along to up front. As for us girls, we keep our heads down and our eyes closed. I feel every turn, fight against the queasiness, and, once again, wish I didn't live so far out in the country. Everybody brought church clothes to go to Mass with us this morning, but no one is actually in the mood to go—including me, but I don't have a choice. *Never have I ever gone to church with a hangover,* I think to myself miserably. I think it's pretty safe to say I'll never drink again.

As we drop each of my friends off on our way to town, I can't help but envy their imminent naps. Sarah is first, and says "thanks" and "good-bye" and really doesn't seem mad so much as sick. Next is Laura, who squeezes past me like I have the plague and thanks my parents for having her over.

Kimi's house is third and she leans back and pats my hand before flip-flopping her way out of the van. "Tylenol, anything greasy from McDonald's, and lots of water," she whispers. "Kimi Wilson's Never-Fail Hangover Cure." I smile weakly.

This leaves Mackenzie and me alone in the backseat, trying to avoid eye contact with each other and with my parents, who keep glancing back at us in their mirrors. A million thoughts race through my mind, a million ways to apologize followed by another million reasons I shouldn't have to. We both like Wolf, yet I know she would have said yes if he'd asked her, never mind my feelings. And yeah, so she called dibs, big deal. It's not like *I* asked *him*. And dibs are something you call on the front seat or remote control, but a boy?

When we drive up to her Barbie Mansion house, I sigh and pull my aching body out of the van to go around back and help her with her bag. I mean, I think she's got an attitude and it's totally unfair, but I get why she's in a bad mood—although leaving me drunk in a cow pie should definitely make us more than even. And like she said last night, New Girls BFFs would never let a boy come between them. So I decide to take the high road and play the peacemaker.

I lift up the van's back door, grab her bag, and give her an apologetic half grin. "Hey, I'm sorry about—"

"Save it," she says, shooting me one last ice-cold stare before plastering a fake smile on her face, waving energetically at my parents, and bounding up her cobblestone sidewalk.

The breeze is cool even though the sun is bright. I pull up the hood of my sweatshirt and tuck the sides of a red plaid flannel blanket around my legs. I lean against a large, flat rock by the creek and scribble in my journal like crazy, retelling my version of last night's events as best I can. It's not pretty.

As I write about the main character, the little nerdy girl who just started a new school only to alienate her best friends in order to make herself look good in front of her dream guy, I feel sick to my stomach. Maybe it's the hangover, but I think about the last time I was out here, when Luke told me that he hoped I wouldn't change on the inside, and feel sick.

I sigh and lie back, closing my eyes and holding my journal against my chest, and listen to the water trickle by. What I *want* to do is crash on my bed and sleep the whole nightmare away, but what I *need* to do is sort out all the drama with a good friend, which is why I'm waiting for Luke. Kimi's Hangover Cure—a McDonald's Happy Meal, two extra-strength Tylenol, and a bazillion cups of water—did make it possible for me to stumble my way out here. It also gave me the strength to withstand Momma's silent treatment and Dad's dinner lecture on "being a responsible teen." I'm not sure what they know, but I'm not offering up any details. And even though it's been two hours and it kind of seems like Luke's not going to show, I don't have the energy to make myself go home and call him again.

I feel Bandit hobble over my legs, but I keep my eyes closed against the overcast sky. It took us a while to get out here, but I feel good about his progress, and I certainly wasn't in a hurry. He's more cautious now, wobbling around the blanket, his nose leading him but not far. He may wander a few steps, but even if he's distracted by a rabbit or a butterfly, he'll watch instead of chase. He cocks his head at every sound, keeping an eye out and constantly looking back at me, making sure I'm still here.

I feel Bandit's nose on my forehead and smile. It's the best I can do under the circumstances. I rub his head, careful of his wounds, and look down at my watch. Almost four o'clock. I stare out toward Luke's house, straining to see a figure on the horizon, but I know he's not coming.

And I could really use one of his hugs right now.

♛

CHAPTER
TWENTY-NINE

"So are we gonna talk about what happened Saturday night?" I ask Luke on the bus Monday morning. He didn't sit with me, but it's not that big of a bus and I moved up to where he was and plopped myself down right next to him. We need to talk.

"What? About you going to homecoming with Wolf? Oh, okay, congratulations," he says sarcastically, looking out the window.

"Oh, is that it?" I ask earnestly. "You're mad 'cause I said yes to Wolf? Join the club."

"No," he says, still looking away. "I mean, he's a douche bag for sure, but I don't give a damn if you go to homecoming with a Jonas Brother. It just makes me sick how you throw yourself at him."

"What?" I ask, indignant.

"Yeah," he says, turning to face me full on. "He only

asked you because he hates that guy Mark. It's so obvious! He's totally using you, and you don't care."

"Ever think he might just like me?" I ask, hoping to convince myself, too.

"He's not that smart a guy," Luke mumbles, looking back out the window.

We bump along in silence for a minute and I grab a hair clip from my backpack. "So you're not mad about homecoming, you're just mad I like Wolf. Is that it?"

He laughs bitterly. "Yeah, that's it. You're going to some stupid dance with some pretty-boy jock and I'm jealous." He lays the sarcasm on pretty thick, although I never brought up jealousy. That actually never crossed my mind. I think back to the day we wrestled by the creek and blush.

"Well, it's just one date," I say, trying to soften things. "I don't know why everybody's getting their panties in a wad. I mean, Mackenzie acts like it's the end of the world!"

"Because it is!" Luke says, totally frustrated. "To people like her, it *is* the end of the world. She's used to getting her way. God, she and Wolf are actually made for each other. They're spoiled rich kids who get by on their looks and money," he says bitterly and turns from the window, leveling me with the intensity of his eyes, "and it makes me sick that you try so hard to be like them. The Ricki Jo I know likes people for their sense of humor and, I don't know, their hearts or whatever. But now"—he pauses, sighs, and lowers his voice, then his eyes—"now it's like you're this other person."

I'm speechless. I want to defend myself, defend my friends, but I'm so stunned that I can hardly think straight. Luke, my loyal, steady, never-talks-about-his-feelings best friend, is having no trouble whatsoever laying it all on the line. And it hurts.

He glances up at me and his expression changes. "You're surprised?" he asks sincerely.

"I just thought you were mad about the Candace thing," I say quietly.

"Yeah, that sucked, too, actually," he says. "That really sucked. The Ricki Jo I grew up with — hell, the one I knew two months ago! — wouldn't have trashed her like that. And she wouldn't have let them talk her into getting wasted. Which reminds me: You're a pretty annoying drunk."

I bristle.

"And, I don't know," he continues. "You used to not care about clothes and makeup and sucking up to everybody. I don't know how to explain it. You're, like, their puppet or something. You do whatever they say and" — he pauses and looks away — "I feel sorry for you."

I feel tears prick my eyes and my throat get tight. But I know this feeling. I'm not sad; I'm angry. Angry to be made to sit here and let my oldest friend tell me how much I suck, let him pity me, just because I've made a few social improvements. So what? I'm a cheerleader, I dress nicer than before, I have cool friends. He should be happy for me. Happy! Not sorry.

And I'm *not* their puppet. Sometimes, I mean, I'm kind of their *project*, but A) that's totally different, 'cause they're just trying to help me and teach me new stuff, and B) I'm the one who wanted a change. And I'm finally pretty sure that I'm totally in the Fabulous Five now, even though things are rocky at the moment.

"I don't need your pity," I say through gritted teeth, fighting the tears. "It's actually me who feels sorry for you."

A single tear falls. I curse it in my head and quickly wipe it away with the back of my hand.

His eyebrows shoot up in surprise. "Me?"

"Yeah," I go on, wanting to hurt him back. "Like, for instance, you're obviously awesome at basketball, but you can't play for PCHS 'cause your dad's a drunk and can't run his farm right without his boys, and so you're jealous of guys like Wolf. And you hate that I have popular friends, and you hate that they have money, and you hate seeing me moving up and out of redneckville."

He stares at me, completely stunned. I expect anger, but see only hurt, and my heart twists. Without realizing it, I mirror his expression perfectly.

I can't believe I just said that.

"Yeah," he says quietly and turns away.

"I'm sorry," I whisper immediately.

"No," he says to the window. "You need those friends."

I look at the back of his head and quiver. I don't know what to say. I'm so angry that I'm shaking, but so mortified, too. I shouldn't have—

"I'm through," he says, his voice cracking, as he pulls on a pair of headphones.

"Through?" I question fearfully, blinking big tears to the corners of my eyes.

"I'm a laid-back guy," he says and then sighs, leaning his forehead against the window, defeated. "I like to laugh and cut up. I hate drama, hate being around those stuck-up idiots. I'm not 'fabulous' and I don't wanna be. I don't like the way I am around you, when you're around them. And I don't like the way you are when you're around them. So I'm through." He looks down at his iPod Shuffle and hesitates before pushing Play. "Ericka."

Then Lynyrd Skynyrd's "Sweet Home Alabama" blares through the headphones and I take the hint—our conversation is over. I slide down in my seat and replay Luke's words over and over in my head. I think about the fact that I'm getting everything I want. And I think about what I may be losing along the way.

As I walk into school, it seems like any other day. The kids around me move through the hallways the same as always, exchanging secrets and high fives and gossiping about their weekends. I duck and weave through the throng, walking quickly toward my locker. A smile creeps onto my lips as I wonder if any of my schoolmates know that I'm going to homecoming with David Wolfenbaker. Then I see Mackenzie's full blond ponytail right in front of me. I slow down and feel my smile fade.

"There she is," Wolf says as I squeeze between him and Kimi.

"Oh my god, Ericka!" Kimi screams. "I was totally going to call you yesterday but I felt like crap and just glued myself to the downstairs couch and watched *Gossip Girl* reruns."

"Ha! I felt pretty bad, too," I admit, moving my hand toward the dial on my locker.

"Allow me," Wolf says, and I realize that he's already got it open.

"I'm gonna have to change my combination," I tease.

"So stupid," I hear Mackenzie say and glance over. She's not looking at me, but from the evil smirk on Laura's face, I can tell that the comment was definitely meant for my ears.

I try to shake it off and refocus on Kimi and Wolf. "I am *never* drinking again."

They laugh with me as the first bell rings.

"Well, never again..." Wolf says, putting his arm around my shoulder. I swoon a little and push my shoulder into him, hoping some of his magic cologne will rub off on me. I'll smell that shoulder all day long. "...until Friday."

I lean away and look up at him. The thought of drinking—just the idea of pouring that poison down my throat again, of the crying and the cow poop and the headache and the vomit, and the fact that Friday is only a few days away—is almost too much.

"Right?" he says, massaging my shoulders a little.

Almost.

Sarah and Jimmy join our group and start making plans.

"I say a stretch limo," she says. "I live by Ericka, so we'll pick her up first and then make the rounds. That way all of us can go together and we won't have to worry about a designated driver, aka parent. Plus, we can totally party in there and nobody'll know."

Jimmy lifts his eyebrows at Wolf and they pound fists, obviously excited by Sarah's plan. She's counting heads and I notice that she includes Mackenzie and Laura, plus whoever they're bringing. That should make for an interesting evening.

"Oh my god," Kimi says, bending down beside me as I unload the contents of my backpack into my locker. "Is that the hair issue?"

She grabs my October issue of *Seventeen* and starts flipping through it madly.

"Yeah," I answer. "We have a meeting for the school paper today and I'm using that to help me with my first article. I think I'm gonna do a quiz."

"Lame." I hear Mackenzie's voice again and look past Kimi to see her still facing away, yet leaning against a closed locker nearby. Laura is covering her mouth, but the giggles burst through. I roll my eyes for her benefit and shoot her a mean stare. I hope she'll pass that one on to her jealous friend.

"I thought so," Kimi answers, turning expertly to a

page in the middle. "Check out this style, girls. It's not exactly what I'm doing, but it's really close to this updo I saw in *Elle*, and it's what you'll see on me Friday night. This is my style. So find your own."

She shows us an elaborate style in the "Hot Homecoming Hair" section, braids everywhere tucked into soft curls and somehow drawn together under a half chignon. I examine the style and feel my eyebrows inch upward. No need to tell me to lay off, 'cause I don't have the patience or number of hands possible to create this look.

"Whoa," I say, wondering how she'll do it with her short bob. I sigh to myself. Like the teen models smiling up at us from the magazine, she'll probably get salon treatment, extensions even, 'cause I know her mom will let her skip school and drive her up to Lexington if she asks. Meanwhile, our small town offers me the choice of doing it myself or asking my cousin Allie to do it after she teaches kindergarten Friday.

"Does it look good with your dress?" Mackenzie asks, half turning toward our group.

"I don't have my dress yet, but it will," Kimi answers confidently.

"Oh, yeah! What's *your* dress look like?" Wolf asks me.

I blush deeply and hate myself for it. I still can't believe I'm going to homecoming with David Wolfenbaker.

"My mom told me to ask you so she'll know what kind of corsage to get," he goes on.

He told his mom about me.

"Um, I'm not sure," I say, hating how high my voice sounds. "I'm going shopping after school."

Actually, Momma's driving me over to Lincoln County so I can borrow a dress from the daughter of a woman she works with; and although I'll never admit that part, it does make me feel better that Kimi doesn't have her dress yet, either.

The late bell rings and we round the corner into Mrs. Wilkes's room. We take our normal seats and I feel like I'm sitting next to a glacier, with Mackenzie sitting sideways in her chair, her back to me. Then she whips around suddenly and reaches her arm across the table to grab Wolf's. "Just make sure to get a wrist corsage," she says, turning on her killer smile. "The kind that pin on tear holes in our dresses."

He looks surprised and nods. Then she turns to me with that same huge smile and I gasp. She lets go of his wrist and then wraps her hand around mine. I flash a relieved smile, glad to be moving on.

"Oh, and Ericka's wrists are super tiny, so maybe get something for a flower girl."

The girls all laugh, some good-naturedly and others rather hatefully, and I feel my ears turn red. I smile back tightly, loosen my wrist from her grasp, and turn toward the speaker as Mr. Bates starts his morning announcements. Wolf catches my eye briefly, widens both of his, and gestures cat claws, clearly loving the attention.

*   *   *

Spanish was always my favorite class, but now, *ay ay ay!*

"Now, I know that homecoming is around the corner and Breckinridge, Kentucky, isn't exactly Mexico City, but I still thought Actividad thirty-eight— 'Common Phrases on a Date'—would tie in perfectly this week," Señorita explains in the middle of class. "So, in your *parejas, por favor,* and share your answers from this afternoon's assignment before turning them in at the end of class. *Sí?*"

The desks screech and kids groan as we turn to face our partners, but I can barely swallow my excitement. Wolf also looks a little pink to me, but my momma says I have an overactive imagination.

"Rosa Juana," Wolf reads out of his workbook, sounding like a total hick. *"Tu pareces hermosa en* your *vestido esta noche."*

I giggle. "Um, nice Spanglish," I say, reaching across his desk and scratching out his mistake.

He laughs and we work through the rest of the assignment together. Since we're both brainiacs (although only one of us actually looks the part), we finish early and spend the rest of the time talking about last weekend.

"So I guess Mackenzie's pretty pissed at you, huh?" he whispers.

I roll my eyes. "What gave you that idea? The fact that she left me lying in a pile of cow poop Saturday night?"

He covers his mouth to keep from bursting out laughing. "Dude. That was sick."

"You think I don't know that?" I whisper fiercely, leaning over my desk toward him. "Trust me, it was sick to the max, and none of you losers helped me up." I throw my pencil at his chest and he fakes like it stabbed him in the heart.

"Loser? That's cold," he says, slipping my pencil behind his small, perfect ear. "Seriously, I hope you got home okay, though."

"Oh, yeah, I'm sure you were *so* worried," I say sarcastically.

"I was!" he says, mocking indignation. "You were really drunk."

"Yeah, well, I could tell you really cared when you called Sunday to check on me."

His smile falters and he clears his throat; he was clearly not expecting that. I keep a little smile on my own face and sit back in my desk with my arms crossed over my chest; I want to keep things light and fun, but it's hard. I was, apparently, pretty messed up Saturday night. A good guy would've called, right? And good friends, too? I mean, somebody should've called.

"Your mom didn't give you the message?" he finally asks weakly.

I laugh out loud as the bell rings, shaking off the brief tension. He can't help but join in. "Pretty lame comeback, Wolfenbaker," I say as I turn my desk back toward the front of the room.

He waits for me to grab my bag and we walk toward the front of the classroom, where Candace meets me outside the door. I hope she hasn't heard anything about my slumber-party drunkenness. As if reading my mind, Wolf grabs my head and whispers down into my hairline.

"Nunca yo tengo nunca," he says, drawing it all out. I giggle at his garbage Spanish, and then flush pink when I realize he's indicating Candace and the lesbian lie.

"I'm not sure that one translates," I say, looking up at him sheepishly.

He grins and squeezes my shoulder. "Later, Rosa J." Then he nods at Candace. *"Roja."*

She rolls her eyes at him and I hide a smile.

"I don't know what you see in him," she says.

Watching his skinny frame walk away, the way his shoulders slant from side to side as he struts through the crowds, I don't see how she misses it.

" 'Best Friends Forever . . . or Never?' What do you think?" I ask Candace.

We're at a table in Miss Davis's class, working on our articles for the school paper. I'm totally happy for an excuse to miss lunch period with the rest of my fabulous friends, since some of them need to get a life. And since I'm currently submerged in a major BFF crisis, I thought a friendship quiz would be a great way to start off my "Terrible Tales of Teenagedom" column.

"I think I saw something like that on MySpace," she replies.

I shoot her a dirty look and blow air through my bangs. "Whatever, Candace."

She gives me a funny look and puts her hands up in defense. "Easy, Hard Charger," she says. "What's with the 'tude?"

I sigh and write down my BFF title. "Just Mackenzie stuff. And Laura stuff. And Luke stuff." I pause for dramatic effect, then look up at her mischievously, baiting her so that I can dish. "And, oh yeah, Wolf stuff."

She smirks but doesn't comment, which actually ticks me off. I want her to either judge me — tell me that she was right and I'm changing and the new me sucks — or ask me all about Wolf and be the one friend I can gush to about homecoming. I stare at her frizzy red braids and want to jerk one.

"What about something like, 'Your friends usually call you when...' and then give, like, multiple-choice answers?" I ask tightly.

"Sounds good," she mumbles, not looking up.

I don't know why, but I suddenly realize that I'm really mad at Candace. Why should I have to fight her battles? Why's Luke got to get mad at me when, number one, I didn't start the stupid girls-kissing-girls thing, and number two, she wasn't even there? If anybody acts too good around here, too stuck-up or whatever, it's the two of them, always judging everybody.

"A, they want to talk about boys..." I read out loud as I write, hoping to annoy her. "B, they want help with their homework…" I snort, remembering certain "friends" of mine.

"Or C," Candace mutters, pressing down hard on her notebook, "their other friends are mad at them."

I gawk, stunned. I'm sure she feels my eyes on her, but she doesn't look up. I start to say something, to defend myself or deny her shot at me, but I close my mouth and look down at my paper, knowing I can't do either because she's right. So instead of battling, I write down Candace's answer as C and try to think of something neutral for D.

"Oh," I say to myself, chewing on my eraser. "Just to talk."

Novel idea, I think as I write it down.

We finish the hour in awkward silence, taking notes from Mitch here and there whenever he checks up on us. He's a pretty hands-on editor, at least for the freshmen, and has a lot of catty suggestions for my multiple-choice answers. A lot more helpful than Miss High and Mighty sitting across from me—and who uses MySpace anymore, anyway?

I finish up the quiz right as the bell rings and turn it in, eager for Mitch's notes. Candace actually waits for me at the door and we walk toward our lockers together, although we still can't find much to talk about. When I see Wolf down the hall, hanging off my already open locker door and grinning my way, I say a quick "later" and make a beeline for him, feeling all the day's tension float away. I have a date this weekend…and I can't wait.

CHAPTER THIRTY

I have never been so stoked for a football game!

I could barely concentrate all day long, and the teachers pretty much gave us all a pass. The football players and Boys' Varsity cheerleaders wore their uniforms to school and the whole place felt different somehow. Alive. We even had a pep rally after lunch, and if you didn't have school spirit before, you'd be hard-pressed not to have it now.

Although I've been looking forward to homecoming since the first day of school, I show up fashionably late. From the parking lot, I can hear the crowds yell and the band explode. Excitement rushes through me as I shut the car door.

"Five minutes," I warn Momma again through the passenger window. She rolls her eyes in response and Dad laughs as they slowly move forward through the parking lot to look for a spot. She agreed to drop me off a few car lengths past the gate, and they promised to wait a few minutes before coming in themselves. As a freshman, I must protect my budding reputation.

I pay my five bucks and squeeze through the people gathered at the entrance. Everybody and their momma came out tonight, high school sports being major social events in a small town like mine and county rivalries really raising the stakes. I want to get down to the student section at the far end of the field before my family comes in and decides to start snapping pictures or something; but at the same time, I can't very well sprint through this crowd or appear overly eager.

So I sashay around the track, weaving through the throngs of people in my cute skinny jeans tucked tightly into my tall brown boots. I scan the bleachers for my *date* as nonchalantly as possible, my cold hands tucked deep into the big pocket of my PCHS fitted hoodie. Today's ensemble: Game wear. Casual, yet cute.

Near the far goalpost, I spot Wolf yelling from the bleachers and nearly lose my breath. He is standing in the glow of the enormous lights, bare-chested, with maroon and gold war paint smeared all over his skinny torso and face, pumping both hands into the air and high-fiving a crew of fellow fanatics.

I stop. And stare. And admire his cut-up abs and ribs as he cheers on the Stallions.

"Ericka!" he shouts. "Ericka! *Aquí! Arriba!*" I smile at

him and scramble up the bleachers double-time so he'll stop screaming my name and waving his arms, which is enough to both please and embarrass me at the same time. Although I don't get to sit right beside him (his chest is the C in PCHS), I squeeze in with a few older girls who are in my same situation, dates of the other football-fan warriors.

"You're Ericka?" a pretty brunette asks me. I nod and smile big. I totally recognize her. Donna Mays, student body president. "Cool. I'm Donna. Nice to meet you."

"You, too," I say and force my eyes to the football field before my uncontrollable smile scares her away. I'm sitting beside the student body president, and she knows my name!

That's yet another fantastic thing about being David Wolfenbaker's date. Even though he's a freshman—just like me—he runs with the upperclassmen. One, because of his older brother, and two, because he plays basketball with the big boys. I sit perched in the student section, happier than I've ever been and extremely nervous around this crowd. This is my first big game as a PCHS Stallion and I want to fit in.

So as Sarah and Mackenzie (who look totally amazing out on the field) lead us through chants and cheers with their squad, I'm right in the moment, hollering and stomping on the aluminum stands with all my might, while keeping it controlled and pretty. *Seventeen*'s "Homecoming Tips" said that guys like girls who are interested in sports, but that they still like *girls*, so keep your face soft and your voice girly but not screechy. I don't understand football, so I pretty much follow Donna Mays's every move, while constantly remaining aware of myself so I won't come off as a stalker. The few times I do cheer of my own accord have nothing to do with the game of football and everything to do with my spunky friends on the sidelines. The way Sarah catapults herself into the air without a running start seems scientifically impossible. And Mackenzie's bounce and pep are contagious, which fills me with both pride and sadness. But my favorite moments during the game, while cheering the home team on to victory, are when Wolf leans forward to check on me, smiling or reaching for a long high five.

"So I guess I'll see you in a little while?" he asks as we make our way to the front gate, inching forward with the massive crowd.

"Yep," I say, tongue-tied and embarrassed. "We'll probably pick you up after Kimi."

He flashes my favorite mischievous grin and cold chills pop up all over my body, as usual. Then his friends grab him and start a "P-C-H-S" chant. He goes crazy with them, obnoxiously ramming people as they cheer and pump their arms. I shake my head and giggle, then lose him in the crowd.

Finally able to relax, I move forward as if I'm floating. The band is still playing our school song and the buzz in the air is invigorating. As I head toward the front gate, stepping on confetti and basking in the bright lights of the field, I can see why "the big game" is so big. Homecoming is magic. I take a deep breath of the brisk autumn air and think about how worried I was on the first day of school about fitting in with my fellow PCHS Stallions. Moving along with the crowd, wearing their colors and knowing their chants, I finally feel like I'm one of them.

And now it is officially Friday *night*. The part of Friday night that required me to shave my legs, paint my nails Strawberry Explosion, and borrow Momma's perfume. The part of Friday night that means Ericka Jo Winstead will be going to the homecoming dance with David fill-in-the-blank Wolfenbaker.

Sarah's limo will be here any minute. I'm usually the kind of girl who runs late, but since I started my homecoming body prep at four o'clock this afternoon, the moment I got off the school bus, the only thing I have to do between the game and the dance is change clothes and fix my hair. I'm counting the seconds 'til she gets here, listening to the Rihanna playlist I made for my iPod. I pace around my room in my underwear and high heels, checking my hair every few minutes to make sure it hasn't moved.

I ended up going with a *Seventeen* style after all, although not one as complicated as Kimi's. They call it the half-pinned style and they swear it takes only forty-five seconds. I scrunched a little gel in my naturally wavy hair and then went to work on random pieces with a big curling iron. Then I parted it on the side and swept it up just above my left ear with a bobby pin. Last, I smoothed my bangs over to the right side and left the rest loose. Simple. And it only took thirty minutes.

I peek between the slats of my bedroom blinds, looking out the window for the millionth time. Still no limo. I'm waiting 'til the last possible minute to slip into my dress so that I don't A) spill something on it or B) sweat through it in my nervousness.

I turn back to my room and admire the reddish-pink dress hanging from my closet door. It drapes off the shoulders and ends right above the knee, but what I really love about it is that, for the first time in my life, I look like I've got shape…an hourglass shape at that. The thick material is scrunchy and fits tightly across my chest and waist, then flares out dramatically at my hips like a Judy Jetson dress. This is exactly what that salesgirl from the mall, Rachel, meant about "dressing to your strengths and downplaying your weaknesses." I'm still trying to decide if it's too dressy to wear again to church on Sunday before my momma has to take it back to her friend.

"Ricki Jo!" my dad calls down the hall.

My heart stops.

"Your friends are here!"

I squeal, clap, twirl around, and jump—then collect myself, moving with lightning-quick speed while remaining acutely aware of maintaining the integrity of my hairstyle. I dab at my armpits one last time with a kitchen towel and then unhook my dress.

"Momma!" I shout at the same time that she knocks on my door.

She enters my room, smiling, and holds my dress open as I step into it. She pulls it up and I slip my arms through, feeling the smooth liner against my body. I smile wide and start to hyperventilate.

"Breathe," Momma says gently. Before I need to warn her, she oh-so-carefully moves my hair to one side of my back while pulling up the zipper. Then she turns me around to face her and does the unbelievable: She produces makeup.

"Close your eyes," she says, unwrapping a new vial of LashBlast mascara and sweeping the wand lightly over my eyelashes. "There," she says, stepping back to admire her handiwork. "Now pucker." And, to my surprise, she twists the lid off of a brand-new tube of Berry Cherry lip gloss and slides it over my lips. She stands back and looks at me, fighting the hug I know she's dying to give. "You look beautiful," she says with a sigh.

I grin widely up at her and step in front of my full-length mirror. I *feel* beautiful.

We hear the doorbell ring and a shiver runs from my toes to the top of my head. I open my bedroom door and step out into the hall. I see my dad laughing and slapping his knee and have a small panic attack. He's telling corny jokes. I just know he's telling his corny jokes to Sarah.

"Dad," I complain, clacking down the hallway in my new gold heels. And then I freeze, mortified, when I walk into the living room and see just who he's telling his corny jokes to.

"Wow," Wolf whispers.

Back at ya, I think to myself, taking him in. He looks more handsome than I ever thought possible. The black suit he's wearing looks like it was cut just for him, from the three-button jacket and straight pants down to the cool black shoes that put my dad's tasseled church loafers to shame. His black shirt underneath is smooth, with the collar turned down crisply over a sleek black and deep pink tie. And it's not only *what* he's wearing, but *how* he wears it. Like he's comfortable. Like James Bond, sexy and smooth.

And I guess it's not only that, but also the way he's looking at me. The way his lips seem permanently turned up on the ends; how his eyes can't seem to meet mine but never leave me, either; the surprising bashful quality he has when he finally steps toward me with my corsage. It's all like my best dream coming true. When he's next to me, opening the plastic box containing my small corsage (two white roses bound by a dark pink ribbon), I notice two small beads of sweat at his temple, very close to his hairline. *He's nervous.* I hold out my hand and silently curse it for shaking. He slips the elastic over my hand and I look down at my wrist, unable to stop smiling.

A flash goes off in my peripheral vision, snapping me out of my love trance. My face flushes a deep red and I'm suddenly embarrassed and very aware that my parents are watching us like spectators at a zoo.

"You look…" Wolf pauses, searching for the right word. "Awesome."

Awesome? I giggle. He took a while to find the right word and came up with *awesome?*

"It's really me," I joke lightly.

Everything is lighter with him tonight, better, like it always is when it's just the two of us. I grab his boutonniere from the top of the sofa and concentrate on pinning it to his lapel without stabbing my finger. His cologne is overwhelming. I take a deep breath and bite my tongue because what I want to say is, *You make me want to bathe in Abercrombie cologne, you look like you just stepped out of a Calvin Klein ad, you are the only guy I know who can pull off a pink tie, you make a simple black suit look like a freaking tuxedo, and you absolutely take my breath away.*

"Let's you two get over by the fireplace for a quick picture," Momma says, interrupting my visual feast and motioning us over.

We pose awkwardly, neither of us quite sure where to stand or put our hands. Then Momma sits me in her reading chair and positions Wolf behind me. When she tries to get us outside on the front porch, I draw the line.

"Momma, they're waiting," I say.

"Oh, all right, sweetie," she says, rolling her eyes. "You kids have fun. You left me the limo driver's number? And David's cell phone number?"

I blush again. "Yes, on the counter," I say.

She leans in and kisses me, while my dad and I just share an awkward wave. I head for the door, but Wolf shakes my dad's hand and says, "I'll take good care of her, Mr. Winstead. Good night, Mrs. Winstead."

I grab the doorknob and suppress a laugh. The boy really knows how to work a room.

"Ericka, you look gorg!" Kimi says as I climb into the limo. Hip-hop is pumping over the speakers and the inside is lit up with white Christmas lights. I guess the limo pickup order got switched around, 'cause the car is already half full.

Kimi and Sarah are perched on either side of their QB hunk of meat, Jimmy James, at the far end of the car, with their backs to the driver. I feel like I'm a million miles away. For a brief second, I don't know if I should shimmy up closer to sit sideways beside them and hope with all my might that I don't get carsick, or just stay put back here. Luckily, Wolf climbs in behind me and pulls me back next to him, facing forward.

"Your dresses are stunning," I say loudly, and I really mean it. The blue satin strapless dress Sarah's wearing wraps around her like water, understated and perfect. Kimi's, on the other hand, is a vibrant orange, which would totally wash me out, but she manages to pull it off. And there's no surprise that it's cut low and high for ample cleavage and thigh, respectively.

"What?" Sarah hollers. She literally flows down the

leather seats to get closer to us, pulling Jimmy behind her. Then she pushes a red button and says into a small speaker, "We're good." On cue, the car rolls forward, down my driveway, and out onto the small country road.

"Stunning," I repeat, pointing up and down at her and Kimi. Sarah smiles big and leans in to give me a kiss. I feel her gooey lip gloss on my cheek and smile, wiping it off quickly. I also smell the alcohol on her breath and my stomach flips.

"Want a drink?" she asks us mischievously.

"You know it," Wolf says right away. I can't help but raise my eyebrows at the eagerness in his voice. "You know, I wanted to wait until I'd talked to your parents, in case they could smell it on my breath or something."

"Smooth operator!" Jimmy says, giving him props. Wolf half grins, beaming back at the upperclassman. I cock my head to one side, having one of those lightbulb-going-on-over-my-head moments. Is Wolf trying to fit in? Like he has to try!

Kimi opens a compartment and passes him a beer. Just the sight of it gives me the heebie-jeebies, a major full-body tremor. She looks at me with a question in her eyes, but I shake my head.

"Two words," I say, holding up one finger and then two. "Cow. Poop."

Everyone laughs heartily and I realize that, as disgusting as last Saturday night's nightmare in the pasture might have been, I now have my "out" for drinking.

"We'll let it slide for now," Wolf says, putting his arm around my shoulders. I shiver. "But once we're back in town and the whole gang's here, you gotta at least do one toast. I mean, at least to this guy right here!"

He gets rowdy and Jimmy responds. They do some type of guttural man sound and pound fists across the car.

"Yeah, and I got a bottle of champagne, which tastes way better," Sarah says, taking a swig of beer. "We can toast Jimmy's big game!"

"Yeah! You scored, like, a million points," Kimi gushes. Sarah shoots her a quick back-off glance and Kimi smiles at her like a total brat. I giggle.

As the stone fences rush together outside my window, I turn my attention to the sky, dazzling with a bajillion stars, and sigh. Everything is perfect. As we climb the hill before the Fosters' house, I start feeling weird about making a stop here to pick up Paul instead of Luke. I don't even know if Luke will come to the dance at this point, and I'm fighting with myself about whether I should go inside with Kimi.

But it's a moot point, I realize, as Paul is waiting at the end of his driveway in a simple gray suit. The limo doesn't pull in, but slows to a stop in the middle of the road. Paul climbs in, Kimi gravitates toward him, and we're rolling again in less than twenty seconds. Guess Mrs. Foster isn't as sentimental as Momma, 'cause she didn't get to snap a single shot. And part of me hoped Luke would be hitching a ride, but I guess that option's out now.

"Is Luke coming to the dance?" I ask Paul over the music.

He's pretty focused on opening the bottle of beer Kimi just passed him, but after a big gulp he sighs, smiles, and shakes his head. "Don't know."

I want to ask more, but Paul's lips are suddenly tangled up in Kimi's, their bodies sending out Do Not Disturb signals.

"Get a room!" Wolf yells at the top of his lungs, and everyone laughs. Paul takes another swig and turns right back to the tongue tango, which seems to inspire Sarah and Jimmy. The hip-hop turns, right at that moment, to an R&B throwback, Usher's "Nice & Slow," and Wolf's knee starts bouncing as he looks out his window. I'm looking out mine as well, awkwardness emanating from both of us.

I want a first kiss. I want it tonight. And I want it from Wolf.

But I don't want it in front of my friends, 'cause I don't have the practice and I don't want to embarrass myself. I am über-aware of my hand, perched on my knee next to Wolf's and tingling like crazy. I see his pinky finger flinch toward mine and almost gasp out loud. *Is the "smooth operator" about to make a move?*

"Jimmy!" Wolf yells suddenly, kicking him hard in the calf. He laughs and covers his head as Jimmy breaks angrily away from Sarah and lunges forward.

"Ow! What the hell, Wolfenbaker?" he yells.

"Dude, did you really make the Lincoln County quarterback cry today?"

If Wolf's plan is to break up the kissing and get everybody back to normal, it works. Jimmy forgets all about making out as he talks about his real first love, reliving every moment of today's game for the entire fifteen-minute drive to Mackenzie's house. We laugh, make jokes, and get play-by-plays of the game. And although he might as well be speaking Chinese for all I know about football, I'm glad to be having fun again. I even get a good one in, making fun of Wolf when his voice cracks once, which prompts him to squeeze my knee until I melt into my seat from the warm tingles that run all the way up my thigh.

At the Watts' McMansion, we pull up to see Mackenzie and Laura posing on the front steps with Mark and his date. I still haven't caught my breath from flirting with Wolf and wonder if the whole night can sustain this electricity. I feel like I'm on fire. Wolf leans way over my legs to get a good look out the window at Mark's date, unaware that his touch to the bare skin above my knee sends a shock wave through my system. I don't move a muscle — I can't breathe — but the seconds drag by endlessly while he's draped across my body.

"Ah, she's not even that cute," he finally says to no one in particular before peeling his forehead from my window and settling into his seat again. I finally take a breath. *He was really interested in Mark's date,* I think to myself, but then I push the thought out of my mind quickly. He chose *me*.

"Hey, y'all!" Mackenzie suddenly yells, throwing open the limousine door. I nearly fall out, not realizing how much of my weight was leaning on my elbow. She climbs over me without care and sits sideways next to Sarah. Laura, her clone, follows suit and comes inches from stepping on my foot before plopping herself down.

"Did you like that?" Mackenzie giggles. "My new accent? *Y'all?*" As tired as the I'm-the-new-girl-from-Minnesoooota act is getting, this actually gets a few chuckles from the group. Wolf reaches for a beer and passes it toward her. "No thanks," she says perkily. He shrugs and passes it to Paul, who's always ready for another beer.

I gape. *"No thanks," and that's it? Meanwhile, I have to say "cow poop"?*

Wolf suddenly puts one arm around me and reaches over again to lower the back window. "Later, Watts!" he says, leaning forward and gripping my shoulders. Mark barely waves as he opens the door for his date, totally focused on her, a really gorgeous sophomore who's on Girls' Varsity. I smile weakly, glad to know I was right about Mark not pining over me but hoping Wolf won't realize it, too, and trade me back for Mackenzie.

"Oh, that's my jam!" Kimi cries as Justin Timberlake croons from the speakers. "Turn that up!"

Sarah willingly obliges and the limo begins to resemble a party wagon again. Mackenzie looks drop-dead gorgeous as usual in the closest thing I've ever seen to a real-life Miss America pageant dress. Laura looks nice, too, but her simple black dress is nothing compared to the heavenly white masterpiece Mackenzie has on. It's floor length, satin, and bejeweled. Plus, her hair is perfect. She definitely brought someone in from out of town to get that done, 'cause Aunt Edna's Beauty Shop never could've pulled that off. She flashes me a brilliant smile and I wilt into my seat, effectively intimidated.

Wolf's eyes are glued to that white dress.

Mackenzie starts snapping pictures of the group, classic photographer that she is, singing along to the pop music and dancing as well as I've ever seen anyone dance sitting down. Jimmy and Sarah have their hands up and are rocking back and forth to the music, and Kimi astounds us all by doing sitting body rolls against Paul's chest.

I'm so proud of myself for listening to Top 40 jams all week in preparation for the dance that I join in, fighting for the attention of my date. I bump shoulders with Wolf and pull faces, knowing that attitude is everything. Basically, I am working it.

"We decided to go stag!" Mackenzie yells over the music, aiming another one of her obnoxious comments my way. "When you go stag, you can have your way with all the boys, right, Laura?"

They crack up and fall into each other on the leather seats. I feel my smile falter but try to shake them off. I'm on my way to the homecoming dance with David Wolfen-baker, haters be damned.

It's all exactly how I imagined it. The football booster moms transformed the cafeteria into an enchanting ball-room, conjuring a celestial theme complete with glittery spray-painted cardboard moons and suns, and more sil-ver and blue balloons than I've ever seen in one place in my entire life. I'm in a beautiful dress and in the arms of David Wolfenbaker as we rock back and forth to Leona Lewis's "Bleeding Love." The girls on the sidelines, includ-ing upperclassmen, are watching me with a mixture of awe and jealousy. His breath is close, his lips right at the side of my face, and every time he speaks it feels like but-terfly kisses on my cheek. Yes, it's all exactly how I imag-ined it, except one hundred million times better.

"You having fun?" he asks me.

I pull back and look up into his face. Oh my gosh, it's so close. I try to speak. Can't. Nod.

"Good," he says and squeezes my sides.

The song comes to an end and our bodies separate as an undanceable rock number starts blaring over the speakers. I take a breath. He looks down at me and smiles. "Take a break?" he asks.

I'll do anything you want me to do, I think, but instead resort to Old Faithful, the smile and nod. He smiles back and does something that stops my heart completely: He grabs my hand.

David Wolfenbaker is holding my hand.

He leads me off the dance floor and over to the table our group claimed when we first got here. I follow, but I can't stop looking down at our hands. That's mine. And that's his. And there they are, pressed together, his long, skinny fingers intertwined between each of mine. My whole arm is tingling and my face is on fire as we weave through the crowd.

It takes us only half a minute or so to work our way over to the table, but it feels like an eternity in heaven. When we reach our group he gives my hand a squeeze and lets go, reaching across a sour-faced Mackenzie for his bottle of water. I briefly catch her eye, but we both look away quickly. I don't know whether she saw him finally make his move, and I don't want anything to ruin the euphoria of it all.

It seems weird that the prettiest girl in our whole freshman class has been sitting over here by herself most of the night. I look around for her shadow, Laura, and when I finally spot her springy curls, I'm a little surprised to see her grinding on the dance floor with that guy Trevor from my old school. I mean, he was in her top five and everything, but last weekend at my house she acted like Luke was the be-all and end-all.

"You wanna dance?" I hear Wolf ask. I swing my head back toward him with a big smile on my face. Of course I want to dance—want to be close to him, breathe in his scent, sway my hips with his, keep my mouth positioned alertly in first-kiss mode.

But then I realize that Mackenzie is scootching back in her chair and standing up...that Mackenzie is flashing her dazzling smile and nodding up at Wolf...that Mackenzie is the girl he's talking to. "You don't mind, right, Ericka?" he asks me, grinning.

Like, one second ago, I put my heart in this boy's hands, and now he's holding that same hand out for a girl who's eight million times prettier than I am, richer than I am, and cooler than I am. A girl he almost asked to the dance. A girl who has stated, on the record, that she likes him...like that.

And he wants to know if I *mind*?

Sure that my eyes have already given me away, I pull my shoulders back anyway and look up defiantly at the two most perfect-looking human beings I've ever met. "I don't even like this song," I say with a shrug, summoning up all the nonchalance I can muster.

He flashes a big smile and gives me a nod before pulling her along. She flashes me a similar smile and I want to scratch her eyes out. Or yell, "He's still *my* date!" or "He still chose *me*!" But instead I cross my arms and watch her float off after him, her soft white dress a vision under the lights. Pouting, I flop down grumpily into a seat at our table and crane my neck to keep an eye on them. At least it's a Michael Jackson song. Hard to get too romantic or bump-and-grindy to "Billie Jean."

"I'm having the best time!" Laura gushes from out of nowhere, plopping down beside me at the table and completely startling me. Her face is so close to mine and so exuberant that she effectively diverts my attention from my Wolf-Mackenzie stakeout. She has a silly smile splashed across her face and her eyes are dancing as she grabs my hands. "This is the greatest night of my life."

I roll my eyes. *I felt the same way about five minutes ago.*

She fishes for a tissue in her purse and launches into an enthusiastic monologue about Trevor and how she's liked him *all year* and how Mackenzie dared her to ask him to dance and how now they're practically already in love. I listen in awe, shocked that she's even speaking to me. Then again, she could have been sent as a diversionary tactic for Mackenzie. I narrow my eyes at her as she raves about Trevor's adorable dimples while still keeping tabs on the dance of betrayal going on behind us.

"Isn't he the cutest?" Laura squeals, clutching my forearm. She pulls me up and we walk toward the window next to our table.

"Totally," I say, playing along as best I can.

She cranks the window open and I feel a gust of cool air blow through. Wow. I hadn't realized how hot it is in here. I touch the sides of my hair and discover that it's soaking wet. Gross. I stand up on tiptoe and see that every one of Mackenzie's hairs is in place, which only makes me want to rip them all out. I realize how tightly my fists are clenched at my sides, how tense my jaw is.

As Michael Jackson finally brings things to a close

(yeah, we get it—she's not your lover), I impatiently tap my foot double-time and Laura dabs at the sweat on her face with a tissue in one hand while fanning herself like crazy with the other. I grab my new lip gloss from my purse and prepare for Wolf's return. So he's done the nice-guy thing, dancing with somebody who was obviously not having a good time, and now he'll come back to me, sheepish, hoping I'm not upset. I'll pretend I'm hurt, he'll hug me tight, we'll forget his moment of temporary insanity, and he'll dance only with me the rest of the night. I sigh, feeling better.

But when other couples break up to regroup and Ne-Yo's crooning voice comes over the speakers, Wolf closes the space between them and brings Mackenzie's hands up behind his neck. Then he wraps his own arms around her waist and they start to sway back and forth, their eyes locked.

I watch this happen in shock and awe. It's like they're the only couple on the dance floor, moving in slow motion. I don't want to look, but I can't pull my eyes away. Their bodies move as if they were made for each other. He says something in her ear and she laughs, throws her head back, and turns around. He puts his hands on her stomach and pulls her up against him. And as if I'm watching a horror movie made especially for me, he starts to grind against her, his hips thrusting forward against her butt. She pulls away quickly, spins back around, and laughs up at him, then glances over at me, a guilty look on her face. I look away, feeling sick.

Laura prattles on, but I can't hear anything but my own thoughts telling me what a loser I am—telling me how stupid I must be to think that Wolf would really like me over Mackenzie.

CHAPTER THIRTY-ONE

"Hello?"

"Momma," I say into the telephone. My voice starts shaking as soon as I hear hers. That always happens. It wasn't easy plastering a smile on my face, asking to borrow Laura's cell phone, or making my way through the crowd and out of the cafeteria while keeping my tears in check. But the minute I hear my momma's voice —

"You having a good time, sweetie?"

I fall apart. Tears stream down my face, silent and quick. I wipe at my eyes, glad for the first time all night that I'm not wearing much makeup.

"Um, will you come and get me?" I squeak out.

"What's wrong, Ricki Jo?"

I take a deep breath, try to get it together. Even though I'm hiding in the girls' locker room, I can hear the music and the chatter from the dance echoing faintly down the corridor. The other end of the phone line is quiet.

"It's just—" I start, the words spilling out, one on top of the other. I can't keep myself together as I cry into the phone. "I just really thought he liked me! I mean, he asked me to the dance, and it's like everything was perfect and he—" I hiccup and feel stupid, but I can't stop. "And now *Mackenzie!*" I wail, not really making sense. "My *supposed* best friend is all over him, and she's—There's no way I can—"

Momma knows me. She's patient. She lets me vent and cry. She lets me sob like a baby, and she probably doesn't understand half of what I'm actually saying. I am sitting on the locker room bench, my elbows on my knees, my head hanging low in the prettiest dress I've ever worn, on the night that was supposed to be some kind of dream come true. And I'm crying…over a boy…over *the* boy.

"Ugh," I mumble, shaking my head.

I'm so *mad* at myself. I feel like a fool. *Flirting. Puh-lease.* I always let him off the hook, every time he acts like a jerk: the paper football, the cheerleading tryout, leaving me passed out in the barn, asking me to homecoming as his pity date. I look so hard for the good in that boy, which is stupid because all the bad is right out there in the open.

I can hear the other kids in the gym corridor outside, taking a break from the dance, getting snacks and taking pictures. They're laughing and screaming and having a great time. And then there's me, crying on the phone to my mom. Pathetic.

"So you want me to come get you?" Momma asks softly. "Or do you want to maybe stay at the dance a little longer and see if you can work things out?"

I roll my eyes. "Momma, how am I supposed to work things out? You should've seen how he was. No. I just wanna come home."

"Ricki Jo?"

My head snaps up at the sound of a voice that's not my momma's and I nearly pee my pants. I totally thought I was alone in here, but Candace must've been in one of the bathroom stalls the whole time. She's standing across from me, her face the mirror image of what mine must look like—splotchy-pink and wet—and I wonder why she's upset. Then I feel the blood rush to my ears when I realize she must've heard me crying like a baby over Wolf.

"I'll call you back," I say to Momma, furiously wiping my face with the back of my hand. I snap the phone shut and stand up to face Candace. "What are you doing in here?"

She's leaning against a bathroom sink in a cute green maxi dress and gold flip-flops. As I walk toward the sinks myself, eager to splash some water on my face and check the damage, I see that she's wearing a little eye shadow and lipstick and her normally frizzy red hair is calm, framing her face in soft curls.

"I heard," she says to me in the mirror as soon as I'm next to her.

"So what?" I say meanly. "Guess you wanna brag? Say 'told you so' and all that?"

She looks baffled, shakes her head, and wipes at her eyes again with a mutilated tissue.

"No, seriously, you have every right," I continue, shooting all the anger I have for myself at her. "Congratulations. Wolf's a jerk. You were right. Happy?"

And at that, a weird look crosses her face. "Am I *happy*?" she asks incredulously.

The tension is still there, thick between us, and I'm struck by how stupid it is. We got off on the wrong foot at the beginning of the year, and we haven't been able to put things back together. Good Lord. I don't have to be her best friend, but since when did I stop treating people right?

"I'm sorry," I say, sighing and dropping my shoulders. "I've been a jerk. This whole year I've treated you like crap. And I don't really know why," I confess.

She dabs at her eyes with the tissue in her hand. "Oh." She shrugs. "I guess a week at Four-H camp doesn't mean we're gonna be thick as thieves. We probably both just had weird expectations. I thought, since we kind of knew each other, that I could show you around and stuff. But you made your own way, and that's cool. I shouldn't have taken it so personally."

It's funny to me that she's able to say all of that so easily. Usually she drops an F bomb and stalks off when people (even teachers) confront her. But tonight she's different. She just lets the words tumble right out, barely even looking at me. Like she's far away.

I don't know what else to say. And I guess she doesn't, either.

"Um," I manage to say, "are you okay?"

"It just sucks," she finally says. "All night, I figured he just stood me up."

"Oh," I say, finally understanding why Candace was hiding out in the bathroom, same as I was. I guess I'm not the only one with boy troubles. At least mine showed up. I give her a confident smile with a touch of attitude, totally in her corner now, and say what I want someone to say to me: "Well, it's his loss."

She gives me a puzzled look. "Ricki Jo!"

"What?" I say. And then, because I've never seen her so dressed up and because I mean it, I add, "You look really pretty tonight."

And she starts to cry all over again.

Geez. What did I say?

"I was so excited when he asked me last night," she says, sniffling, still staring like a zombie and walking over to the benches. "He called me and we were just joking around like always and he asked if I was going to homecoming. I wasn't gonna come. I mean, the game, yeah— I'm in the marching band—but the dance? Not really my scene." She wipes at her cheeks and smiles at me. "But we started joking about it, and then, I don't know. It felt good to be asked. And me and Luke are good friends, you know? So I just went out to the Fashion Bug after school today and grabbed this dress—and it was on sale—and the whole time I was getting ready, I got more and more excited."

She wipes at her eyes and cheeks with the already crumpled tissue and takes deep breaths, trying to calm herself. I take a deep breath, too, trying to steady myself because I'm completely stunned.

Luke asked Candace to homecoming?

"And so when he didn't show up, and still didn't show up, and I saw Paul Foster here...I don't know." She unfolds the tissue from her hand and blows her nose into it for what must be the second or third time. I watch her as if she's moving in slow motion.

Luke asked Candace to homecoming. I'm seriously dumbfounded. First of all, Luke doesn't even like Candace that way, or at least he's never said anything about her to me. I mean, I didn't know he liked anybody like that, let alone enough to take someone to a high school dance. And second of all, I don't know, it just seems like she's not really his type. I mean, he's no Casanova, but I figured him to like more laid-back girls—spunky, maybe, but less chip-on-the-shoulder and more bounce-in-the-step. I squint at the locker in front of me and feel my forehead wrinkle like it does in algebra when I'm trying really hard to understand a difficult equation. And then suddenly, it hits me: I'm jealous. I'm actually jealous of Candace Baker.

I shake my head and smile wryly. This night just keeps getting better.

"I was gonna egg his house tonight before I ran into Paul," Candace says bitterly, snapping me back to the conversation.

"Wait, but Luke wouldn't stand you up," I say with certainty.

"I *thought* he stood me up," she says. "I've been cussing him out in my head for the past two hours, while he's been laid up at the hospital."

She grinds her jaw, obviously mad at herself, but I shut her out. I can't breathe. I can't have heard her right.

Laid up at the hospital.

No. Impossible.

"Luke's in the hospital?" I finally ask.

Then it's Candace who has the surprised look on her face. "I figured you knew."

I stare at her, speechless, because these days, I probably wouldn't know about anything concerning anyone but myself.

"What happened?" I ask, fear coursing through my body.

She sighs and turns to face me. "Okay, so I was pretty pissed off, like I said. We were supposed to meet by the back doors of the gym at ten thirty, you know, fashionably late or whatever. I waited and waited and called his house and nobody answered. I just kept thinking how dumb I was to get all dressed up for this, you know? Spend all that time getting ready just to be stood up. It wasn't even my idea to come! I think school dances are lame, but Luke begged me."

He begged her? Luke thinks school dances are lame, too. For the gazillionth time, I wish Luke and I weren't in this stupid fight. I should have known all of this, everything, and hearing it from Candace is pretty much killing me.

"Anyway, I was about to leave just now, when I saw Paul Foster running out of school like a bat out of hell. I caught up to him and grabbed his arm and...I don't know, he was pretty wasted. But he said his mom had just called and something bad happened at home while Luke was, I guess, getting ready for the dance. I don't really know the details, but Paul was so upset...and said it like"—she takes a deep breath and looks up— "like it had something to do with their dad?"

The question in her voice hurts me and I nod slightly, hoping I'm not betraying Luke's trust. I lie back on the narrow bench and think about the other times, think about that day at the vet's office when Luke talked about making a stand, protecting his momma, becoming a man. I close my eyes, feeling sick to my stomach.

She finishes. "And now he's in the hospital."

I clench my teeth together, angry.

"And I'm a jackass. I was so mad at him for not being here. Not *worried* about him, but angry." She shudders. "I know I shouldn't, but I feel *guilty*. It's like he's this fun guy at school, you know? Everybody likes Luke. Nobody could've guessed—"

I moan loudly, like a growl almost. I feel everything she says like a knife to my gut, twisting with each word. Candace reaches out for my hand but I shake her off, get up, and walk around and around the bench, my heels *click-clack*ing on the concrete. I pound a locker with the bottom of my fist. *I* knew. *I* could have been there for him. *I* knew there was pain behind those smiles. *I knew.*

Finally I grow tired. I let out a huge, shaky sigh and force myself over to the sinks. I lean down and turn on the cold water and splash my face. It feels good, cool, soothing. I turn off the faucet and reach over for a paper towel, dab my face dry, study myself in the mirror.

I hate what I see.

"I gotta get over there," I say determinedly as I reach for the door to the cafeteria.

"We can't," Candace says, following me. "Visiting hours aren't 'til tomorrow!"

I ignore her. No way I'm abandoning Luke now. I swing the door open and, confident for the first time in these high-heeled shoes, I start to cross the room, focused on one thing and one thing only: getting to my real best friend and begging him to forgive me. I fight my way through the throng of students heading outside, getting knocked around but standing my ground and pulling Candace along behind me. I look at the sweaty student body in front of me like a puzzle, see a hole in the crowd, and sidestep into it just as someone else comes barreling through.

"Sorry," Mackenzie says, slamming into me hard. I glare up at her, and when our eyes meet I see that she's teary, too.

Oh, great, I think to myself. *Some dance.*

"Are you okay?" Candace yells to her over the music.

I roll my eyes and tug at Candace's hand. *Who cares? Luke is waiting.*

"I…" Mackenzie starts. Then she looks at me and grabs my shoulders. "I'm sorry, Ericka. I really am."

This is possibly the only thing in the world that could have delayed me from grabbing my things and figuring out a way to get to the hospital. I have to see Luke, no matter what the visiting hours are, but Mackenzie's hands are pushing down on me hard and her blue eyes are pleading.

"Here," Candace says, handing her a wad of toilet paper. Mackenzie looks surprised. "We haven't really had a great night, either."

Mackenzie tears off a long piece and folds it, carefully dabbing at her bottom row of eyelashes. "He's not worth it," she says loudly, looking intently into my eyes. "He's scum. He's trash. I…I was so stupid. Your friendship is worth—" She fights her tears, and once again I am struck by how pretty she is absolutely all the time. Candace and I looked like freakin' lepers when we were crying, but Mackenzie pulls it off. Still, I stiffen, having fallen for this act a couple of times already.

"Yeah, you've said all this before," I say drily. I mean,

I'm not trying to be a jerk, but I'm finally getting perspective on who my real friends are, and I don't want to be as naïve as I've been before. "And to tell you the truth, it looked like my friendship was the last thing on your mind when y'all were out there rubbing all over each other on the dance floor."

She looks down at her own hands. "Yeah, I know. Apparently, he got the same idea, because he—" Mackenzie stops, takes a deep breath, and looks up at us, her eyes a mixture of rage and embarrassment. "Because he *spanked* me. He slapped me on the butt so hard that I actually almost fell down." She shakes her head in disgust and looks out toward the dance floor. "I hope his hand falls off."

I sigh. Wolf is Wolf. And although I wish his heart were pure gold, I guess I've always known that it's more of the brass variety.

I stand on tiptoe, getting pushed and shoved from all angles. I've got to get out of this crowd, get around all this chitchat, grab my stuff, and get to Luke. I feel bad for Mackenzie, but I'm actually glad it wasn't me out there after all. Candace squeezes my hand hard and I look at her. She's giving me that same look that Luke used when I fought with her—that kiss-and-make-up look, that play-nice look.

I roll my eyes and sigh. "I guess I didn't have to be so—"

But before I can make any apologies for my own behavior, the jerk of the hour spins me around by the waist.

"Ericka!" Wolf shouts, looking very pleased to see me. "I've been looking all over for you!"

"Oh, please," Mackenzie says with a snort, turning away and rolling her eyes at Candace.

"It was just a joke!" Wolf yells, shaking his head and obviously just as annoyed with her as she is with him. Then he looks down at me and flashes that grin of his.

I raise an eyebrow, surveying the state of my date. He's ditched his jacket, his sleeves are rolled up, his collar is loose, and his tie is wrapped around his head, hanging off to one side. His hair is soaking wet and his face is glistening as if he just played an entire game of basketball.

"You got all sweaty looking for me?" I ask dubiously.

His expression falters a tiny bit before the music changes and he dodges the question completely. His eyes light up like a kid at Christmas. "The Electric Slide!" he yells, dipping his shoulders and twisting my hips to the music. "Awesome!"

I narrow my eyes and really see him for the first time. Wolf's a hunk, for sure, but I finally see the ugly under all that handsome. I can't help but think about Luke, and how Wolf isn't even half the man he is, and how blind I must be to have taken this long to see that.

"I'm leaving," I yell over the music. As impossible as it may have been only hours ago, I easily wiggle my hips free from his hands and walk right past him, weaving through our grooving student body to get my things from our table. Everybody looks worn down, hairstyles wet from sweat and strapless dresses getting hiked up all over the place. I grab my purse and pull my coat out from under a big pile. Mackenzie appears at my side and seems to have the same idea.

When I turn around, Wolf is right behind, staring at me in total shock. I grin. *That* feels good.

"See you in Spanish," I say, and walk toward the exit.

Candace meets me outside and I'm grateful for the nip in the air. Mackenzie surprises me by following us outside, too.

"Ericka!" she calls. "I really am sorry."

"I can't believe y'all were fighting over *Wolf*!" Candace says, nudging me. Then she adds, quieter, "Don't worry. That's the closest I'll come to a told ya so."

I crack a small grin—it's still not *that* funny—and look at Mackenzie. "Yeah, me, too."

"I shouldn't have been so mean to you this week," Mackenzie continues. "And I shouldn't have danced with him so much tonight, but I knew that would make you mad, and I've just been so jealous."

I am again amazed that someone like her could be jealous of anyone. And then I shake my head, eager to get out of here and get to Luke. "Listen, Mackenzie—"

"I just—ugh! I feel so gross, you know?" She absentmindedly rubs her lower back and I can see she's still in shock. I nod up at her. It does feel gross. Not that I was spanked, but it *is* gross that this and all of Wolf's other pranks and stunts are giggled at and taken in stride just because he's so good-looking.

"I learned my lesson, though," Mackenzie continues, putting her hands on my shoulders and looking me straight in the eye. "I shouldn't have let a boy come between us. New Girls BFFs?"

I hesitate and really think about the way a best friend—a truly *best* friend—should behave. And it isn't the way she's treated me. And it isn't the way I've treated, well, anybody lately.

I look Mackenzie in the eye and, for the first time, see someone who's not perfect, someone really similar to the person I was looking at in the mirror earlier, and now that I know I'm just as good as she is, and maybe just as bad, I think our friendship might have a chance.

"New Girls," I say, holding off on the BFF part, 'cause you need to be a good friend before graduating to the Best category. And I can think of only one person who deserves that title right now. I just want to get to the hospital.

Mackenzie hugs me fiercely. "I've missed you," she says and I hug her back, happy to smell her salon-washed hair again.

"Listen," I start to say again, trying to free myself from her grip.

"I know," she says abruptly. "We've got to go. Candace filled me in while you were telling off Wolf, and Mark's waiting in the car."

"What?" I ask, wondering what in the world her brother has to do with anything.

But without answering, she loops me with one arm and Candace with the other and marches us through the parking lot. In the front row, Mark flashes his lights at us, and we all climb into the backseat of his brand-new Ford Explorer. His date pouts in the front seat, making it pretty obvious that it was not her idea to leave the dance early. I don't know what's going on exactly, but I'm anxious, excited, and eager to see Luke.

And Mackenzie, of all people, has a plan.

CHAPTER THIRTY-TWO

"Home, James," Mackenzie says to Mark in a snobby voice. He grins at us through the rearview mirror.

"Sorry to hear about Luke," Mark says sincerely.

I meet his eyes and nod, surprised at how quickly the lump in my throat comes and goes. Now is not the time to cry. Now is the time to call Momma and fill her in on what's going on...sort of.

As Mark pulls out of the parking lot, I grab Laura's cell phone from my purse and dial. Whoops. I'll have to get that back to her.

"Momma?"

"Feeling better, baby?"

"Yeah, it was okay. I guess I overreacted."

"So you worked things out with David? And Mackenzie?" she asks.

I cringe. "Well, yeah, me and Wolf are still friends, I

guess, but that's it. But the really great thing is that I made up with Mackenzie!"

Mackenzie silently claps her hands next to me and leans in to listen. I turn the volume up and put it on speaker so she can really enjoy the ego stroking.

Momma coos. It's her thing. And she loves Mackenzie. "I'm so glad, Ricki Jo. I think she's a good friend. She seems like a really sweet girl."

Mackenzie bats her eyes and puts her hands together like an angel. Candace makes a gagging gesture. I try not to giggle.

"Yeah, and she asked me to sleep over tonight. Can I?"

"Oh, well, I don't know," Momma says. "It's awfully late notice, and—"

"Pleeeeeease, Momma? I've had such a crazy night and I just want to work everything out with Mackenzie," I say, playing on my momma's sympathies.

"And she called her mother?" Momma asks. "You're sure she's okay with a surprise guest?"

"She's used to it, Mrs. Winstead," Mackenzie says into the phone, laying the manners on thick. "I had loads of slumber parties back home."

"Okay then, girls," Momma says. "Y'all have fun, and make sure to get some sleep. Ericka, I'll come in to get you around lunchtime after Ben's rec soccer game."

"Thanks, Momma!" I say, giddy that the plan is working perfectly. "Bye! Love you!"

I snap the cell phone shut and give high fives to the

girls as we pass the Dairy Queen, getting closer and closer to Luke.

"Hi, Betty," Mackenzie says as we enter the sliding front doors of Preston Memorial Hospital. I follow her nervously across the lobby to the stairs, worried that the night nurse will stop us. But Betty looks sleepy, and even though visiting hours are way over and three teenage girls just strolled through the front doors in semiformal dresses, she barely glances up from her crossword.

In the elevator, the tension is heavy. "I called my dad, so I knew we wouldn't have any trouble," Mackenzie explains, even though she seems a little nervous, too. Candace and I nod. What is it about elevators that make everybody so quiet? You're shoulder to shoulder with people, but you never know what to say. And of course, since the hospital was built, like, a century ago, the elevator crawls upward at a snail's pace. We look at our reflections in the mirrored walls and I think how much I'd like to have a ponytail holder so I could get the sweaty hair off my neck.

"Guess I overdid it for Preston County, huh, *y'all?*" Mackenzie asks out of the blue, hip checking me as she gestures to her bright red acrylic nails. Candace and I both gape at her. "I mean, my spaghetti straps have rhinestones, and my hair won't move."

I burst out laughing. Mackenzie is a knockout, but she's right. A long white gown and baby's breath wound in her

French twist? I'm no fashion expert, but I do know small-town Kentucky, and that isn't it. Candace is laughing, too, even though in my opinion she actually undershot the dress code with her flip-flops and jersey dress. Next week, maybe I'll pitch a "Homecoming Review: Hot or Not" article for my column in the school paper. I mean, I've already got wardrobe material, and some great trauma and drama, Wolf serving as the perfect inspiration...especially since calling "The Electric Slide" awesome is so obviously a major *Not*.

"Yeah, you're kind of Homecoming Barbie," Candace says, which makes me tense up, since she and Mackenzie aren't really friends. But Candace seems to mean it as a compliment, and Mackenzie soaks it up, moving her body in weird robotic gestures like a real plastic doll.

Tears well up in my eyes again, but this time they're happy tears. It feels so good to laugh with these girls. To make up with my friends and sort out who they really are.

Ding!

We're here. Fourth floor. Our laughter dies down in an instant as the elevator doors creak open and the three of us peer out into the dim, empty hallway.

"It's so quiet!" I whisper, or at least I hope it was a whisper. My pulse is pounding so hard in my ears that I can barely hear myself talk.

"Yeah," Mackenzie says quietly, the first to step forward. "These small hospitals are like that at night. Not a lot going on and, you know, most normal people sleep at night." She winks at me. "Even the sick ones."

I follow her lead and we make our way down the hall. Candace's flip-flops are like gunshots while our heels echo in a staccato rhythm. After a few steps we all walk lighter, my whole weight lifted up onto the balls of my feet. My hands and arms are freezing, but I still feel sweat trickling from my armpit down the side of my body. For one thing, I'm kind of scared of hospitals. For another, I'm kind of scared of the dark. And finally, I'm totally scared of jail, although I'm fuzzy on whether or not what we're doing is wrong. Mackenzie said she called her dad, but she's acting just as jittery as I am.

"How will we know which room he's in?" I ask.

Mackenzie frowns. "Well, I guess we can just look at the name plaques on the outside of each room 'til we make it to the nurse's station."

I gulp, conjuring up a pretty scary mental image of the night nurse.

"Peters...McGaughey...Edwards..." she whispers on her side of the hall. *Jones...Fox...Calloway...*I read to myself on mine.

I keep my eyes trained on the names and numbers, reading the plaques as we pass each oak door. Fryman... Allen...Turner...Bryant...Jacobs...Nantz...Suddenly Mackenzie stops.

"Here it is," she says.

Room 404—Foster.

We stand outside his door for a second, not saying anything and not moving for the door handle. I feel like the wind has been knocked out of me. I guess there was still some small part of me that hoped it was just a bad dream, but Luke really is here. He really is hurt. And he really is right on the other side of this door.

Something loud crashes to the floor around the corner and we all freeze. "Okay, you guys go ahead," Mackenzie whispers urgently. "I'll keep watch from down there on those couches."

"Keep watch?" Candace asks, her eyes bugged out.

Mackenzie's cheeks flush a light pink. "Um, I did *call* my dad, but I didn't actually *talk* to him.... It went to voice mail." Candace and I look at her in shock. She raises her hands quickly to defend herself. "I knew if we had any problems, it'd be fine. It's just, since you found his room already and I don't really know him that well, I'll go sit in the waiting area and stall the nurse in case she makes a night round while you're in there."

"So we *can* get in trouble for sneaking in?" Candace asks.

Mackenzie shrugs, but the answer is obvious. Yes, we can get in trouble, and she's gone as far as she's willing to go. My hands are sweating and I chide myself for being so nervous. It's Luke; trouble or not, I'm going in. Candace has been in trouble her whole life, so I'm surprised that she has any reluctance at all about breaking the rules.

And then I cock my head and look at her differently. She may cuss a lot, talk loud, wear cheap gaudy jewelry, and be trailer park proud, but she's also in the band and on the school paper, and she gets really good grades. It hits me like a ton of bricks that maybe I'm not the only one who's trying to change.

"Why don't you take a minute first, Ericka?" she says nervously. "See if he's awake."

"Yeah, we'll be right down the hall," Mackenzie says as she presses down on the chrome door handle and pushes me inside, my heart pounding in my ears.

"Knock, knock?" I say lightly, moving toward the giant bed near the window.

Luke is in there somewhere. In the light of all those monitors, hooked up to those tubes, under tightly tucked-in covers, Luke is there. I walk carefully across the floor, already shocked by what I see in the moonlight. His chest is bare, one arm in a cast resting across it at a right angle, and his head is wrapped in gauze. I take a deep breath and continue. The room is small; it should take only about five steps to cross, but I'm taking my time, inching toward him.

"Anybody home?" I try to keep my voice light, wanting him to know that I'm here if he's awake, but really not wanting to disturb him if he's not.

"Ricki Jo?" he asks hoarsely.

My eyes well up. I stop and look up at the ceiling tiles, blinking hard and wiping the tears away, then move forward again. I can see his outline pretty clearly by the light of the machines next to him. Enough to see that his pretty blue eyes are closed, bruised, swollen shut. Dried blood coats the bandage above his eyebrow, and there's a bit on his cheek as well, from where it's seeped through the gauze. An oxygen tube runs up to his nose and lies across his swollen cheekbones. There are so many bandages on his body that I hesitate to guess what's broken, fractured, cut, or bruised. But I can see enough in the darkness to feel my heart break in two.

"As bad as Bandit?" he asks softly.

I laugh, one of those nervous laughs that you can't keep inside.

"Oh, Luke, I'm so sorry," I say, rushing forward and grabbing the railing on his bed. The tears run freely now. "I'm so sorry about everything. It's so stupid. I'm so sorry about what I said on the bus. And just...all year, I've been so busy trying to fit in, be cool or whatever. Ugh! I don't know why I needed new friends when you're the best friend I've ever had. Ever. Ever. You're—"

"Shh..." He groans. "Take it easy."

"No, I just—I just care about you so much, and I got so scared when I heard what happened. I'm so sad that you were hurt and you probably hate me and you have every right to, but you mean so much to me and—"

"Hey, hey," Luke whispers, and he reaches his good hand (although it's also scraped up) toward mine. "Breathe."

I inhale and exhale a few times, deeply, and feel a little better. I take his hand lightly and spin that worn leather band round and round his wrist.

"I hate that I wasn't there for you," I whisper.

"What could you have done? Fight him for me?"

"No, I mean that I haven't really been there for you . . . all year. As a friend."

I sniff and reach for the box of tissues by his bed. I know what I look like when I cry this hard for this long, and the selfish thought comes to me that I'm glad his eyes are closed, although I despise the circumstances and kind of feel evil for even thinking that. I shake my head and blow my nose. He breathes a shaky breath. I put my hand back on his and he gives my thumb a slight squeeze.

"I could have told my parents," I say, a little more steady. "I could have told them what I saw. What I knew."

"It wouldn't have mattered," he said. "This is our problem. The only person who could have done anything was my momma." His voice turns hard. "And she wouldn't."

"But she will now," I say. "Right?"

He actually manages a barbed grin. "She has to, or the state will. I already talked to the police and some lady from social services about domestic violence or whatever. They're gonna come back tomorrow when I'm feeling better, and, you know, when there aren't a ton of doctors and nurses around. But it's child abuse. And I'm not covering for him."

I squeeze his hand involuntarily; I'm so proud of him. "Ow."

"Sorry!" I cry, removing my hands immediately. He starts to laugh really hard, then he coughs violently, and each spasm obviously causes him more pain. I panic, looking at the IV thing and the huge remote on his lap, wondering if I'm supposed to do something if he goes into shock like on those hospital shows on TV. "Luke? Luke, what do I do?"

He holds his hand up and starts to regain control of his breathing as the cough finally dies down.

"So, basically," he says, as if the conversation hadn't just been interrupted by him almost dying on me, "Dad's going to jail. And I don't know for sure, but I think Momma will pretty much have to divorce him."

"Divorce?" I say quietly. I note that, through it all, his voice has remained oddly upbeat, considering the words he's said. There is no remorse, no worry, no fear—only resolve.

"Yeah, divorce. Or else we'll go to foster care."

I giggle. "Haven't you kind of been in 'Foster Care' your whole life?"

Luke moans, but grins. "Oh, god! Your jokes are as corny as your dad's!"

I giggle harder. I'm so happy to be here with him, to stroke his arm, to feel the golden soft hairs against my fingers. So happy to make him feel better, even a little. Leaned over him like this, I feel like I'm right where I'm supposed to be.

"Wow," he says.

"What?" I say quickly. "Should I get the nurse?"

"No." He grins. "I just peeked. Nice dress."

"You can see?"

"Barely," he says. "He got in a couple of good punches, in case you hadn't noticed, but if I lift my chin up I can kind of see through my left eye. And tell me if I'm dreaming or if it's the drugs, but I think a pretty girl just broke into my hospital room."

I smile, widely and giddily and happily, and feel a couple more tears slip out. I feel tingles all over my body and fill myself up with one of those huge breaths that make you feel like your lungs could explode through your ribs. *Luke thinks I'm pretty.* I feel the cog turn like the wheel on the tobacco setter as our relationship evolves in this quiet moment to more than friends. Of course we're more than friends. We maybe always have been — like, we're meant to be together or something.

"Thanks," I say softly, hesitantly brushing a piece of his soft blond hair off his forehead. He starts to ask a question, but I think I spot a smirk on his busted-up lips and interrupt: "Don't ask."

He chuckles, coughs a couple of times, and says, "Told ya so."

"You sound like Candace," I say.

He sighs. "I bet she hates me right now."

"Nah," I say. "She cussed you pretty good, but now she feels awful. She's here, actually. Want me to go get her?"

"No," he says quickly and squeezes my hand tighter, then winces from the pain. I had only half turned away from the bed, anyway. I hadn't really wanted to get her, but the real me doesn't always put herself first. Still, I smile smugly—I can't help it. I guess they *are* just friends. He must see the self-satisfied look on my face, 'cause he adds, "I wouldn't want you girls to fight over me."

My impulse is to flick him on the forehead, but I manage some self-control, given all of his injuries. I chide myself. You put a dress on the tomboy, and she's still a tomboy.

Speaking of...

"Hey, you gonna be in the hospital a long time?" I ask.

"I don't know," he says. "At least 'til tomorrow, and maybe the day after. Why?"

"And then how long 'til you're all better? I mean, totally back in working condition."

"The doctor said maybe six weeks. I don't know. My arm's broken."

"Hmmm...but you could strip tobacco with one arm, probably, right?"

Luke groans. "Ah, you're already complaining about strippin' season?"

"Hey!" I say, wondering if he can see my smile, but knowing he can hear it in my voice. "You go and pull a stunt like this, do it on the off months. Geez. Now my dad's gonna have me working the Foster farm twenty-four/seven."

"Aw, shucks," he says, barely pulling his lips up on each side.

"Scoot over," I say, lightly swatting at his legs. I lower

the railing, and of course he can't really move much, but an advantage of being freakishly small is fitting into tight spaces. I oh-so-carefully lie down next to him and feel those tingles again. I wonder if he feels them, too. I gently lay my head on his shoulder, breathe him in, and focus on his chest, trying to match my breathing to his.

Up and down, his chest expands and contracts, and I think about what an idiot I've been. I've been so caught up in changing, while Luke's always liked me the way I am. I've been searching for new friends, when he's the best there is. I've been dreaming of the perfect guy, when he's been right under my nose my whole life.

"Thanks for coming," he whispers, his hand brushing my back. "And I'm sorry, too. I wondered if you would even come tomorrow, you know, to see me."

I look up at his face and see the tiniest sliver of blue looking down at me. I choke against the tightness in my throat, marveling at how fractured our relationship had gotten, at how bad a person I'd become, that he could possibly think I wouldn't be right here at his side in a heartbeat.

I squeeze him, very lightly. "Wolves couldn't keep me away."

He chuckles, closes his eyes, and takes a deep breath.

"I've missed you, Ericka," he says softly, his hand absentmindedly working through my hair as if it were the most natural thing in the world.

I smile up at him, my whole body happy and light. "You can call me Ricki Jo."

ACKNOWLEDGMENTS

It started out as a few words on a page. Write what you know, they said. So I took a dash of my childhood, added a heavy dose of drama and make-believe and a pinch of wit and charm, and stirred it all into a broth of small-town Kentucky.

So thank you, Cynthiana, for being a great place to grow up. Thank you, Mamaw and Papaw, for westerns, the game show network, Easter egg hunts, chauffeur services, and cheering at the top of your lungs for me at every single extracurricular activity in which I participated. Thank you to my own Momma and Dad, for believing in me always, for taking me to slumber parties and letting me host my own, for blending into the background when you chaperoned my dances, and for honking loudly and waving maniacally when I missed the bus on purpose in order to look cool getting dropped off in front of school. Ahh, the things that shape us.

Thank you, Matt, for agreeing to read this book, and thank you, Bobbie Jo, for reading everything. Thank you, Whitney, for running so slow at soccer practice that we could jog along together and forge the friendship of a lifetime.

Thank you to Micol Ostow, Mediabistro, and the women I worked with there while writing this book. Thank you for your input, and for being a champion for Ricki Jo from day one. And to Micol especially, thank you for all your feedback, and for showing me the business side of writing.

To Alyssa Reuben, the best agent in the biz, thank you for answering my phone calls, keeping me sane, and believing in both Ricki Jo and me. I am so happy to be working with you.

To Elizabeth Bewley, thank you for taking little RJ under your wing and helping her reach her Queen potential. And to Cindy Eagan, thank you for giving us a home at Poppy. I am so blessed to have an editor who believes in and connects with my work, and a publishing house to call home.

Thank you to my early readers, especially Cindy Johnson, Becky Bennett, and my mom, Vicki Whitaker. Your feedback kept my feet on solid ground. Thank you, Ms. Burgess, for pulling me aside in the tenth grade and giving me an application to the creative writing program at the Governor's School for the Arts (GSA). And thank you to GSA for opening my eyes to the arts as career, not hobby. And also, thank you to Ms. Andrews for actually making me work for my A's in English.

And a gigantic-sized thank-you to the two most amazing men I have ever known: my husband, Jerrod, and my son, Knox. Jerrod, for believing in my talent enough to move to NYC and allow me to chase after this dream full-time, for turning off the TV and completely ignoring me when I tried to procrastinate, and for loving me. And to Knox, for simply being born, and for every bright smile you flash my way.

Matthew 7:7

Where stories bloom.

poppy

Visit us online at
www.pickapoppy.com